Praise for the authors of *Drop-Dead Blonde*

NANCY MARTIN
National bestselling author of the Blackbird Sisters mystery series

"Great clothes, great mystery, great fun!"
    —*New York Times* bestselling author Jennifer Crusie

ELAINE VIETS
National bestselling author of the Dead-End Job mystery series

"Wry sense of humor, appealing, realistic characters, and a briskly moving plot."   —*South Florida Sun-Sentinel*

DENISE SWANSON
National bestselling author of the Scumble River mystery series

"I enjoy every minute of every book in this series."
                                        —Charlaine Harris

VICTORIA LAURIE
Author of the new Psychic Eye mystery series

"Abby Cooper is a fresh, exciting addition to the amateur sleuth genre. Author Victoria Laurie has talent to spare—she's a writer to watch!
                        —J. A. Konrath, author of *Whiskey Sour*

DROP-DEAD BLONDE

NANCY MARTIN
ELAINE VIETS
DENISE SWANSON
VICTORIA LAURIE

A SIGNET BOOK

SIGNET
Published by New American Library, a division of
Penguin Group (USA) Inc., 375 Hudson Street,
New York, New York 10014, USA
Penguin Group (Canada), 10 Alcorn Avenue, Toronto,
Ontario M4V 3B2, Canada (a division of Pearson Penguin Canada Inc.)
Penguin Books Ltd., 80 Strand, London WC2R 0RL, England
Penguin Ireland, 25 St. Stephen's Green, Dublin 2,
Ireland (a division of Penguin Books Ltd.)
Penguin Group (Australia), 250 Camberwell Road, Camberwell, Victoria 3124,
Australia (a division of Pearson Australia Group Pty. Ltd.)
Penguin Books India Pvt. Ltd., 11 Community Centre, Panchsheel Park,
New Delhi - 110 017, India
Penguin Group (NZ), cnr Airborne and Rosedale Roads, Albany,
Auckland 1310, New Zealand (a division of Pearson New Zealand Ltd.)
Penguin Books (South Africa) (Pty.) Ltd., 24 Sturdee Avenue,
Rosebank, Johannesburg 2196, South Africa

Penguin Books Ltd., Registered Offices:
80 Strand, London WC2R 0RL, England

First published by Signet, an imprint of New American Library,
a division of Penguin Group (USA) Inc.

First Printing, February 2005
10 9 8 7 6 5 4 3 2 1

Copyright © Penguin Group (USA) Inc., 2005
"Slay Belles" copyright © Nancy Martin, 2005
"Killer Blonde" copyright © Elaine Viets, 2005
"Dead Blondes Tell No Tales" copyright © Denise Swanson Stybr, 2005
"Blind Sighted" copyright © Victoria Laurie, 2005
All rights reserved

Ⓟ REGISTERED TRADEMARK—MARCA REGISTRADA

Printed in the United States of America

CONTENTS

SLAY BELLES

A BLACKBIRD SISTERS MYSTERY

NANCY MARTIN

It's a pleasure to be among such esteemed company. Elaine, Denise, and Laura: When next we meet, I'll buy the champagne!

Chapter 1

In the hope of starting a Christmas tradition that didn't end with throwing food at a sibling, I took my niece Lucy to visit Santa at Haymaker's department store. Afterward, we snagged the best table in the Mrs. Claus Tearoom on the mezzanine, where Lucy licked the sprinkles off half a dozen cookies and told me family secrets while we waited for her mother.

"Mummy says she has too much juice in her caboose right now, Aunt Nora, and she can't face Christmas," Lucy volunteered. "So she's getting a massage every afternoon from Jason and yelling about electrolysis and her chin. What's electrolysis?"

After I told her, I asked, "What kind of massage does Jason give, exactly, Luce?"

My niece was saved from ratting out her mother when Libby arrived. "Hello, darlings!"

My sister swept up like a zaftig Italian film star with her whoosh of auburn hair and a red sweater so revealing that three of Santa's teenage elves nearly suffered whiplash as she sailed by. She carried enough shopping bags to cripple a Nazareth donkey, and dropped the loot on an empty chair with triumph. "What a night!"

"Mummy," Lucy said with a Machiavellian gleam in her eyes, "Santa didn't ask if I was good this year."

I said, "We were very relieved. Waiting in line was beginning to feel like a perp walk."

"What about you?" Libby skewered me with a look as she sat down. "Have you been naughty or nice lately?"

"Santa didn't ask me."

"You hardly look angelic," Libby observed. "In fact, you

have a distinctly postcoital glow. Have you been seeing the gangster again?"

"He isn't—"

"Because I just bumped into Alan Rutledge at the top of the escalator. And he's looking adorable these days."

"Does owning a department store make a man adorable?"

"It helps." Libby fluffed her hair and adjusted her décolletage. "He isn't bad to look at, really. Rather like a teddy bear—cute ears and that little tummy, of course. And he always smells divine."

My sister had been widowed twice and still enjoyed men of all shapes, sizes, and proclivities. With her uncanny radar for available partners, I firmly believed she could find an eligible man if she were cast adrift in the Amazon River. I said, "You got close enough to smell him?"

"It was a friendly holiday greeting, that's all." She took out her compact and checked her lipstick for damage. "I'm not interested in him in the least, despite all his money. I need someone with more fire. But you've been a widow for two years now, and Alan might be exactly the person to bring you to your senses."

"Too late," I said.

She forgot about her lipstick. "Oh, dear heaven, you haven't eloped, have you?"

"No. Alan's engaged."

"How disappointing! Not to Bitty Markham, I hope. Ever since her poor Stanley's little financial mixup, she's been looking for another meal ticket."

"Poor Stanley bilked his best friends, Libby, and it's formally called investment fraud, which is why he's in jail. No, Alan is engaged to Cindie Rae Smith."

"You're kidding!" My sister dropped her compact and stared at me with round eyes. "Cindie Rae? The *Penthouse* girl with the X-rated Web site?"

Lucy looked up from her cookies. "Mummy, what's a *Penthouse* girl?"

"A woman who lives in an apartment, darling." While her daughter frowned, Libby said to me, "That gold digger finally hit her jackpot, huh?"

"I guess her Web site isn't as lucrative as she hoped."

"Taking requests from perverts on a live camera?" Libby

cried. "How can that not make scads of money? She'll perform anything with that hilarious fluorescent dildo she's got for sale."

"Mummy, what's—"

"An extinct bird, sweetheart. Would you like some hot chocolate? With marshmallows?"

While Lucy scrambled off to order a diversionary drink, I sat back in my chair to better gauge the seriousness of my sister's pre-Christmas hysteria. Although the wills of her late husbands left Libby financially capable of rearing her children, she didn't have enough extra cash for a Christmas blowout. And the flash in her eye looked more manic than simple holiday high spirits. I wondered what crisis might be brewing.

But I said, "You seem to have a thorough knowledge of Cindie Rae's Web site, Libby."

"I feel it's important to keep my computer skills up-to-date. Haven't you peeked? Honestly, Nora, she's utterly icky. No romance, no mystery. It's just plumbing, and not very nice plumbing at that. What would Alan's parents say if they were still alive?"

"Maybe they'd say it's about time Alan did something with his life besides go to matinees."

Libby sat up straighter, aquiver with indignation. "You mean a job? Why should a man with his resources have to work for a living?"

"Because sloth is a deadly sin that kills the soul?"

"Oh, you're just sorry that we lost our own fortune, aren't you?" She patted my hand. "It's natural to grieve. Admit it, Nora, you thoroughly enjoyed the life of leisure before Mama and Daddy left. The hardest work you ever did was decorating the charity balls."

Ever since our parents absconded from Philadelphia to sail off for South America with our trust funds tucked in their matching Louis Vuitton luggage, my sisters and I had struggled to make ends meet. I'd found employment as the lowly assistant to a newspaper society columnist, while our younger sister, Emma, tried to make a career out of training show jumpers for the Grand Prix circuit. Libby, however, had bounced from one scam to another in the pursuit of a line of work that could simultaneously support five kids and unleash her spiritual and sensual potential. Most of the time, I just hoped she wasn't going to get herself arrested by the vice squad.

With a smile, I said, "A job isn't the worst thing that's happened to me."

"Well, Alan should be allowed to enjoy his money and leisure time while he's got them. You should have moved in on him, Nora. If you keep seeing the Mafia prince, you'll end up like Bitty Markham—languishing at home with no sex life while your man sits in jail."

"Libby, Michael is not involved in his father's business."

"That's what they want you to think, isn't it? Nora," she said with a perfectly straight face, "it's possible for a vulnerable woman to be blinded by great sex. Personally, I've always been able to prioritize even in the arms of an excitingly primitive lover, but you're venturing into a new phase of your life that could be very—"

Lucy saved me from the same lecture that had been driving me crazy for months. She returned to the table with her lower lip pouting. "They aren't making any more hot chocolate, Mummy. They say the store closes in ten minutes."

My sister reacted as if she'd been jabbed with a cattle prod. "Oh, heavens, and I haven't found anything to wear to this weekend's reawakening!" She jumped to her feet and grabbed Lucy's velvet coat. "I've got to find the plus-size department immediately. Why do these stores always hide the large sizes? Do they think size sixteen is contagious?"

While Libby gathered up her shopping bags, I helped Lucy fasten the toggles on her coat. " 'Bye, Luce. Thanks for coming with me."

" 'Bye, Aunt Nora!" She gave me a sprinkle-encrusted kiss. "You're coming to my school play, right? On Friday. I play the Third Pickpocket."

"Typecasting," said Libby. "I'm in charge of the PTA refreshment table. We're doing Christmas cookies and raffling off a day-spa treatment with the delicious new man at Jason's."

"I'll be there," I promised.

Holding hands, Libby and Lucy set off through the crowd like mother and daughter killer whales cleaving the rough waters of the North Atlantic.

"Who the heck is Jason?" I asked their departing figures. "And what on earth is a reawakening?"

I pulled myself together with the firm admonishment that I didn't want to know.

Putting my loopy sister out of my mind for the time being, I gathered up my handbag and stepped around Santa's workshop—still teeming with the last few howling children and camcorder-carrying parents of the night. The frazzled elves hurried their final customers out, and I was willing to bet that Santa would sell his soul for a boilermaker. Only the animated reindeer looked tireless as they blinked and nodded in their white plastic wonderland.

With Bing Crosby's croon fading behind me, I headed on my way, passing first into Haymaker's luxury bedding department. Immediately, a display bed blocked my path, and I slowed my pace to admire it. Heaped with red satin cushions, the sensuously plush mattress was covered with a polar bear faux fur and draped with a gauzy white curtain— a perfect spot for Mrs. Claus to await Santa's return from his rounds.

But standing beside the bed was no long-neglected wife hoping to make a little Christmas merriment with her overworked husband.

"Alan?"

Alan Rutledge lingered at the marble mezzanine railing in exactly the same spot his father had stood at closing time every evening, and his grandfather, too. The diminutive owner of Haymaker's smiled down upon his domain like a kid who couldn't tear himself away from the final innings of a crabby baseball game. He obviously didn't see hundreds of crabby customers slapping down their credit cards one more time before rushing off into the night. A much more serene fantasy transfixed him.

I almost hated to disturb his pleasure, but I touched his arm and tried again. "Alan?"

He shook himself as if from a trance and turned to me with a sweet-natured smile. The corona of his strawberry-blond hair glowed like a halo behind his receding hairline and caused his round ears to stand out from the sides of his head exactly like a teddy bear's.

"Nora Blackbird!" he said. "How nice to see you."

I bent down so he could give me a kiss on the cheek and

noticed that Alan did indeed smell divine. I wondered if he hadn't been spritzed as he wandered through the men's cologne department. He often ambled daydreamily around Haymaker's as if lost in a paradise. Vigilant store employees sometimes managed to spiff him up as he floated by. Tonight he wore a perfectly tailored suit that screamed Brioni and disguised his rotund shape. Handsome Italian shoes must have been slipped on his feet by an alert clerk when he wasn't looking.

"Happy holidays, Alan."

"Don't you look fetching." He held my hand and gave me an appreciative once-over. "The working life must agree with you."

"Why, thank you, Alan. I understand congratulations are in order? I hear you're getting married."

For a man of thirty-odd years, he could still blush like a teenager. "Yes, I am. Have you met Cindie Rae? She's a lovely girl."

"She's beautiful." Floundering for something genteel to say about a woman who had exposed every portion of her body—and a few portions of its interior, also—to anyone willing to plunk down a few dollars to buy a magazine or sign on to her Web site, I said ineptly, "I hope you'll be very happy together."

"We're very well suited," Alan said. "She's so full of energy."

Well, *energy* was one euphemism, I supposed. I noticed he carried his own coat as well as a voluptuous fur over his arm. "Are you on your way out this evening?"

"Yes, Cindie Rae and I are going to the theater tonight."

I checked my watch. "Oh, dear, you've missed the curtain!"

The news didn't spoil his amiable mood. "I suppose we have." He gave a little shrug. "We'll catch the second act."

"How disappointing!"

"Not really." With a shy smile, he admitted, "We saw the show last night, and the night before, too."

"My goodness. Cindie Rae must share your enthusiasm for theater."

"Well, I hope she'll learn to enjoy it as much as I do." Alan's face glowed with a rhapsodic bliss. "There's nothing like a great play. I'm lucky she puts up with my obsession."

A more cynical man might think his future wife "put up with him" because he was worth millions and had access to the world's most luxurious goods at wholesale prices. But Alan seemed flattered to have a fiancée who made him miss the overture.

He focused on me again. "Are you doing some Christmas shopping tonight, Nora?"

"I'm going to a party shortly, but first I must pick up a package for a friend. From Popo Prentiss."

Alan's sweet smile faltered only for an instant. "Popo never stops working, does she?"

"She must be a great asset to the store."

"Oh, yes."

With a nearly invisible frown, Alan considered his premier personal shopper—the sales associate who pampered high-end customers into spending astronomical amounts of money in Haymaker's store. Everyone from blue-blooded heiresses and the trophy wives of the nouveau riche, to time-strapped executives or discerning consumers of high-priced goods—they all used Popo. She dashed around the store to personally select merchandise that best suited her demanding clients. With her innate sense of style and ability to predict trends, Popo helped even the most hopeless cases build fashionable wardrobes and enviable lifestyles. Many former fashion failures could attribute their best-dressed status to Popo's skill and energy.

Alan gave a quick head shake to resummon his good cheer. "Popo is remarkable. I hope we never lose her."

I said, "I'm sure Popo stops working when the store closes, so I'd better dash. Enjoy your show, Alan."

"It'll be wonderful," he assured me, brightening again at the prospect of his evening entertainment.

I couldn't stop myself from giving Alan a farewell kiss on the cheek, and he went down the escalator, smiling with anticipation.

Although a grown man had a right to marry anyone he chose, I couldn't imagine shy, low-profile, and culturally sophisticated Alan Rutledge mixed up with a woman of Cindie Rae Smith's very public persona. Her exploits had been splashed all over the local newspapers and magazines to the extent that any living adult would have to be a hermit to not know who she was. Her Internet Web site had triggered an uproar that still—six months after its opening day—raged around the city.

Alan hardly seemed the type to have a liaison with such an astonishingly different person.

But lately people had begun saying the same about me.

Mulling over the oddities of human attraction, I threaded my way through the luxury bedding department. I got half-way into Gucci goods before I managed to bump into Popo Prentiss herself.

"Hey!" She stiff-armed me out of her personal space. "Watch where you're— Oh, it's you."

As tiny and snappish as a terrier with a toothache, Popo glared at me. With one arm raised, she carried several dresses on hangers—enough couture to settle the national debt. In her other hand she held one of the jumbo water bottles she was never seen without, and from one finger dangled a ring of keys—no doubt her access to all the inventory storerooms in Haymaker's. She wore a pair of trim, black Italian jeans and a loose black Dolce & Gabbana cotton shirt printed with vintage travel posters. On her feet she proudly wore running shoes—proof that she never stopped hustling.

"Hello, Popo. I was just on my way to see you."

"Oh?" Popo's small eyes narrowed on me through the white-blond spikes of her signature punk hairdo. Her unspoken question was, "Can you afford Popo now?"

Before my family nest egg got scrambled, I had been one of the first clients to use Popo's services as a personal shopper. For me, Popo had been a big time saver. Oh, I'll admit I could pull out my credit card just as fast as any shopaholic in town, but I had more interesting things to do than poke through hangers at the YSL sale rack. It had been easy to phone Popo and pick up a few pretty things before jetting off to London for a weekend of museums. I'd recommended her to many friends.

But when my parents took the money and ran, and my husband quit doing cocaine long enough to be murdered by his drug dealer, I'd discontinued my relationship with Popo. I couldn't afford her anymore. Nothing like a dose of the real world to set a girl straight.

Popo's hostile expression reminded me that she not only resented my departure as a client, but also that I'd known her when she first got started and needed my help—before she started referring to herself in the third person.

She certainly didn't need anyone's help anymore. I'd recently heard that Popo's work with wealthy clients raked in tens of millions of dollars for the department store every year—far exceeding any other Haymaker's employee. To better facilitate her sales, she had been given her own boutique, a private salon tucked in a corner of the store where she plied her clients with light salads, chilled bottles of Cristal, and plenty of personalized salesmanship.

Popo's expert gaze swept over my ensemble—my faithful Calvin Klein skirt and a well-cut jacket that had seen me through many examinations by fashion Nazis. Although I told myself I didn't care what anyone thought of my clothes, I suddenly hoped I didn't look threadbare.

Unwillingly, Popo said, "You don't look bad, Nora. Is that jacket Carolina Herrera?"

"Yes, as a matter of fact. You have an amazing eye, Popo."

"Popo is the best," she corrected. She flicked through the hangers in her hand and pulled out a long wisp of beaded chiffon. "You should buy this Alberta Ferretti dress. Just the thing for a Christmas party. Good with your coloring. Only twenty-four hundred."

"Thanks." I swallowed hard and tried not to calculate how many rolls of generic toilet paper I could buy with twenty-four hundred dollars. "It's . . . gorgeous."

Popo dangled the dress in front of me like juicy bait at the end of a sharp hook. The garment probably weighed as much as a handkerchief and looked as if it might cling to my curves like melted butter. Popo smirked. "You could make your boyfriend crazy with this dress."

"Uhm . . ."

"Maybe he'd buy it for you. I hear he's a rich bad boy. C'mon. Only takes a minute to try it on."

I gave myself a mental slap. What was I thinking? Even a Kathie Lee Casual from Wal-Mart was beyond my budget. "I can't," I said firmly. "I'm here to pick up a package for Lexie Paine."

Popo immediately snatched the dress back, and gave up trying to tempt me. "Lexie's box is inside." She jerked her head toward the glass door of her salon. "Check with Darwin. He'll find it for you. Just duck before you ask for the package."

"Duck?"

"Yeah. Darwin's not your biggest fan. He might throw something at you."

I couldn't imagine why Popo's assistant could possibly care about me. "Why should Darwin want to hit me?"

Her grin was more of a death-mask grimace than a smile. "He heard about your recommendation."

"My—"

"You told Alan Rutledge not to promote Darwin."

"I never—"

I stopped myself. At the intermission of a benefit performance of a Broadway show months ago, Alan and I had spoken briefly on the subject of Darwin Osdack, Popo's assistant. With a flush, I remembered Alan asking if I thought Darwin was ready to become a personal shopper and start taking clients of his own. My response had been guarded—definitely lacking in enthusiasm. I suddenly realized now that Alan had taken my lukewarm answer as a negative comment on Darwin's abilities.

"You were right, of course." Popo slugged some water from her enormous plastic bottle. "That goes without saying. Darwin's not ready. But he decided it was you who tipped off Alan about the shrinkage problem."

"Shrinkage problem?"

"You know—employees walking off with merchandise. Darwin thought he was getting away with it, but you must have sharper eyes than Popo does. Nobody suspected Darwin was the thief."

"But I didn't know anything," I said. "If Alan inferred that I believed Darwin was doing anything wrong—"

"Store security couldn't prove anything," Popo assured me. "If they had, Darwin would have been history right away. But he's definitely on probation, and he didn't get the promotion."

"Because of me."

Again, Popo gave one of her ghastly smiles. "Yep. So duck when you pick up the package."

"Thanks for the warning," I said. "And for the package. I'm sure Lexie will appreciate the work you've—"

"Popo, darling!" A trilling voice interrupted us.

From around a rack of Gucci belts came a tall, skinny woman wearing a mink coat and enough gold jewelry to sink a pirate ship. She carried two Haymaker's shopping bags that bulged with her booty.

"Sage, darling," Popo cried, giving double air kisses. "Just in time to see the David Yurman necklaces before they're all gone!"

"You kept a few back for me, right, Popo? You're the best!"

In the presence of a paying customer, Popo was instantly a different person. Her eyes sparkled with enthusiasm, and her energy level spiked to match her client's. She seized Sage's arm and guided her toward the escalator. "Let's run down to Fine Jewelry this instant. I found the most perfect diamond pendant, just the thing to go with that Valentino for New Year's Eve. And earrings to match!"

"What would I do without you, Popo?" Sage gushed.

Popo never looked back at me. She had work to do for worthier customers.

"Merry Christmas," I murmured after their departing figures.

I stood for a dreadful moment, thinking about Darwin Osdack's situation. About how my stupidly unenthusiastic comment in a social situation to Alan may have spoiled Darwin's chances for advancement.

From my handbag emerged my dog, Spike, awakened perhaps by the proximity of a creature with even fewer appealing qualities than himself. He snarled sleepily.

Spike had been a gift from my driver's mother, and I'd been struggling to adjust to coping with a pet ever since. He was ten pounds of pure dynamite with many bad habits, and I had taken to carrying him around in an old Balenciaga handbag to keep him from destroying my home while I was out. Trouble was, he'd been badly injured a few weeks earlier, and his recovery involved plaster casts and sometimes a little wheeled cart to support his hindquarters. Mostly, however, he seemed content to snooze in my bag. But with a flicker of his old bad temperament, he glared after Popo's departing figure and growled.

"Don't let her bother you," I said, patting his bristly head. "There's no chance I'll be doing business with Popo anytime soon."

Spike, an ugly little fiend on his best day, gallantly suggested he pee on her foot.

"Go back to sleep." I stuffed his head back into my bag.

Outside Popo's salon stood a headless mannequin wearing a spectacular Oscar de la Renta gown—a fountain of ruffles, and cut on the bias, too—enough camouflage to hide the figure flaws of a camel. No doubt Popo had placed the dress there to entice one of her customers needing a last-minute grand entrance to a holiday party. Popo was smart that way—she always knew what her clients needed before they did. But looking at the Oscar, all I could think about was the beaded dress Popo had shown me. It was even more beautiful than the one on display.

But now I had to face Darwin.

I took a deep breath for courage and pushed through the door to Popo's private enclave, and found myself in a wonderland of the most expensive goods sold under Haymaker's roof. Piles of handbags designed by celebrity wives, mounds of featherlight lingerie, racks of sequined party dresses—all evidence that Popo continued to do what she did best—push the priciest products on very willing customers.

But not all her customers were happy.

As I stepped into the salon, a female voice snarled, "There's only one thing we can do. We'll have to kill Popo together."

Chapter 2

Behind Popo's cluttered desk, Darwin Osdack clutched a tiny leather handbag protectively against his puny chest and brandished a silver letter opener. "What, are you crazy?"

Two customers faced the desk, their backs to me. One was a slim young blonde wearing a black satin corset over spandex pants that clung to her body like the skin of a greyhound fresh off the racetrack. The heels of her tight boots were too high and stiletto-thin. Her hair cascaded around her shoulders like yellow cotton candy. She leaned over the desk and presented her perfect butt to me for admiration while jamming her finger into Darwin's solar plexus. "I want that handbag, Darwin. Yesterday I told Popo I'd strangle her with my bare hands to get it. You're not man enough to keep that bag away from me now."

"I can't give it to you!" Darwin's foxy face puckered with the effort to keep from weeping. "Popo already promised it to somebody else!"

"I'm here now, and I want it."

"But Popo says—"

"Dammit, my fiancé owns this dump!" The blonde slapped a clear spot on the desk so hard the platoon of Popo's various beverage bottles jumped. "That means I get anything I want!"

Maybe because I felt guilty about Darwin, I suddenly found myself protecting him.

"Excuse me," I said.

Cindie Rae Smith spun around. Her flawless, Botoxed face was flushed, but uncreased despite her rage. Platinum hoops danced furiously in her ears. A vein throbbed in her

15

throat. Her bosom—two astonishing monuments to modern surgical technique—quivered with suppressed fury.

"Who the hell are you?"

"Hello, I'm Nora Blackbird." I put out my hand to her. She ignored my hand and tried to narrow her eyes, but the Botox did its duty. "Is that supposed to mean something to me?"

"I'm an old friend of Alan's. I just spoke with him. He's looking forward to seeing a play with you tonight."

"Let him wait. That damn *Titanic* takes longer to sink on stage than it did in the ocean." Cindie Rae's lips— unnaturally puffed with collagen—curled into a distorted smile that had to be painful. "Darwin's about to give me the Lettitia McGraw handbag I want."

"No," said the other customer. "Darwin's going to give it to me."

The aristocratic woman who towered over the desk was none other than Pinky Pinkerton, the elderly heiress to the Jiffy Kitty Litter Box fortune. Although Pinky lived in splendor on Philadelphia's Main Line with a tennis court, swimming pool, and golf and archery greens to keep her fit and feisty, she wore a threadbare Burberry coat and a pair of faded khaki trousers that belied her tax bracket. With a stubborn Hepburn jaw and white, boyish haircut, Pinky generally radiated patrician disapproval, but tonight she appeared to be appalled to find herself in the presence of the infamous Cindie Rae.

"Hello, Pinky," I said. "I haven't seen you since last year's tennis finals."

Although bruised from heaven only knew what kind of sporting accidents, Pinky still looked capable of whipping the youngsters who dared set their pretty white sneakers on her tennis court. At the very least she seemed ready to flatten Darwin with the ratty umbrella gripped in her right hand.

"Hello, Nora," she said, stiffly summoning her composure. "I'm sorry you walked in on this ugly scene."

"Oh, my gawd!" Darwin put the letter opener to his own throat. "As if my day wasn't crappy enough! First these two harridans, and now you! I might as well kill myself."

"Do it," Cindie Rae said. "And I'll get the handbag."

"You'll do no such thing, Mr. Osdack," Pinky snapped.

"I was promised that bag for my granddaughter's Christmas gift, and you're going to hand it over immediately."

Cindie Rae thrust out her armored chest. "You'll have to go through me to get the bag, you old battle-ax. So back off—unless you want to try shoving a pillow over my face like you smothered all your husbands."

Darwin gasped. I nearly swallowed my own tongue.

Upon hearing the long-whispered accusation spoken aloud, Pinky drew herself up to her full rangy height and sent a lightning bolt of a glare down at Cindie Rae. "You, young lady, are a tramp, pure and simple. I won't listen to that kind of talk."

"So hit the road," Cindie Rae said. "And good riddance."

Pinky skewered Darwin with an equally electric glare. "If I hear you've given that bag to this gold digger, young man, I'll do worse than murder you. I'll make sure you never work in this city again."

I thought Pinky might sweep out of the salon with her head high, but no such luck.

With her umbrella, she whacked the letter opener from Darwin's grip and made one last grab for the handbag. Darwin shrieked, but he was trapped behind the desk and couldn't escape. He whipped the bag over his head to keep it from Pinky's long-armed grasp.

Cindie Rae saw her chance and lunged.

"Ow!"

"No!"

When all three sets of hands latched onto the Lettitia McGraw handbag, Pinky began beating Darwin's head with her umbrella, and I saw Cindie Rae grab a handful of his hair. Darwin shrieked. The three of them crashed down on the desk in a grunting tangle. Popo's water bottles and carefully organized merchandise flew off the desk in a whirling hurricane of debris. I was hit by a Jimmy Choo and dodged the splashing contents of one of Popo's cans of Slim-Fast. The can clattered to the floor, spraying chocolate glop in all directions, and a six-pack of water bottles tumbled down into the mess.

The melee woke Spike, who muscled his way out of my bag with an unholy snarl. Quicker than an angry rattlesnake, he flashed his teeth at the nearest target—Darwin's protruding left ear. I heard the sickening crunch of cartilage, then Darwin's scream. Spike—startled by his success—immediately released his prey. But the tantalizing scent of Slim-Fast caught his attention. Before I could grab him, the dog made a dive out of my bag. He hit the floor and splashed into a sticky chocolate lake at my feet.

"A rat!" Darwin snatched his feet off the floor. Pinky leaped onto the desk, too, pinning Darwin under her knee, but hanging on to the handbag for dear life. Somehow Cindie Rae had commandeered the umbrella, and she began beating Pinky's shoulder with it.

I bent and grabbed a bottle of water from the floor. With a snap, I opened the cap. "Stop it! Stop it, all of you!"

I splashed water on the writhing heap of humanity as if breaking up a vicious dogfight.

Cindie Rae reeled back first. "My hair!"

Darwin scrambled out of danger. "This shirt is pure silk—dry clean only!"

Only Pinky had the composure to stand back in rigid silence, straightening her coat with the last vestiges of her dignity.

"That's enough," I snapped. "You're all behaving like crazy people. Darwin, give me the bag."

His hand trembling, Darwin obediently placed the Lettitia McGraw bag in my upturned palm. I took possession calmly.

"Now," I said. "We've had quite enough violence for one night. We're going to let Popo decide who gets this bag. It's her job, and she does it extremely well."

Darwin made a rude noise with his lips.

Cindie Rae was still rearranging the mane of her hair. "We'll see about that. If I have any say in the matter, Popo is history!"

Pinky said, "I think I know how to solve this impasse. Here, young man. Surely you can spend this wisely."

She placed a crisp one-hundred-dollar bill on Popo's desk, but Darwin recoiled from the money as if it might be contaminated. "Take that back! Do you want to get me fired? I'm not taking bribes!"

"Since when?" Pinky demanded. "Popo makes no bones about it."

"Take it back, take it back!"

"Oh, stop screaming." Pinky snatched up her money. "I'm going to find Popo this minute. I'll get this straightened out one way or another."

She made a stalking exit, the hem of her Burberry coat flying out behind her skinny frame.

"That woman is a menace!" Cindie Rae went to the mirror and checked her hair. "Why hasn't she been convicted and electrocuted by now? Everybody knows she killed both her husbands."

"That's enough," I said.

"Who do you think you are? And you," she said to Darwin. "If you breathe a word of this catfight, you'll regret it. I'll tell Alan everything that happened here."

Satisfied with her hair, she gathered up a shopping bag and followed Pinky out of the salon with a hip swivel that would have done spinal damage to a person with less muscle tone.

"There," I said, handing the Lettitia McGraw back to Darwin. "You'd better put this bag in a safe place."

He sniffed. "I'll take it down to the store safe in the security office."

"Good idea."

"What a mess!" He rubbed his bitten ear as he surveyed the chaos of Popo's carefully arranged merchandise. Hysteria threatened again, but Darwin bravely gathered his courage. "I have to get this cleaned up before Popo gets back."

"Let me help."

"God, no." He shuddered at the thought of spending another instant in my company. "I'll manage somehow. It's past closing time. All customers should be out of the store by now. Including you."

"Listen, Darwin, I'd like to talk with you."

Still standing stiff and wounded behind the desk, he said, "About what?"

"There's been a misunderstanding, and if I was part of it, I need to make things right."

"I don't know what you're talking about."

Spike stopped lapping up the spilled Slim-Fast and began scrambling around underfoot, dragging his hindquarters and panting with excitement. He tracked chocolate paw prints all over Popo's floor.

I picked up Spike and held him away from my clothing.

He dripped with Slim-Fast. "First let me clean up the dog in the lavatory. Then we'll have a discussion."

Silently, Darwin pointed.

I ducked into the bathroom at the back of the small salon and plunked Spike in the sink. At once he sensed what was coming and tried to climb out, but I was too quick for him. Pinning the dog in place, I carefully scooped warm water over his rough coat to avoid soaking his casts.

"You are a menace," I told him.

At last I turned off the water and held Spike down with one hand as I stretched to yank a handful of paper towels from the dispenser.

Which was when the lights went out.

"What in the world . . . ?"

Silence. The lavatory had no window, so the darkness was complete. Spike gave a nervous yap.

"Quiet," I told him, and blindly tried to dry him off with the towels. Over my shoulder, I called, "Darwin?"

I heard someone jiggle the locked doorknob.

"Darwin? What's going on?"

No response. I put Spike on the floor and felt my way to the door. I grabbed the knob and twisted to disengage the lock, but when I tried to pull the door inward, it didn't budge. "Darwin!" I called. "I'm locked in here!"

Still no answer. And no lights. Panting and whining with excitement, Spike hobbled around my feet in the small bathroom.

The bathroom lock was on the inside of the door, I reasoned. So why couldn't I let myself out? It was as if the door had been dead-bolted from the outside.

In total darkness, I rapped my knuckles on the door. Then I pounded. I shouted. I kicked the door as loudly as I could. To accompany me, Spike barked and finally began to howl.

But Darwin didn't come to open the door.

Nobody did.

"That little bastard locked us in here for the night," I said to Spike.

The puppy sat down on my foot and whined.

After five minutes of fuming, I finally got an idea. I went to the door and felt around the edges to locate the hinges. "Aha."

Groping in my handbag for something to use as a tool, I poked myself with a metal nail file. I pulled it out and tested its strength. It was flimsy, but it would have to get the job done. Cautiously, I wedged the nail file up into the hinge and pushed. I felt the bolt give way, but only slightly. Getting the door off the hinges was going to be a tedious process.

When the first hinge was disassembled and the second bolt nearly wiggled out, the lights suddenly came on again. I checked my watch. Nearly forty-five minutes had passed, and I'd broken three fingernails. The palms of my hands were going to be bruised. I ran cold water into the sink to soak them for a minute, then went back to inching the hinge apart.

I let out a cry of relief when the second bolt fell out and hit the tile floor with a musical *ding*. Wrestling the door out of position was harder than I imagined. It didn't just fall into my arms. I had to shove and wiggle and heave to inch the heavy door out of place.

At last, the weight of it fell sideways. A rush of cool air entered the lavatory. I looked out and realized that someone had tied one length of a rope around the doorknob and fastened the other end to a sturdy coatrack on the opposite wall.

"Darwin, you little fink!" I said to the empty salon.

No sign of the weasel.

I gathered up the contents of my bag and shoved it back where it belonged. Then I stepped over the rope and picked up Spike. "Let's get out of here."

Just as eager to leave as I was, Spike let himself be dumped into my bag. I pushed out of the salon and into the darkened department store.

It was eerie, deserted and quiet. The usual rumble of escalators, heating system, and muffled music had been silenced. I didn't see a single person. Even the reindeer in Santa's Wonderland were still. I headed for the escalator.

At the edge of the luxury bedding department stood the display bed I'd noticed earlier. But something was different this time.

I stopped still at the foot of the bed. "Popo?"

The sprawled body of Popo Prentiss lay in the bed-clothes, the sheets wildly twisted around her. Popo didn't move. Her eyes were half-open and unfocused. One of her hands lay upturned and flaccid. The other still gripped her plastic water bottle, now empty and dented. I realized I was standing in a splashed puddle of water.

"No," I said, already feeling the floor begin to tilt around me.

I didn't need to touch her to know she was dead. Her stillness was complete. I could see that a plump needlepoint pillow with a Ralph Lauren tag had been abandoned beside her head. A thin line of foamy drool ran from the corner of her mouth. The blond spikes of her hair were damp. She had tried to fight off her killer with the water bottle.

"No," I said again. I backed away from the bed and bumped into a display shelf. A rack of brilliant yellow towels cascaded around me, and I cried out. I pushed away and rushed for the escalator. I stumbled on the top step, then caught my balance on the railing and clattered downward. I must have shouted, but the panic was deafening.

From below, a rush of darkness swirled up to me. Not an electrical blackout this time, but a different kind of darkness. I had to find help before I passed out.

At the bottom of the escalator, a figure in a uniform appeared. I made out a bald head and a name tag that swam before my eyes. He reached for me, but I couldn't see his face, only the Haymaker's logo embroidered on his shirt. A security guard.

"Call the police." I gasped. "Popo's been murdered."

Chapter 3

My best friend, Lexie Paine, greeted me at the front door of her home. "Sweetie, where have you been? I was ready to send a Saint Bernard to go search for you."

"Sorry I'm late." I stepped inside and reached for the edge of a table to support myself.

Lexie lived in a converted Victorian-style boathouse along the famous Boathouse Row on the Schuylkill River, a picturesque curve of storybook houses that were maintained by various boating clubs. With her powerful connections and bottomless personal bank account, my friend had managed to score one of the abandoned boathouses and had renovated the second floor into luxurious living quarters.

Behind her, I could hear the buzz and hum of party guests along with soft jazz and the scent of expensive flowers from Neppo.

Summoning some self-control, I said, "You, on the other hand, look stunning. Which rapper did you have to mug to get that necklace?"

Slim and sinewy from beating up bulls and bears on Wall Street, Lexie wore a smoky black cashmere ensemble and double strand of serious bling. She toyed with one of the diamonds at her throat. "I had a good week in the Asia markets. You won't believe how desperate American manufacturers are to get themselves into pathetic Chinese villages so they can exploit the workers and make billions. I could spend every day playing matchmaker if I didn't get bored with all the upstanding, two-faced executives from Omaha."

"Nobody would ever mistake you for two-faced, Lex. You tell it like it is."

Lexie closed the door and gave me a hug. "Sorry about the rant. Now, sweetie, what's happened? You look white as Christmas snow. My God, you're shaking!"

"Careful," I said. "I don't want to spoil your party."

My friend popped her eyes wide and held me away from herself to get a better look at my face. "What's happened? You didn't discover another dead body, did you?"

"As a matter of fact—"

She cursed prayerfully. "You're kidding! Who was it? Anybody I know?"

"Popo Prentiss."

Aghast, Lexie pulled me over to the staircase and we sat down together on the bottom step. I put my bag gently on the floor, and Spike slept on. Hugging my knees, I told Lexie the whole story, keeping my voice low so as not to disturb her guests.

"And you were locked in the loo while it happened?" Lexie put her arm across my shoulders for comfort. "My God, Nora, it could have been you!"

"I doubt it," I said.

"What do you mean?"

"I've had a couple of hours to think about it. If you were a random killer, would you commit your crime in the middle of a department store shortly after closing? With all those security cameras going?"

"You think someone deliberately murdered Popo? Hell, what am I saying? Of course she was deliberately murdered. Half the people in this town despise her!"

"And the other half suck up to her so she'll get the dresses they want for the Christmas galas." I gave a hiccough and realized I was fighting back tears.

Lexie tightened her arm around me. "You've had a terrible shock. I'm so sorry, sweetie."

"I'm okay. The police came right away. They were very nice to me."

Her expression reflected genuine concern. "Did you faint?"

I blanched. "Yes. Dammit, I wish I could get over that tendency. It makes me feel like such an idiot."

"You're just empathic. But there's nothing to worry

about now. Surely the police are looking at videotapes this minute. There must be security cameras all over that store. The killer will be caught in no time."

"That's the thing. Somebody tampered with the security system." I told her about the power outage. "All the cameras went off-line."

"You mean someone from inside the store shut off the electricity?"

"Not just electricity, but the backup generator for the security systems, too. Someone really knew what they were doing."

Lexie blew a sigh and shook her head. "This is certainly going to be more bad news for Haymaker's."

"More bad news?"

Lexie smiled wryly at my question. "You listen to all the wrong gossip, sweetie. Haymaker's is performing poorly. It's the dreaded third-generation syndrome."

"The what?"

"Alan Rutledge is the third generation to own the store. His granddaddy started by selling pencils on the street and built Haymaker's from nothing. Then Alan's father joined the biz and made it into a regional chain. The two of them worked like dogs to build Haymaker's, but they never showed Alan how to get his hands dirty. Now he's on his own, and he doesn't know how to mind the store. He'd rather go see a musical. It's a classic business story. The third generation bungles the family store."

"Haymaker's is going out of business?"

"No, but the vultures are circling. I've heard a couple of big retailers are looking to buy out Haymaker's."

"Maybe that's a good thing," I said. "Alan will be free to enjoy what he really loves."

Lexie nodded. "He's a closet song-and-dance man. I heard a wild rumor he got engaged to Cindie Rae Smith. That can't be true, can it?"

"It can, and is. I saw Cindie Rae at the store tonight. She was acting as if she owned the place already. I think she's the closest Alan could get to a leading lady."

Lexie leaned closer. "Did you get a good look at her? I mean, is she as . . . enhanced as everyone says?"

"Put her in the warm sunshine and she'd melt like a Hershey bar."

"Ugh. I hear her Web site is beyond revolting, too. What is Alan thinking?"

"We both know what he's thinking."

Lexie shuddered. "Everybody knows I'd rather make money than love. I have no sex drive whatsoever. It's so messy, for one thing, and all those dreadful emotions that make people do crazy things like— Oh, sorry, sweetie. I didn't mean you."

"No offense taken."

Lexie wagged her head. "But Alan . . . What a waste of a solid family fortune."

I took a deep, steadying breath and let it out slowly. "I can't believe Popo is dead."

"Me neither. She may have been universally hated, but she was indispensable to a lot of my friends."

Just a few minutes with Lexie had made me feel better. But I didn't want to spoil her party. "Look, I should go. I'm sorry to bring bad tidings. I should have waited until morning to call you. But I thought I'd better stop by to apologize for not picking up your package in case it was something you needed tonight."

"Oh, forget about that! Heavens, you shouldn't have bothered. It was only a little evening bag I planned to use next weekend."

"A little evening bag?"

"Right. Popo called and said it would match a dress I'm wearing to a charity ball on Saturday. A Lettitia McGraw handbag."

I couldn't help myself. I laughed.

She cocked her head. "What's the story?"

"It's a very popular bag tonight, that's all. Look, I'd better run along. You have a lovely party to host, and I—"

"Don't beg off," she commanded, getting to her feet and extending her hand to help me up. "You have to stick around. If nothing else, you could use a stiff drink, I'm sure. And everybody wants to see you."

Although I simply wanted to go home to my own bed, I could hardly walk out without saying a few hellos. I picked up my bag with the sleeping puppy inside and shouldered it. "All right. Tell me who's here."

"The usual suspects." Lexie linked her arm with mine to pull me into her home. "That nutty writer, what's-her-

name, with the book about cloning babies or something.
And the new curator for the museum."

"Belinda, the one with the red glasses?"

"Yes. It's a good blend, although I accidentally invited
too many politicians. It seems everybody's running for
mayor except that handsome John Fitch, who's also here.
You've met him before, right? I think he has a shot at the
Senate. Plus a handful of my best friends for sex appeal."

"And there must be one of your billionaire clients or
two in the mix."

She grinned. "Of course."

"Are you raising money for the museum?"

"Always. Tonight I'm targeting Vince Scuddy. Do you
know him? He owns a truckload of cable television stock,
so he can afford to spend most of his time playing street
hockey with underserved kids in South Philly."

"Sounds like a mensch."

"Who needs something cultural to balance his résumé,
and then I suppose he'll run for mayor, too."

We arrived in her living room, which was packed with
guests. For a woman of her income and a family history at
least as old as my own, Lexie lived in remarkably small
quarters. Her boathouse was sparsely and inexpensively
furnished, but hung with spectacular art from the collection
her mother had inherited and Lexie's own investment
pieces. The president of the art museum board, she had the
combination of serious scholarship, instinctive good taste,
and the gargantuan disposable income needed to possess
paintings and sculpture that were the envy of many long-
time collectors.

"You moved your Warhol out of the bedroom." I observed the pop-art portrait that dominated the living
room wall.

"I moved a Vermeer oil study over my bed instead,
which is ever so much more restful."

Two friends approached and gave me air kisses, and
someone offered to get me a drink. I tried to make conversation, but I felt as if my body were floating on the ceiling
as the party whirled around me. I tried to fake being socia-
ble. The mental image of Popo Prentiss's body kept popping into my head. Even handsome John Fitch couldn't
distract me with his usual intelligent charm.

Soon one of the hired waiters came over and murmured into Lexie's ear. She nodded, then leaned close to me and said quietly, "Why don't you take a few minutes in the kitchen? I understand there's someone waiting for you there."

I gave her a grateful squeeze and excused myself from John. With a smile that was more relieved than festive, I slipped through the crowd until I reached the swinging door to Lexie's kitchen.

There, the catering staff was quietly preparing more canapés, washing up glassware, and efficiently keeping bottles opened and trays filled. I recognized my childhood friend Jill Mascione, as she whipped a tray of caviar blintzes out of the oven. I had met her long ago at the parties my parents threw and her parents catered. We had played marbles under the bunted tables while the adults drank champagne above us. Now she ran her family's business, and I saw her often at social events.

Jill caught my eye and grinned, too busy to do more. Then she shot a pointed glance across the room, and I followed her gaze.

The door to Lexie's small wine cellar stood open. It was more of a closet than a cellar, of course—just a few square feet of floor space with a small table surrounded by racks of wine bottles. A shaft of kitchen light knifed into the room, illuminating the figure inside.

A man with hulking shoulders ate from a bowl of pasta, both elbows on the table, half in shadow. The kitchen staff respected his presence by tiptoeing about their chores and sending uneasy glances in his direction. He frowned at Lexie's wine labels as he twirled his fork, the rough planes of his face set in the glower of a man with a mean hangover.

I went to the door and leaned in. "I see you're out of jail."

He looked up at me and the hangover expression disappeared. He smiled. His eyes were the same intense blue as an acetylene torch, but reflected more heat. "Hey."

"You're making everybody nervous."

"I haven't even threatened to break any kneecaps yet."

"I guess you just look like a man who could hurt a few people before dessert."

"There's dessert?"

I kissed his mouth. "What are you doing here?"

Michael "the Mick" Abruzzo, son of the infamous New Jersey mob boss "Big Frankie" Abruzzo, had given up his life of crime for love. So he claimed. Tonight he looked like an unreformed wise guy in faded jeans and a black sweater loose enough to conceal a weapon. He'd slung his leather jacket over the chair back. His blunt, Roman nose had been daunting even before it was broken, and the dent in his chin was courtesy of a long-ago prison-yard brawl. These days I failed to see what was so frightening about his face, but I was in the minority.

He said, "We left things up in the air the other night."

"So you tracked me down for a rematch?"

Mischief danced in his gaze. "I'm game. Hungry?"

"No, thanks." The idea of food made my stomach give a little roll. "How did you score dinner for yourself? The rest of the guests are only getting hors d'oeuvres."

"I dunno. Maybe the cook thought I'd stay out of trouble if my stomach was full." He looked down at his bowl. "She made this just for me. It's good stuff. White truffles. Sure you don't want a taste?"

I touched an unruly curl of his dark hair. "I'm sure."

In a different tone, he said, "Want to go home?"

"Yes, please."

He got up, a tall, powerful body that radiated comfort and something much more magnetic. Touching the point of my chin, he said, "Let's blow this joint."

"Why don't you come inside and meet some of Lexie's guests first?"

"No," he said.

I slanted a glance up at him. "Are you afraid to meet my friends?"

"Nope."

"Because they're dying to meet you."

"I'm not going to scare the shit out of your aristocratic pals just for the entertainment value. Anyway, you need to get home, I think."

I carried his plate and silverware to the sink and spoke briefly to my friend Jill. Waiting by the back door, Michael drained the glass of red wine he'd been sipping and left it on the counter. We went out the door into the cold air. The harsh, damp smell of the river washed up to us as we walked around the side of the boathouse and past the long line of vehicles Lexie's guests had parked in her driveway. There were German cars and Rovers, plus a Hummer and a Jag or two.

Under a no-parking sign, Michael had angled one of his many muscle cars. This battered one looked ready for an Ozark stock-car track, with a low nose and a spoiler on the back. He saw me into the passenger seat before going around and getting in behind the wheel. Then he started the engine and thumbed the heater full blast before turning sideways toward me.

He said, "You going to tell me what happened now?"

"Is it that obvious?"

"You look plenty shaken up. Who's dead?"

Chapter 4

Later, at Blackbird Farm, after I'd told him everything and spent a couple of tumultuous hours reaffirming life, I once again heard Michael's unique perspective on crime.

With one shoulder propped against the headboard, he said, "It's the assistant."

"You think Darwin killed Popo?" I filed my broken fingernails with an emery board while deciding if we were tired enough to sleep or had just reenergized ourselves for a long night. "Why?"

"The twerp assistant has the best motive. He wanted her job. And he's probably got access to the security system."

"But he didn't have enough time. He locked me in the bathroom, and then— Wait, that's why you want to see him arrested, right? Because he locked me up?"

Michael grinned slowly. "If he'd hurt you, he'd be in a hell of a lot more trouble."

"From you? Tell me, Tarzan," I said, dropping the emery board on the bedside table, "precisely how does your family exact revenge on the reckless fools who mess with your women?"

"Is that what you are now? My woman?"

"Let's not get ahead of ourselves," I said.

"Nora—"

"Let's just be happy that you're not in police custody at the moment, shall we?"

Reminded of our recent argument, he rubbed his face as if to erase the events of the last several days. "They didn't arrest me. It was the usual drill, a bunch of questions. The whole thing was blown out of proportion in the papers."

"Michael," I said with mock solemnity, "please tell me you didn't throw a dwarf."

"Monty's not a dwarf. He may be altitude-challenged, but he's technically not a dwarf. Anyway, he makes up for his size in orneriness. The crazy son of a bitch has been known to bite. And nobody likes a biter."

"The papers say his nickname is Monty Python."

"Yeah, well, you don't want to know why. He's liable to show you."

I had learned not to challenge Michael when it came to matters of taste. "So Monty once worked for the Abruzzo family?"

"For a couple of years, yeah, he did collecting—you know, debts. He was very good at it. He could crawl through doggie doors when customers refused to let him inside."

"But now he's going to testify against your father? Over the racketeering thing?"

"He was lined up to testify. But he fell into a Dumpster and got a few bruises." Michael shrugged. "A junkie snitch told a cop that I— Look, I wasn't even in the same county at the time."

"Really?"

"I was at a truck auction with a couple of hundred witnesses, so the cops let me go. Simple."

"Even I'm not naïve enough to believe it's simple, Michael. Intimidating a person from testifying against your father's organization is tampering with a witness. That's a felony."

He shrugged. "The police claim he's being coerced, but they can't prove it."

"The papers say somebody stole property of Monty's and is holding it hostage for his silence. What property might that be?"

For a moment he considered not answering, then said, "An Elvis suit."

I blinked. "He likes Elvis?"

"Monty's very big into Elvis. He puts on a little white suit and jumps out of cakes as Elvis. It's a good line of work when you're a dwarf."

"You've seen him jump out of a cake dressed like Elvis?"

"Only pictures. It's mostly a girl thing."

"You mean he takes off the suit?"

"Parts of it."

I debated whether to ask Michael if he knew who was currently in possession of the little Elvis jumpsuit and decided I didn't want to know the answer. He watched me think it over and smiled.

I said, "Just promise me you won't get your picture taken with him, Elvis costume or not. You're nearly two feet taller than Monty. The two of you will look like something in Ripley's Believe It or Not."

Michael rolled over and pinned me to the pillows. Without his clothes, his body was lean and hard. He said, "I promise. You're cold again. What do you have against central heating?"

"It's expensive."

I'd returned to my family's drafty homestead when my parents gave me the deed to the family farm. I'd moved into the ramshackle mansion with a firm vow to keep the family legacy out of the hands of land developers, and ever since then I'd fought a hard economic battle. In addition to the estate, my parents handed over to me their delinquent tax bill, which amounted to an impossible two million dollars. After the shock wore off, I'd sold everything of value to organize a tax repayment plan, then gotten a job and drafted Lexie to help me find creative ways to pay the monthly bill. So far, I was keeping my head above water. But barely.

Michael had been the first creative source of income. We'd met when he and a friend purchased five acres of my prime riverfront farmland. I'd received enough money to hang on to Blackbird Farm a little longer, and Michael had promptly built Mick's Muscle Cars, a used-car lot that I could see from my bedroom window. Since our relationship had evolved, however, I didn't feel right about accepting money from him. It felt too much like my old life.

Michael said, "Why don't you move over to my place for the winter? It's not a palace, but at least we won't be Popsicles by spring."

I traced the line of his collarbone with my fingertips and didn't answer.

He said, "Don't be upset about Monty. This thing will blow over."

"And then what?"

"I'm doing my best," he said, already nibbling his way down my ribs one by one. "It takes a while for the tiger to— What did you say before? To change his stripes?"

"Michael . . ."

"Hmm . . . ?"

His mouth felt better and better, and I sighed. "Never mind."

Later, we slept tangled up in each other's limbs, breathing in sync and perhaps dreaming together, too. Only once, when my subconscious mind began to churn with images of Popo's death, did Michael nudge me awake.

"You're having a nightmare," he murmured, half-asleep himself.

I held him tighter and tried to forget about crime.

In the morning, he dressed and went out to buy a newspaper while I showered. In my pajamas and with wet hair, I went downstairs and found coffee made and Michael reading the paper at the kitchen table. He read aloud while I puttered with oatmeal at the stove. Spike trundled his little cart around the kitchen, his front paws propelling him while his hindquarters healed from his accident. When the bell chimed in the front hall, Michael and I exchanged a look.

"Expecting company?" he asked.

"Not at this hour."

"Want me to get scarce?"

I ruffled his hair. "No need."

Spike dragged his cart to the entry hall. When I hauled open the front door, I found a former *Penthouse* Pet on the porch.

Cindie Rae Smith glared at the sagging doorjamb and the warped porch floor. "God, does this museum even have indoor plumbing?"

"Hello, Cindie Rae," I said. "Is it cookie season already?"

Cindie Rae's morning attire did not resemble a Girl Scout uniform. She wore a hilarious attempt at a business suit—pinstripes with a white blouse that actually bow-tied under her chin. But the jacket barely buttoned around her wasp waist, and her breasts threatened to explode from their prison any moment. The pants were tighter than the skin of a tomato, and she tottered precariously on very high heels. She had managed to stuff the hugeness of her blond hair into a Monica Lewinsky beret. No amount of Botox or plastic surgery on her face could have hidden the fact that she hadn't slept much since I'd seen her the night before.

"I need to talk to you," she said.

"I can guess what this is about, Cindie Rae, and I don't think the police would be pleased to hear we tried to get our stories straight."

"I don't care what your story is," she snapped. "I need your help."

She pushed past me into the house. "Boy, that's an ugly dog. Do I smell coffee?"

She headed for the kitchen, hesitating only when she arrived in the butler's pantry and couldn't figure out which door to choose. I led the way into the kitchen. Spike followed Cindie Rae, ready to bite her if she made a wrong move.

Michael lowered the newspaper and looked at Cindie Rae over the tops of his reading glasses.

She stopped dead at the sight of him, too. "Oh, wow."

"Morning."

"You must be . . ." She simpered, awaiting a formal introduction.

Briskly, I said, "Cindie Rae, this is Michael Abruzzo. Cindie Rae Smith."

Michael appeared not to notice the jiggle in her blouse or the camel toe in her pants. He picked up the newspaper and went back to reading. I suspected he was playing it safe.

I could almost see the steam rising from Cindie Rae's overtaxed brain as she desperately tried to figure the best way to engage Michael in a conversation that dealt with her area of expertise. Before she reached a decision, I poured her a cup of hot coffee and pushed it into her hands. "Here you go. Sit down."

"Thanks." She took a tentative sip and eased her bottom into the chair opposite Michael's. She leaned sideways to peer around his newspaper. "I, uh, hope I'm not interrupting."

"What's on your mind, Cindie Rae?" I knocked my

knuckles on the table to get her attention. "You said you needed my help."

From behind his paper, Michael shot me a grin.

"Is it safe to have a discussion while . . . we're not alone?"

"Safe?" I said. "That depends on your definition, I guess. Why don't you try, and we'll see what happens?"

Cindie Rae sighed. "I don't have a choice, is that it? Well, surely you know all about last night. Popo dying, I mean."

"Popo's murder, you mean."

"Right. Somebody said you locked yourself in the bathroom. I'd like to know what you saw before you ran in there."

"I didn't run or lock myself anywhere, Cindie Rae. And I've already told the police what I heard and saw. If they want to know more, I'm sure they'll ask."

"But . . ." She set down her coffee cup. "Okay, I'll put my cards on the table. Early this morning, the police arrested Alan."

"Alan!" I sat down hard. "You're kidding. For Popo's murder?"

"Yes, they say he's the only one who could have turned off the electricity and the security systems. How silly is that? My little Pookums wasn't in the store at all. There's a tape that shows him leaving. And besides, why would he murder his best sales associate? The store is worthless without Popo."

"Who told you that?"

"It's what Alan says. Of course, he could have mentioned that teensy detail a little sooner!" She worked her oversize lower lip into a huge pout. "How was I supposed to know Popo was so damn valuable?"

Michael put the paper down. "Exactly how valuable?"

Perhaps annoyed that Michael hadn't sufficiently noticed her yet, Cindie Rae unbuttoned her jacket to reveal her weapons of mass seduction. "Alan says other retail companies have offered to buy Haymaker's, but only if Popo's employment contract was renewed."

"And now that Popo is dead?" I prompted. "The store is less valuable?"

"She sold a lot of shit," Cindie Rae said. "Apparently, she was more important than I thought she was."

"So why did the police arrest Alan?" I asked.

"Because there's a tape. The same one that shows when he left the store. Earlier in the evening, Alan and Popo had a big fight. And it was caught on one of the security cameras."

"What kind of fight?"

"A lot of yelling, that's all I know." Cindie Rae directed her answers to Michael, although I had been the one asking questions.

I said, "I presume Alan has a lawyer?"

"God, yes, the executive suite is crawling with them."

"Not a corporate lawyer, a criminal lawyer."

"Why would he want a criminal lawyer?" She dragged her attention away from Michael to frown at me. "Oh, I get it! You don't mean a criminal who's a lawyer, you mean— "

"Cindic Rae, what exactly do you want from me?"

Michael got up from the table and ambled over to the stove to stir the oatmeal. Cindie Rae watched him with a carnivorous expression. "Alan says you can figure out how that Pinkerton woman killed Popo."

"Pinky? That's ridiculous."

Sensing I might turn her down, Cindie Rae focused the full force of her personality on me at last. "Alan says you'll do it because you're old friends. He says you can do a better job than the police. And you heard what she said last night."

"I'm sure Pinky never meant—"

"She's a menace! She shouldn't be walking around. She killed *both* her husbands, didn't she? She's as bad as you Blackbirds."

We heard a clatter as Michael dropped the wooden spoon.

I said, "Her husbands died of natural causes, Cindie Rae."

"That's the official story, but she has friends in high places. She probably bought her way out of both of those murder charges. I saw it on *Stripperella* once. Pamela Anderson figured it out. It shouldn't be too hard for you."

"Miracles do happen." I sighed. "I don't know, Cindie Rae."

"You should ask around. You're naturally nosy, right? And my Pookums seems to think you're relatively smart."

"Thanks," I said dryly. "But—"

"He said you'd help. He said you valued friendship very highly, and you'd prove Mrs. Pinkerton did it because you're a nice person."

I stewed for a moment. I liked Alan, and I was sorry to hear he'd been arrested. Although I was reasonably sure Pinky hadn't laid a finger on Popo, it wouldn't hurt anyone to ask a few questions. And, frankly, I wanted to know who had locked me in the bathroom.

I didn't realize I was frowning.

Michael said, "I know that expression."

"Oh," said Cindie Rae brightly. "Have you seen my Web site?"

Chapter 5

While I dressed in a suit that had belonged to my grand-mother—a woman of discerning fashion sense and a penchant for trips to Paris to indulge her taste—Michael re-arranged his schedule for the afternoon. When I went downstairs, he told me he liked the Dior skirt.

"I wish I'd had a chance to see the old girl wear these duds." Michael touched my skirt, perhaps to better judge the tailoring, but I doubted it. "She must have been almost as easy on the eyes as you."

As he drove me over to the Main Line, the winter sun shone bright and warm through the windshield. Michael took the back roads out of Bucks County. Occasionally he interrupted our conversation to speak on his cell phone to various business associates. I couldn't help thinking he had begun to sound like a mogul.

When he disconnected for the last time, I said, "Are you starting another business?"

Among his many concerns, Michael ran a used-car dealership, a motorcycle garage with an attached tattoo parlor, a fly-fishing outfitter, a limousine service, a grass-growing venture called the Marquis de Sod, and, of course, Gas 'n' Grub, a gas station that had blossomed into an enormously successful chain of gasoline and convenience stores. While I scraped every penny that came my way, Michael was suddenly swimming in money.

He said, "I'm thinking of investing in automotive parts."

"Factory authorized?"

"Used."

"Do I want to know anything about that?"

"It's perfectly legal," he said. "Tell me about the woman we're going to see."

"Pinky Pinkerton. She used to play doubles with my grandparents."

"Doubles?"

"Tennis," I said. I checked on Spike in my handbag and found him snoozing peacefully. "She had a serve that looked as if it had been fired from a bazooka. Pinky could play just about any sport, as a matter of fact. If she'd been born in another era, she'd probably have become a professional athlete. Her granddaughter is an up-and-coming pro golfer. Kerry Pinkerton. Have you heard of her?"

"Uh, we didn't follow golf at the correctional institution."

"Did you follow Cindie Rae's career instead?"

He smiled at the road. "Probably. I don't remember her."

"You didn't look at their faces?"

"She's had a lot of work done on her face, hasn't she?"

"And a few other places. She hardly looks human to me. Did you find her attractive?"

"Is there any way I'm going to come out good in this conversation?"

"Probably not."

He patted my knee. "You're the one who makes my temperature rise, sweetheart. Besides, she could be one of your suspects, right?"

"Technically, yes," I said. "Pinky made threats against Popo, but not as vicious as the ones Cindie Rae made."

"Would Cindie Rae have a motive to kill the shopping lady?"

"Only to get her hands on more merchandise, which seems a little flimsy. And why would she come to me for help if she was the one who murdered Popo? Or was she fishing for information?"

"I don't think she's on the short list for any Nobel prizes. Anyway, I still like the assistant."

"We'll find Darwin next. But first— Oh, turn here."

"Here?" Michael peered up through the windshield at a set of iron gates pinned open to reveal a long, meandering driveway paved with cobblestones. "What is this? A monastery or something?"

"It's the Pinkerton house. Careful. Pinky has a gazillion little dogs. If you hit one, you'll have to move out of the country."

Michael turned the car into the shady lane. "Is that a golf course?"

"Just three holes. It's very pretty in the springtime." I pointed. "See the barn? They used to keep Shetland ponies there. My cousin Brophy and Pinky's son Kelpy were best friends, and Brophy brought me here a few times."

"Why can't you people have normal names?"

"Like Big Frankie and Monty Python? Or Johnny the Cap and—"

"Okay, okay. Which way?"

We had come to a fork in the driveway. I indicated a left turn, and we arrived a moment later at a wide curve of cobblestones in front of a tall house fashioned after a Norman abbey. A stone statue of a medieval pilgrim stood by the front door, his hands outstretched to accept a tithe or to hold the reins of a visitor's horse.

I rang the bell and heard it echo inside the vast house.

A chorus of barking convinced us the doorbell had been heard. A minute later the door was opened by a wizened man wearing an apron printed with KISS THE COOK. Half a dozen little pug dogs swarmed around the dusty bedroom slippers on his feet, panting and barking in hoarse hysteria. Their agitation whipped up a distinctly doggie smell. Bunton, the Pinkertons' aged butler, bore the pandemonium with Zen-like calm. I always suspected he was partially deaf.

"Hello, Bunton," I shouted over the ruckus. "I'm Nora Blackbird, here to see Pinky. Is she at home?"

Bunton gave Michael a slow blink, then stepped aside and waved us indoors.

As we stepped across the threshold, Spike heard the call of his brethren and poked his head out of my Balenciaga bag. Michael prevented bloodshed by scooping Spike out of the bag and pinning the puppy in the crook of his elbow.

Making no effort to make himself heard over the yelping pugs, Bunton turned and scuffed down a long, black-and-white checkerboard marble corridor lined with faded tapestries and some very ugly Victorian furniture. As Michael and I followed, I noticed the ball-and-claw feet of the chairs and tables had been chewed almost to oblivion.

We passed a faded dining room with a crusty chandelier and a library with few books and dozens of sporting trophies, until we finally arrived in a large solarium at the back of the house. Bunton opened the beveled glass doors.

Lined with tall windows and packed with too many yellow sofas, the solarium had obviously been decorated by an interior designer who planned the whole room around the vivid yellow dress on the woman depicted in a life-size portrait over the mantel. She was a leggy brunette swinging a golf club—Pinky in her youth. The painter had captured the tensile strength in her lean yellow-clad body, and the decorator drew attention to it by his color choices in the room. Now the furniture was faded, but the yellow dress in the portrait shone as brightly as the day it was painted.

It had been a lovely room at one time, but today the place looked worn and smelled strongly of dogs.

Bunton paused in the doorway. "Miss Nora Blackbird, ma'am, and friend."

The pugs pushed past Bunton and raced into the solarium. They leaped onto the lemon-yellow furniture, snarling and yapping at each other for the best seats in the house.

Pinky Pinkerton sat in state in the middle of one of the yellow sofas with a lap desk across her knees. Two more ancient pugs flanked her, snuggled up to her legs and snoring wheezily. As we stepped into the room, Pinky dropped an ice pack down into the cushions of the sofa.

"Good God." She waved us off. "Bunton, show them out immediately. I'm not to be disturbed this afternoon."

Perhaps the cacophony of barking prevented him from hearing correctly, because Bunton muttered something inaudible and departed back the way we'd come.

I took my cue from Bunton and walked across the solarium, pretending I didn't hear her command. "Hello, Pinky," I said cheerily. "Sorry to bother you today!"

"I'm busy." She indicated the piles of paperwork.

"My goodness, what a mess." I knelt on the carpet and picked up some of the paper scattered there. Bills, I noted with a quick glance. From a hotel chain, a sporting-goods store, and a suburban boutique. On the lap desk lay a pair of scissors, and I realized Pinky was cutting coupons from the newspaper.

I put the bills back onto her little desk. "Here you go, Pinky. You've got quite a project going here. Can I help in any way?"

"Of course not. I can manage quite well." To prove her mettle, Pinky picked up her scissors and brandished them. But her grip faltered, and she bobbled the scissors.

Still on the floor, I picked them up for her. "You've hurt your wrist, Pinky."

"It's nothing," she snapped, covering her bruised hand and wrist with the sheaf of bills. "I've had worse injuries. It's just a bump."

"Here's your ice pack." I passed her the pack, then sat on the plush sofa opposite her.

Brusquely, Pinky accepted the cold bundle. "Young man, what are you doing over there?"

Michael had strolled to a library table that displayed three golf trophies—all of them deep silver bowls etched with a woman driving a golf ball into the distance. Absently, he stroked Spike's head to keep him quiet. "This is a lot of hardware."

"Yes, it is. Don't get any fingerprints on them."

"Did you win all these?"

"Of course not. Can't you read the dates? Those belong to my granddaughter. This year she'll start winning the big tournaments. You mark my words."

"She must take after you." Michael tipped his head toward the portrait above the mantel. "Can she beat you yet?"

"Certainly she can. Kerry's much better than I ever was. Of course, I taught her a few things."

He sauntered back to us. "I bet you still teach her things."

Pinky bit back a small smile. "Maybe I do," she said. "Come over here."

Michael obeyed, standing above her and rocking back on his heels as he held Spike captive in one arm. "Close enough?"

She put on her glasses and gave him a long appraisal that ended with his face. "Maybe too close," she said at last. "You're nothing to write home about, are you?"

"You're not so hot yourself anymore."

She took off her glasses again. "You look as if you could swing a club, though. Do you play?"

"Golf?" He shook his head. "The closest I get to a country club is . . . well, nothing you want to hear about."

She snorted. "You think I don't know what men do outside the gates when they have to cover their side bets? Is that what you do? Finance weakness?"

With a shrug, he said, "I do a little of this, a little of that."

"Hmph. Well, I can see you've got good red blood in your veins, none of this thin blue stuff." She pointed her scissors in my direction. "What are you doing here, may I ask?"

He nodded at me. "I go where she says."

Pinky seemed to relax. She shifted her fierce gaze to me. "All right, Miss Blackbird. If he isn't here to collect a debt, I can guess what brings you to my doorstep. But I'll tell you right up front—I'm not going to spill anything to the police that didn't really happen."

"I wouldn't dream of asking you to do that, Pinky. Have you spoken with the police?"

"Of course. They were here first thing this morning. Woke up Kerry, in fact." Pinky's fingertips slipped to the bruise on her wrist. "She's in training and needs her sleep. So I told them what happened, and they left in good order."

"I wonder if you'd mind telling me what happened last night?" I asked. "After you left Popo's salon, I mean. Did you see her in the store?"

Pinky eyed me with suspicion. "Why do you want to know? Are you helping that milquetoast, Alan Rutledge? I hear he got himself arrested."

"I don't think he killed Popo. Do you?"

"I doubt it. That boy was under his mama's thumb too long to have enough gumption to hurt a fly. He's not much of a man, is he?" She couldn't help glancing up at Michael as he sauntered over to the tall windows with Spike.

I said, "If Alan didn't kill Popo, the real killer is still on the loose. And from what happened in Popo's salon last night, I'm guessing she was murdered by someone who was there. I heard some very ugly talk."

Pinky's fierce gaze sharpened. "Are you accusing me?"

"No. But I wonder if you know something about Darwin, something that maybe you didn't tell the police."

"Popo's assistant? That little mole with the pointy nose?" Pinky bristled. "I only know him as Popo's gatekeeper."

"I couldn't help noticing that you . . . well, you tried to give him some cash."

"A Christmas gratuity," she said quickly. "I'm as generous as possible during the holidays, especially to service people."

"But he reacted as if you were trying to bribe him."

"I did no such thing!" Pinky moved with such agitation that her lap desk overturned and landed on top of one of the sleeping pugs. He snarled, but subsided when Pinky put her hand soothingly on his back. More calmly, she said, "It was a tip, that's all. Can I help it if he refused? He's been in trouble at that store, so he's probably playing it safe."

"Do you know about his trouble?"

"Only gossip, which you don't expect me to repeat, I'm sure."

"Of course not."

"He nearly lost his job before," Pinky said promptly. "He was in hot water over some missing merchandise. Even Popo suspected he was the culprit."

"Did you hear that from Popo herself?"

She looked uneasy. "I don't remember. But Popo disliked her assistant. I believe she was trying to get him fired."

"How do you know that?"

Before Pinky had time to respond, we were interrupted by the arrival of Kerry Pinkerton, a tall, powerfully built young woman with none of her grandmother's natural physical grace, but plenty of brute strength showing in her shoulders.

She strode into the room without noticing me. "Where the hell is Bunton?" she demanded. "He was supposed to have my towels ready when—"

"Hello." I stood up. "You must be Kerry. I'm Nora Blackbird. What a pleasure to meet you."

I moved to shake her hand, but Kerry skidded to a stop several yards away. Dressed in damp running clothes, she had pulled her dark hair back into a no-nonsense ponytail to exercise. Her face, suntanned and shining with perspiration, had a stormy set to the jaw and brow, but I saw her throw a mental switch that engaged her professional expression instantly—a bland smile, a superior tilt to her nose, no light in her hazel-eyed gaze.

"Hello," she said coolly, keeping her distance. "I hope you don't mind if I skip the handshake. I have to keep my grip healthy for the tour."

"Of course. Congratulations on your success. Your grandmother tells me you're going to be a big winner this year."

Kerry walked closer, hands on hips, her athletic stride long-legged and loose. Her running shoes were caked with wet crumbs of dirt, as if she'd been jogging on the grounds of the estate. Ignoring the carpet, she came close enough to loom over her grandmother. "Really?" Her voice had an edge. "What else have you been saying about me, Gramma?"

Pinky's upright posture seemed to shrink before my eyes. Instinctively, her left hand moved to cover the bruise on her wrist again.

I said, "Your grandmother is very proud of you. Justifiably so. Are you going to any tournaments soon?"

"Not soon enough." Belatedly, Kerry tried to make the words into a joke by smiling coldly. "I'm supposed to leave day after tomorrow to start training. Last night my coach gave me a farewell party. What are you doing here, if you don't mind my asking? I'm a little protective of Gramma, you see. She's getting old, and people take advantage of her sometimes."

"I came to talk about last night. I was at the store with Pinky, too, and—"

"Oh, were you the one who got my handbag?"

"No, I—"

"Because the cops say it disappeared."

"Disappeared?" I frowned. "Darwin was going to take it to the store safe last night. He told me—"

"Obviously he didn't make it," Kerry snapped. "Because I phoned this morning. He said the bag disappeared. Maybe he was lying, though. Everybody's conspiring to keep that bag away from me."

"Kerry, honey—"

"Quiet, Gramma. If you had gotten the bag for me last night like you were supposed to, maybe that shopping lady would still be alive. Did you think of that?"

Pinky looked down at her lap. "No, I—"

"So shut up." Irritated, Kerry lifted her hand to adjust her ponytail.

Pinky flinched, as if ready to dodge a blow.

In Michael's arm, Spike snarled. Michael came out of the shadow cast by the curtains at last. He'd stood so still that Kerry hadn't noticed him before, but when he stepped into the light, she moved away from her grandmother instinctively.

"This is Michael Abruzzo," I said.

Kerry opened her mouth to speak, then reconsidered. Michael said nothing.

Pinky broke the short silence. "What kind of dog is that?" she asked. "He's not very attractive, is he? I prefer a pug to any other kind of dog. They have such human expressions, don't you think?" She gathered up one of the sleeping dogs beside her and lifted the animal to her own face. She made kissing sounds before chattering on. "My wonderful little pugs—sometimes I think they're my old friends, reincarnated. This one, doesn't he look like my own father?"

Kerry sighed. "I never knew your father, Gramma. You're losing your marbles. Am I going to have to hire someone to look after you? So you don't keep making stupid mistakes? I'd hate to see you lose all your money because you can't take care of yourself."

Pinky didn't answer. She petted her dog and didn't look at Kerry.

Chapter 6

In the car, Michael said, "That little bitch deserves a spanking."

I hugged myself to stop shivering. "She abuses her grandmother."

Michael nodded. "I think she beats the shit out of the old lady on a regular basis."

He let the engine idle while we looked at the Pinkerton house and imagined what might be happening inside at that very minute.

I said, "Pinky pays Kerry's bills. I saw the receipts. Last month somebody spent over three thousand dollars at a boutique I know. I'm sure Pinky doesn't wear shoes from that particular store, so it must be Kerry. And the hotel bills are near golf courses in Florida."

"Yet Gramma cuts grocery coupons to keep herself in food."

"And the house hasn't been updated in years. I wonder what it costs to finance a career in professional golf?"

"I'll bet it's not pocket change." Michael's white-knuckled fist rested on the steering wheel.

"Pinky isn't as helpless as Kerry pretends she is."

"She's a tough old bird," Michael agreed. "But the kid has her spooked."

"Besides forcing her to pay bills, I wonder what else Kerry might be pushing Pinky to do. Pinky was obviously more desperate to acquire the handbag for Kerry than I'd first thought. If she returned home empty-handed, maybe she risked a beating from her granddaughter."

Michael tapped his fist lightly on the wheel. "I'm going back inside."

I reached for his arm to keep him in the car. "They'll have you arrested," I said. "And that doesn't help anyone."

"It'll help me feel better."

"A confrontation may escalate things at this point. There's a better way. When Kerry leaves day after tomorrow, I'll come back and talk to Pinky alone. She needs an ally before she goes to the authorities."

Michael glared out the windshield at the house.

I leaned across the seat and kissed his cheek. "Down, boy," I said.

Unwillingly, we left the Pinkerton estate and drove into Philadelphia.

We discovered that Haymaker's department store was closed for the day because of the police investigation. Printed signs had been taped to all the locked doors. I could see employees inside, however, gathered in small groups. A uniformed police officer stood outside beside a forlorn Santa who dutifully rang his bell for the Salvation Army, despite the lack of shoppers. Michael slipped him a few bills.

"I suppose I can wait until tomorrow to talk to Darwin Osdack," I said as we walked to the Four Seasons for an afternoon snack.

We ordered a cheese plate and a bottle of a wine Michael had been wanting to try. It was delicious—very dry, yet hinting of berries in hot Italian sunshine. We talked about Popo's murder for a while; then Michael's cell phone began to chirp. While he gave monosyllabic answers to his caller, I sipped the wine and watched him, wondering if the time would ever come when I might want to know exactly what he was doing.

Michael closed his phone with a snap and said he had things to take care of and did I want to go home. I needed to attend a cocktail party for a small historical society in my role as the assistant to the *Philadelphia Intelligencer*'s society columnist, so he agreed to take Spike and dropped me at the home of Trenton Aquinas of Society Hill.

"Nora, don't you look lovely," Trenton said when he opened the door and I identified myself.

"How would you know, Trent?" I stepped carefully around his Seeing Eye dog, Buster, and gave his whiskery cheek a kiss.

"Well, you smell wonderful," he said on a laugh. "Very feminine. Welcome to my party. Are you here on official newspaper business, or in response to my private invitation?"

"Can I be both?" I asked.

"Of course. But I heard a rumor that your boss gets testy when you're invited as a guest and she's not. I don't want to get you into trouble."

"I can handle Kitty," I said, although I wasn't sure I was telling the truth. Even six months after I started working for the newspaper, Kitty Keough was still jealously trying to make my life miserable. She hated that I'd been born into a world in which she would always be an outsider.

Trenton pulled me inside and closed the door. For the evening's festivities, he wore a Brooks Brothers sport coat over flannel trousers, a pin-striped shirt, and a tie decorated with reindeer—all carefully chosen by his wife. His beard was neatly trimmed, his hair impeccably combed. "How do you like having a job? Evie thought you might have trouble adjusting."

"Actually, the hours suit me very well. I go to parties in the afternoons and evenings, and I do my writing at home on my computer. I can e-mail my pieces anytime before midnight."

"Sounds like a great gig. I wonder if I could get Evie hired somewhere? She spends my money faster than I can make it."

Trenton Aquinas didn't need any more money, no matter how fast his wife could spend it. He had inherited a fortune from his father, who invented a pump for oil wells, and he was due to receive an even bigger inheritance when his elderly mother—one of the Kendricks of Main Line—passed away. Perhaps Trenton's academic career brought in a little pin money, but it hardly paid the taxes on his Federal-style house that had once been a boarding school for young men of society.

Before I could respond, Evie appeared and greeted me cheerfully. She was a petite woman several years her husband's senior, but she strove to keep her figure trim enough to wear expensive, tailored fashions. Tonight she looked svelte in plum silk with a pearl necklace and matching earrings. She swept me into their home to meet the other guests and admire her decorating skills.

The grand salon of the Aquinas home showed Evie's penchant for endless shopping. Flowered chintz pillows and dozens of fussy bibelots mixed with fine Hepplewhite furniture that had come from Evie's old-money Philadelphia family, the Cardomans. Heavy Scalamandre draperies hung in swags from the tall windows. The rose, powder blue, and buttercream colors were also echoed in velvet upholstery and the subtle shades of the enormous floral rug. Nautical prints hung at precise intervals on the walls.

Unlike Lexie, who had the confidence to live in a simple, self-effacing sort of home, Evie seemed to need to acquire more and more belongings to confirm who she was.

"Your home is more stunning than ever," I told her. "Every little addition you make enhances the elegance."

Having heard satisfactory praise for her efforts, Evie happily went off to find me a drink.

I saw Lexie Paine talking with friends by the grand piano. She spotted me at the same instant and met me beside a tray of hors d'oeuvres on a sideboard. Lexie looked fabulous in an understated Valentino suit cut to emphasize her slender figure. In her ears, diamonds and sapphires sparkled together.

"Sweetie," she said, giving me a hug. "You ran off last night without a word!"

"I'm sorry, Lex. I should have said good-night, but—"

"No excuses required."

"Michael got me home before I fell apart."

Lexie's brows twitched. "Did you really fall apart? I'm so sorry, darling. You had a very rough night. I hope you feel better today."

"Actually, I had a surprising visitor this morning."

"Do tell."

Lexie nibbled on mushrooms and made appropriate exclamations when I told her about Cindie Rae's call, Alan's arrest, and my visit to Pinky Pinkerton's home.

"Do you know Kerry Pinkerton?" I asked.

"Only from an occasional country club wingding. She's not very social. And she hasn't any money of her own, so she doesn't need my services."

"No money at all? Didn't her parents leave her something?"

Lexie shook her head. "Her mother's still alive, living in California and hoarding her cash in case she decides to open a yoga studio or something. Kerry's got a trust fund somewhere, but she doesn't take possession until she's thirty. Until then, she's on a shoestring, I gather. That is, unless a sporting-goods company asks her to be a spokesperson. Then she'll be rolling in dough."

"But she has to become a better player first, I assume?"

"She's getting to that level. I always assumed Pinky took care of her."

"Yes," I said.

"What is it?" Lexie asked.

I attempted to wipe my expression clean. I didn't want to spread rumors about Pinky and Kerry, even to my best friend. Not until I was sure.

I changed the subject. "What about Alan and his department store, Lex? Last night you told me the store might be for sale."

"The drumbeats were noisy all day today. I understand the retailers who wanted to buy Haymaker's are rethinking their offers. With her sales figures, Popo was one of the big assets. Of course, a murder in the store isn't exactly great publicity either."

"Do you know anything about shrinkage?"

"Stolen goods? Sure." Lexie ate another mushroom and reached for a napkin. "All stores have shrinkage."

"I mean goods stolen by employees."

"Haymaker's is no different from any gift shop or mall emporium. A lot of goods disappear." She chewed thoughtfully and wiped her fingers. "Now that you remind me, I think Haymaker's had a big number in their shrinkage column."

"Popo mentioned something to me before she died. She blamed a fellow employee."

"I wouldn't put it past Popo to have some sticky fingers herself."

"Why do you say that?"

"I dunno. Even with her Christmas bonuses, how could she afford that wardrobe of hers, let alone the money she gave me to look after?"

"She had some cash put away for a rainy day?"

"You bet. For a monsoon, in fact."

Lexie didn't talk to me about her clients unless they were dead. Still, I knew I was expected to be discreet.

"Maybe Popo had a sugar daddy?" I asked.

"Who would be attracted to the likes of her? Hell, she was more prickly than I am!"

"I know plenty of men who are attracted to you, babycakes."

She tossed the napkin down. "Keep the list to yourself, sweetie. Oh, here's Evie."

Evie Aquinas pressed a glass of very good pinot noir into my hands and engaged Lexie in a conversation about buying jewelry. Lexie glanced surreptitiously at me and rolled her eyes.

I eased away to sip my wine and make small talk among the other guests. Writing mental notes, I composed my newspaper piece in my mind. Trenton Aquinas had revived a small historical society, and the members were pleased to be invited into his home for their first annual holiday gathering. The crowd was mostly university professors. I saw a few friends, met a newcomer or two, and tried to make an early escape once I had a rough draft of a story in my head.

"Nora!" Evie Aquinas caught me in the foyer. "Lexie tells me you're interested in Popo Prentiss's death. Are you as shocked as the rest of us?"

Why hadn't I thought of Evie sooner? Of course, she had probably been one of Popo's most frequent clients.

"I'm very shocked," I assured Evie.

"She was practically my best friend," Evie said quietly. A sparkle of tears welled up in her eyes. "I could always call her just to talk when I was feeling down. I don't know what I'll do about my spring clothes. Popo planned to order everything for me in the next few weeks."

"Maybe Darwin can help."

Evie winced. "Or maybe I'll try another store. Darwin's not exactly my type. He doesn't have Popo's joie de vivre."

"Or," I suggested, taking a chance, "her access to the best merchandise?"

Evie laughed awkwardly. "Oh, you know Popo. She always had a few little treats tucked away. For special clients. She called them her small investments."

"Investments?"

Tears forgotten, Evie started to blush. "To tell the truth, I suspected she bought the things herself for later resale. Why, last summer she suddenly realized she had some of those Hermès ties that were so hard to find months earlier—the ones with the sailboats? Just in time for Trenton's birthday. I feel certain she kept them just for me."

"But you think they came from Popo, not the store? From some kind of special stash?"

"Well, that was my suspicion." Evie began to look distressed. "She hand-delivered personally. Come to think of it, she didn't provide store receipts either. I wanted those ties so badly that I never—"

"Evie, this is important or I wouldn't ask. Do you think Popo might have stolen the ties from the store?"

"Of course not!" Evie mustered some indignation. "No, I think she purchased the treats with her own money and simply resold the ties to me later. She really went the extra mile for special clients. We were friends, honestly."

"Do you know where Popo kept her little treats?" I asked. "The things she held back for her pals?"

"Not at the store," Evie said slowly. "Last May she invited me to an after-hours sale at her apartment. I was so flattered to be asked. Popo has a condo in Rittenhouse Square. In fact, it might be the same building you lived in before your husband— I mean, before now. She gave us caviar and a tour of the things she wanted to sell. Some of it was out-of-date, but she had a lot of new merchandise, too. I bought a Lettitia McGraw tote."

So Popo had been hoarding merchandise for years and reselling it to her most trusted clients. Now I needed to find out if the merchandise had been legitimately hers to sell or if she'd stolen from Haymaker's to keep her side business well stocked.

But I wasn't going to learn more from Evie. She pulled herself coolly together, obviously sorry she had told me anything. "It was so nice to see you again, Nora. Thank you for coming."

She couldn't get me out the door fast enough.

I decided to hike across town to Rittenhouse Square. If Popo truly lived in my old building, perhaps I could chat up the doorman. He might have some insight into Popo's private boutique.

But the weather had gotten ugly, and I made it only a few blocks before stopping to dry off in a coffee shop. I didn't want to ruin my shoes in the slush, so I found a pay phone and got lucky. Well, sort of.

Twenty minutes later, my sister Libby pulled up in front of the coffee shop. I ran out across the sidewalk to the street and popped open the passenger door of her minivan.

"I was picking up a few more gifts! Shopping is such an adrenaline rush. Almost as good as aerobics, don't you think?" She chattered with even more animation than usual as I climbed in. "I had a fabulous day. First I went to the King of Prussia mall; then I dashed into the city for another look around Haymaker's, but they're closed. Can you believe it?"

"Are you taking those metabolism herbs again?"

"Of course not! I'm just enjoying the season! Look, I even bought a few things for myself. There was an Elizabeth Arden special bonus *and* a Vera Bradley diaper bag discount, so I went crazy."

I glanced into the backseat and saw a mountain of bags and packages. "Boy, you're not kidding."

"You don't have to hurry home, do you? Can you have dinner with me?"

"Don't you have to get home to the baby? Aren't you still nursing?"

"I'm weaning him. I don't mind the extra cup size, but the leaking has become a problem. You should have seen the puddles I made on the massage table last week."

I remembered I wanted to ask Libby about her massages, but she bulldozed over my voice.

"It's time to wean, anyway. I can't put my own life on hold forever," she rattled on as she pulled into traffic. "And that child can thrive on Bright Beginnings just as well as my milk, which is probably tainted by preholiday stress."

"Why don't you let me help with your shopping, Lib? You could stay home and enjoy the children."

"Dear heaven, I'm trying to get *away* from home! The twins are driving me insane. Lucy's invisible friend gives everybody the creeps, and who knows what Rawlins has been doing. He's hardly ever at home anymore. I think he needs a father figure, a strong man to be a role model."

I began to suspect that the blaze in my sister's eyes was a hormonal surge, not seasonal mania. "Are you doing something about that? The father figure, I mean?"

"Of course not! I'm not dating anyone. Or seeing anyone at all, in fact." Her madly cheerful front began to crumble. "Who would want a lactating cow like me? What man could possibly enjoy spending time with a widow with five children when he could have anyone in the world, b-b-but he chooses another *man* over me, for crying out loud, because I'm too *disgusting*?"

"Are we talking about—"

"J-J-Jason, of course! He's *gay*! How come nobody ever *tells* me these things? Attractive gay men should be required to wear name tags so women don't make fools of themselves! I-I-I felt like such a *breeder*!"

"Libby," I said, "let's go get some dinner and talk."

She burst into tears.

She wobbled the van next to a fire hydrant, set the brake, and bawled for a while. I made soothing noises and calmed her down with some platitudes, pats on the back, and finally a butterscotch Life Saver that I found in the glove compartment. She blathered a lot of nonsense and soaked through her own handkerchief and mine. Nobody could have hysterics the way my sister could. I think there was even runny mascara on me by the time she was finished. But she emerged from the handkerchiefs looking radiantly beautiful.

Eventually, she was able to drive again. She made a beeline for a Friendly's, and we skipped dinner to order gargantuan ice-cream sundaes in a booth near the jukebox.

"For five seconds I thought about trying to change him." She scraped the last molecules of whipped cream and chocolate sauce from the bottom of her dish. "But remember what Mama used to say?"

"That you can't change a man unless he's in diapers?"

"It's true, I know. But I thought if anybody could get Jason to change his tune, it's me."

"Right," I said.

"I'm not unattractive, you know."

"I know."

"I may have a few more curves than some women, but I'm very firm. He told me that. I have firm flesh. He said it."

"I'm sure he meant it."

"He has wonderful hands." Libby's eyes began to glaze over again, and not from the shock of all the ice cream she'd just ingested. "I've never had a massage like he gives. So sensual. So caring. Jason really leans into his work, and when he touches my—"

"Libby."

"Right," she said. "There are lots of fish in the sea."

"Exactly," I said.

"More men where Jason came from."

"Even better men."

"I need a passionate, but spiritual person, somebody who understands my subconscious needs. Someone whose desires meld with my unique chakras, who will interface with my physical and nonphysical being as we travel beyond this plane to a self-actualized illumination. Are you going to finish your ice cream?"

I passed my dish across the table. "Have you heard from Emma?"

"She phoned this morning. Maybe that's part of my problem." Libby swirled chocolate sauce into the melting ice cream. "Now that Emma's out of commission for a while, I feel as if I should be wreaking havoc on the male of the species on her behalf."

Our youngest sister, Emma, could attract men wherever she went. Of the three of us, she was the incredibly gorgeous one, the sister who exuded sexual invitation the way other human beings perspire. She handled men as deftly as she managed the wild horses she trained. They obeyed her every command.

But gradually Emma's social drinking had gotten out of hand. Libby and I had risked a powerful sisterly bond by insisting Emma get some help. She had checked into a rehab program just a week earlier.

"How's she doing?" I asked.

"She's still pissed off. But less than before."

"She's taking rehab seriously?"

"I think so. Look, we can't worry about her every moment, Nora. We have to allow Emma to make her own mistakes."

"She's made more than her share," I said.

"We're all at turning points." Libby licked her spoon and eyed me.

"What is that supposed to mean?"

"That man of yours . . ."

"Libby—"

"I just want you to know that it makes no difference to me if you're having a fling. As a reject from the Common Sense Club myself, I encourage an occasional wild, sexual adventure, especially for someone as repressed as you are, but—"

"Hey."

"But I hope you're being very careful, Nora. You don't want to be mixed up with a dangerous man for the long haul."

"I'm not a teenager," I said. "So you can lay off the motherly lecture."

"Can I help it? I care what happens to you! And I know That Man is not the kind of partner who's best for you. You need a dependable, hardworking, sensitive person who can help you come to terms with the disaster of your first marriage and move—"

"Can we stop talking about this?" I asked.

"Do you honestly see yourself eating spaghetti and meatballs the rest of your life?" she demanded. "Bailing him out of jail every time he gets arrested? A nice, normal sort of man won't cause you any more heartache. You've had your share already, Nora."

I waved to the waitress. "Check, please!"

"When are you going to wake up? That Man is a criminal."

I grabbed the check out of the startled waitress's hand. "Let's go home."

On the way back to Bucks County in the minivan, I distracted Libby by asking about Cindie Rae's Web site. My sister knew everything.

"It's sorta like QVC, only Cindie Rae has most of her clothes off when she talks about her product."

"Does she make much money?"

"Well, I noticed she uses a nine-hundred number, which means the customer gets charged for making the phone call to her. She takes requests, you know. There must be a bunch of weird regulars who watch all the time and call in to chat. I don't know if she sells many of those crazy-colored dildos. I didn't watch for very long. The fuzzy screen gave me a headache."

"She can't be on camera twenty-four hours a day, of course."

"No, no. She's got her Web cam on all the time, although she's not always on-camera. She puts up little signs to advertise when she'll be back. It's adorable." Libby heard my choke and said quickly, "In a very yucky way, of course."

Libby dropped me off at Blackbird Farm. The house was empty, and I found myself actually missing Spike's annoying presence.

I went upstairs and took a long, soaking bubble bath with a book, then put on my pajamas and took my laptop to bed. Sitting Indian-style, I typed up my notes on the Aquinas party and e-mailed the piece to my editor.

Then, still wide awake and feeling brave enough to take a look, I located Cindie Rae's Web site on the Internet.

Chapter 7

Maybe I have a delicate stomach, but when the grainy picture finally came into focus, *yucky* did not begin to describe how I felt.

I heard her voice first.

"And if you're feeling frisky, boys, you can try this fun toy outside in the fresh air. Just be careful, because somebody might be watching! Some naughty person could be spying on you. Ooooh . . . For under twenty dollars, you can please yourself or your lady friend. And if you act now, I'll throw in a special gift, just for you."

As she giggled, the camera honed in on something large, long, and neon pink. Cindie Rae's talonlike fingernails scored the length of it as she brightly began to describe the various ways she could employ such a grotesque item. While she spoke, the camera blurred as if run by an amateur photographer, then landed on Cindie Rae's bare thigh and began a leisurely tour of parts better left unmentioned.

I clapped my hand over my eyes. "Oh, God!"

"And girls," Cindie Rae continued, "if you're planning a wild and crazy bachelorette party, let me show you a few fun games you can play with your girlfriends. No, wait— I think I hear a caller! Hello, baby, are you there?"

"Uh, yeah, Cindie Rae, how you doin'?"

"I'm doing great! What's your name, honey?"

"Uh, Dick."

"Hi, Dick! What can I do to make you happy tonight?"

I peeked between my fingers. Cindie Rae's face filled my computer screen, and her smile was perkier than the Friendly's waitress had been.

I turned the sound off, got up, and went into the bathroom for a Tums.

Padding back to the bed, I heard a whistle from downstairs and then the sound of footsteps on the staircase. With a rush of guilt, I allowed my finger to hover over the "quit" button.

"I'm up here!" I called, still debating.

Michael came in crooning "Are You Lonesome Tonight?" in his best Elvis impression. He carried a glass of milk in one hand. With the other, he plopped Spike into his basket. "What did you do? Take a really hot bath? You're all pink."

"Not as pink as some people." I turned the screen so he could see.

He took a slug of milk first and climbed onto the bed to kiss me on the mouth. "Whoa," he said when he caught a glimpse of the action on my computer. "This is a side of you I didn't expect."

"It's a onetime deal. Look, it's Cindie Rae."

Michael twisted his head sideways. "How can you tell?"

"The implants. See?"

"Yikes. Even scarier without the clothes." He slurped some milk. "May I ask what you're doing?"

"Libby thinks I'm repressed."

He grinned. "And this is your answer? Watching Internet porn? Look, if you want to cut loose, I have some better ideas."

I tweaked his ear. "I thought we'd done it all."

"We've hardly scratched the surface." He offered me his glass.

I accepted the drink. The milk was warm and smelled slightly of rum, but I handed it back without sipping. "No, thanks. My stomach is a little upset. No, look at the background. Behind Cindie Rae."

"If you're looking at the background, maybe your sister is right."

"No, look." I pointed at the screen.

"Yeah," Michael prompted. "What am I looking at?"

"A handbag. See? Hanging on the back of the closet door. To be specific, it's a Lettitia McGraw handbag."

"Okay. What's the significance?"

"Cindie Rae was in Popo Prentiss's salon looking to buy exactly this handbag. Why would she want one if she already had this one at home?"

"Maybe this is the purse in question."

"Yes, Watson, you could be right."

"What the hell is she doing now?" Michael asked. He squinted at the computer screen. "The camera is too damn fuzzy."

"The lousy camera work," I said, "means there's somebody else in her studio. Someone's running the camera."

"It's not her fiancé. I hear he's still in jail."

I didn't ask how Michael knew that information. He had various twisted lines of communication that reached all echelons of law enforcement. "Is Alan all right?"

He hesitated. "Rutledge isn't great. Somebody broke his nose. He's got bruises that would scare Mike Tyson."

I forgot about Cindie Rae in a hurry. "Michael! What happened?"

Unwillingly, Michael admitted, "Where he's locked up, things can get out of hand very easily."

"Is he safe?"

"The quicker he gets sprung, the better."

So I had to work faster, I thought. Alan Rutledge didn't belong in jail, where he was incapable of defending himself.

"So who could the cameraman be?" I asked.

"Why don't you phone Cindie Rae and find out?" He pointed at the nine-hundred number displayed above Cindie Rae's now writhing body.

"No way!"

"Why not?" With a grin at my squeamishness, Michael put his glass of milk on the bedside table and pulled his cell phone from the pocket of his jeans. "Here. You want to talk? Or should I do the honors?"

"Michael, don't!"

He laughed at me as he punched in the phone number. "It's not a crime. She's got a legitimate business going."

"Your definition of legitimate and mine—"

"It's not very appetizing, I'll admit, but she's earning a living."

"At what cost? She's perpetuating the perception that women don't have to be treated like human beings."

"The lady is making a buck with the talent God gave her. Okay, a plastic surgeon helped. He ought to be sued, if you ask me. See that pucker near her navel?"

"I thought that *was* her navel."

He pinned the cell phone to his ear with his shoulder. "She's contributing to the economy. For all we know, she could be a member of the Better Business Bureau. Hell, maybe she belongs to the Rotary Club and— Hey, Cindie Rae, great show tonight!"

I stifled a cry of humiliation and flung myself down on the bed. I yanked the pillow over my head so I couldn't hear whatever conversation Michael had in mind. Soon I heard him laughing.

When he disconnected a couple of minutes later, he patted my behind. "It's safe to come out now."

I threw off the pillow, but remained prone on the bed. "What did you learn?"

"I can get three of Cindie Rae's gadgets for the price of two if I act before midnight."

"What would you do with them?"

"They might make nice roadside flares." He shut down the computer and closed the screen. "And her cameraman is a guy by the name of Calvin. He's camera-shy, though. I didn't see his face. Or any other part of him, thank God."

"Calvin," I murmured, trying to dredge up some kernel of information that niggled in the deepest part of my brain. "I don't think I know any Calvins."

"You suspect Cindie Rae killed the shopping lady now?"

"Yes. No. Why would she ask me to help exonerate Alan if she was the one who murdered Popo?"

Michael finished his milk in a long gulp and unlaced his boots. "Can we think about this in the morning?"

I watched him peel off his sweater and start to unbutton the shirt underneath. "They're not married yet. If Alan is convicted, Cindie Rae won't get his money. She'll have to continue to make her living by that Web site."

"Not a lot of career options for someone with her background," Michael agreed.

Absently, I ran my fingertips along the curve of his bare back. "Did you have any luck finding Elvis tonight?"

"Who said I was looking?"

"You only drink a toddy when you think you won't be able to sleep. I assumed you were working on your Monty Python situation."

"Monty is my father's problem, not mine."

So where had Michael been tonight? What problem was so knotty that he needed help to shut off his brain for the night?

The forces of Michael's life had begun to tangle darkly around mine, and no matter how intensely we both wanted to build a future together, there were still circumstances neither of us could control. I didn't want to think Michael's choices might alter the relationship we were still so tentatively forging.

If I didn't ask, he didn't need to tell.

Or to lie to me.

Michael got up and kicked off his boots. He went into the bathroom to brush his teeth and came back a few minutes later without his clothes. He pulled the cord on the lamp and slid into bed with me, all warm muscle and peppermint. I slipped into his arms, but Cindie Rae's explicit Web cam antics had cooled all carnal thoughts for one night. It felt good just to hold on tight.

In the morning, Michael woke with his usual ardor and left me weak as a kitten in the bed while he showered. An hour and a half later, my nephew Rawlins showed up to hide from his "crazy mother" in front of my television. He volunteered to look after Spike, so Michael and I were free to go into the city unencumbered.

On the highway, I caught him glancing into the rearview mirror more often than usual. "What's going on?"

"One of us has a tail."

"A . . . ? You mean somebody's following you?"

"Or you," he said, already reaching for his cell phone. He made a call, spoke briefly, and clicked the phone closed a moment later. "Okay, it's me," he admitted. "Dammit."

"Is it the police? Are you going to be arrested?"

"I doubt it. But I hate your being in the car when they stop me. Let's do a little fancy driving."

"Michael, you can't outrun the police!"

"I'm not outrunning them." But he squeezed his car between two tractor-trailers, where no other vehicle could fit without endangering lives. At a perfectly moderate speed, he drove the rest of the way into the city between the two trucks, humming along to the music on his radio. Finally, we scooted off an exit. Among the city streets, Michael ran a traffic light on the yellow and zipped into a parking garage. He took a ticket from the automated machine, drove up two floors and back down again to exit on the other side of the city block. When he paid the confused attendant, he turned onto the one-way street and down a few more blocks to another garage. He passed several open parking spaces until he found a spot he liked between two very large SUVs.

"You've done this before," I said.

"What would you think about going up to New York before Christmas?" he said. "We could see the decorated windows, have a nice dinner someplace expensive, go ice-skating . . . ?"

"You can ice-skate?"

We got out of the car and Michael opened the trunk. From inside, he dug out another license plate.

"Is that legal?" I asked as I watched him swap the new plate for the one already on the car.

"Technically?" He dropped his screwdriver and the original plate into the trunk and closed it. "Maybe not. I just happen to have two cars the same make and color. Confusing the plates might be an honest mistake."

"Hmm."

We walked across the street and into Haymaker's department store. As far as I could see, nobody followed us.

"There are a lot of cameras in this place," Michael observed on the escalator. "Somebody really knew what they were doing when they shut down the whole system."

"Maybe Popo's murder wasn't a one-person job," I said.

We arrived at Popo's salon, where the sentry at the door was still the mannequin wearing the Oscar de la Renta dress. Inside the salon, Darwin Osdack gave a squeak of terror when we walked in.

"What are you doing here?" he cried, seizing a leather coat off the nearest rack and holding it against himself as if it were a bulletproof shield. He stared from me to Michael and back again. "Oh, my God, you're going to kill me!"

"Don't be ridiculous, Darwin. I just want to talk."

"Who's he?"

"A friend."

"You're kidding, right?"

Michael ignored us and took a tour of the merchandise that crammed the salon. He flipped over a price tag or two, picked up a spike-heeled shoe decorated with dragonflies, and nudged a thousand-dollar suitcase with the toe of his boot.

"Don't let him do that!" Darwin hissed. "It's worth more than my monthly salary!"

"Darwin, how about telling me a little more about the night Popo died?"

"Why?"

"Because I'd like to know what I missed after you locked me in the bathroom."

He flushed. "I did no such thing."

I sat down in one of the Louis Something chairs that stood before Popo's desk. "I'm sure the store security cameras recorded the truth. Shall we find out?"

Darwin lowered the leather coat at last. "All right, so what if I did lock you up? You deserved it."

"Darwin, if I promise to help your career in whatever way I'm capable, will you please drop the wounded act and talk to me? The fate of this store is probably at stake."

He took a tentative step toward me, unable to resist the drama. "It is? How?"

"Trust me when I say that Alan Rutledge's future is the key to the store's future, too. After you made sure I was stuck for the night, what did you do with the Lettitia McGraw handbag?"

"I told you. I put it into the store safe."

"Try again," I said. "It never arrived. Did you sell it to Cindie Rae?"

"What if I did?" Darwin demanded. "She's going to be Alan Rutledge's wife! I didn't see any point in denying her what she wanted."

"But Popo had other plans for the bag, right? Like maybe she planned to keep it for herself?"

Darwin frowned at me. "I don't think I should discuss this with you."

"I know about Popo's business on the side, Darwin. She

was stealing from the store, wasn't she? And reselling goods privately at parties she conducted at her apartment."

"That would be very wrong." Darwin staunchly defended his mentor. "Any employee would be instantly fired for stealing store merchandise."

"But Popo blamed the shrinkage on you. Why are you protecting her now?"

Darwin glanced nervously at Michael, who made a pretty good pretense of looking through some dresses on a rack. Darwin jerked his head. "Is he okay? I mean, really?"

"He's not working for store security, if that's what you mean."

Darwin sighed and drooped into the chair beside mine. "All right, here's the real deal. Popo planned to let Cindie Rae have it. But Cindie Rae jumped the gun and came here to the store to get the bag. That was supposed to happen at Popo's house."

"How do you know?"

"I'm not dumb. But Cindie Rae certainly is." He edged his chair closer to mine. "She left a message on Popo's voice mail. Which I am supposed to check every hour. When Cindie Rae showed up for the bag that night, Popo was furious."

"Because she hadn't had a chance to steal the bag for herself yet?"

Darwin nodded. "Plus she realized I finally figured out what she was doing. I've been taking the blame for months, and it was Popo all the time!"

"Did the two of you argue?"

"We had customers," Darwin said with a lift to his nose. "Popo and I would never be so unprofessional as to have a disagreement in front of customers."

Michael sauntered closer and leaned against a tall mirror. Darwin's loyalty crumbled entirely.

"We were *going* to argue," Darwin admitted. "But Popo died before I could confront her."

I sighed. "Do you see my problem, Darwin? As far as I can figure out, you're the only person with a real motive to kill Popo."

"Then you haven't looked very far."

"Oh?"

Darwin leaned in and whispered, "Popo was boinking somebody."

I tried to comprehend such an impossibility. "You're joking, right? Who would have an affair with Popo, of all people?"

Darwin looked me in the eye. "You promise to help me get a new job if I get fired from this one?"

"I promise."

"Okay, then. It was Mr. Rutledge."

"Alan?" I cried. "You're saying Popo and *Alan* were seeing each other? But he's engaged to Cindie Rae."

"He was seeing Popo before he met Cindie Rae. As soon as his parents kicked the bucket, Popo went after Mr. Rutledge like a barracuda. They met every week at the Four Seasons before his Wednesday matinee." Darwin shuddered. "I don't even want to imagine what that scene must have been like. But then he met Cindie Rae. And when he tried to break things off with Popo, she went ballistic."

"Let's get this straight," Michael said. "The dead lady was having a little WrestleMania with the store owner. Then she blew a fuse when he found true love with the *Penthouse* Pet?"

"Yes," said Darwin.

"So who smoked Popo?" Michael asked.

Behind me, I heard another customer arrive at the salon door. Darwin looked up and turned a color that made me fear he had thrown an embolism. I turned to see who had come in and got hastily to my feet.

A store security guard walked in, followed by two men I knew instinctively were police officers. One wore an Eagles jacket with a green scarf double-wrapped around his neck, and the other had a Columbo-style trench coat.

The cop with the scarf showed us his badge and made a pretense of courtesy. "Mick Abruzzo? We'd like to ask you some questions. Will you come with us, please?"

Agog, Darwin gave a squeak.

The security guard stood aside and allowed the police to do their business, but his hand rested tensely on the pistol that hung on his hip. He was a gangly young man with pale eyes and a shaved head.

"Don't go anywhere by yourself," Michael said to me as he departed with the police. "I'll be out in a few hours."

I followed them out of Popo's salon, but the store security officer blocked me from entering the employees-only elevator with them. He said, "Sorry, ma'am. You'll have to take the next car."

"All right." I found myself suddenly staring at him. "Aren't you the security guard I met night before last?"

He peered more closely at my face, and recognition dawned. "Sure, I remember you. How are you feeling?"

In the instant before the doors met, I looked at his name tag.

It read, CALVIN REILLY."

Calvin.

Darwin said to me, "Are you okay? You look like you're going to faint."

I pushed past him and ran for the escalator. Half a dozen shoppers clogged my path, but I wiggled through them all, apologizing as I headed down. At the bottom, I heard someone call my name.

"Nora! For heaven's sake, wait for me!"

Libby bore down on me, laden with shopping bags. "I spent some time thinking last night," she reported without preamble, "and I decided to return most of the things I bought so far. I don't know what came over me, but shopping seemed the best medicine at the time and now— My God, what's wrong?"

"I just figured out who killed Popo Prentiss."

"What!"

"I have to hurry. The police are taking Michael now and—"

"Oh, my God, *he* killed Popo?"

"Of course not!"

"Then who—"

"I don't have time to explain." I rushed away from her, hoping to catch the police officers before they left the store.

"Wait!" Libby called.

I reached the main entrance of the store, plunged through the revolving door, and dashed onto the sidewalk.

And collided with the Salvation Army Santa who stood ringing his bell just outside the door. When I hit him, he gave a startled grunt and sprawled on the pavement, knocking his bucket off its tripod and causing such a clatter that every pedestrian for two blocks turned to look. His bell clanged onto the sidewalk and proceeded to bang its way into the street, where it was run over by a bus.

Libby burst out of the revolving door and crashed into me: "Oh, my God, Nora, you've killed Santa!"

"I'm so sorry," I said in a gasp, kneeling down to help the poor man. "I'm so, so sorry! Are you hurt?"

"M-merry Cwithmuth." Santa lay stunned on his back, blinking dazedly up at the sky.

I tried to loosen the big black button at his throat, but I couldn't paw my way through his synthetic beard. "Oh, God, I think he's got a brain injury! Libby, call an ambulance."

Libby dropped her shopping bags and leaned over us to peer more closely at the man in the red suit. "He doesn't have a brain injury! His hat and wig broke the fall."

Santa sat up unsteadily. "Whath happem?"

"But he can't speak!" I cried.

My sister bent down and used a Kleenex to retrieve a small item from the sidewalk. She held it up to the sunlight. "Because he knocked out his false teeth. Here, bub, try this."

"Twanths," he said, accepting his teeth. He slid them into his mouth without a care for hygiene and waggled his jaw around. Then he grinned up at Libby. "You're a life-saver as well as a looker. Want to get a cup of coffee with me?"

Libby put her hand down to help him to his feet. "You're a charmer, Santa. Feeling okay?"

"Not bad." He stood up unsteadily and dusted off his velvet pants. "How about we check my vital signs over coffee?"

"I'm too young for you." Libby handed his bucket back to him.

"You won't know what you're missing until you try."

I scrambled to my feet and put the tripod upright again. While Santa tried to pick up my sister, I grabbed Libby's gifts that had tumbled onto the sidewalk and stuffed them back into their shopping bags. I found a rolling pin and slid it into a Williams-Sonoma bag. The boxed bottle of Chanel perfume went into the Haymaker's bag. The heavy autobiography of a former president had come out of bag marked

BARNES & NOBLE. The red leather bustier, coming unraveled from its tissue paper, flummoxed me.

Libby snatched the bustier and stuffed it into her purse without missing a beat. "You took that hit like a real tough guy, Santa. Do you work out?"

"Down at the Y, sure. Aerobics class three days a week. Some free weights on Tuesdays and Thursdays."

"It's paying off." She felt the muscle in his arm. "You must have played football in your younger days."

"Linebacker at Rutgers," he said with pride. "Now that I'm retired, it's easier to stay in shape, though. You ought to think about power lifting. You've got the build for it. You don't mind my saying, you're built like a brick outhouse."

"I hope that's a good thing. You really okay?"

"Sure." Manfully, Santa pulled himself up to his full height.

I handed all the bags back to Libby. "I can't believe you."

"Hey, you're both pretty cute," Santa said. "How about an early lunch? There's a place around the corner that makes a top-notch grilled cheese sandwich. My treat."

"Sorry." Libby tucked a twenty into his bucket. "But we've got to track down a criminal."

"Oh, yeah? You girls undercover cops or something?"

"Or something," Libby agreed.

As I tried to calm my heart into a normal rhythm again, I saw a familiar figure come out from around the corner of Haymaker's and cross the street. I grabbed Libby's arm. "Look! It's Calvin!"

"Who?"

"The security guard who probably shut down the electricity to the store when Popo was murdered. There he goes."

"Must be his lunch hour." Libby squinted after Calvin as he strode away from us. "He's kinda cute."

"He's bald," said Santa. "I've got all my hair, see?"

"I'm going to follow him," I said.

"Not without me," Libby shot back. "You've already knocked down one innocent bystander."

"Who you calling innocent?" Santa asked.

I took off after Calvin with Libby in hot pursuit. She wobbled on her high heels and struggled a little with her heavy shopping bags, but she kept up the pace. We tailed Calvin for two more blocks, keeping a safe distance so he wouldn't observe us. The lunch-hour crowds hadn't hit the sidewalks yet, but plenty of holiday shoppers made good cover for us. I explained to Libby more fully about what Darwin had told me and Calvin's connection to Cindie Rae.

Eventually Libby began to limp. "I didn't plan a ten-mile hike when I got dressed this morning. These shoes are killing me."

I stopped dead and ducked closer to the nearest building. "Look, Calvin is window-shopping."

Libby bumped into me from behind. "For what?"

We hung back and watched as Calvin slowed down and peered into the window of Victoria's Secret.

Libby said, "Here's an Easy Spirit store."

I was afraid to tear my gaze from Calvin. "Uh-huh."

"If I keep walking on these shoes, I'm going to be crippled. I'm going in. Wait for me here."

"I'm not waiting, Libby!"

"It'll just take a minute. Here, hold some of my bags."

She handed me two enormous shopping bags and disappeared into the shoe store. A moment later, Calvin started walking. I followed. He went another block before pausing again, this time in front of a take-out deli. I watched as he pulled out a cell phone and made a call.

Two minutes later, Libby reappeared, out of breath but no longer limping. "These Easy Spirits feel great! You should try some. Very comfy. Not terribly attractive, maybe, but I didn't have time to be choosy. What's he doing?" She leaned over my shoulder to watch.

"Ordering some lunch, I think."

"I could use a bathroom myself."

"Libby, why don't you go back to Haymaker's and finish your shopping?"

"Because I'm making sure you stay out of trouble. Look, he's going inside that take-out shop."

We watched Calvin haul open the door and step into the deli.

"I bet there's a restroom in there," Libby said.

"You're not going in."

"Why not? He doesn't know who I am. I could slip inside and figure out what he's doing."

"He's reading the menu board."

Libby stewed for another two minutes. "I'm going in," she declared. "It's unhealthy to walk around with a full bladder."

"Libby—"

"Here, hold a couple more of my bags, will you?"

My sister thrust two more shopping bags into my hands and dashed for the deli before I could grab her. I had to admit she was lighter on her feet in her new shoes.

Chapter 8

When Libby disappeared, I shifted all the shopping bags from one arm to the other, straining under the weight of gifts my sister planned to return, but keeping my eyes on the small restaurant. Minutes ticked by, and my feet began to get cold.

Libby came out of the deli. With her fingers, she oh-so-casually combed her hair away from her face. Then she tossed her hair over her shoulder and strolled toward me, hips swinging.

I recognized all the signs. "Tell me you didn't try to pick up Calvin while you were in there."

"Of course not. He looks terribly callow up close. But there was a very charming gentleman waiting for a latte, who—"

"Are you so desperate for male company that you— Never mind. What is Calvin doing?"

"Waiting for his lunch. He must be a hearty eater, by the way. He ordered two meals to go—a burger and a Greek salad."

"Maybe he's picking up for somebody else."

"I suppose he— Look, here he comes!"

We dodged into the doorway of a stationery shop and pretended to admire a display of Christmas cards. I tried to hide in Libby's shadow.

Calvin walked past us, holding a clear plastic bag by its handle. Two Styrofoam containers were inside. He headed back in the direction we had come.

"He's going back to work," Libby said.

But he turned right instead of left, heading away from Haymaker's.

"Let's go," I said, already in pursuit.

We tailed Calvin for four more blocks and ended up on a short residential street lined with apartment buildings that had been designed in the days of fallout shelters. Scraps of newspaper tumbled in the street, and a homeless person slept on a grate, wrapped in trash bags and guarded by a scraggly cat on a leash.

Abruptly, Calvin jaywalked and opened a plate-glass door to let himself into one of the buildings. Libby and I watched him disappear inside.

"Now what?" Libby asked.

From behind us, a male voice said, "Ho, ho, ho, girls. Want some company?"

It was Santa. He carried his collection bucket in one hand, and his eyes twinkled roguishly behind his synthetic beard.

"Are you following us?" I demanded, prepared to play tough in order to get rid of him. "Because we'll call a cop if you are."

"No need for that." He held up one hand to calm me. "I *am* a cop. Or was. Retired after twenty-two years of service in the Lancaster County sheriff's department."

"Well, you can't give speeding tickets to any Amish buggies around here," Libby snapped. "We're on a serious mission."

"Me, too," said Santa. "I'll do anything to have lunch with you, doll face. Even lend a hand in your covert operation."

"How old are you?" Libby asked. "Take off that beard."

Santa pulled the beard down low enough so we could get a better look at his face. He wasn't bad, actually. Kind of wrinkled, maybe fifty-something. He said, "Don't get fooled by the false teeth. I got my real ones kicked out by a kid who resisted arrest."

"All right, you can stay," Libby said.

"No, he can't," I said.

"I can be helpful."

I sighed. "You two wait out here and flirt with each other. I'm going into the building."

Libby said, "My sister is very impulsive. I have to keep an eye on her."

"And I'll keep an eye on you," said Santa. "See? Things are starting to work out for us already."

We went into the apartment building and found ourselves in a small lobby with plate-glass doors on both sides, one of them cracked as if it had been kicked. Someone had tried to repair it with masking tape. A line of mailboxes with buzzers greeted us from one wall.

I read the names on the mailboxes, hoping to find Calvin's. My finger stopped on apartment 3B, however.

Cindie Rae Smith.

"I'll be damned," said Santa, tilting his head to read through his bifocals. "Is this the real Cindie Rae Smith?"

"How would you know her?" Libby asked with a new edge in her voice.

"She's in the papers all the time. She's the one, right? The *Penthouse* girl?"

"Yes," I said.

"How do we get into this building?" Libby asked. "Without letting Cindie Rae know?"

I laid my hand flat on six buzzer buttons at the same time and leaned on them all. Seconds later, a variety of voices squawked on the intercom.

"UPS!" I yelled. "Delivery!"

Immediately, the door buzzed open and we went inside.

"Stairs or elevator?" I asked.

"Definitely the stairs," Santa said with new respect.

Libby eyed him doubtfully. "Can you make it three flights?"

"Can you?" he asked.

We trooped up three flights with Libby bringing up the rear. To lighten her load, Santa and I split her remaining shopping bags between the two of us.

The third-floor hallway was L-shaped and smelled like incontinence. We checked the numbers on the doors and found Cindie Rae's apartment at the end of the hall. We edged closer to listen, but a television blared in the next apartment, drowning out all other sound.

"I can't hear anything," Libby whispered.

"Shh."

"I don't mean to stick my nose in your business," Santa said, "but is anyone armed in this situation?"

"Calvin is," I said. "At least, he was wearing a gun in the store."

"Jeez," said Santa. "I was afraid of that. We need to call

the Philly cops. It's foolhardy to bust in on somebody with a gun."

Libby pulled out her cell phone and checked the screen. "I'm not getting a signal in here."

"You should get a new service," Santa advised. "My ex-wife uses Verizon and gets great reception."

Libby glanced up from her phone. "You're divorced?"

"Three years," Santa reported. "I hate living alone, but what's a guy with false teeth supposed to do? I volunteer for the Salvation Army and the Meals on Wheels and the—"

"Could we get back to business here?" I asked. "Somebody go call the police."

Libby said, "She has man trouble. It makes her testy. I'll go down the hall to see if I can get a signal there."

"I'll help you," said Santa.

They walked away, leaving me in front of Cindie Rae's apartment door holding shopping bags. I listened for voices, but across the hall a new burst of game-show music began.

Suddenly the door opened from inside. Cindie Rae stood there in a tank top, flannel pajama bottoms, and flip-flops, holding the door for Calvin as if she'd just ordered him off the premises. She had a sleeping mask pushed up on her forehead and circles under her eyes. Without makeup, her face looked even more surgically ballooned than ever. Her breasts defied the laws of gravity inside the tank top.

"If you can't remember the salad dressing, what good are you?" she asked.

Calvin continued to mope for another instant until he realized I stood in the doorway. He said, "Hey. It's her."

Cindie Rae's head whipped around, and she stared at me. "It's you."

"It's me," I said.

Cindie Rae grabbed my arm, pulled me into the apartment, and slammed the door.

"What are you doing here?" she demanded. "How did you find this place?"

Her apartment looked like an entire sorority house had exploded. Discarded clothes, shoes, and take-out containers littered the floor. A glimpse toward the kitchen convinced me the health department should be making a call very soon. But the living room was draped in luminous cur-

tains—a television-friendly background for the round honeymoon bed in the center of the room. In the middle of
the bed stood a hand-lettered sign that read, BE BACK TO-
NIGHT! The letter i was dotted with a heart.

A mounted camera stood in front of the bed, its red
light blinking softly. Two large lamps with photographer's
reflecting umbrellas bounced ambient light onto the bed.
Electrical cables ran all over the makeshift studio—even
hanging over doors. Around the bed, someone had abandoned a variety of predictable props—handcuffs, a ratty
feather boa, and a life-size cardboard cutout of a German
shepherd.

Stacked within handy reach stood several dozen packing
cartons. I saw one of Cindie Rae's fluorescent sales items
sitting on the topmost box, looking like the horn of a radio-
active rhinoceros.

"You asked me to help get Alan out of jail," I said,
delicately pretending not to notice my surroundings. "I
came to report what I've learned."

"Oh," she said. "You proved the Pinkerton lady did it?"

"Um, not exactly." I indicated Calvin. "Perhaps your
friend should leave so we can talk?"

Calvin's jacket hung open far enough for me to see his
sidearm. To Cindie Rae, he said, "She must have followed
me here."

"Really?" Cindie Rae blinked at me. "Why?"

With luck, Libby and Santa had made contact with the
police by now. It was only a matter of keeping Cindie Rae
occupied until the cavalry arrived.

"Because she knows," said Calvin.

He unsnapped his holster and drew the gun. My heart
skipped, and I froze as he leveled it at me. He spread his
legs and supported the barrel of the gun with both hands
as if preparing to mow down a squadron of Columbian
drug dealers in a made-for-TV movie.

"Calvin," I said, "let's stay calm."

"How does she know?" Cindie Rae asked.

"You probably said something dumb."

"Me?" she demanded hotly. "What about you, Einstein?
If you hadn't gone wandering around the store that
night—"

"That's my job! I'm supposed to patrol."

"Look," I said. "Why don't we sit down and relax for a minute?"

"Good idea." Cindie Rae pushed me to the only spot to sit—the edge of her round bed. "Get comfortable right here while we think up what we should do."

I dropped the shopping bags and sat down hard on the honeymoon bed.

"Tie her up." Calvin pointed the gun at me.

"I don't have any rope."

"Use the handcuffs!"

I couldn't take my eyes off the gun, which bobbled in Calvin's hand as he scratched his ear. "Look, there's no need to get carried away. Let's just—"

"Shut up," said Cindie Rae.

"Don't move," Calvin ordered.

Cindie Rae got down on her hands and knees and began groping through all the junk on the floor. "I should have figured out Alan was up to something when he sent me to you in the first place. He told me you'd dig up dirt on the Pinkerton lady! Why am I a sucker for cute guys?"

"He's not so cute," Calvin said.

"Are you kidding? Half the sales clerks in that stupid store were sleeping with him." She came up with the handcuffs.

"Well, duh! He's rich! And you're not going to get any of his money if you can't figure out a way to get married, Cin."

"You expect me to marry that jerk now? I'm not sharing him with all those other women! That's disgusting! Hold still," she said to me. "Cal, she won't hold still."

Calvin stepped closer and pointed the gun at my nose. "Hold still."

I allowed Cindie Rae to fasten the handcuff on my left wrist. She snapped the other bracelet around a leg of the nearest light stand. I said, "You must be devastated, Cindie Rae. To learn your fiancé has been unfaithful must have been a terrible blow."

"Yeah," she agreed with a pout, "a really terrible blow. I mean, last month I sat through eight performances of *Phantom of the Opera* for that guy. All those people shrieking the same song over and over? I deserve a really big wedding for that alone!"

"And to learn Popo was one of his paramours—"

"His what?"

"One of his girlfriends. You must have been furious."

"Yeah, especially because she was jerking me around about the Lettitia McGraw handbag. I mean, what does it matter if I pick it up at the store or not? She was such a bitch. When Alan said we had to get rid of her, I—"

"Alan suggested killing her?"

"He said we had to get rid of her before we got married because she could make trouble. I *thought* he meant killing her. But when I visited him at the jail, he started blubbering about firing her, and who could have killed her, and I—"

"Didn't Alan know you killed her?"

"Pookums thinks I'm his sweet babycakes. And when I told him what really happened, he . . . he said you could help, that you could prove the Pinkerton lady did it because everybody thinks she already murdered her doddery old husbands. She deserves to go to jail for that anyway."

"She never—" I thought better of arguing. "So it was you and Calvin who figured out the plan of shutting off the security system?"

"It was mostly my idea." Calvin waved his gun around the room. "It was the least I could do to help Cin land the big fish. We've got bills to pay around here. All this camera stuff doesn't come cheap, y'know. Every caller we get on the nine-hundred line pays us a few bucks, of course, but we aren't moving the product fast enough." He pointed to the boxes of dildos.

"You are Cindie Rae's business partner as well as her cameraman?"

"I'm her director," Calvin corrected. "And her brother. The security guard gig is just my day job."

The phone rang. Startled, Cindie Rae bolted upright. "We've got a caller! And I don't have my false eyelashes on yet!"

She scampered for the bathroom while Calvin headed for a multiline telephone and hit a button. I suddenly became aware that the camera was pointed directly at me, solo, handcuffed in the middle of the bed.

"Hello, uh, Cindie Rae?" said an uncertain, amplified voice. "It's, uh, Dick again. Remember me?"

From the bathroom, Cindie Rae called, "Hi, Dick! Of course I remember you!"

"Uh, I really like your girlfriend," said the caller. "When does she take her clothes off?"

I gave up on the plan to keep things calm until the police arrived. "Forget it!" I shouted in Cindie Rae's direction. "No clothes are coming off! None!"

Calvin dropped the gun beside the phone and hurried to the camera. He peered through the lens and began to make adjustments.

I yanked at the handcuff. "I don't want any part of this!"

The caller said, "Are you girls going to do some nasty stuff together?"

"No!" I said. "We're not doing anything together! Cindie Rae, get in here right now!"

"Here," said Calvin. "Hold this and look like you're turned on."

He held out the fluorescent dildo to me.

Instead of reaching for it, I plunged my free hand into the Williams-Sonoma shopping bag and came up with Libby's rolling pin. I swung hard and knocked the dildo out of Calvin's grasp. Like a home run headed for the bleachers, it sailed over the camera and hit the kitchen wall. The momentum of my swing combined with my left hand being trapped by the handcuff sent me falling back on the bed.

"Hey!" Calvin yelped.

"Oh, yeah," said Dick on the telephone.

While Calvin went to retrieve the dildo, I struggled to sit up. I dropped the rolling pin and rummaged in another shopping bag. One-handed I came up with boxed perfume. Frantically, I tore open the box and fumbled with the bottle. By the time Calvin came back to me, I was ready. He bent to put the dildo on the bed, and I squirted him in the eyes.

He screamed and fell onto the bed with me, clutching his face.

"Oooh, yeah, baby!" Dick yelled.

Cindie Rae dashed into the room with one false eyelash hanging drunkenly from her eye. "What's going on? Calvin! Calvin! What are you doing?"

She leaped on the bed and rolled her brother over. "Let me see, Cal, honey. Are you hurt?"

"Hurt him some more!" bellowed Dick.

Cindie Rae straddled him and began doing chest compressions on her brother. Calvin choked on the perfume and wept streaming tears. The fluorescent dildo rolled into my lap. I reacted as if it were a Molotov cocktail and threw it into the air.

Which was when the police burst through the door. The first cop snagged the dildo out of the air like a football.

Libby and Santa burst in right behind him.

"Oh, my God." Libby surveyed the scene with me front and center. "You get to have all the fun!

Chapter 9

Later that evening, Michael arrived at Blackbird Farm bearing steaks and wine. He opened the bottle first, and we sipped a very nice Beaujolais in the kitchen while I told him everything. Reluctantly, I even told him about the tussle on Cindie Rae's bed.

He listened with a suspiciously straight face while preparing a potato gratin, complete with cheese shaved from a chunk he'd been saving in the fridge.

"You think maybe Calvin made a tape?" he asked when I finished the tale. "Because I'd pay a lot of money to see it."

"There is no tape," I said firmly. "I had Libby and Santa double-check."

Michael cocked his head toward the living room, from where Libby's giggle and Santa's lower-timbred laugh floated back to us. "What's his real name, anyway?"

"I don't know. I don't think it matters."

"He's not the lasting type?"

"Stranger things have happened," I said. "I just hope he doesn't break her heart before Christmas. She's already on the edge."

Michael sipped some of his wine. "And the police arrested Cindie Rae and her brother?"

"Yes. But it looks like Alan was the mastermind all along. He planted the suggestion of getting rid of Popo with Cindie Rae and let her plot the murder with Calvin. It was his way of getting rid of both Popo and Cindie Rae. He figured she'd be too inept to get away with the crime. To help the investigation along, he told her to get me involved."

"So the cops got the right man this time?" Michael shook his head in disbelief. "I guess it's time to break out the snowshoes in hell."

"Michael," I warned.

He slid the gratin in the oven and put a sauté pan on the stove to heat. He doused the pan with a splash of olive oil, adjusted the flame with care, then came over to the table, where I sat on one chair in the dress he'd bought for me from Darwin, the dress Popo chose and set aside with my name pinned to the low neckline. She'd been right—I looked fabulous in it. To tone down the glamour, I had my sock feet propped up on the opposite chair.

Michael picked up my feet and sat on the chair, warming my toes with his hands. "You look beautiful."

"Thank you. I love the dress. But it's too expensive. You have to take it back."

He shook his head. "It's a Christmas gift, and it's worth every penny. Popo really knew what she was doing. It makes me think about what you'll look like when I take it off."

"What will I get for you? I'm completely broke."

"You'll think of something."

We heard Libby laugh again; then a loaded silence told us Santa was well on his way to giving Libby some Christmas cheer.

Michael smiled. "You can't stop love."

I smiled, too. "You sure about that?"

"I am," he said with conviction. "Nora—"

"I know," I said. "I'm sorry. I should have waited instead of chasing off on my own. But I saw Calvin coming out of the store and knew it was my chance. I had to follow him."

He nodded. "I know what you'll do for the people you care about. But when somebody loves you the way I do, you have a responsibility. You have to take care of yourself now. For me."

I put my glass down and reached for his hand. I squeezed. "I will. I promise I'll be more careful."

He accepted that by kissing my fingertips. "Are you sorry your friend is going to jail?"

"Not if he really planned Popo's death. I think he actually wanted Haymaker's to fail. If he no longer had the store, he would be free to go to the theater as much as he liked. Cindie Rae said he even hoped to buy a theater for himself."

"Maybe he'll still get his chance. He can afford good lawyers. That makes a big difference."

I allowed that observation to hang in the air for a moment.

Michael caught my eye and gave a wry smile. "I'm doing what I can, you know."

"Are you, Michael?"

He focused on gently kneading the arches of my feet. "I look at my life and know I've wasted a lot of time. I want to come home to you every night with a clear conscience. But I can't clean up a lifetime overnight."

Quietly, I said, "I heard about Pinky Pinkerton's granddaughter, Kerry. It was on the news. She hurt her hand."

Michael looked up, but his face betrayed nothing. "She did?"

"On her way to the airport. A car-service driver slammed her hand in a door. She's hurt badly. The surgery is complicated and may take over a year to heal. She won't play golf for a long time. And the car-service driver has disappeared. Nobody's even heard of the company before."

"No kidding," he said.

"The good news is that she got a job offer. A sports network starting up in California wants her to do golf commentary. So she's moving to the West Coast."

"Lucky for her grandmother, huh?"

"Michael," I said, "we both want to start our lives over. More than anything, I want us to end up together every night, too. But there are things I can't accept. I have some experience with men who live by their own rules, who are self-destructive, and it's . . . it's too painful to go through again."

"The last thing I want to do is hurt you," he said. "I'm going straight. I promise."

"All right," I said. "I trust you."

"That," he said, "is the best Christmas gift I've ever received."

He kissed me as if to seal the bargain.

Read on for an excerpt from the next
Blackbird Sisters mystery by Nancy Martin

Cross Your Heart and Hope to Die

Coming in hardcover from NAL in March 2005

I was still in bed recovering from Christmas when the phone rang.

On the other end of the line, I heard the roar of a chain saw.

No, on second thought it was the voice of my boss, Kitty Keough.

"Get your coat, Sweet Knees," she squawked. "And get your ass into the city right away. I need you to cover a fashion show that starts in less than an hour."

"Kitty," I said, "I could use a little more warning when it comes to assignments."

"Oh, barf," she shouted in the same dulcet tones as before. "Are you whining? Because nobody's going to kiss your tiara in the newspaper business, honey. You want to stay at home and count silver spoons? Or you want to get paid this week?"

I could hear the blare of traffic in the background and figured she was phoning from a taxi that careened through the snowy streets of Philadelphia, speeding Kitty to a high-society party that somehow outrivaled the assignment she was tossing over her shoulder to me. No doubt her brassy blond hair was blowing in the wind and she was whipping her driver with the moth-eaten feather boa she carried to formal events in the misguided belief that it lent glamour to her appearance. "Quit playing footsie with the Mafia Prince and get your butt in gear."

"He's not—" I stopped myself from giving her further ammo to use against me and reached for a pen. "All right, give me the details."

Which is why I threw a fur coat over my nightgown,

slipped on a pair of Chanel boots, and headed out for an evening that promised to be legendary. It was go, or lose my job.

And oh, baby, I needed the job.

I applied lipstick and three coats of mascara while my sister drove into Philadelphia. Michael had other business to tend, so I'd called Libby to go with me. On the way, she told me about her new business venture.

"Donald Trump says a successful entrepreneur has to be passionate about what she does," she informed me as she fearlessly drove her minivan through the snow.

"What does that mean?"

"So I found my passion. My greatest wish is to electrify the romantic relationships of everyone I know."

"Electrify? Sounds like you're selling vibrators."

"At Potions and Passions, we call them intimacy aids."

I nearly scratched my cornea with the mascara wand. "You're kidding, right?"

"Adult products are a booming business! I'm an official Potions and Passions consultant now. I get my first shipment of sex toys this week. Except we're supposed to say erotic enhancements." With a charmingly demented smile, she asked, "Don't you want to know what the buzz is about?"

While she laughed, full of delight and adventure, I said, "Libby, why couldn't you pay off your Christmas debt by going to work as a telemarketer or something? You could sell lawn mowers to bedouins!"

"I'm not passionate about lawn mowers. I am passionate about sex."

For Libby, the path to self-fulfillment was a long, winding highway with many roadside attractions. Still a few years shy of forty, she visited the graves of two husbands and at least one "very dear friend." Before her children were born, Libby had been a rising painter, not to mention a founding member of the local erotic yoga society. But nowadays she was always flinging herself into diversionary pit stops that sometimes made me long to strangle her.

"Anyway," she said, "I need to make a living. I hate being penniless, don't you?"

Poverty was new to both my sisters and me. Groomed for debutante balls and advantageous marriages, we had been badly burned when our parents lit a match to the Blackbird family fortune. They spent our trust funds faster than drunken lottery winners could buy a fleet of Cadillacs, then ran off to South America to practice the nuances of the tango.

Mama and Daddy left me to cope with Blackbird Farm—a difficult challenge in itself with its crumbling roof and ancient plumbing. But the $2 million debt of back taxes really threw me for a loop. Maybe it's an old-fashioned notion, but I couldn't let the family legacy be bulldozed to make room for a Wal-Mart, so I sold everything I could to start a tax repayment plan, and then I ventured gamely into the world of employment for the first time in my life.

Okay, so I hadn't been reduced to eating out of Dumpsters, but my lifestyle went from frocks and rocks to macaroni and cheese in a hurry. I had to get a job. My blue-blooded ancestors were probably rolling over in the Blackbird mausoleum, but now when Kitty Keough, the society columnist for the *Philadelphia Intelligencer,* called, I came running.

"Why can't Kitty go to this big-deal fashion show herself?" Libby asked. "It's just her kind of thing, right? Famous people sucking up and free goody bags, too? Why send her assistant instead?"

"I don't know. She didn't say. It's probably part of her plot to get me fired. But I have to go, don't I?" I tucked the mascara back in Libby's handbag and checked my watch. "And it starts in ten minutes."

"We'll get there," Libby promised, and she floored the accelerator of her minivan.

KILLER BLONDE

A DEAD-END JOB MYSTERY

ELAINE VIETS

To the real Margery Flax,
who is not and has never been blonde

Chapter 1

"Some women are born blond," Margery Flax said. "Some achieve it. Being blond doesn't have anything to do with your natural hair color. It's an attitude. A true blonde knows she can get away with murder."

"Can she really?" Helen Hawthorne said. "Did you ever know a successful blond killer?"

"I knew one," Margery said. "It was more than thirty years ago. It was a blonde-on-blonde crime. The blond killer was never caught. Her blond victim was never found."

Helen, a brunette, was sitting out by the pool at the Coronado Tropic Apartments with her gray-haired landlady, Margery Flax. It was one of those soft south Florida twilights where women who've had a little wine tell each other secrets.

Helen would never have guessed that Margery knew an uncaught killer. But there was a lot she didn't know about her landlady. There were a few things Margery didn't know about her, either: Helen was on the run from the law in St. Louis. So far, the court hadn't found her.

South Florida was a good place to hide. Helen wondered how many lawless types like herself were sitting out by their pools tonight, sipping wine.

She couldn't answer that question, so Helen concentrated on what she did know about Margery. Her landlady was seventy-six, she loved purple, and she smoked Marlboros.

Now Margery seemed ready to reveal something from her past. She poured them both more white wine from the box on the patio table and set fire to another cigarette. Her lighter flared yellow, then her cigarette tip glowed orange in the deepening dark. It was oddly comforting, perhaps because it was unchanging. Margery's smoking ritual would have had the same flare and glow in the last century.

"Keep in mind this happened some thirty-five years ago," Margery said. "America was a different country. Nixon was president. We were still in Vietnam. There were riots and protest marches. But the summer of love was long gone. In 1970, the Beatles broke up, Janis Joplin OD'd, and four students were killed at Kent State. Everything the sixties stood for was coming apart. Something dark was loose in America. I could see it even at the office where I worked."

"I thought you ran the Coronado," Helen said.

"I had a husband," Margery said. "He ran the Coronado. I had to get out of the house."

Margery never talked about her husband. Helen didn't know if he was dead or divorced. She'd never seen his picture displayed in her landlady's home.

"Never mind where I worked in Fort Lauderdale," Margery said. "We pushed paper, like most offices. Young women can't understand what offices were like then. Women's rights were still something people debated, and they weren't sure we should have them. Strong-minded women were condemned as libbers and bra burners.

"It's also hard to picture the daily office routine. There was no FedEx. Fax machines weren't common, so important documents were sent across town by cab or messenger. Computers were the size of Toyotas. Office workers didn't have PCs or e-mail," Margery said.

"People used typewriters, big clunky metal things in battleship gray. Men used to brag that they couldn't type. It was women's work. It was definitely my work. I could type seventy words a minute. Most typists still used carbon paper. I carboned the back of a letter or two in my time.

"This was so long ago, I was still a brunette," Margery said. "I always will be, no matter how gray I get. Brunette is an attitude, too."

Helen did a quick calculation. Margery must have been forty in 1970, two years younger than Helen was now. She tried to imagine her landlady at that age and couldn't. Then she remembered a photo she'd seen of Margery from that period. She was wearing a purple miniskirt and white Dallas cheerleader boots. What did they call them? Go-go boots. Margery's hair had been a rich brown, and her face was nearly unlined. Helen thought she'd looked young and sassy.

"Let me tell you about the boss," Margery said. "Vicki ran our department back in the days when women bosses were rare. She didn't know much about business, but she understood office politics. Some said she got her promotion because she had a special friendship with Mr. Hammonds, the CEO. They always said that about successful women then, but in Vicki's case, it might have been true.

"Vicki was one of those blondes you love to hate. She was a snippy size two. She wore spiked heels that turned her walk into a pattering little sway. She liked pink and ruffles."

Margery blew out a cloud of smoke, and Helen could almost see Vicki in the swirling wisps.

"Men thought Vicki was cute. She knew how to flatter them. She didn't waste soft words on the women at work. She certainly didn't waste any on me. I was the department manager. But I could stand up for myself, and I knew where all the bodies were buried. Vicki was a little afraid of me, and I liked it that way. I trusted that woman as far as I could throw her."

Helen thought her landlady was capable of lobbing Vicki across the pool. She was a strong woman, in all senses of the word.

"The one I felt sorry for was Minnie. The poor girl was a mouse. Even her name belonged to a mouse. Minnie was short for Minfreda, which she said was a family name, but she couldn't get anyone to call her anything but Minnie. She was not a forceful person.

"Minnie's hair was mousy brown. I guess that color takes an attitude too, but it wasn't one I wanted. The rest of her was mouselike. She had a small, pointed chin and a sharp nose that looked like it was twitching for cheese.

"Vicki loved to pick on Minnie. I swear she used to spend her nights dreaming up ways to torment her. It wasn't fair. Minnie worked harder than anyone else in that office. She was the best qualified, too. She had two degrees and ten years' experience. She was more than book-smart.

Minnie understood the business better than any of us. She should have had Vicki's job. Heck, she should have had Mr. Hammonds's, except she'd need a sex change to get it.

"I was always giving her pep talks," Margery said. " 'You have to stand up to her, Minnie,' I'd tell her. 'That Vicki is nothing but a bully. It's the only way to get her off your back.'

" 'You're right, Margery,' Minnie would say in her wispy little voice.

"I'd see her standing at the entrance to Vicki's office, trying to summon the courage to tell her off. I'd silently root for her, but she never stood her ground. Minnie would start to knock on Vicki's door. Her mouth would open and shut like a goldfish's. Then the bold words would dry up in Minnie's throat and she'd scurry away.

"Poor Minnie would work harder, desperate to please Vicki," Margery said. "We knew that was hopeless. Hard work didn't impress this boss. Vicki favored some of the worst goof-offs in the office. I wanted to take Minnie and shake her. She was a doormat. Vicki wiped her feet on Minnie."

Margery might pity Minnie, but she would have no patience with her, Helen thought. The fearless cannot understand what it's like to be afraid. But Helen knew. She was afraid her ex would find her, afraid she'd have to go back to St. Louis, afraid she'd once more be standing in front of the bald, wizened judge who'd ruined her life.

"Minnie was as colorless as our office," Margery said. "Now, when I tell you this story, you're going to wonder *how* I know some of these things. I ran the department. Vicki couldn't type for beans, so I did her typing. I filed the memos from on high. I had the payroll and personnel records on everyone in the department."

"Sounds like you found some useful information buried in those boring files," Helen said.

"Oh, I did," Margery said. "I saw and heard even more. I answered the phones, so I knew when a man's wife was angry at him. Even the nicest wives couldn't always keep the sharpness out of their voices. I also figured out that when a married man wrapped his hand around the receiver and started whispering all lovey-dovey, he probably wasn't cooing to his lawful wedded wife. I was friends with Mr.

Hammonds's personal secretary, Francine, so I picked up a few things that way. If I needed to hear or see something interesting, I wasn't above changing a typewriter ribbon at a nearby desk, or getting down on the floor to look for dropped paper clips."

Helen imagined Margery's office, circa 1970, with its clunky gray metal desks, creaky leather chairs, army-green filing cabinets, piles of paper in gray metal in and out boxes, and heavy black five-button phones. Wooden coat-racks were festooned with men's suit jackets. The walls were painted institutional green and curdled cream. Sitting at most of the desks were white men in gray suits.

The twilight turned into darkest night as Margery talked and Helen listened. The only other sounds were the creak of the chaise longues, the rustle of small things in the bougainvillea, and the glug of the wine box when Margery refilled their glasses from time to time.

Her landlady's voice, with its smoker's rasp, was hypnotic. Helen didn't dare say a word. She was afraid Margery would suddenly stop her revelations.

Helen sat back and listened as Margery told her story of blond betrayal, murder, and a secret burial in an ordinary office.

Chapter 2

God, I loved the early seventies fashions. I know everyone laughs at them now, but they were wild. The men dressed like Regency rakes. They looked romantic in long hair, velvet frock coats, and ruffled shirts. Well, some men looked like that. Rock stars, mostly.

These were Margery's words. Helen kept silent, afraid to interrupt the flow. Margery's memories seemed dredged from some place deep.

Her landlady continued, almost to herself:

The men in my department never made the sixties, much less the seventies. They could have walked out of any office in 1959. They didn't even have the lush seventies sideburns. One guy did show up at the Christmas party wearing a turtleneck and a peace symbol. Our CEO, Mr. Hammonds, gave that ornament such a cold stare he nearly froze it off the guy's chest.

The next day Mr. Peace and Love was back in suits, shirts, and strangulation ties.

It's too bad, really, you have to neuter yourself for a corporation. I understand the idea of dressing for success. It creates a more professional atmosphere, but it doesn't have much flair. So I was lucky. When I worked in an office, women didn't have to know about proper corporate dress. I suppose my clothes were in bad taste for a work environment, but how does that saying go—"Good taste is merely the fear of the beautiful"?

I had no fear.

I used to wear white go-go boots and purple miniskirts. The first time I bent down to get some papers out of the U-to-Z file drawer, half the men in our department nearly keeled over from heart attacks. I was careful how I moved after that. I wasn't a tease.

I was still pretty cute in those days, before my chest fell to my knees and my face wrinkled up like a prune. I was a bright spot, sitting behind my big old battleship of a desk at the department entrance. The delivery boys weren't sure whether to fear me or flirt with me. In the end, they did both. I shooed them away, just like I did the office Romeos.

Men hardly noticed Minnie, but why should they? Minnie sat hunched at a dun-colored desk, her face to the wall. Minnie's resemblance to a mouse could not be denied, even by me, and I liked her.

And that Vicki. There was a piece of work. She wore these short pink suits with a froth of ruffles at the throat, as if she were exploding with femininity.

She'd sit at her desk, flipping her long blond hair, which drove the men crazy. Like most young women then, she wore her hair straight and parted in the middle. It gave her an innocent look—something else I didn't trust about her.

I thought Vicki was slick as an icy pond the first time I laid eyes on her. I was right, too. You know what she did? She gave herself a private office. Up and did it late one night.

Vicki bribed the maintenance guys with beer and eye-batting. After the office staff left, the maintenance men put up a door and two metal-and-glass dividers, enclosing Vicki's corner of the office, including a window.

Windows are coveted in offices. People get claustrophobic shut up and staring at blank walls. When you got an office with your own window, you were on your way. In our department, that window was supposed to be for everyone, but Vicki hijacked it.

Once her new dividers and door were in place, Vicki stayed up most of the night, painting her office pink and putting down a square of hot-pink shag on the mold-green tile floor.

When the staff came in the next morning, they saw Vicki's new corner office. You should have heard the uproar.

Everyone except the very top bosses sat in a big open area, so we became a herd of faceless white-shirted workers in a bullpen. Now there was a pink tumor growing out of its side. Vicki smiled sweetly in her newly painted office. I sat back to watch the show.

Six men marched into Mr. Hammonds's office in an angry delegation. Privacy is precious in any office. Vicki had stolen hers at their expense, so their mood was a lot like the pitchfork-wielding villagers in the old *Frankenstein* movie.

Mr. Hammonds laughed at them, and it wasn't a pleasant sound. He wasn't much to look at, either. Imagine Donald Rumsfeld sucking a lemon, and you had our CEO.

Mr. Hammonds let Vicki keep her coveted private office.

"She's smart. I like that in a woman—or a man," he told the angry delegation. "She didn't take an inch more than she was entitled to, she just used the space better. And no, you cannot have your own offices. I've issued orders to maintenance that there will be no more late-night office raids. She was first and she was fast. You lost. Now take it like men."

After that, Vicki built her empire a little at a time, so most people hardly noticed. But I did. Her desk was sleeker and more expensive than the others. She hung a painting on her wall, something psychedelic in pink and orange. Mr. Hammonds thought this meant she was in touch with the youth market, which was vital to our business.

A pink rose in a vase on Vicki's desk showed she was a woman. A big, heavy coffee mug that said WORLD'S BEST BOSS was a testimony to her management skills. Vicki claimed it was a gift from the staff at her last job. Some people suspected she bought it herself.

Vicki slyly kept the men stirred up. She sweet-talked them and did little favors for them, like giving them a sick day when they were really hungover. She teased them without mercy.

Vicki was supposed to be engaged to Chris—who we never saw, by the way—but that didn't stop her from flirting with every man at the office, married or single. I thought she liked to get the guys jealous by bragging about how "Chris did this" and "Chris did that."

Chris took Vicki away for a romantic weekend to a bed-and-breakfast, which was a lot racier in 1970 than it is now. Chris bought a fifty-dollar bottle of wine at the best restaurant in Lauderdale when that was a decent day's pay. Chris beat up a man who stared at her too long in a bar. Vicki was especially proud of that story.

But Vicki never brought Chris to the company dinners or the Christmas parties. She always said, "Chris can't make it. My Chris is such a go-getter, always working late and on the weekends."

There was one more key character in this story: Jennifer, Minnie's best friend at work. Jennifer was blond and beautiful, but everyone forgave her for that. We managed to overlook her platinum-blond hair, pale skin, and wide brown eyes because she was so sweet.

At first, you had a hard time believing Jennifer's sugarplum-fairy act. But after a while you realized there was nothing sneaky or calculating about Jennifer. She really was as kind as she was beautiful.

Jennifer urged Minnie to get a job someplace where the management would appreciate her. "You can't bury yourself here, Minnie. You have to leave." Jennifer was too nice to say, "You let Vicki pick on you."

But Minnie heard it anyway. "If I leave here, I'll only have problems with someone else," she said. "At least Vicki is the devil I know. I've had too many bad bosses. You know what? They've all been blond."

"Oh, Minnie," Jennifer said. "Not all blondes are bad. I'm blond." She ran her slender fingers through her white-gold hair. She did that a lot, as if she couldn't believe anything so fine belonged to her.

"You're not a boss," Minnie said.

"I want to be one," Jennifer said. Her brown eyes looked like twin pools of chocolate syrup. "I have a good chance of being promoted to department manager if I get a favorable evaluation. Do you know what a manager is?"

"No," Minnie said.

"A mouse in training to be a rat."

Minnie laughed. Vicki was a department manager.

"The rumor mill says Vicki will be moving up to division head," Jennifer said. "I want her job."

"I'd love to work for you," Minnie said. "It's my idea of heaven."

"First, we have to survive the evaluations," Jennifer said.

But neither woman seriously expected a bad report. They were the office workhorses. They saw a rosy future at our company: Vicki would get promoted to division head. Jennifer would take Vicki's old job and her pink office, and Minnie would live happily ever after.

But Vicki couldn't resist trying to wreck their careers. She had the ultimate corporate power to destroy, and she was in love with it.

Vicki tried to ruin them both and signed her death warrant.

Chapter 3

Evaluation week was a nerve-wracking time at our office. Raises and promotions depended on our supervisor's rating. The right word or the wrong fork at lunch could mean another thousand a year in a pay envelope—or not.

There was another reason why the staff had nightmares during evaluation week: It was the only time our jobs were in jeopardy. A bad evaluation could start the process to get rid of the "deadwood."

Mr. Hammonds usually selected one person a year to be deadwood, and chopped without mercy. It kept the others on their toes.

The boys in my department knew they were prime timber for cutting. They had their own survival plan for evaluation week. The boys. That's how I thought of them, anyway. What kind of grown men had first names that ended in y?

There were three boys.

Bobby had a prep-school accent, seersucker suits, and polka-dot bow ties. He looked down his long, bony nose at everyone. Those who failed Bobby's exacting standards for clothes, accent, or address were condemned as "trailer trash." Poor Minnie flunked all three categories.

Bobby said he was a Stillman Rockefeller. Vicki was impressed by his pedigree. I wasn't. I knew how to find out things. I had Bobby's birth date and Social Security number. A few phone calls, a trip to the microfilm archives, and I discovered that Bobby was born in a trailer park in Macon, Missouri. The closest he got to a Rockefeller was the spinach on his oysters.

I kept my mouth shut until Bobby ordered me to hand-

address the envelopes for his next party, as if I were his
social secretary. Then I whispered two words in his ear:
"Shady Oaks."

That was the name of the natal trailer park. Bobby never
again asked me to do anything that wasn't connected to his
job, and I never said "Shady Oaks" at the office.

Jimmy, the second boy, was the office skirt-chaser and
self-proclaimed expert on camping and canoeing. I thought
he spent more time popping the tops on six-packs than
paddling canoes.

Jimmy would swagger into the office sunburned and bug-
bitten after one of his trips, and Vicki would listen wide-
eyed to his tales of camping and cruising for women. Jimmy's
conquests were mostly sad bottle blondes he picked up in
country bars. He called them his "sleeping bags." These
women seemed to expect bad treatment from men, but they
didn't stick around long enough to know for sure.

The boys and Vicki loved to gather 'round while Jimmy
lied to his wife, Juliet. "Yeah, honey," Jimmy would say,
his voice all sticky-sweet. "I've gotta stay late again tonight.
I won't be home until after eight. No, don't worry about
supper. Yes, I agree, honey. That Vicki is a regular slave
driver."

Jimmy would give Vicki a wink. She'd giggle. After he
hung up the phone, that no-good would light out for the
local no-tell motel.

Vicki carried on like he was the last of the red-hot lovers.
It made me mad. I talked with Jimmy's wife when she
called the office. She was always pleasant and polite. Juliet
deserved better than him.

Jimmy was such an experienced rake, he kept a bar of
Dial in his glove compartment, the same brand he used at
home. He'd shower with it at the motel, so he didn't come
home reeking of unfamiliar soap. He kept a fresh white
shirt in his trunk, in case his own was smeared with another
woman's lipstick. Worse, he bragged about his conquests.

Jimmy also had *The Sensuous Woman* by J to entertain
his lady loves. That book was pretty risqué for 1970. Jimmy
would bring his copy to the office and read the naughty
bits out loud to Vicki and the boys. Poor Minnie would
blush. Vicki would get this mean little smile.

Jimmy was an unlikely lothario. He was short, pudgy,

and freckled. But he knew how to make women laugh, and
they'd overlook a lot for a few jokes. Jimmy hit on me one
hot summer day when Vicki was at lunch. Jimmy's head
didn't reach the top of my chest.

"I'm married, sport," I told the little weasel.

"Good. I like married women." It sounded like a line he
used often.

"You got one at home," I said. "Ever wonder why your
wife swallows your stale 'Honey, I'm late' stories? Maybe
she's having her own fun while you're banging the headboard at the no-tell motel. Juliet's indifference says it all,
Romeo. If you were any good in bed, she'd be protecting
her property."

I said that for Juliet's sake. I didn't really think she was
running around. Jimmy slunk off with his tail, or something,
between his legs.

He never hit on me again.

The third one, Irish Johnny, had the face of a ruined
choirboy. He was losing his hair and wore a hat to cover
his bald spot, but he was handsome. Everyone loved
Johnny. He was bone lazy, fond of the bottle, and had the
backbone of a slug, but he made those faults endearing.
He had the Irish gift of gab—and of betrayal.

People told Irish Johnny things they'd never tell anyone
else, and he took them straight to Vicki. He fed her information about everyone in the office.

I kept my files locked. One day I found Irish Johnny
trying the handles on my file cabinets.

"I was looking for the vacation schedule. What do you
do with that key, darlin'?" Irish Johnny said.

"I take it home with me, Johnny dear. There's a lot of
information you wouldn't want out," I said. "Including how
much money was actually in the bowling-shirt fund you
handled."

Irish Johnny went dead white and never touched the file
drawers again.

There were other men in the office, but the three boys
dominated our department. They were Vicki's chief
courtiers.

During the dangerous evaluation week, the boys' suits
were freshly pressed, their ties were free of soup stains,
their shirts a little whiter. They sat up straighter at their

desks and stayed later. And they laughed louder at Vicki's jokes.

Vicki was the queen of our department during that week. The men treated her mildest whim as a command. Her desk was loaded with their bribes: slices of coffee cake, flowers, and chocolates with cherry-pink centers.

Everyone waited for the dreaded moment when Vicki said, "I have your evaluation." She enjoyed that little frisson of fright even the most secure felt when they heard those words.

Vicki had a pecking order, and the boys were at the top. She took most of the men in the department out for drinks or coffee when she gave them their evaluations. They'd be gone anywhere from fifteen minutes to an hour.

The three boys got lunch.

On Monday, about eleven thirty, she said, "I have your evaluation, Johnny."

Irish Johnny's handsome choirboy face turned pale. Vicki smiled and showed pretty predator's teeth. He clapped his hat on his brown curls and followed her out the door, shoulders hunched, head down, like he expected a beating.

Three hours later they came back together. Irish Johnny was filled with boozy good cheer and prime rib from Harper's, an old city steakhouse. He got a good review, better than he deserved.

I typed it up later, and my fingers twitched on the keys as I copied the undeserved praise for this goldbrick. I itched to change those sentences, but I couldn't. Vicki would read my work, then personally deliver it to Mr. Hammonds.

Vicki came back from every man's evaluation giggling and pink-cheeked, as if she'd been at an assignation. The men were always smiling.

By Friday, I knew all the men got good reviews, even the drones and drunks. Vicki, like many bosses in those days, considered alcoholism a manly vice—until the man started making embarrassing scenes. Then, like a cute puppy who'd grown into an unruly dog, he was out on the street.

I got my evaluation on Friday morning. Vicki made me wait, but what she said was fair. More than fair. Vicki praised me to the skies, so I knew she was still afraid of me. My evaluation didn't come with giggles and prime rib, but I didn't want to spend any more time than I had to with Vicki.

There were no lunches, drinks, or even a soda from the company cafeteria for Jennifer and Minnie. Vicki made them endure a wretched weeklong wait. By three o'clock Friday, they still hadn't had their evaluations. Jennifer wasn't worried, but Minnie was a wreck.

I didn't know what comfort I could give her. From the way Vicki was prancing around the office, I was sure she was up to no good.

Vicki dropped Jennifer's and Minnie's evaluations on their desks at five o'clock Friday. Then she flounced out the door without a word. Vicki had typed them herself, and I could see the X's crossing out her mistakes. Too bad Vicki wasn't evaluated on her typing.

Jennifer read hers, then slammed it down on the desk and said, "That miserable bitch. I'll get her if it's the last thing I do."

I raised an eyebrow. Gentle Jennifer never talked like that.

Minnie read her evaluation and wept. "It's not fair," she sobbed. Her sharp little nose was red and dripping. Her eyelids were pink and swollen. "I've worked so hard. I don't know what else I can do to please her."

"You can't do anything, Minnie," Jennifer said. "Haven't you got that through your head yet?"

I'd never heard Jennifer speak so harshly to her friend. Minnie only cried harder, but for once, Jennifer didn't try to comfort her.

"Come on, ladies, you've had a horrible week," I said. We didn't use expressions like *stressed-out* then. "Let me buy you a drink."

"No, thanks," Jennifer said. "I have work to do, Margery. I think you understand."

Jennifer had a fire in her brown eyes I'd never seen before. She rummaged in her desk until she had a big pile of papers. Jennifer shoved them in her briefcase, along with her accursed evaluation, and marched out.

Minnie gathered up her fat black leather old-lady purse and put on a sad brown scarf. "Thanks, Margery, but I just want to go home," she snuffled. Minnie's reaction wasn't healthy. I wished she had the same angry fire as Jennifer.

At eight thirty Monday morning, drab little Minnie was at her desk, slaving away in a hopeless effort to please Vicki.

At nine A.M., Jennifer walked into Vicki's office without knocking, a thick file under one arm. Her step was bold. Her long blond hair waved defiantly.

I was out of typing paper, which I kept in a cabinet near Vicki's office. While I rooted around for it, I could hear everything Jennifer said. Dear, sweet Jennifer had quite a mouth on her when she was riled. I liked the little blonde even better for that.

"What do you mean, giving me a poor evaluation, you incompetent twit?" Jennifer's low voice cut like a knife.

Vicki made a gurgling sound. No one, not even me, spoke to her that way.

"Do you know how many times I've saved your bacon?" Jennifer said. "Obviously you need a reminder. So here's a complete list of your mistakes and my corrections."

I heard the slap of that fat file hitting a desktop.

"Without my intervention, this company would have lost $67,457.16," Jennifer said. Now the other staff members were straining to hear, but only I could catch what she said.

Vicki was speechless. At least, I didn't hear her reply.

"Let's start with the Harrison project," Jennifer said. "You forgot to add the shipping fees when you prepared an estimate—"

She proceeded to chronicle Vicki's mistakes for the next half hour. Jennifer was sweet, but that didn't mean she was stupid. She must have distrusted Vicki as much as I did, because she kept backup files. Jennifer had copies of Vicki's original orders and proposals, signed and dated, and then her own clever catches and corrections. She was one sharp little blonde.

"Now, you have your choice," Jennifer said, when she finished her staggering list of Vicki's errors. "You can redo my evaluation, or I can take this file in to Mr. Hammonds. You have one hour to reconsider. If I don't have that revised evaluation on my desk by ten thirty, I'll have a talk with Mr. Hammonds. And it won't make any difference how much you coo at him. He's a hardheaded money man. When he sees this, you'll be out on your twitching pink tail."

At ten twenty-five, Vicki called me and asked if I would summon Jennifer. I escorted Jennifer to the pink office, then hung around outside, in case the boss needed me.

"Here's your evaluation," Vicki told Jennifer.

That's all she said. Vicki had also typed this one, and it was full of slipped letters and misspellings. But she was dead-on about Jennifer this time. That young woman got the praise she deserved.

Vicki decided to play it safe and revise Minnie's evaluation. It didn't give Minnie nearly the credit she deserved, but it raised her rating from a lousy F to a B-minus.

Minnie quit sniffling and actually smiled. "I knew if I came in early today and Vicki saw me working hard, she would change her mind," she said. "Hard work conquers all."

It wasn't my place to set poor Minnie straight.

Jennifer spent the morning at her desk, typing furiously. I wandered over to check the coffee machine and saw what she was working on: a résumé.

My, my, I thought. Things will get interesting now. Jennifer will be snapped up fast by our competition, the Bradsco Corporation. Mr. Hammonds will want to know why this rising star was hired away.

On Wednesday, Jennifer called in and said she felt sick. She had a doctor's appointment and wouldn't be in until noon. I didn't believe her. Jennifer was healthy as a horse.

Thursday night, Jennifer stayed later than anyone, even Minnie. I forgot the Tupperware container I used for my lunch and went back for it. Those things smell to high heaven if you leave them unwashed overnight in this climate. I found the lights still on in our department. Jennifer was packing up the contents of her desk.

"Congratulations," I said. "I hope the Bradsco Corporation is paying you lots more money."

Jennifer looked startled, but then she smiled sweetly. "I should have known I couldn't fool you, Margery. I got them good, all of them." I didn't think she meant Bradsco.

Friday morning, Jennifer announced she was leaving.

"Don't bother with your two weeks' notice," Vicki said in her snippiest voice. "The guard will escort you out now. Margery will pack up your things and send them to you."

"Good-bye," Jennifer said. That's all she said. She was smart, that young woman.

Jennifer stopped by Minnie's desk. She was hunched over her calculator, a long strip of white paper and black numbers rolling down her desk.

"Minnie, please come with me to my new job," she said. "You're too good to work for Vicki. I'll make sure you get the money and the appreciation you deserve. We'll make a terrific team."

With her white dress and long pale hair, Jennifer looked like an angel pleading for Minnie's soul.

But Minnie wasn't the first—or the last—to refuse an angel's plea. "Vicki's getting better, Jennifer," she said. "Look how she changed her mind about my evaluation."

Jennifer was too modest to take credit for Vicki's change of heart. Instead she said, "Did Vicki give you the A-plus you deserve for your work?"

"No." Minnie's sharp nose turned a discouraged red, like a squashed plum. "But nobody's perfect. I know that."

"Minnie, why do you stay with that woman?" Jennifer said.

"She needs me," Minnie said. "You only like me."

"What kind of answer is that?" Jennifer said. "You must like being abused. Vicki gives you nothing, yet you run after her, hoping she'll change for the better. She's never going to like you."

Minnie stayed silent. She didn't know why she stayed with Vicki. Some people didn't believe they deserved good treatment.

Jennifer sighed. "I can't save you if you won't save yourself," she said sadly.

I waited until Jennifer was gone about an hour. Then I told Vicki that it appeared our former employee had already taken everything from her desk, including her Rolodex with hundreds of client names and addresses.

Vicki paled. "Thank you, Margery. There's no need to tell anyone else. I'll take care of it."

I bet. Mr. Hammonds would spit a brick if he found out.

Minnie was heartbroken when her friend left. She cried at her desk all day. I found her there, slurping lentil soup and crunching raw carrots. I ask you: Is that food? No wonder that woman didn't have the strength to put up a good fight.

I tried to talk with Minnie. I tried to get her to leave. I

all but ordered her to pack up and follow Jennifer. But she refused, in that stubborn way weak people sometimes have.

Later, I told myself I tried. I really did. I knew it was Minnie's last chance.

But I didn't know everything, the way Jennifer thought I did. I didn't know it was also Vicki's.

Chapter 4

Minnie was different after Jennifer left. She was even quieter, if that was possible. But her silence had an angry edge. Now I heard things slammed around on her desk.

Once, I caught the high-pitched sound of breaking glass. In the mood she was in, I was afraid Minnie might slash her wrists. I ran over to see if she was okay. Minnie was weeping over a broken coffee mug, hot tears mingling with the shattered blue glass.

"It slipped," she said. "It was a present from Jennifer."

But I saw the gouge in the plaster by her desk and the milky coffee running down her wall. Minnie threw that cup in a fit of rage.

So why didn't Minnie get angry when Vicki loaded her with Jennifer's work? Why didn't she demand that Vicki give her a raise for doing two jobs? Why was Minnie such a dishrag?

Little Vicki was a big bully. I knew that. But now I saw that side of her unbridled. When Minnie didn't fight back, Vicki began to openly torment the poor thing. A few men walked away when she started, but the boys joined her. Picking on Minnie became the new indoor sport.

Vicki started it, with her cruelly accurate Minnie imitations. She would hunch her shoulders, screw up her face, cry, and creep about.

Bobby was equally vicious. His cries of "Squeak! Squeak!" followed Minnie down the hall.

Trust Jimmy to use sex as a weapon. He brought in the infamous April issue of *Penthouse,* the first national magazine to show pubic hair. He left the thing open on her desk. It was pretty dirty for those days. Minnie blushed so violently, I was afraid she'd have a stroke. She couldn't bring herself to touch the magazine.

I picked it up and dropped it down the incinerator.

I was sure Bobby put that lifelike rubber mouse on Minnie's desk. It made poor Minnie shriek.

Next, a mousetrap snapped at her sensible shoes.

Then a wedge of port-wine cheese found its way into Minnie's typewriter. What a mess that was. I had to send out the typewriter for cleaning. If Vicki was any kind of boss, she'd have stopped the games right there. That cleaning cost the company thirty-nine dollars. The game was getting out of hand.

Irish Johnny would hang around, waiting for Minnie to make her next ugly discovery. He'd pretend to sympathize, then run back and report every agonized word to Vicki.

I couldn't do anything to stop Vicki and the boys, but I refused to take part in the harassment. I would check Minnie's desk a couple of times a day for mice, cheese, or, once, Mickey Mouse ears. I threw anything I found in the trash.

I could always tell when she'd found another malicious surprise: Minnie would burst into noisy tears. That woman could weep waterfalls. I wanted to hug her. I wanted to slap some sense into her.

"Have you no shame?" I asked Jimmy, when I caught him leaving more cheese in Minnie's typewriter. It was a slice of Swiss this time, a bit stinky but harmless. He shrugged but didn't answer.

"How can you torment that poor woman?" I said to Bobby when I surprised him planting mouse poison on her desk.

"How can we not?" Bobby said with a sneer. "She's such a crybaby."

I wished Minnie would stand up for herself. I tried to coach her. One Monday I found her crying in the bathroom after she discovered a windup mouse spinning in circles on her desk blotter.

"Now listen, Minnie," I said. "Here's what you do: Don't cry when they leave that stuff on your desk. That's what they want. It just encourages them."

"I can't help it," Minnie wailed. "It hurts."

"Thank them for the cute toys. Pretend you like the stuff, and this harassment will stop," I said.

"I c-c-can't." She wept. "I don't like it."

You can't give someone a backbone implant, I decided.

Finally, even these sadists were bored with Minnie's monotonous weeping. Either that, or they got tired of buying mouse novelties at the dime store and lugging cheese in their briefcases. Bobby forgot about a hunk of Limburger one August day and had to throw out a Dunhill briefcase. That made him almost as weepy as Minnie.

When that game ran down, Vicki started another. This one was more subtle. It took me a while to see what she was up to. She was suddenly, suspiciously kind to Minnie—no mimicry, no mice, no mocking laughter. Poor Minnie started coming out of her shell, or her mouse hole. She even smiled a bit.

Then Vicki called Minnie into her office. Our blond boss was at her most charming. She had me fetch herbal tea for Minnie. I stayed outside Vicki's door to hear what she was plotting.

"Now, Minnie," Vicki said. "I need you to work on a special project. The Redacher proposal is vital to our department, and only you can do it. You have to help me by doing the best job possible."

These words were specially designed to appeal to Minnie. She threw herself into the task. Minnie came to work so early and stayed so late, I was worried about her health.

One day, I left a message on Bobby's desk while he was at lunch. I saw a file labeled REDACHER PROPOSAL under his phone. I opened the folder. Inside was a half-finished proposal, with sheets of in-house facts and figures that had to have been supplied by Vicki.

I knew Vicki's game now: She'd put two people on the same job, but had given only one the inside information. Bobby's proposal would be chosen.

I tried to give Minnie one of my "Dutch aunt" talks without going into details. I couldn't tell her I'd been snooping around Bobby's desk.

"You can't trust that woman," I told her. "Did you ask her if you're the only person working on that project? Did she give you any in-house numbers? If she hasn't, Vicki is setting you up for a fall."

"No, Margery, you're wrong. Vicki wouldn't do that. This is my big chance," Minnie said.

She was hopelessly trusting. I'd failed again.

Meanwhile, Vicki invited Minnie for little salad lunches at Renee's Tea Cozy. She even took her shoe shopping, the ultimate female bonding ritual. Minnie bought brown lace-ups that would be too old for me now, and I'm seventy-six. Vicki bought herself frivolous pink heels.

After three weeks of nonstop work, Minnie put her finished project in a serious black binder and came shyly up to my desk.

"Margery," she said, "would you read this for me?"

I read it and declared it was the best thing Minnie had ever done. I meant it. Minnie was overjoyed. But I had an ominous feeling things were going to go very wrong, very soon.

I hung around Vicki's office and saw Minnie proudly hand in her work. Vicki was all pretty blond hair, pink ruffles, and pleasant smiles. She paged through the proposal, while Minnie sat there looking touchingly hopeful.

It took Vicki less than a minute to crush her. "I'm sorry, Minnie," she said dismissively. "It's not what I had in mind. I wanted to give you a chance, but you're not quite good enough. Bobby's proposal is much better."

Minnie looked as if she'd been slammed with a cinder block. She wobbled out of Vicki's office like a punch-drunk prizefighter. I was sure there would be another crying jag in the women's bathroom.

But I was wrong. This time Minnie didn't creep off to cry. I never saw her cry again. It was as if she'd wept away all her tears. Now she was dry and hard.

Minnie straightened her shoulders, held her head high, and walked right out the office door.

Good, I thought. If that young woman has any sense, she'll keep on walking.

Chapter 5

I heard what happened next thanks to Mr. Rick, my hairstylist. He had the most fashionable salon on Las Olas—the Cut Direct.

Mr. Rick believed that he looked like Paul McCartney, so he dressed like the cute Beatle. The hairstylist wore a florid mustache and a coat festooned with braid and epaulettes like Paul on the *Sgt. Pepper's Lonely Hearts Club Band* album.

Alas, Mr. Rick resembled the rogue-nosed Ringo more than Paul, especially in profile. Still, I appreciated his sartorial courage. Except for this one delusion, Mr. Rick's fashion judgment was flawless.

Speaking of courage, Minnie walked into Mr. Rick's salon without an appointment and said, "I'm sick of me. Make me someone else."

Only a desperate woman said that to a hairstylist. It was an act of bravado, a fashion free fall. It was doubly brave in a salon painted with showers of psychedelic stars and rainbows. It took still more courage to say it to a stylist dressed like a Gilbert and Sullivan pirate.

Maybe my lectures about standing up for herself had finally worked. Maybe Minnie had had enough. For whatever reason, she was ready to be a new woman.

Mr. Rick sat Minnie in a red chair and tied a pink plastic cape under her chin. She looked better already with some color near her face.

To the customers in the Cut Direct, Minnie seemed hopeless. But Mr. Rick walked around the red chair, studying her.

He examined her hair closely. It was the color of cold gravy and styled to emphasize her large ears. He considered her sharp nose and pointed chin. He noted her frumpy ankle-length brown jumper and big fat purse. Her flat shoes were styleless canoes.

But he also saw that her hazel eyes were large and intriguing. He watched them change from brown to green and back. He gently lifted her sheepdog bangs and saw a high, noble forehead and well-arched brows. Her skin was clear and unblemished.

Mr. Rick brandished his scissors, shoved back his braided cuffs, and announced, "I'll make you a blonde. You'll have more fun."

"I'm not quite ready for that," Minnie said, gripping the arms of her chair.

"Then I'll give you blond streaks. You can use a little fun," Mr. Rick said.

There was no arguing when Mr. Rick took that tone. He'd used it on me once when he refused to make me a redhead like Vanessa Redgrave in the movie *Camelot*. Eventually I came to my senses.

Mr. Rick got out his mixing bowls and brushes. Streaks were a painful process thirty years ago. Mr. Rick put a plastic cap full of holes on Minnie's head, then pulled the hair he wanted to dye blond through the cap with what looked like a crochet hook. Minnie never flinched or said, "Ouch." After working with Vicki, she was probably used to pain.

Once that was over, the rest was easy.

Mr. Rick brought her a tall iced tea and a frivolous magazine. Minnie seemed quite happy relaxing and reading fashion fluff. I don't think she ever had what we'd call a mental-health day. She even got a manicure while waiting for her transformation.

You probably think highlights were invented a few years back, but they were big thirty years ago, too. Take a look at Mrs. Robinson in *The Graduate*. It's those streaks that make her look so wicked.

Minnie wasn't wicked when Mr. Rick finished his cutting and streaking, but she did look different. She wasn't a blonde exactly, but the drab brunette was gone. Her soft new cut hid her ears and exposed a profile that belonged on a cameo.

The blond highlights gave her round face definition—and cheekbones. They also brought out her hazel eyes. Her sharp nose assumed a classical shape. Her pale skin had a pearly sheen.

"Very nice," Mr. Rick said.

Minnie blushed.

"Promise me you won't wear brown or gray," Mr. Rick said. "It's so bad for your skin. It drains the color from your face."

"But I have to look professional at the office," Minnie said.

"Try navy blue with a plain white blouse, if you're not ready for anything more interesting." Mr. Rick handed her the card of a fashionable shop on Las Olas. "Ask for Marie. She'll help you pick out something."

"Is it expensive?" Minnie asked timidly.

"Of course," Mr. Rick said. "But you're worth it."

Minnie looked as if she'd never considered this before. Then she smiled at her new self in the mirror and said, "Why, yes, I am."

She started to put on that sad brown scarf, but Mr. Rick snatched it off her head. "That's mine," he said. "It's part of my fee."

Minnie handed it over, and he dropped it delicately in the trash.

"But—" she said.

"No buts about it. Head scarves are for old women." Minnie looked bewildered, but she accepted this decree.

"One more thing," Mr. Rick said. "Burn those brown flats."

The next day, Minnie teetered into our office on three-inch heels. She hadn't quite mastered walking in spikes yet, but her attempts were cute, like a new colt learning to stand. She walked with a lighter step, and it took me a moment to see why. The twenty-pound old-lady purse was gone, replaced by a small swinging shoulder bag.

Minnie wore a tailored navy suit and a white blouse. Now you could see she had a smart little figure and sweet, slender legs.

The men in the office, married and single, suddenly sat up and got that glazed look. Jimmy told me that men are suckers for white blouses and neat navy suits. They start fantasizing about parochial schoolgirls and airline stewardesses. We didn't call them flight attendants then.

Vicki tip-tapped into work shortly after Minnie, but she

didn't get her usual adoring reception from the men. Her frothy pink suit seemed overdone compared to Minnie's trim navy number, and her makeup was a little heavy.

Vicki noted Minnie's new look, but she didn't say anything. She walked into her office and shut the door a fraction too hard. When I brought in her morning coffee, Vicki's face was disfigured by an unattractive frown. It gave her deep lines between her brows, and Botox was thirty years away.

Minnie blushed at all the new attention, and the guys found that delicious. Men are suckers for shy women. I knew there would be no more nasty surprises on Minnie's desk, and I foolishly thought our office would settle down. I should have been watching more carefully. Instead I sat there swollen with self-satisfaction, too pleased with myself to pay attention to the danger signs. I thought my lectures had finally gotten through to Minnie. I thought I'd changed things for the better at that office.

Now men stopped by Minnie's desk just to say hi. Instead of rubber mice and smelly cheese, they brought her little delicacies: anise cookies from Angelo's Italian bakery, strong shots of Cuban coffee from the corner bodega, or bagels with blueberry cream cheese from Levine's Deli. At first I thought the gifts were to make up for their bad behavior. Then I realized they were tributes to Minnie's newfound beauty.

The men started showing off like high school boys. "Hey, Minnie," Irish Johnny said, "watch this!"

He lobbed a paper ball into the wastebasket across the room, a decent shot for a desk jockey. Minnie applauded prettily, and Irish Johnny's ears turned red. I wondered if he was going to run back to Vicki with that story.

Even the boys were deserting Queen Vicki.

Jimmy, always a sucker for a pretty face, was the first to publicly defect. He asked Minnie to lunch. I took him aside and said, "You hurt that girl, Jimmy, and I'll fix it so you're singing in the Vatican choir."

"There's nothing wrong with lunch with a colleague."

"No, there's not," I said. "Just keep your ham on your own sandwich, and there's no problem."

Jimmy made sure everyone noticed when he escorted

Minnie to Harper's steakhouse. Irish Johnny slunk over to watch them, but I don't think he saw anything worth reporting. Minnie wasn't that kind of girl.

Bobby was out of the office on a business lunch in Pompano.

For the first time ever, Vicki had to eat a chicken-salad sandwich alone at her desk.

She scowled when she saw Minnie and Jimmy coming back from lunch at two o'clock, laughing over some silly remark. Vicki called Jimmy into her office and scolded him for having scotch on his breath. "You must maintain a professional demeanor at this office," she said. "And that means no two-hour lunches."

Jimmy did a devastating imitation of her lecture later for our benefit. Even Minnie couldn't suppress a smirk.

"Can you believe it?" Jimmy asked. "The bitch is gone for three hours most afternoons, but she has the nerve to criticize me for a long lunch."

It was the first time he'd referred to Vicki as "the bitch" behind her back. Within the week, all the boys called her that. We women already used that name.

As Minnie grew more popular, Vicki pouted and became surly. She no longer flirted and flipped her blond hair quite so often. The men hung around Minnie like she was the last lemonade stand in the Mojave.

Now there were awkward silences when Vicki entered a room and titters when she left. Jimmy did hilarious imitations of Vicki mincing into the office on her high heels, swinging her pink-suited behind.

Of course, no one left Vicki nasty little presents. She was still the boss and they feared what she could do to them. The boys flattered her outrageously, but Vicki knew their overdone compliments were just this side of mockery.

She couldn't criticize them, so Vicki tried to take it out on me. She snapped so much I finally had to put Vicki in her place.

The boss had started using me to run errands for her on company time. I didn't mind, as long as I could get my regular work done. If it was a sunny day, I liked getting outdoors. Vicki would leave a little note on my desk with her instructions, and I'd pick up her dry cleaning or take in her shoes for new heels.

Then she asked me to buy a present for her sister's birthday. Vicki wasn't close to Val, but they stayed in touch for birthdays and holidays.

"I don't know what your sister likes," I said. "I've never met her."

"Just go to the department store and get anything. Val will probably take it back, anyway. I always give her the sales receipt along with the gift. Make sure you spend enough so I don't look cheap."

I bought Val a boxed set of Chanel No. 5 perfume and dusting powder. It looked classy and expensive.

"What a stupid present," Vicki said when she pulled it out of the bag. "My sister is an Avon lady. Take it back right now."

Vicki practically threw the box in my face, as if I were some foolish ladies' maid.

"Then you should have said so before you sent me," I said. "Maybe you'd like to discuss my duties with Mr. Hammonds. I have a list of the times, dates, and stores where you've sent me, along with your memos ordering me to run your errands on company time."

The color drained from Vicki's face. She'd forgotten about those little notes she'd left on my desk. Vicki had made a fatal corporate mistake: She'd put it in writing.

"You'd better go back to work, Margery," was all she said.

I think she took the Chanel set back herself. I'd left the receipt in the bag. Vicki never asked me to run errands for her again.

That was her only mistake. Vicki kept most of her tantrums confined to me and her little pink office. Word of her erratic behavior hadn't leaked out to the important people in the company, like Mr. Hammonds. She was still on the fast track.

Minnie had changed, too. She was still shy and quiet, but it wasn't a sad quiet. She grew more self-assured. As I said before, her crying days were over. Her face never crumpled when Vicki said something mean. Minnie just set her jaw a little, and Vicki would back off.

That's my girl, I thought. You're learning how to deal with a bully.

People make jokes about a yellow streak being the sign

of cowards. But putting some gold in Minnie's hair put steel in her spine. Each month, Minnie was a little blonder—and a little bolder.

She started gently resisting Vicki. She didn't tell the boss off exactly, but Minnie would say, "I can't possibly do the Watkins report in twenty-four hours. I need at least forty-eight."

Minnie didn't sound angry, but she was firm.

Of course, Vicki gave her the extra time. She had no choice. She couldn't have written the report if she'd had a month. Now that she'd chased off Jennifer, she really did need Minnie.

The staff had always appreciated the quality and quantity of Minnie's work, but when she stood up to Vicki a bit, she was treated with new respect. Some people said Minnie would replace Vicki when she was promoted. I wasn't sure that would happen, but I looked forward to the day when we were free of Vicki. Minnie would make a much better boss.

I was proud of her, and I told her so. "Smartest thing you ever did was walk out of this office and into Mr. Rick's salon."

"He wants me to go all blond," she said, "but I don't have the courage."

"Why not?" I said. "All the changes he's made have been good so far."

"I'm afraid." She looked at me so seriously with that little cameo face. "I'm afraid it will set something loose."

"Oh, you don't have to worry about Vicki anymore," I said. "She's thoroughly tamed."

"I wasn't talking about Vicki," Minnie said. "I meant me."

Chapter 6

It was another six months before Minnie was ready to go all the way.

I don't know what triggered the final change. Vicki didn't treat her any better, or any worse. But I could feel something unstable in our office. Everyone had the jitters.

We were a week away from our next evaluation time. There were more rumors than usual. There would be changes this time, bigger than the annual chopping of the deadwood.

A special corner office was being built for the new division manager. Mr. Hammonds had personally picked out the furnishings. Francine, his secretary, showed them to me. I was bowled over. The new office would have an antique partners desk that cost a thousand dollars, luxurious sculpted brown shag carpet, a silver pencil holder that once belonged to John D. Rockefeller, and a leather wastebasket. It was a palace compared to the cubicles for us wage slaves.

I knew the staff would kill one another to sit behind that ornate desk. The competition would be vicious.

Minnie wanted a promotion. She was determined to sit at that partners desk someday. But first she had to make department head. She wanted to pump me for information, so she took me out to lunch. I appreciated the gesture. Vicki wouldn't have bothered.

Minnie didn't get me cheap chicken salad at Renee's Tea Cozy, either. She sprang for steak at Harper's and a decent red wine.

"You know everything and everyone at the company, Margery," she said. That was pure flattery, but I liked it just the same. "I want to be department head. What do you think of my chances? I do most of the work. I should be able to run it."

I chomped a juicy hunk of cow and considered her pitch. This was before we knew about cholesterol. Sirloin steak was almost a health food. With a scoop of cottage cheese on the side, it was a diet dinner. But I wasn't on any diet. I had a baked potato slathered with sour cream and chives.

"I think you have a good shot, as long as Vicki gets promoted to division head," I told her. "If you get promoted over Vicki, there will be hell to pay. You'll spend so much time putting out the fires started by Vicki, you won't be able to get your work done."

I took another bite of sirloin, chewed, and thought some more. "Vicki's your only real opposition. You have a lot of friends in and out of the department. Mr. Hammonds sees himself as forward-thinking, so he wouldn't object to another woman department head. You're definitely being noticed. Just keep doing what you're doing."

I decided to put in a good word with Francine to help things along. But I didn't say that to Minnie.

If Minnie had followed my advice, she'd be running that company today. But she couldn't let well enough alone. Minnie was a born overachiever. That was her fatal flaw.

The staff had become used to the new, good-looking Minnie. As part of her promotion strategy, she decided to stir things up and get noticed all over again.

So that Saturday, Minnie sat down in Mr. Rick's chair and said, "I'm ready. Make me a blonde."

And Mr. Rick did. He'd been waiting for this moment.

"Your true destiny is to be a blonde," he said. "You have a blonde's eyes and skin coloring. Mother Nature simply slipped up. I'm righting her wrong."

Mr. Rick restored Minnie to her rightful place. No more half-blond streaks. Mr. Rick mixed and measured until he had the perfect potion to turn straw-colored hair into gold. There are many shades of blond. He gave her a touch of Marilyn Monroe blond for sex appeal, a bit of Twiggy for youthful style, and a dollop of Grace Kelly for class. It was the perfect combination.

When he finished, Minnie's hair was a shimmering gilded

wave. It bounced on her shoulders like a Breck shampoo ad. Her hair was so beautiful, it seemed alive. The ceaseless salon chatter stopped. Even the hair dryers were silent. Customers and stylists alike were lost in admiration of his new creation.

Minnie had been pretty before, but now she was dramatic. She was a drop-dead blonde. She studied herself in front of Mr. Rick's full-length mirror. "I'm transformed!" she crowed. When she finished pirouetting, she examined her nice navy suit.

"I'm tired of dressing like a nun, Mr. Rick. I need some suits with style."

"Sweetie, I'm your fairy godmother," he said. "My last appointment is at four, and then we'll go shopping."

They made an odd couple, the fey, big-nosed man in the bizarre braided coat, and the cameo blonde in the severe suit. He was proud that he'd spotted her beauty before anyone else.

Mr. Rick said they went on a spree that had Las Olas talking for a week. It was an orgy of high-style purchases—suits, shoes, purses, jewelry. They would take over each store. Mr. Rick would select suits, dresses, and blouses, send Minnie back to the dressing room, then make her model them.

"Oh, I can't possibly buy this," Minnie said, when she appeared in the showroom in a splendid designer suit. "I've never worn anything this expensive."

"Exactly why you should have it," he said.

Mr. Rick egged her on to more and better extravagances, but he made sure she never crossed from daring to outrageous. Everything Minnie bought was for an elegant young executive.

"Are you sure this looks good?" she asked, modeling yet another stunning suit.

"You bet your sweet bippy," Mr. Rick said. That was the catchphrase of the day.

The saleswomen stood back and smiled their approval, then discreetly rang up the purchases. Money was no object, or not much of one. Minnie had squirreled away most of her salary, lived in a modest apartment, and ate frugally. Her blond hair was her one indulgence.

At last, Mr. Rick declared her new killer-blonde wardrobe complete. They ended, sated and weighted with boxes and bags, at a restaurant on Las Olas.

"Dinner is on me, my dear," Mr. Rick said. "You are my most brilliant success. Tonight I will celebrate you."

He ordered Caesar salads with extra anchovies, mushroom-stuffed chicken, and a chilled bottle of Blue Nun wine to toast Minnie, his subtropical Pygmalion.

"Why is a glamour girl like her hanging around with that fruit?" snarled a cigar chomper at the next table. His voice carried to Minnie's large ears, now happily hidden under her golden waves.

Minnie kissed Mr. Rick so hard he blushed. The cigar chomper bit his smuggled Havana in two.

"I know I'm not your type," she whispered in Mr. Rick's ear. "But I wanted to show the old creep. You've changed my life."

"Yes, I have," Mr. Rick said when he recovered. "But I prefer to stay your fairy godmother."

Minnie, who'd had a little too much Blue Nun, giggled immoderately.

"As your fairy godmother," he said, waving his butter knife over her golden hair like a wand, "I give you blond power. Use it to get what you want. Remember, you deserve it."

"I solemnly swear," Minnie said, taking another swig of Blue Nun.

Mr. Rick ordered cherries jubilee for dessert. Minnie stared into the alcohol-induced flames and saw only her bright future.

When Minnie walked into the office on Monday, I nearly dropped the Connors file—all eighty-two pages. Minnie had looked good before, but now she was stunning. She wouldn't remind men of a parochial schoolgirl anymore. Minnie was a blond bombshell.

"Va-va-voom," I said.

Minnie smiled sweetly, but she didn't blush.

She wore what you'd call a power suit. But this was power on two levels: sex and business. Her suit was a shapely black with a soft periwinkle blouse. It was expensive, feminine, and absolutely serious. Her shoes were classic Chanel, and so was her purse.

The newly blond Minnie walked in a golden glow. As she made her progress through our department to her desk, typewriters stopped clacking, phones were dropped, and at least one coffee cup hit the floor.

When two of the boys saw her, they sounded like the cast of *Laugh-In,* the hottest show on TV.

"Sock it to me," Bobby said, reverently.

"Verrrrry interesting," Irish Johnny said, doing his best Arte Johnson imitation, which wasn't very good.

It got even more interesting when Vicki tip-tapped into the office in a hairy pink bouclé suit and hooker heels.

Vicki was blond, but compared to Minnie, her hair was brassy. I noticed she had a lot of split ends and her roots needed a touch-up. Vicki didn't have Mr. Rick to work his magic.

Vicki knew that she was outclassed. She seemed to shrink into herself and look for an escape. But she brightened when her favorite boy, Jimmy, walked into the department. He stopped dead and his eyes nearly popped out of his head like a cartoon character. Then he gave a long, low wolf whistle.

Vicki smiled and simpered.

The smile slid off Vicki's face when he said, "Minnie, you look like a million bucks."

"Thank you, Jimmy," she said sweetly. "But my name is Minfreda."

Chapter 7

Word of the transformed Minnie—excuse me, Minfreda—
spread through the building. Even Mr. Hammonds, our
sour-faced CEO, found an excuse to check her out. Naturally, the great man wanted to keep track of one of the
few females with executive potential. Or maybe he wanted
to take Vicki down a notch.

The whole department trembled when he walked in. Mr.
Hammonds was a balding, mean-mouthed man who looked
like he wouldn't give his grandmother a dollar if she were
begging on the street. But he had a glow of his own, the
kind created by money and power.

Vicki smiled and wrung her hands like a kitchen maid
summoned to meet the master. Mr. Hammonds walked past
her as if she didn't exist, and Vicki's face turned to stone.

He kept on going straight to Minfreda's desk, and spent
nearly ten minutes talking to her. I sailed by once to get
some carbon paper and happened to hear some of their
conversation.

"Unusually cool winter weather we're having," Mr. Hammonds said.

"Why, yes," Minfreda agreed. Everyone always agreed
with Mr. Hammonds.

After a few more scintillating exchanges, Mr. Hammonds
left. Minfreda appeared slightly dazed, as if she were a
peasant girl who'd been visited by the prince.

After Mr. Hammonds's visit, it seemed like everyone in
the office had to find an excuse to see Minfreda. Some
claimed they needed sales figures. Others wanted to know
if she was coming to the company softball game or had

signed up for the midwinter picnic. A few women congratulated Minfreda on her new look and asked for the name of her hairstylist. They got points in my book for being straightforward.

Absolutely no work was getting done that day. Even the extremely proper Francine came back to our department, suddenly in need of a Social Security number I was quite sure she had.

"Maybe I should sell tickets to the show," I said, when Francine left.

Minfreda giggled. It was an engaging sound. I was enjoying this day way too much. I should have known that Minfreda would pay for her triumph.

Vicki sat alone in her pink chamber, taking no notice of the commotion, saying nothing to Minfreda. She was quiet. Too quiet, as the sheriff said in those Westerns before the cattle rustlers attacked the ranch.

About four o'clock that afternoon, Vicki called Minfreda into her office. She was all business.

"Well, you've certainly impressed Mr. Hammonds," Vicki said. "The CEO has asked for long-range planning ideas for 1971, and he is particularly interested in what you think about our company's future. Your next promotion could depend on this report.

"If your ideas are good enough, you could move straight up to division manager. No slaving away as a lowly department head, like I did." Vicki gave a little self-deprecating laugh.

"Mr. Hammonds believes leadership is about ideas, and he definitely wants yours. But you haven't much time. I need your report by nine o'clock tomorrow morning. He'll announce his decision in two days."

Minfreda nearly skipped down the hall to tell me her news.

"I have a shortcut to that corner office, Margery," she said. "Vicki wants me to prepare a long-range planning report. If I do a good job, I'll be the next division head."

"It's a trick," I told her. "Remember what Vicki did to you last time? This makes no sense. If you're the new division head, what happens to her? Vicki won't help you leapfrog over her to a better job."

"She says Mr. Hammonds will make her a vice president." Minfreda looked as trusting as a newborn golden retriever puppy.

Open your eyes, I wanted to shout. Instead I said, "I haven't heard a word about that, and I had lunch with Francine this week. Mark my words: Vicki is up to something. You can't trust her. Don't forget how she had Bobby writing a report the same time as you. He got the inside information and you didn't."

"Things are different now," Minfreda said. "I checked with all three boys. None of them are working on anything."

"Vicki's playing another game they don't know about," I said.

Minfreda patted my shoulder. "Relax, Margery. You worry too much. I'll win. I've been thinking about how to improve this company for so long, I have that report already written in my head. My buddy Jimmy swiped the projected production figures for next year from Vicki's desk. I have my own inside information. I'm a different person now."

She was. But Vicki hadn't changed.

Minfreda didn't believe me. I think she took Mr. Rick's good-fairy wave with the butter knife seriously. She truly believed this was her blond destiny and she had blond power.

I truly believed Vicki was up to no good. I had only a few hours to find out what it was. I waited for Vicki to leave her office so I could search her desk, but she stayed rooted in that chair for the rest of the afternoon. She didn't even take a bathroom break.

When I brought Vicki an interoffice memo, I got a good look at her face. She was so smug and self-satisfied, I shivered. She shouldn't seem so calm after being snubbed by Mr. Hammonds. Vicki was plotting something.

I called Francine and tried to meet her for coffee, but she couldn't get away. I asked her point-blank if Mr. Hammonds was going to make Vicki a veep, but she refused to discuss it over the phone. Francine was so proper, I think she starched her bras.

Every so often I'd look over at Minfreda's desk and see her hunched over her typewriter keys, like the Artur Rubinstein of the Underwood. Her golden hair was a beacon.

Her cameo face glowed with determination. That young woman was typing her heart out, so sure she was that she'd succeed.

Vicki pattered out on her pink heels at six o'clock. I waited another fifteen minutes, just in case she came back. Then I searched her office. There wasn't much to look through: a few stacks of papers on her desk, some private files in a cabinet I had the key to. Still, I was careful and thorough. I spent nearly forty-five minutes searching.

But Vicki had learned from her encounters with Jennifer and me. Whatever she was planning, she didn't put it in writing.

It was nearly seven o'clock when I packed up my things to go home. The office was empty, except for Minfreda. Suddenly I didn't hear the click of the typewriter keys. Minfreda had taken a break. I suspected she was making another pilgrimage to the construction area. I followed her to the future site of the partners desk. Minfreda was so sure this would be her new corner office. She visited it at least once a day.

The work was progressing. The old gray carpet had been ripped up and left in the back hall. The sun-faded curtains were in a heap there, too, along with piles of broken plaster and ceiling tiles.

Most of the room's rickety furnishings and a ripped-out wall had already gone down the chute into the construction Dumpster. The new walls were being painted burnt orange. Hey, this was the seventies. If you wanted good taste, go to a restaurant.

Minfreda stood at the doorway, a dreamy look on her face. I could tell she was measuring herself for a leather chair behind the partners desk.

I hoped nothing would go wrong, but I knew it would.

After her visit to her future office, Minfreda shook her silky blond hair like the woman in the Breck commercial, then sat back down at the typewriter. It didn't make any difference how pretty Mr. Rick made her, Minfreda still believed in hard work.

I put a chocolate bar on her desk. I knew she would be working late into the night and she wouldn't stop to eat. It was the least I could do. I went down in the elevator, sure that I had failed her.

It was two thirty in the morning when Minfreda finished her report. Her name was typed on a separate cover sheet, and the whole thing went into a black folder. Minfreda filed the carbons in her desk as usual.

As she read through the report one final time, she was proud of her work. With ideas like these, Mr. Hammonds was sure to promote her. Minfreda left the report on Vicki's desk under the heavy WORLD'S BEST BOSS coffee mug.

The next morning, Minfreda didn't come in until nine thirty, which was late for her. She looked pale and tired. Vicki had arrived early for a change, even beating me into the office. She thanked Minfreda for her report, but said no more.

We all waited. We all wanted rid of Vicki.

The announcement came two days later. Mr. Hammonds sent out a memo to everyone in the company. We found it on our desks at nine that morning. I read it with growing excitement:

It is unprecedented to promote someone this young to division manager, the memo began. *Another precedent has been broken: This is our first upper-level female executive.*

Yes! I cheered quietly. Yes!

But I was deeply impressed with the far-reaching suggestions in this report. Consolidating the Miami Springs and Hallandale offices is a bold cost-cutting move. Reorganizing the shipping department is sadly overdue. The changes in our accounting and billing systems are brilliant.

I kept reading. *These ideas are so innovative, so important to our company's progress, I have no choice but to promote . . .*

The words blurred before my eyes. Surely I read them wrong.

But then I heard an agonized cry: "That miserable bitch!"

Minfreda was shaking violently. She pointed to Mr. Hammonds's memo and said, "Those are my ideas. Every one of them. Vicki stole my report."

Her face was pale as candle wax, but her eyes flared with anger. She was so furious, I thought she would ignite.

I'd never seen Minfreda like that, but I was glad. She was burning with healthy rage.

Okay, I thought. This is bad for us, but good for her. She'll give Jennifer a call over at Bradsco. Won't her old friend be surprised to see how Minfreda has changed? I was sorry to lose Minfreda, but maybe it was for the best.

Minfreda pawed through her desk, looking for her carbons, so she could prove that Vicki had swiped her ideas. She spent the whole day tearing apart her desk, but the file was gone. Without it, she couldn't go to Mr. Hammonds. She'd look like a lunatic.

"Thief," Minfreda muttered, mostly to herself. "She steals everything. She stole her first office. Now she's taken this one from me. She won't get away with it this time."

Vicki sat in her purloined office, looked insufferably pert in pink. I figured she'd stolen Minfreda's ideas and retyped the report's cover page with her name. I wondered if she'd made up another report for Minfreda, or simply told Mr. Hammonds that Minfreda couldn't make the deadline. Probably the latter. It would give her rival a double black eye.

Vicki was slick as a greased snake. Now she was going to slither into a cushy office and take the promotion Minfreda should have had.

Minfreda paced back and forth by her desk mumbling something I couldn't make out.

I knew there would be a confrontation when the office cleared out that evening. But I wasn't worried about leaving Minfreda alone with Vicki. She was no longer a mouse. She was a tawny blond lioness.

It was her turn to roar.

Chapter 8

The miserable day was finally over. Most of our department was already in the bar at Harper's getting plastered.

Believe me, they weren't celebrating Vicki's promotion. They weren't holding a wake, either, although their hopes were dead. This was survival time. The men eyed each other warily, like dogs about to turn on one another. Every man there was drinking so he could do what he had to do—something scummy to keep his job.

Next Monday was the start of evaluation week, and it would be payback time for Vicki. The now all-powerful executive would wreak revenge on everyone she thought had snubbed her or laughed at her.

The boys remembered the times they'd done Vicki imitations, flirted with Minfreda, or taken the cameo blonde to lunch. Vicki was vindictive. The office deadwood could hear the echo of the ax.

As the day crawled on, the boys realized they would have to do some serious puckering to save their jobs. They were a spineless lot. I knew they'd turn on Minfreda. I couldn't completely blame them. They had wives, college-bound children, and thirty-year mortgages.

I had principles, but I could afford them. I didn't care about being promoted. The worst Vicki could do was fire me, and then I'd sit by the pool at the Coronado, drinking screwdrivers.

That's what I planned to do tonight. That blasted memo from Mr. Hammonds was going to send me to the vodka bottle. Every time I read it, it got worse. I think it was the third time through that I noticed something new. Vicki was staying on as the head of our department *and* running the division. There would be no promotion for Minfreda. Vicki would force her out. Minfreda was a reminder of her boss's own treachery.

Minfreda understood this. She knew she had nothing to lose. That's why she was preparing for a showdown with Vicki tonight. If she lost, she wouldn't have a desk, much less a corner office. I watched Minfreda's cameo face freeze into a marble mask. Her hands clenched and unclenched. I could almost see her gripping a sword. She was a warrior princess, preparing for battle.

In a fair fight, Minfreda would win. But Vicki didn't fight fair.

I looked up Jennifer's phone number at Bradsco, and left it on Minfreda's desk. I didn't say anything. I squeezed her shoulder and went back to my desk.

It was after six P.M. when I put the plastic cover on my Underwood, watered my philodendron, and locked my desk. Only Vicki and Minfreda were in our office when I left.

What happened next is guesswork, but I think it's accurate, based on the evidence I found the next morning.

When the elevator doors shut on me, Vicki was in her purloined office. She'd stayed late to plan her ascendency to the division throne. No more girlie pink for her. Her new corner office would have power colors, burnt orange and brown. Vicki sat at her desk making little sketches of how she'd arrange the furniture and what she'd put on the walls. I suspected she'd buy herself a new wardrobe to match. Couldn't have her suit clashing with her sculpted shag carpet.

Vicki didn't notice that Minfreda was still in the office, but why should she? Minfreda always worked late.

Minfreda didn't bother knocking on Vicki's office door. She was bolder now. She swept into Vicki's office, blond hair swinging like a battle banner. Her eyes blazed with righteous fury.

Vicki looked up and said in a sugary voice, "Why, Minnie, working late again?" Her pale pink blouse had a pussycat bow. She had canary feathers on her pink lips.

"My name is Minfreda."

"You'll always be Minnie to me. Underneath that dyed blond hair is a scared little mouse."

"Not anymore." Minfreda slammed Vicki's door shut so hard the glass rattled. For the first time, Vicki seemed nervous. She glanced around the room.

"Don't bother looking for help," Minfreda said. "They're all gone. It's just you and me, and we're going to have a serious talk."

"There's nothing to talk about." Vicki sounded like she was trying to convince herself that she was in charge.

"Oh, yes, there is." Minfreda moved toward her, lithe as a golden cat. "You stole my ideas and you stole my promotion."

"I did nothing of the kind." Vicki sounded more snippy than scared.

"Liar!" Minfreda screamed. That single cry unleashed years of buried rage and humiliation. Minfreda grabbed the pussycat bow around Vicki's neck and twisted it tightly.

"Stop!" Vicki gasped, clawing at her own neck to pull away Minfreda's fingers.

But Minfreda only twisted tighter. Vicki's color went from delicate pink to stroke-out red. "Not till you tell me where you hid those carbons."

"File . . . M." It was all Vicki could manage, but it was enough.

"Don't move," Minfreda ordered as she marched to the file cabinet. There was no chance that Vicki would run away. She could hardly sit up. She was gasping and trying to catch her breath.

Vicki's natural color was coming back by the time Minfreda said, "Aha!" She had the pilfered carbons. "What's your name doing on this title page?"

"I . . . I typed it," Vicki said. She had a sandpaper rasp after her near strangling.

"So you did. But I typed the rest of this report."

"You can't prove it," Vicki said.

"Oh, but I can. The page you typed was done on a different machine. You're not as good a typist as I am. Notice how your Ts float and your Ws jump? Even Mr. Hammonds will be able to see that. And if he can't, I'll hire an expert to explain."

Minfreda could feel the tension loosen in her neck and shoulders. She had the proof of Vicki's theft. She would sit at her beloved partners desk after all.

"Now you're going to write a confession," Minfreda said.

But Vicki felt bold now that she could breathe again. She laughed, a sarcastic sound, sharp as a slap in the face. "After you tried to strangle me? Over my dead body." Then she added a mocking, "Mouse."

Hot new rage flowed over Minfreda's old, impacted anger, and it ignited with a deadly roar. "That can be arranged," she said.

Vicki's desk was loaded with lethal weapons: a daggerlike letter opener, a pink granite paperweight, a silver memo spike. That last was so dangerous offices don't allow them anymore.

But Minfreda had sought the unconscious irony. She hit the world's worst boss with the WORLD'S BEST BOSS coffee mug. She hit her once, and felt the fragile bones on the side of Vicki's skull crack. Vicki stared at her in dazed surprise, as if her stapler had learned to talk. Her lip curled into a nasty sneer, but she didn't get a chance to speak. Minfreda hit her again. And again and again. Minfreda kept hitting her until the heavy mug broke and the side of Vicki's head was soft and squishy.

Blood spattered Vicki's blond hair and ran down her cheek. There was an ugly abrasion over her ear. But Minfreda had mostly battered the white bones beneath the pink skin. Vicki was deader than last year's vacation schedule. She sat in her executive's chair with a death's-head grin on her face.

The old mousy Minnie would have panicked when she saw her battered boss. The new Minfreda kept her cool blond head. She calmly considered what she needed to do.

Vicki's blood was dripping on her suit and heading for the floor. Minfreda whipped off her neck scarf and wrapped it around the dead blonde's head. Better, but blood was seeping through it already. Minfreda looked around for something else and saw my typewriter cover. I was the only person in the department who used one. The others didn't care about their machines. The cover was gray plastic. She bundled it around Vicki's dripping head.

She had to get rid of the body. Vicki was not tall or heavy, but she was a deadweight, no pun intended. Minfreda was strong, but she couldn't move the body without help. She went back to the construction area.

The old sun-faded curtains from the corner office were still in a heap in the back hall. She also saw a lumber cart, like the ones you get at Home Depot nowadays for hauling large purchases.

Minfreda bundled the curtains onto the cart and trundled them back to Vicki's office. She spread the curtains out on the lumber cart, then tipped Vicki's chair forward. The exterminated executive landed in the dusty drapes with a deadweight thud.

"It's curtains for you, boss," Minfreda said out loud, and tried to suppress a giggle.

The cart was harder to maneuver with the body on it. Minfreda had to shove Vicki's desk aside to get the cart through the door. The dead blonde's foot caught in the door frame, and her pink heel was pried off. Minfreda tossed it on top of the body, then cleared a path through the department, carefully moving waste cans and steering around desks until she got to a clear aisle.

Minfreda was sweating like a construction worker. The cart was heavy and awkward. She was worried someone would come back to the office. She kept her ears open for the *ding!* of the elevator doors. But Minfreda was no mouse. Her fear didn't paralyze her. It made her think more clearly.

Once in the dingy back hall, Minfreda pulled the cart near the old torn-up carpet and spread the rug out flat. Then she tugged on the curtains until the body slid off the cart and onto the carpet. She heard the rotted, sun-faded fabric rip, but not before she'd moved Vicki.

Minfreda had a sneezing fit from the dust, but she rolled up the carpet with Vicki inside. A Vicki taco, if you will. No, a Vicki crepe with a poison pink center.

Minfreda grabbed the carpet roll and dragged it to the construction chute, rejoicing that the opening was close to the floor. She was about to drop Vicki headfirst down the chute when she saw a pink heel on the floor. Minfreda put it on the dead blonde. Vicki's foot was still warm, and she had pale pink polish on her toes. They looked small and sad.   •

Minfreda shivered a little. But then she remembered what Vicki had done to her. She straightened her shoulders and walked resolutely back to Vicki's office.

As she stood in the doorway, she could feel the rage she'd set loose in the room. But Minfreda had work to do. Fragments of the shattered coffee mug had flown everywhere. She even found one chunk on Vicki's filing cabinet. She brushed broken bits off the desk, then crawled along the pink shag carpet looking for pieces buried in the thick looped pile.

She threw the shards in the rolled-up carpet. She was about to send the dead blonde down to the Dumpster when she panicked and remembered something important. The plans! Vicki's plans for her corner office were still on her desk. Minfreda shoved them into the rolled-up carpet.

Now, at last, she slid the bundled body down the chute. The carpet made a good solid landing, and stayed rolled up. No pink-painted fingernails showed, no pink shoes peeked out. There were no telltale hanks of blond hair.

But Minfreda took no chances. She threw plywood scraps, broken plaster, torn-out molding, and discarded ceiling tiles down the chute until Vicki was covered by a foot-thick pile of construction debris.

"Sorry I won't be in tomorrow, but I'm feeling just a little bit under," Minfreda said, and fought the urge to giggle again. If she started laughing, she wouldn't stop. She wanted to run through the building yelling, "Ding-dong, the witch is dead."

When Minfreda went back to Vicki's office, the atmosphere seemed less poisonous. She pulled Vicki's desk back in place, straightened her desktop, and righted the vase with the pink rose. She even refilled its spilled water. She vacuumed Vicki's rug. The office cleaning crew could be haphazard. She also vacuumed the hall and the path she took through the department, making sure there were no traces of the fight or the body removal.

When she finished, Minfreda's hands were grimy. She caught her reflection in the bathroom mirror. She was a mess. Her suit was torn under one armpit and streaked with dirt and grayish-white plaster dust. She had runs in both stockings. Her golden hair straggled down her back, and her makeup was smeared.

Minfreda washed and repaired her face and combed her silky blond hair. She threw away her laddered stockings, figuring bare legs would be less noticeable. She shook the dust off her clothes. She couldn't do much about her torn suit, but she had a plan to disguise it.

Now she had to write a farewell letter. Minfreda rummaged in the janitor's closet until she found a pair of yellow rubber gloves. They made her hands feel thick and clumsy. Good, she thought. She would type more like Vicki that way.

Minfreda pulled out a sheet of Vicki's pink personal stationery with her name on the top. She sat down at Vicki's typewriter and wrote:

> Business is no longer relevant to my life.
>
> I want to live! I want to love! I want to follow my heart! Call me wild, call me crazy, but call me gone. Please don't try to follow me. I want to be free.
>
> Before I go, I'd like to set one thing straight. Minfreda should have had my promotion. I stole her ideas. I put my name on the report she prepared for Mr. Hammonds. Her original carbons on my desk are the proof. I was co-opted by the Establishment.
>
> By resigning today I will lose my job, but regain my soul. Try not to judge me. I am leaving to be a new woman and a better one.
>
> Good-bye and good luck.

Minfreda typed one last word at the end: *Vicki.* She wasn't going to attempt her late boss's signature. It was too flowery.

Minfreda bent her golden head, rereading and admiring her work. All those *me*s and *I*s. That refusal to accept any responsibility. It was so Vicki. It was so brilliant.

Minfreda typed one more letter and put it in a pink envelope. She took that one with her. She didn't want it found right away.

She checked her watch. It was eight thirty. The cleaning crew arrived at nine. She had to leave now, but her work wasn't done yet. She knew Vicki rented a small house off U.S. 1. Minfreda looked up the address in the company directory.

Minfreda found Vicki's purse and keys. She put on Vicki's pink coat, plus the head scarf and gloves she found in the pocket. She was glad it was a chilly night.

The security guard at the lobby door said, "Good night, Miss Vicki."

Minfreda said nothing, which was typical Vicki. Her late boss didn't waste words on the hired help.

She drove Vicki's 1968 pink Mustang convertible. Minfreda longed to put the top down and feel the wind in her hair, but she didn't dare. She didn't want anyone looking at her too closely.

Vicki's home was in a subdivision with square houses on square blocks. It was pink, of course. Minfreda let herself in with Vicki's keys.

Inside, the place was a pulsating pink. The living room was pink and black, a sleek modern design that Minfreda liked. She thought it looked sophisticated.

The bathroom was pink, right down to the pom-pom poodle cover on the toilet paper.

The bedroom was a mad welter of pink ruffles on the bedspread, the lamp shades, and the curtains. It was like walking into a live peony. All that throbbing color left Minfreda queasy, but the only thing she could find to soothe her stomach was Pepto-Bismol.

Minfreda kept on Vicki's pink gloves while she packed her boss's clothes, shoes, and makeup in three pink suitcases. She also took Vicki's checkbook and savings account passbook, plus three hundred in cash she found in Vicki's lingerie drawer when she packed up her clothes. She cut up the credit cards and left them on the kitchen table, along with the note she'd typed at the office. It was addressed to Vicki's sister.

Dear Val, it said. *It's time you had a little fun. I won't be needing my Mustang convertible where I'm going.*

That was certainly true. But Minfreda hoped Val believed her sister had taken off for Tahiti or Timbuktu. She also hoped that if Val got the Mustang, she wouldn't look too hard for Vicki.

The keys are on the kitchen table, the letter said. *My rent is paid through the end of the month, and there's a first and last months' security deposit to cover any other expenses. Please give anything you don't want in the house to Goodwill.*

Minfreda took an empty shopping bag, then locked up Vicki's house.

Fort Lauderdale has miles of canals. Minfreda drove to a deep-water canal and dropped the heavy suitcases off a bridge. She stood on the bridge, waiting to see if the luggage burst open and the clothes floated to the top. Her luck held, and so did the suitcases. They sank like concrete.

Minfreda neatly folded the pink coat, gloves, and scarf into the shopping bag and took a bus back to the office. It was midnight when she got to the company parking lot and slipped into her own car.

At eight the next morning, Minfreda put on the pink coat, scarf, and gloves one last time. She stopped at the bank and withdrew all Vicki's money. Minfreda planned to use the money to maintain her blond hair. She would never be called Mouse again.

She dropped the pink coat, scarf, and gloves in an apartment Dumpster on the way to work. Minfreda tucked the pink bundle under an old carpet, which gave her a sense of completion.

Minfreda was at the office at nine A.M., looking refreshed and rested.

And why not? She'd gotten away with murder.

Chapter 9

Suddenly, there was silence.

Helen realized it was not 1970. She was back in the present, sitting by the pool at the Coronado. Her wineglass was empty. Margery's cigarette glowed in the darkness, like an alien eye.

"That's it?" Helen said. "How did you know Vicki was dead? Or that Minfreda killed her? Did Minfreda confess?"

"Oh, no," Margery said, refilling the glasses. "She never said a word."

Helen felt woozy from the wine, and oddly cheated.

Margery seemed to read her mood. "This blonde got away with murder, remember? People who get away with crimes don't go around bragging that they killed someone."

Right, Helen thought. I've been on the run for more than two years, and I haven't exactly announced it to the world. Even Margery doesn't know. Then Helen thought about the afternoon she'd caught her husband with their neighbor, Sandy, and how she'd picked up a crowbar and smashed her world. And I'd do it again.

Helen shrugged. "Makes sense that Minfreda wouldn't talk," she said. "But how did you figure it out? Did you see her hit Vicki?"

"No, I missed the dramatic moment." Margery stopped then, and her silence was louder than anything she'd said. Helen saw the slow burn of her cigarette. She wished she could see Margery's face.

"I put it together from the evidence I found," her landlady said. "First, there was the resignation letter in Vicki's typewriter. I saw it when I got to the office the next morn-

145

ing. I knew there was something off about it. Vicki was a terrible typist.

"Minfreda, on the other hand, was excellent. She'd tried to type in a clumsy manner, but the letter looked like a good typist trying to be a bad one. She had a steadiness to her touch that bad typists don't have. The letter had to be Minfreda's work.

"I also found a shard of the WORLD'S BEST BOSS coffee cup under Vicki's desk. I picked it up and put it in my pocket. Minfreda saw me do it, but said nothing.

"Plus my plastic typewriter cover was missing. And there was a dime-sized spot of blood on Vicki's desk. I wiped it up."

Helen was shocked. "You removed evidence of a murder."

"She could have had a nosebleed." Margery blew smoke, which Helen thought was appropriate.

"The ripped-up carpet and the old curtains were in the back hall when I left work that night. The next morning I got there before the construction crew came on, but the curtains and a huge pile of debris were gone. The janitor didn't throw things down that chute. It wasn't his job."

"No one reported that the trash was gone?" Helen said.

Margery gave one of her Seabiscuit snorts. "You can't steal trash. Dumping debris is hot, sweaty work. Who's going to complain because someone did his work for him?

"I talked to the night guard, Sam, and got some interesting information. Sam told me that Vicki left about twenty to nine, before the cleaners arrived. Sam was a fat old guy, who slept at his desk most nights, but he kept an eye on the pretty women.

" 'Queen Vicki was her usual snobby self,' he said. 'Didn't bother saying good-night to me. I'm not important enough to notice—but she expects me to put my ass on the line for her if she's attacked.'

" 'That's Vicki all over,' I said. 'But she sure likes to get noticed. Did you see those weird earrings she was wearing?'

" 'Can't say I did,' Sam said. 'Her face was hidden by that big pink scarf, like she was Julie Christie avoiding her adoring fans.' "

Helen was confused. "What earrings?" she said.

"I made them up," Margery said. "I wanted to see if

Sam had really noticed her face. When he said that, I knew he didn't see Vicki leave. He saw her pink coat and scarf walk out the door."

"That doesn't prove anything," Helen said.

"There's more," Margery said. "Sam told me Minfreda came back for her car at midnight, like it was big gossip. He couldn't wait to tell me that part. 'That nifty little black suit was half-torn off her, too,' he said. He'd thought she'd had a hot date, the old lecher."

"Date? That sounds like date rape," Helen said.

"You're looking at it thirty years later," Margery said. "Anyway, I knew for a fact Minfreda wasn't seeing anyone. That young woman was married to her job at the time. She tore her suit hauling Vicki's body."

"That sounds reasonable. Maybe," Helen said. "But how did you know some of that stuff, like that bit about the dropped pink high heel and Vicki's warm foot?"

"Oh, I made that up," Margery said a little too quickly. "I don't really know if Minfreda talked to herself when she moved the body, but I know I would. Little details like that make a better story. So I added a few here and there.

"But if you insist on just the facts, ma'am, here's what I know for sure: Vicki was never seen dead or alive again. The cops may have bought the story that she sailed off into the sunset, but I didn't. Vicki was a corporate creature. An office was her natural habitat.

"Here's another fact: Minfreda was extra jumpy all that week. She haunted the back hall by the construction chute. She would stand there, pale as a ghost, staring down at that Dumpster, which got fuller each day. Lucky for her, it was a chilly week in Lauderdale."

"Why was that lucky?"

Margery sighed. "Use your head, Helen. What do you think one hundred pounds of spoiled meat would smell like in hot weather?"

"Oh, yuck," Helen said, when she thought about it.

"Minfreda didn't relax until the construction company carted away that Dumpster a week later. Then she was a different person. She smiled for the first time since Mr. Hammonds's stupid memo.

"One more thing: She never went near the back hall again."

Helen's head was spinning, but she didn't know if it was from too much wine or too much information.

"How did the office react when Vicki didn't show up?"

"I was the first to know," Margery said. "I found the letter in Vicki's typewriter. I took it and Minfreda's carbons straight to Mr. Hammonds's office. Francine read the letter, examined the carbons, and clucked, 'Margery, I never did like that young person.'

" 'Me, either,' I said.

" 'No sense of responsibility,' Francine said. 'What's she thinking, running off with her boyfriend like that? Mr. Hammonds gave her an opportunity no other woman at this company has ever had. Selfish, I call it. She makes all women look bad.'

"People talked that way then. You weren't a good or bad boss. You represented the entire sex.

" 'There's another deserving young woman here,' I reminded her.

" 'Yes, there is. And we must not forget those were really her ideas and that Vicki person misappropriated them,' Francine said. 'We must right this wrong. Wait here, Margery, while I talk with Mr. Hammonds.' She went straight into the CEO's office. Francine was a determined woman, with a strong sense of what was fitting.

"I waited maybe half an hour. Then Francine came out. 'Mr. Hammonds would prefer you say nothing about this until he makes a decision,' she said.

" 'I'll have to tell people something,' I said, 'or the rumor mill will go crazy.'

" 'Then say that Vicki has taken an unscheduled leave of absence. That is the truth.' "

"Speaking of the truth," Helen said. "Did you mention your doubts about the resignation letter?"

"They were doubts, not facts," Margery said. "Mr. Hammonds didn't like anything that wasn't cut-and-dried."

"And you liked Minfreda."

"I did. I still do.

"Our department went through the motions for the next week. Everyone was asking me: Was Vicki gone for good? Was she still our boss or not? Everyone but Minfreda. She knew the answers, of course. She didn't ask me anything. She seemed curiously lifeless.

"The boys didn't know whether to wear black armbands or break out the champagne. They had the lip balm ready and were prepared for some career-saving smooching. But Vicki's posterior had vamoosed, and they weren't sure if Minfreda would be sitting on the departmental throne.

"Our CEO took his own sweet time deciding, too. Evaluation week was canceled for our department, but that made everyone even more nervous. It wasn't natural.

"Mr. Hammonds's announcement came the Monday after evaluation week. We found his memo on our desks first thing in the morning.

"It said that Vicki had resigned. Period. That was all on that unlovely subject. Then the memo said, 'Because of her impressive record and innovative ideas,' Minfreda was our new division head and the head of our department.

"There was no explanation for why Vicki resigned and no mention that she'd stolen Minfreda's ideas. Mr. Hammonds couldn't admit that he'd made a mistake promoting Vicki. I had the feeling that Minfreda would always be a little tainted because of her connection with the episode. Not too tainted, though. Minfreda was now the highest-placed woman in the company.

"There were whoops of glee throughout our department. We were finally, officially, Vicki-free. 'Congratulations, Minfreda, I knew you could do it,' Bobby said, though he knew nothing of the kind.

" 'I've been behind you one hundred percent,' said Irish Johnny. With his knife at her back.

"Jimmy just said, 'Congratulations, blondie, you deserve it.' He was the most honest of the three boys.

"Oh, the celebration we had in Harper's bar that night. By rights, I should still have the hangover. Minfreda didn't join us. She was smiling but subdued.

"She moved into her new office the next day, and she looked like she'd been born behind that partners desk. That dark wood and burnt-orange walls made her golden hair into living fire.

"As one of her first acts, Vicki's pink office was dismantled. The purloined walls were removed, the pink shag carpet was thrown out, the window and its hijacked sunshine were restored to the whole department.

"The staff saw this decision as a sign that Minfreda really

cared about office morale. I suspected she had other reasons. Now all trace of Vicki's reign—and her removal—was gone. But things were about to get sticky."

"What happened?" Helen said.

"The cops showed up. And then Minfreda started acting strange."

Chapter 10

It was almost midnight. The moon rose white and cold.

Helen heard odd rustlings in the bushes near the pool, then a terrified squeak was cut short. South Florida was a strange, primordial place, freshly ripped from the swamps. Predators of all kinds abounded. What did anyone here know about their neighbors?

In Helen's hometown of St. Louis, everyone was connected in some way. One phone call, and Helen would know all about a man: where he went to high school, if his dad carried a briefcase or a lunch box to work, if his mom was a church lady, a lush—or both.

In south Florida, people have no families and no pasts. We are all freshly remade and newly hatched, Helen thought. Including me. Including Minfreda, who may or may not have been a murderer.

"It was nearly three weeks later when the police investigated Vicki's disappearance," Margery said.

"Her sister, Val, called them after Vicki didn't show up for a birthday dinner. It was Vicki's birthday this time. Val and Vicki weren't close, but they never missed their birthdays. Val didn't even have a key to her own sister's house. The cops broke in Vicki's door and found the typed goodbye letter. Oddly, it was the letter that made Val suspicious.

" 'Vicki has never given me anything I've ever wanted,' her sister said. 'She wouldn't give me that Mustang. She'd sell it and take the cash.'

"It was funny reasoning. The cops didn't buy it. But when Val told me, I thought it made sense. Remember, I got sent out to buy Val's birthday present.

"The police came here. I talked with a Detective

151

Mowlby, I think it was. He had an odd name. He was very impressed with himself, but I wasn't impressed with him. He struck me as one of the boys in a trench coat.

"Mr. Hammonds, the CEO, showed the detective Vicki's resignation letter. Mowlby questioned everyone in the office, including me."

"Did you tell the cops you suspected Minfreda?" Helen said.

"I told them what I knew for sure," Margery said. "That Vicki was a lesbian and Chris was a woman."

"What!" Helen nearly dropped her wineglass on the concrete.

"Sure. I saw them together at a restaurant in Miami."

"But Vicki flirted with all the men."

"Yes, she did. Vicki was what we used to call a lipstick lesbian. I don't know if that term is proper anymore. She was excessively feminine. She loved to lead men on. But she lost her heart to a woman with tattoos and a hairy lip.

"When I thought back to her stories about Chris, she'd never said 'he.' And Vicki was so proud when Chris beat up the man who looked at her too long. That story made more sense when you understood that Chris was a woman."

"But why was Vicki jealous of Minfreda and the attention she got from the men?"

"It wasn't about sex," Margery said, as if she were talking to a large, slow child. "It was about power.

"After Detective Mowlby heard that, he was even less interested in digging. He confirmed that Vicki was a lesbian and had a lover named Christine. He confirmed that Christine had quit her job, closed out her bank accounts, and skipped town, leaving no forwarding address.

"Detective Mowlby figured Vicki and Chris took off for San Francisco or some equally open-minded place. Remember, people ran away from dull marriages and boring jobs a lot more in the sixties. It was an unstable time. Mowlby had more work than he could handle. Most of it was either hopeless or solved itself. The missing twenty-year-old daughter would usually turn up on her own, with VD and track marks, or she'd been living in some crazy commune. Either way, she'd want her middle-class life back, and in most cases Mommy and Daddy were more than happy to welcome her home.

"The detective told me that Vicki's bank accounts had been cleaned out by a blonde in a pink coat the morning after she wrote that letter. Her clothes, makeup, and purse were gone. He thought the letter giving her car and personal effects to her sister was a nice gesture. The detective said Vicki might have committed suicide—people often gave away their favorite possessions before they stepped off a bridge. Mowlby checked all the morgues and hospitals, and no blondes like her turned up.

"Val laughed at that idea. 'Suicide?' she said. 'Not a chance. My sister drove people to suicide, but she wouldn't take herself there.'

"Val called, wrote letters and browbeat the cops. The detective went through the motions. He looked through Vicki's office files in our storage room and had her typewriter dusted, but didn't find any useful prints. Too many people had used it since Vicki left."

"Left?" Helen said. "She was murdered. She was dropped headfirst down a Dumpster. Didn't you tell the police about the Dumpster and the broken coffee cup?"

"Coffee cups break all the time," Margery said.

"But you found blood on Vicki's desk," Helen said.

"One drop. Maybe she cut herself when she broke the coffee mug. Sure, I thought the rolled-up rug went down the Dumpster, but I had no proof a body was in there. I never looked."

"You didn't want to look," Helen said.

Margery shrugged. "If Detective Mowlby had asked me, I would have told him what I suspected, but he didn't bother. I was just a secretary. What did I know? Besides, the cops weren't looking for a killer. They knew the staff didn't like Vicki, but most people don't like their bosses. Mr. Hammonds's memo didn't mention that Vicki had stolen Minfreda's ideas. We all followed the CEO's lead. We didn't mention it, either.

"After a while, Val quit pushing the police and they quit asking questions. Val was thrilled to have that snappy little Mustang convertible. I don't think she missed her mean little sister much. I sure didn't.

"The way I figured it, if Vicki was buried in a landfill somewhere—and I didn't know that for sure—she brought it on herself."

"So Vicki got the death penalty for stealing?" Helen wished she didn't sound so sanctimonious.

"No, she got it for attempted murder of a career, the worst possible corporate crime. That kind of killing has no recourse under the law, but it does irreparable damage. A smart, talented young woman would have been unemployable if Vicki had had her way—not that I'm saying Minfreda murdered that lying slimeball of a boss."

Margery lit another cigarette. The yellow flame illuminated her face for just a minute. She was grinning, but I couldn't tell if she was laughing at me.

Helen sat in the heavy silence and wondered: Did Margery really add those details to make her story more realistic? Or did she actually touch that dead foot with the sad pink polish?

The dropped high heel . . . she could have made that part up, maybe. But the warm foot and the pink toenail polish sounded too real.

Helen could feel the hair go up on the back of her neck. It was midnight, and she was drinking white wine with a woman who'd helped a murderer get away.

Maybe I should be glad, Helen thought. Maybe if the cops come for me, Margery will help me escape, too.

No, that couldn't be right. Margery didn't see anything.

Okay, she was an accomplished snoop. Most good office managers were. Helen had seen some sterling examples at the Coronado. She could imagine her landlady loose in an office. Margery would enjoy her power over the confidential files. She'd like being wallpaper and watching the little personal dramas.

Margery had known there was going to be a confrontation that night. Did she sneak back to the office with some trumped-up excuse? Did she see a murder instead of a fight?

Did she watch, hidden behind a desk, while Minfreda moved the body—or did she help?

She remembered Margery's careful wording: *I missed the dramatic moment.* Not, *I didn't see any murder.*

Did Margery miss the murder, but see the corpse? Was that why she knew those details?

Did she watch her battered boss go headfirst down the

chute into eternity? Did she throw plaster and wallboard on Vicki's grave, instead of roses and dirt clods?

Your imagination is wilder than a college kid on spring break, Helen scolded herself. Margery is a law-abiding citizen. She's seventy-six years old.

But Helen saw her landlady on the chaise longue in the silvery moonlight, smoking cigarettes and swilling wine, wearing sexy purple shoes. Margery was not your sweet old grandmother.

"Did you . . ." Helen started to ask, Did you help move the body?

But the words died on her lips. Margery fixed her with a look that made Helen feel like a butterfly on a pin.

Margery wouldn't actually commit a murder, Helen decided. But she might keep silent if she approved. Margery might believe that old Southern defense, "She needed killing." Margery didn't always believe in the law, but she always believed in justice. Justice said Minfreda should have had that job.

"Did I what?" Margery demanded.

Suddenly Helen was nervous. The moon gave the night a graveyard glow. I've been listening to spooky stories and scaring myself, Helen thought.

But she was never sure about Margery. She did know Margery was not fond of the police. Whenever possible, she solved the problems at the Coronado without calling the cops. There was some history there that Helen didn't understand.

"Did I what?" Margery demanded again, and Helen's last questions about Margery's role in the murder died in the cold moonlight.

"Did you find out why Chris, her lover, never came forward?" Helen said. "Maybe they really did run off together. Otherwise, why wasn't she looking for Vicki?"

"Because they'd had a fight right before Vicki's death and broke up," Margery said. "Chris never wanted to see Vicki again. She said so. I knew that because Chris called her once. It was the only time she called Vicki at the office. I happened to pick up the wrong extension and heard them fighting."

Right, Helen thought.

"When Vicki missed her own birthday dinner, Val called Chris looking for her sister. Chris knew she'd be the number one suspect if her lover was mysteriously missing, and the law was not kind to homosexuals. Chris really did take off for San Francisco. She lived happily ever after with another woman. I ran into the couple on a trip a few years ago."

"Did you ever see any signs that Minfreda felt guilty about what she'd done?"

"Was she wracked with murderer's guilt?" Margery said. "No, not that I could tell. I think she was glad Vicki was gone. I certainly was. Our office was a better place without her.

"But the murder and the double promotion did make Minfreda crazy. She started believing she was all-powerful. Minfreda flirted outrageously with the boys. Really, it was shameful, and they were married men, too. I was disappointed in her behavior. I think she may have actually had an affair with Jimmy.

"She ignored the deserving women in our office, and even made fun of the hardest workers. Minfreda's pretty blond head got fat on all that flattery."

"It's almost as if, after killing Vicki, she turned into her," Helen said.

"Maybe," Margery said. "Or maybe all that gorgeous blond hair went to her head. Or maybe she thought she could get away with anything.

"Minfreda forgot that hard work got her promoted. She started coming into the office late and leaving early. She took long, boozy lunches with Jimmy, Bobby, and Irish Johnny while the rest of us slaved at our desks. People were starting to say that she was no better than Vicki, and maybe a little worse.

"The last straw was when Minfreda started ordering me around like I was some kind of servant. I didn't mind picking up her dry cleaning and taking her shoes in for new soles. But one day she handed me her grocery list. She wanted me to do her shopping on my lunch hour. She was one of those nitpicky shoppers, too. 'I want the Smuckers grape jelly in the six-ounce size, not the eight-ounce,' she told me. That kind of stuff can make you crazy. I wasn't going to put up with it.

"I went to the store, all right. I put one brown bag on her desk and said, 'They were out of everything but this.'

"Minfreda opened the bag. Inside was a WORLD'S BEST BOSS coffee mug. A nice thick mug.

"Minfreda turned pale when she saw it. 'Thank you, Margery,' she said. 'That will be all for today.'

"That was all, period.

"Minfreda became a lot more polite to the women in the office. She stopped flirting with the men. She no longer went for three-hour lunches with the boys. Most days, when she didn't have a lunch meeting, she brown-bagged it at her desk. She stayed later and worked harder than all of us put together.

"Her behavior became perfectly professional. All in all, she was a good boss. We all liked her.

"She started dating nice men, on her professional level. The whole office chipped in and bought her a silver chaffing dish when she married a corporate lawyer and moved to Arizona two years later. They had three children, all blondes. That's funny, when you consider Minfreda and her husband both had brown hair. I guess Mother Nature righted that wrong in the next generation. Last I heard, Minfreda was vice president of some accounting firm. She is well respected.

"Just like she was at our company, once she straightened up and started flying right. She was known to be a bit strict, but fair.

"Well, she did make one exception. I have to say, she treated me like a queen," Margery said.

"But then, like all good secretaries, I knew where the bodies were buried."

Read on for an excerpt from
Elaine Viets's next Drop-Dead mystery

Just Murdered

Coming from Signet in May 2005

"Uh-oh, here comes trouble," Millicent said.

If this was trouble, Helen Hawthorne wished she had it. A Rolls-Royce Silver Cloud pulled up in front of Millicent's Bridal Salon on Las Olas Boulevard.

This was a vintage Rolls, the car of new movie stars and old money. Its long, sculpted curves were the color of well-polished family silver. The shiny new Porsches, Beemers, and Ferraris on the fashionable Fort Lauderdale street looked like cheap toys next to it.

The driver's door opened and out stepped a chauffeur in a uniform tailored to show off his broad shoulders and long legs. His pants hugged the best buns beyond the Gran Forno bakery. His hint of a beard would feel deliciously rough on bare skin.

The chauffeur jogged to the rear passenger door with an athlete's grace.

"Baby, you can drive my car," Helen said.

"Sorry, sweetie, Rod's taken," Millicent said, "and it's battle stations. They have an appointment here."

The chauffeur opened the door, Helen saw a candy-pink spiked heel like something from Barbie's dream closet. Was the woman wearing a size-four shoe? Did they make a size four? Helen was six feet tall and didn't know much about petite-people wear.

This woman might reach five feet. She had on a sleeveless pink dress with a flirty pleated skirt to match her pink stilettos.

"Oh, my God," Helen said as the woman slid out of the car. "She's not wearing any panties."

"Typical," Millicent said. "Kiki can spend so much

money and still look cheap. That dress is two thousand dollars, and it's suitable for a child of fourteen."

"On a woman of forty," Helen said.

"Forty!" Millicent said. "Kiki Shenrad is fifty if she's a day—and tucked so tight she has hospital corners."

Kiki threw her arms around the hunky chauffeur and pulled him toward her for a deep kiss, while running her slender leg along his muscular one.

"She'd better pick out a dress quick," Helen said. "I think they're going to consummate the marriage right on the sidewalk."

Millicent didn't hear her. She was too busy pulling wedding gowns from the racks. Helen knew she should help her boss, but she couldn't tear herself from the show outside the shop window.

A small, shy figure emerged from the huge Rolls and crept around the nearly copulating couple. Miss Meek was about twenty with no-color hair scraped into a messy ponytail. Her gray sweats were baggy, but Helen guessed a slender figure was buried underneath the lumpy cloth.

"You'd think Kiki would give her maid a decent cast-off dress," Helen said.

Millicent looked up from the snowstorm of white chiffon and satin on the silver display stand. "Maid? That's the bride—Desiree Shenrad."

"Uh-oh," Helen said. "We've got trouble."

Kiki finally pried herself off the chauffeur, slapped his perky posterior, and sent him back to stand by the car. She flung open the salon door and yelled, "Millie!"

Millicent winced. Only big spenders called her that. She hated it.

Miss Meek scurried in her mother's magnificent wake. The shop's pink paint was designed to flatter most complexions. The mirrors made double chins vanish. But they couldn't transform dreary little Desiree.

Kiki started to air-kiss Millicent, then swiveled her head so abruptly, Helen thought she'd get whiplash.

Kiki had seen the rose dress.

"I want that," she said. Helen had never heard a soft voice sound so hard.

Every woman who came into Millicent's wanted the rose dress. There was nothing quite like it. The strapless gown had a beautifully beaded bodice. But the skirt was the showstopper. Made of dark red taffeta that shaded to black, the skirt was swirled to look like an enormous bouquet of velvety roses. If Helen ever won an Oscar, she'd want to wear that dress onstage.

"I'd like to wear that to my daughter's wedding," Kiki said.

"That's not a mother-of-the-bride dress," Millicent said.

"I am not going to wear some pathetic little powder-blue dress," Kiki said.

"I don't sell pathetic little dresses," Millicent said. "But my customers leave here properly dressed for special occasions."

"I'll decide what's proper. You!" Kiki pointed at Helen. "Take the rose dress to fitting room A."

She picked the largest room, naturally. Helen looked at Millicent for approval, who gave her a slight nod.

"Oh, yes," Kiki said. "We should get something for my daughter, too." The bride was an afterthought at her own wedding.

"And when is the wedding?" Millicent said.

"Saturday," Kiki said.

"June, July, or August?"

"This coming Saturday, December fourth," Kiki said.

Millicent looked stunned. "Impossible. Three months is a rush job. We can't order the dresses in time for a wedding in a few days."

"Then we'll buy something in stock. And you'll have to alter it here. Money is no object."

Millicent's eyes narrowed. "You'd better tell me what happened, and why you're coming to me so late. I won't help you until I know the whole story."

"It's that bitch at Haute Bridal. I saw what she got in for the wedding and canceled everything. The fabrics looked cheap. The colors were horrible. Nothing was as she promised."

"But bridal sales are final," Helen said.

Kiki laughed. "My ex-husband is a lawyer. Nothing is final."

"It is at this store," Millicent said. "Do what I say, and I'll make you look like every one of your thirty million dollars."

Millicent was pointing a red talon at Kiki, punching each word for emphasis. Helen thought the bloodred nails were the mark of Millicent's success. She'd clawed her way up to the chicest shop on Las Olas with only a small divorce settlement and one major talent: She had a gift for making women look good.

Millicent knew how to emphasize their good points and downplay their figure flaws. She was her own best example. Her hair had turned snowy white years ago. Millicent had the courage to leave it that dramatic color. It made her look younger than most of the highlighted salon jobs in her shop. An unface-lifted fifty, Millicent looked forty. Colorful tops drew attention to her remarkable chest, held high by a cantilevered bra. Dark pants minimized generous hips. But she couldn't hide her clever, appraising eyes.

Kiki shrugged like a spoiled child. "Millie, darling, help me into the rose gown."

Kiki stepped out of her pink dress and revealed an even pinker body. Her blond pubic hair was sculpted into a dollar sign.

Helen gaped.

"Any man who gets me hits the jackpot," Kiki said, and winked.

It took Helen and Millicent both to wrestle her into the rose dress. The skirt had four layers, including the only hoop Helen had seen since *Gone with the Wind*. Helen had to admit that the outrageous gown fit Kiki. She had the carriage and the attitude to wear a skirt the size of an SUV.

"I have to have it," Kiki said.

"So buy it," Millicent said. "But don't upstage your daughter at her own wedding."

"No one can upstage the bride," Kiki said. "I'll take the dress."

"Only if you promise to buy another dress for the church service," Millicent said. "You cannot wear a ball gown to a daytime wedding, Kiki. You'll look like a joke."

Those words got through to Kiki. She settled on a sleek black knit for the church and a gauzy gold gown suitable for a minor goddess for the rehearsal dinner. She insisted on putting the rose dress back on.

Finally, Kiki remembered her daughter. Desiree stood silently in the corner like Cinderella. Helen didn't know whether to offer her a chair or some ashes by the fireplace.

"I want a wedding dress with a full skirt and a cathedral-length train," Kiki said.

"That's a ten-foot train," Millicent said. "A petite bride like Desiree will be swallowed by all that fabric."

"Not if she stands up straight." Kiki's French-manicured nail poked her daughter between her slumping shoulder blades.

"I want something expensive," Kiki said. "I want snow white, not that off-white color. It looks like dirty teeth."

Desiree stood there, mute.

"What do you want, Desiree?" Millicent asked. "It's your wedding."

"It makes no difference. I won't get it." Desiree's little voice was drowned in disappointment.

What was Millicent doing? Helen wondered. She was too smart to get between warring mothers and daughters. Did she forget that Kiki was paying?

Desiree tried on a simple white strapless gown. Her mother said, "Oh, Desiree. You're only twenty years old and I can see you as a nun."

"And I see you as an old tart." That soft voice. Those hunched shoulders. That meek expression. Yet she'd insulted her mother with acid-stinging accuracy.

For five hours, Desiree tried on dresses while her mother stabbed her with stiletto slashes. Desiree seemed sad and beaten. Only later did Helen realize the meek young woman had fought back with feline ferocity.

Helen did know one thing: She was worn out from being in the same room with that rage. Hauling the heavy wedding dresses didn't help. They were encrusted with scratchy crystal beading and itchy lace. Many weighed twenty pounds or more. Helen had to hold the hangers over her head to keep the long skirts off the floor. Her arms ached, and her neck and shoulders screamed for relief.

When she ran for yet another dress, she saw the chauffeur, Rod, sweating in the shimmering sun. It wasn't fair to keep him standing by the car in the brutal Florida heat. Helen pulled a cold bottle of water from the fridge and went outside.

"You look like you could use this." She handed the frosty bottle to Rod. A little sweat improved the man. The chauffeur's black curls were tousled by the Florida breeze—or an expensive stylist.

Rod turned pale under his tan and backed away. "Don't let her see you," he said. "You could ruin everything." He sounded really frightened.

"I'm sorry," Helen said. "I don't want you to lose your job. It's a hot day and—"

"Job? You could cost me a lot more than any job. Get away from me with that."

Why would a water bottle frighten a big, strong man? Helen didn't have time to think about it. She heard Millicent calling her: "Helen, where's that dress I sent you for?"

Helen ran inside, grabbed it off the rack, and hurried back with a pearl-and-crystal concoction. Desiree put it on like a hair shirt.

"It's regal," Kiki said, after Helen fought the dress's one hundred white satin buttons.

"I look like a homely Hapsburg princess," the despairing Desiree said.

She was right, Helen thought. She did look like a sad, chinless royal bride. Desiree was one of those women who looked her worst in white.

The desperate Millicent went into the odd closet, where she kept her mistakes. She brought out the spider dress. The bride had broken her engagement and defaulted on the seven-thousand-dollar gown. The spider dress had been impossible to resell. It looked bad on a hanger and worse on most women. The color was peculiar: Its pale pink undertone looked dingy next to the true white gowns. The style was odder still, a cobwebby lace that floated on the air like cat hair. Helen itched every time she saw it.

Desiree tried it on and, for the first time that day, smiled.

Helen quit shoving a beaded gown back on the rack and stared at the little bride. She had never seen a dress make such a dramatic transformation.

Mousy little Desiree lived up to her name for the first time in her life. She was beguiling in that dress, a fey fairy princess. The lace was a gossamer web. The crystal beads gleamed like enchanted dewdrops. The subtle pink color turned Desiree's flour-white complexion creamy and put highlights in her dull hair.

On this bride, the odd dress looked elegant and extraordinary.

"It's perfect," Millicent said.

"I love it," Helen said.

"I want it," the bride said.

"You can't have it," her mother said. Kiki was still wearing the rose dress. But she was no longer a showstopper. Now she looked overblown in the extravagant gown. "That wedding dress will never do."

Of course not, Helen thought. You can't have your daughter outshine you.

"Then I'll buy it myself," Desiree said.

"Using what for money?" her mother said. "It's seven thousand dollars. You won't come into your grandmother's trust fund until you're thirty."

"Daddy will buy it for me," Desiree said.

"Daddy is fighting off bankruptcy," Kiki said. "Daddy the hotshot lawyer spent millions on that computer-stock class-action suit and lost. Daddy can barely pay his half of the wedding."

"Why do you keep running up the costs for Daddy?" Desiree cried. "I wanted a simple beach wedding, not a sit-down dinner for four hundred."

"What you want is beside the point," Kiki said. Helen thought those were the truest words ever spoken in that store.

"A beach wedding is fine when a secretary marries a mechanic," Kiki said. "But for our sort, weddings are for the parents. We're paying the bills. Your father will invite his important clients. I will invite patrons of the arts. They will expect to see a traditional bride walk down the aisle, not some hippie. I will buy that one."

Kiki indicated the Hapsburg princess dress. Its wide, stiff skirt looked like a satin pop-up tent. Its ten-foot train was loaded with crystal beads. Helen wondered how the tiny bride could drag all that fabric down the aisle.

Desiree hated the dress. So did Helen and Millicent.

"Mother, I can't dance in that at the reception. Not with that huge train."

"We'll bustle up the train," her mother said.

"Can't," Millicent said. "It's too bulky. It will look like a bale of fabric on her back."

"Is the train detachable?" Helen said.

Millicent raised an eyebrow at Helen's faux pas.

Kiki's smile dripped malice. "Let me guess. You had your reception at the VFW hall next to the turkey-shoot posters."

"Knights of Columbus Hall," Helen said. "And it was the Holy Redeemer rummage sale."

Millicent frowned. Helen shut up. She'd let a detail from her old life slip out in her anger. Her fingers itched for the crowbar she'd used to end her marriage. She was on the run, but she never regretted the satisfying crunch she heard when she first started swinging and connected with her target. The cries and crunches felt good. Kiki was a candidate for just such a shattering experience.

The silence stretched on. Then Kiki said, "We shall buy two wedding dresses. One for the church ceremony and one for the reception. If Desiree will wear the dress with the train for the wedding ceremony, I will buy her the hippie dress to dance in."

The bride said yes, happy for even a half victory.

Helen was surprised that Kiki would compromise. Thank goodness for the trend among rich brides for two dresses—and Kiki's eagerness to run up bills for her cash-strapped ex.

"We'll take these and come back tomorrow to pick out the veil and bridesmaid dresses," Kiki said.

Another welcome surprise. Helen didn't think she could survive another five-hour fight. She did some quick calculations. Kiki would be spending maybe sixty thousand dollars on dresses, accessories, and alterations at Millicent's. Helen would have to work more than four years to make that much at her dead-end job.

Kiki left in a tornado of promises and air kisses, invigorated by the afternoon battle. Desiree trailed listlessly behind her. Rod, the delectably sweaty chauffeur, opened Kiki's door. She slid inside decorously.

When the Rolls pulled away from the curb, Helen and Millicent collapsed into the pink chairs. They were soft, but not too yielding. A tired woman could get out of them with dignity. No woman ever sat on the gray "husband couch." She knew her eyes would glaze with boredom if she went there.

Helen sighed and kicked off her shoes. Millicent fanned herself with a bridal consultant's brochure.

"The things I do for money," Millicent groaned.

"Rod the chauffeur is doing something strange for the big bucks," Helen said. "You won't believe this, Millicent. He was afraid to take a bottle of water from me. I mean, really scared. He said, 'Don't let her see you. You could ruin everything.' He acted like I was handing him a bomb. Why is he so afraid?"

"Because Kiki is a jealous bitch. She doesn't want her chauffeur talking to a younger, better-looking woman."

"I wasn't coming on to him. I'm happy with Phil." Boy, am I happy, Helen thought.

"Then don't interfere," Millicent said sharply. "Kiki's name should be Kinky. She likes watching her chauffeur stand by that car and sweat. She probably does him that way. Don't feel sorry for Rod. That's his job. Don't cater to him like he's married to a client. He's not a husband, although God knows he has some of the same duties."

"At least Rod is well paid," Helen said.

"He thinks he is, the fool," Millicent said. "Kiki's had many chauffeurs. She pays them minimum wage and puts them in her will for a million bucks. When she bounces them, she writes them out. Gets herself cheap help and first-class service that way. It must be a shock for those young men to go from millionaire dreams to minimum-wage reality. I can't imagine what it's like."

I can, Helen thought. I used to make major money and live in a mansion before I caught my ex-husband with my next-door neighbor. I'd kill Kiki if she pulled that on me.

"How do you know these things?" Helen said.

"It's the talk of the town," Millicent said.

Which town? Helen wondered. No one discussed it where she lived.

"This chauffeur will get his walking papers soon," Millicent said. "Kiki didn't grope him when she got back into the car."

Millicent talked so easily about the outré world of the overrich. Helen felt like a stranger in a parallel universe. "Well, they're gone," she said. "I'm glad it's over."

"Over?" Millicent said. "It's just begun."

DEAD BLONDES
TELL NO TALES

A SCUMBLE RIVER MYSTERY

DENISE SWANSON

In memory of Sara Ann Freed (1945–2003),
who gave me my first big break

Chapter 1

Blonde, But Not Forgotten

"Bunny!"

"Ruby!"

"Girlfriend, you'll never believe . . ."

The Sunday-morning silence inside the bowling alley storeroom was shattered by the excited squeals coming from near the building's entrance. Skye Denison paused in midreach to listen. She recognized one voice as being that of Bunny Reid, the alley manager, but who was Ruby?

Scumble River, Illinois, was a small town of only three thousand people, most of whom Skye knew, and the name Ruby didn't ring a bell. And what would Bunny never believe? Skye pursed her lips; she hadn't been able to hear the end of that sentence.

Oh, well, it really was none of her business, and the shrieking had stopped, so Skye shoved a strand of chestnut hair behind her ear and went back to reshelving boxes of napkins and paper towels. Someone had gotten in overnight and thrown all the supplies into the middle of the floor, then tossed around the loose items in the rest of the bowling alley. Nothing was missing or broken, but there was quite a mess to clean up.

This was a far cry from Skye's usual occupation. Forty-two weeks of the year she was employed as a psychologist for the Scumble River school district, but as of last Friday afternoon, Skye was on spring break for nine days.

She had briefly considered going somewhere warm for the holiday—the end of March in central Illinois was generally cold and miserable—but the precarious state of her checkbook, along with her boyfriend Simon Reid's plea for help, had convinced her that taking the job he offered was a better move.

Simon was both the county coroner and the owner of Reid's Funeral Home. In addition, a few months ago he had bought the town bowling alley for his mother, Bunny, to manage. Bunny had reappeared in his life after a twenty-year absence, needing a job and a permanent address in order to avoid going to jail for misusing prescription drugs.

Against his better judgment, Simon had decided to help Bunny. He didn't quite trust her—all was a long way from being forgiven or forgotten—but in the end he couldn't let his mother be locked up.

So far, Bunny had proven to be good at running the alley, but her recent idea to increase business—the Spring Break Bash—had worried Simon, and he had installed Skye to both help his mother and keep an eye on her. Skye was thankful that Bunny had been amused rather than insulted by her son's tactics.

As Skye put yet another box of paper goods back where it belonged, she was already questioning her decision to help Simon rather than raid her savings account and fly to Florida for the week. When she heard an angry male voice roar Bunny's name, Skye was pretty sure she had made a bad choice in staying home. And when that same voice boomed even louder, followed by a woman's scream, Skye knew she'd made a big mistake.

Since it was too late to leave for Fort Lauderdale now, she'd better find out what was going on. Skye dropped the carton of straws she had been holding, and took off running.

As she flew out of the stockroom, the shouting became louder and more strident. When she rounded the corner, she gasped and ran faster. Near the front door, Scumble River's police chief, Wally Boyd, stood with a tall, full-figured blonde in handcuffs. That was bad enough, but the real cause of Skye's distress was the redhead beating the chief with a bowling pin.

Skye was used to Bunny's impulsive behavior, but this time she'd gone too far. Assaulting a police officer was not in the same category as greeting your gentleman friend at the door wearing nothing but Saran Wrap, or unwittingly hiring a drug pusher to manage the alley's grill. Had Simon's mother completely lost her mind?

Once Skye got closer, she noted with relief that at least the pin was a Styrofoam decoration and not the real thing. Bits of white plastic were lodged in Wally's black hair, and a snowdrift of pellets was forming at his feet. The expression in the chief's usually warm brown eyes did not bode well for either the redhead's or the blonde's future.

Although he didn't look it, Wally had turned forty a few weeks ago, and he hadn't been in the best mood since then. Normally, Skye would have stepped in right away—she had found coping with Bunny wasn't very different from dealing with the teenagers at school; it was a good idea to nip any misbehavior immediately in the bud—but Skye and Wally were not currently on the best of terms, so she hesitated trying to figure out the most advantageous way to approach him.

Skye's pause was just long enough for Bunny to throw away the remains of the disintegrated Styrofoam bowling pin and pick up an umbrella hanging on a nearby coatrack. As Bunny drew back, looking like Babe Ruth about to make a game-winning home run, Skye flung herself forward.

Depending on one's perspective, her timing was either perfect—she saved Bunny from being charged with assaulting a police officer—or it was a little off—the brunt of the swing caught Skye across the face, and she went down like a seven–ten split knocked over by the ball of a pro bowler.

For a moment there was complete silence; then Wally roared, "Son of a bitch!"

Bunny threw herself on Skye, wailing, "I'm so sorry. I'm so sorry. Are you all right? Say you're all right."

Wally wrenched the redhead away, ordering her, "Get a wet rag and a cold compress." He knelt by Skye's side and gently cupped her chin. "Do you need an ambulance?"

"No." Skye struggled to sit up. She could taste blood in the back of her throat, and was afraid she would vomit if she didn't lift her head.

"Lie still for a minute." Wally put a hand on her shoulder and pressed her back. "Let me get a good look."

Skye fought back tears of pain as he ran his fingers lightly over her cheeks and nose. He'd had EMT training, and she trusted him to make an accurate assessment of her injuries.

"I don't think anything is broken. Your nose is bleeding, but it looks intact, and your cheekbones seem okay, too. How's your vision?"

That was a good question. Skye squinted. How many Wallys were there? She could make out three—no, four. After she blinked a few times his multiple faces merged into one. "I can see fine."

A subdued Bunny returned with the first-aid items. Wally took the wet cloth and ice-filled dishcloth without acknowledging her, all his attention on Skye. Bunny hovered near his shoulder, wringing her hands.

Wally murmured reassuringly to Skye as he cleaned away the blood from her face. At last he handed her the cold compress and instructed, "Hold this across your nose and cheeks."

"Okay, but I need to sit up." She felt too helpless lying on her back.

He put one arm under her shoulders and the other under her knees, then lifted her into a chair Bunny had brought over from the bar.

Skye was impressed with his strength. She was no lightweight, yet he had picked her up as if she were a size six.

Once Skye was settled, Wally turned on Bunny, his voice controlled, and as chilly as his eyes. "Care to explain yourself?"

"You're the one who barged in here, grabbed poor Ruby, and slapped her in handcuffs." Bunny crossed her arms under her surgically enhanced breasts and scowled. "You explain."

Skye moaned from beneath her ice pack. Bunny was taking the exact wrong approach with Wally.

The chief's expression hardened, but he said in an even tone, "You go first."

Bunny opened her mouth, a stubborn look on her face, but before she could speak Skye loudly cleared her throat and, despite the sharp pain it caused, wildly shook her head no.

Some sense of self-preservation must have finally kicked in, and Bunny's expression changed from petulant to shrewd. She moved closer to Wally, running a long red nail studded with rhinestones down his chest. "I am so sorry, Chief. I don't know what got into me." She fluttered her fake eyelashes. "I guess it was seeing great big old you manhandling my best friend in the whole world."

Wally's response was an exasperated, animal-like grunt as he moved out of her reach.

"Now, don't be like that," Bunny cajoled, fluffing the pile of fire-engine-red curls artfully arranged on the top of her head. "You're just so big and strong that I was scared you were going to hurt my friend."

"Right." He raised a dark eyebrow, his tone skeptical.

Bunny pouted, but wisely kept quiet.

Wally turned to Skye. "I'm guessing you won't be pressing charges, considering she's Reid's mother?"

Skye nodded, then regretted it as new pain shot across her cheeks.

"Now that we've settled that . . ." Wally paused and looked around. "Shit! Where did she go?"

The blonde in handcuffs had disappeared.

Chapter 2

Never Judge a Blonde by Her Cover

Skye had abandoned both her chair and the cold compress, and was once again standing between Wally and Bunny. At least this time no one had weapons in their hands, although Wally's fingers *were* caressing the grip of his gun.

They had searched the bowling alley and there was no sign of Bunny's friend. Ruby's car was still parked outside, but she had vanished.

Wally blew out a puff of exasperation. "You mean to tell me neither of you saw her leave? She's got to be six feet tall and weigh over two hundred pounds; how could she vanish? She was handcuffed, for crying out loud."

"I never saw a thing." Bunny's voice was admiring. "But Ruby was married to a magician for a couple of years, and that man taught her some neat stuff."

Skye wondered just what tricks Ruby knew, but restrained herself from inquiring—Wally didn't seem in the mood for long explanations. She would quiz Bunny later, after he left. Now, she asked, "Why were you arresting her, anyway?"

"It started out as a routine traffic stop." Wally shoved a hand through his hair, visibly puzzled as to how things had gotten so out of control. "She was driving down Basin and kept weaving over the center line, so I pulled her over, thinking she was drunk."

"And?" Skye prompted.

"She didn't have any liquor on her breath, and she explained she had been putting her makeup on—something about a heated eyelash curler and her false eyelashes starting to smoke. Anyway, I was going to give her a warning ticket for reckless driving when I noticed the paraphernalia in her backseat."

"What? Ruby doesn't do drugs," Bunny bristled. "Her son died of an overdose. She'd never—"

"I didn't say it was drug related," Wally interrupted. "These were . . . uh . . ." He trailed off, a flush creeping up from under the starched navy collar of his uniform shirt.

"They were what?" Skye's curiosity was fully aroused. Wally wasn't usually shy when it came to speaking the plain truth.

"Obscene materials and devices." Wally's tone became official.

"What?" Skye asked, confused.

Bunny snorted. "Sex toys."

"You're kidding." Skye felt her cheeks redden to match Wally's.

"Ruby owns a store in Las Vegas called Sexploration. She must have been bringing me some samples."

"Why?" Skye asked without thinking, then could have bitten her tongue. This was not a subject she wanted to explore with Bunny.

"Why not?" Bunny smirked, smoothing tight brown velour leggings over her hips. "Or did you think you were the only one in town with a sex life?"

Skye's faced burned with embarrassment, and she took a quick peek at Wally, who was frowning at her. Although they had never dated, Skye and Wally had an emotionally charged history.

There had been chemistry between them since she was a teenager and he was a rookie cop. Nothing had happened back then, since she was underage, nor when she returned to Scumble River as an adult, because by that time he was married. Since then, his wife had left him, and Skye had become involved with Simon. She and Wally had a sort of Scarlett-and-Ashley type of relationship—their timing stank. Lately they had taken to acting as if the attraction didn't exist.

Wally continued to study Skye for a long moment before taking up where he had left off. "Upon seeing the obscene materials, and ascertaining that the suspect had a sufficient quantity to constitute wholesale promotion of the devices, I ordered her to exit the car."

Bunny blurted out, "You mean dildos are against the law in Illinois?"

"Scumble River has a city ordinance stating that it's illegal to 'wholesale promote' devices that simulate sexual organs or materials marketed as useful primarily for the stimulation of human genital organs." Wally was expressionless as he recited the regulation.

Bunny, a bright note of query in her brown eyes, questioned, "How many makes it wholesale?"

"Six or more."

Skye was afraid to find out why Bunny wanted to know the exact number; instead, forestalling further inquiries from Bunny, she hastily asked Wally, "What happened when you told Ruby to get out of the car?"

"She stomped on the accelerator and roared off." A scowl twisted Wally's handsome features. "I was originally just going to give her a warning and tell her to get out of town. I thought she was probably a prostitute getting ready to set up shop around here, and I wanted to make sure she knew that would be a bad idea."

"You thought Ruby was a prostitute?" Bunny yelped.

Wally gave the huffy woman a level look. "She drives a bright pink Cadillac, has a backseat full of sex toys, and is dressed straight out of a Victoria's Secret catalog. You add it up."

Bunny's gaze was defiant, and she sullenly flicked imaginary lint from her tiger-patterned velour top, but for once she kept quiet.

Wally went on as if he hadn't been interrupted. "I pursued her with lights and siren. She drove several blocks, then illegally parked in front of the bowling alley and ran inside."

Bunny flicked a sidelong glance at Skye. "Ruby had only been here a minute or two, and we were hugging when he"—she paused dramatically and pointed an accusing finger at Wally—"burst through the doors, grabbed her, and slapped handcuffs on her."

"Which is when she"—Wally jerked his thumb at Bunny—"grabbed the Styrofoam bowling pin from the window display and started to hit me." He brushed at a stray white pellet clinging to his navy uniform pants. "I should arrest her for assaulting an officer."

"But you won't," Skye coaxed. "After all, you'd look pretty silly charging a middle-aged woman with assault by plastic bowling pin."

"Who are you calling middle-aged?" Bunny challenged.

"I'll let it go this time, but she needs to watch it," Wally declared, ignoring Bunny.

"So what will you do now?" Skye asked, also ignoring the redhead.

"Obviously Ruby will have to come back for her car. I'll nab her when she does." He put his hand on the door and added, his expression stern, "And you two better let me know if she turns up."

Bunny sketched a cross on her chest and said, "I promise."

Skye rolled her eyes, then gave Wally a "what can you do?" look.

After he left, Skye said to Bunny, "Do you want to call Simon and fill him in, or shall I?"

"We don't really need to bother Sonny Boy, do we?" Bunny wheedled.

"Yes, we do. You or me?"

Bunny heaved a put-upon sigh. "I'll do it."

"That would be best," Skye said, then went back to the storeroom. She needed to finish sorting out the mess in there, since she had a feeling she'd have a new mess concerning Ruby and Bunny to sort out in the near future.

Chapter 3

The Case of the Disappearing Blonde

"Okay, where is she?" As soon as Bunny called him at the funeral home, Simon had hurried over to the bowling alley.

His mother was preparing her monologue as emcee for Monday night's talent show and didn't raise her eyes from her clipboard. Tuesday was Team Trivia, Wednesday was karaoke, Thursday afternoon they were having an Easter-egg hunt, and Friday's Marilyn Monroe look-alike contest would cap off the alley's Spring Break Bash. "I told you, I don't know."

Simon looked over at Skye, who was draping the stage with pink, purple, and yellow bunting. "Do you have any ideas?"

She stapled a fold of cloth to the side of the wall and tried to think where a six-foot-tall, two-hundred-pound blonde, dressed in red capri pants and a matching halter, could hide. "Wally looked in all the obvious places, but if she was married to a magician, Ruby might be able to fit into smaller spaces than we thought."

"She's double-jointed, too," Bunny contributed. "And her third—no, fourth husband was a contortionist."

Skye cringed. She could tell Simon was nearing the end of his patience. His usually crisply styled auburn hair was standing in spikes like the crown on the Statue of Liberty, and the lines radiating from his golden-hazel eyes were not caused by laughter.

She spoke quickly to divert his attention from his mother. "Let's think about this logically. We were standing by the entrance. There are lockers on one side of us, and the coatrack and bathrooms on the other. If Ruby had left through the door, we would have heard the swooshing sound it makes, so she had to have gone either right or left."

"The lockers are only two-feet-by-two-feet cubes, so there's no way she could have fit in one of those, contortionist or not," Simon said. He shrugged off his charcoal-gray suit coat and hung it on the back of a chair.

Skye set down the staple gun and went over to him. "Then it has to be the bathrooms, but we checked them."

"Even the men's room," Bunny added.

"Let's look again." Simon rolled up the sleeves of his buttercup-yellow shirt.

As they approached the bathrooms, Skye examined the area carefully, but could see no trace of the missing blonde. Of course, by now the woman could be in Chicago or points south; nearly an hour had elapsed since she had disappeared. Skye wisely refrained from pointing this out to Simon, who did not seem in the mood to receive helpful observations.

Having inspected the men's lavatory and found nothing, Bunny, Skye, and Simon crowded into the ladies' room. To their right a sink, soap dispenser, and paper-towel machine hugged the wall. To their left were two stalls. There was no sign of any recent occupation.

Skye let her gaze wander, starting at the floor and traveling slowly upward. Suddenly she gasped and pointed to the ceiling. A telltale swatch of red spandex clung to the white acoustic tile.

Simon left the room to fetch a chair from the bar. He returned, loosened his tie, and climbed on. He pushed the white acoustic tile aside and poked his head into the opening. Less than a second later he descended and said, "She was there, all right. The dust's been disturbed, and there's another sliver of red cloth caught on one of the struts. But she's gone now."

"At least we know where she hid." Skye took his arm as they all moved out of the bathroom. "I was beginning to think she really had vanished into thin air."

"That's right." Simon squeezed Skye's hand. "And she can't have gotten far without her car."

Bunny grinned, sitting back down and picking up her clipboard. "You never know. Ruby's very resourceful. You should hear about the scrapes she used to get us out of when we were in the big show together at the Golden Nugget."

"It's too frightening to contemplate." Simon looked at his mother through narrowed eyes.

"Don't tell me one of her husbands was also a car thief."

"No, but she dated a cop who worked the stolen-vehicle squad." Bunny's voice was dreamy. "That man could pick a lock and hot-wire a Corvette faster than a professional car thief."

Simon heaved a sigh, then headed to the bar. "I need a drink. Anyone else want something?"

Before either Skye or Bunny could respond, a throaty voice from the doorway said, "I'll take a martini, straight up, two olives. Don't be stingy with the vodka. It's been quite a day."

"Ruby!" Bunny catapulted out of her chair and embraced her friend. "Are you okay?" Her voice was muffled in Ruby's cleavage, since Bunny was a good seven inches shorter than the blonde.

"I'm fine. I was just over at the police station straightening things out with that gorgeous police chief. Sorry if you were worried." Ruby squeezed Bunny back and then zeroed in on Simon. "Don't tell me this handsome man is Sonny Boy."

He shot his mother a dirty look before holding out his hand. "I prefer Simon, and you must be Ruby . . . ?"

"Oh, don't worry about last names. When you've had as many as I have, you sort of lose track." Ruby moved closer to Simon, ignoring the hand he held out and instead enveloping him in a smothering hug. "Bunny, you never told me Scumble River was so full of good-looking men."

Skye had been standing to the side, watching the proceedings. Now she made a mental note to ask Wally what last name appeared on Ruby's driver's license.

Simon had managed to wiggle out of Ruby's grasp—no easy task, since the blonde was a whole lot of woman, and he clutched Skye's hand like a lifeline. "This is my girlfriend, Skye Denison."

Ruby answered, "We've met, although not under the best circumstances." She took Skye's chin in her fingers and examined her face. "You're developing a couple of impressive shiners. Remind me to give you some makeup I've got that will cover them up." She peered at Simon from beneath her lashes and drawled, "We don't want everyone in town thinking Sonny Boy beats you."

Simon made a noise deep in his throat, but before he could respond, Bunny tugged her friend away and settled her into a chair. "It's so good to see you. Tell me what everyone has been up to since I left."

"Well, Benny's back in jail." Ruby dangled a high-heeled red sandal from her toe and leaned back. "Although hopefully not for long."

Simon followed the two women and sat down. "Before you start catching up, I have just a couple of questions."

"Oh?" Ruby's eyes were guarded.

"Bunny, were you expecting Ruby?"

"Sure. She called a couple or so days ago and said she was driving up from Vegas to visit me. I told her it was perfect timing because of the Spring Break Bash. Ruby does a great Marilyn Monroe impression. She'll be the star of our show Friday night."

"I see." A line appeared between Simon's eyebrows, but he kept his expression pleasant. "Ruby, what made you decide to visit right now? It can't be our great weather."

"Just wanted to see my friend Bunny."

"Bunny said you own your own business. Was it hard to get someone to take care of your store while you're gone?"

Ruby waved her hand. "I had to shut it down. I lost the lease on the building. That's why I had the leftover merchandise in my car when Chief Boyd stopped me."

"That's too bad. What will you do now?"

"I'm not going to worry about that." She shrugged. "Something will turn up. It always does." She squeezed Bunny's hand. "And with the store closed, I have time to travel and visit friends."

Bunny elbowed Simon in the side. "If you're through interrogating us, maybe you could fix Ruby that martini she asked for, and I'd like a—"

"Coke." Simon cut her off. Bunny had come to Scumble River addicted to prescription pain medication after hurting her back. She had gotten caught trying to use a fake prescription, and as part of her probation she wasn't supposed to consume any narcotics or alcohol.

"Right, a Coke." Bunny jutted her chin out. "That's what I was going to ask for before you interrupted me."

Simon and Skye exchanged glances. His mother always meant well, but somehow she invariably managed to get into predicaments that other people avoided. Bunny was trouble waiting to happen.

"Just one more question." Simon stared at Ruby, unmoved by his mother's irritation. "How did you fix things with Chief Boyd? From what I heard, he sounded extremely angry."

Ruby's tone was offhand, but her gaze was sharp. "He and I understand each other."

"So if I call him, he'll tell me everything is fine with you?"

"Yes." Ruby examined her manicure. "You know, lack of trust is not an attractive trait in a man."

Skye noticed Simon's jaw tightening, so she took his hand and tugged him toward the bar before he could respond. There really was nothing more he could do unless he wanted to call his mother's friend a liar, which she was afraid might be exactly what he was about to do. His and Bunny's mother-son relationship was still too fragile to withstand an affront like that.

As soon as they were out of earshot Skye whispered to Simon, "Do you believe her?"

"Not for a second."

"What are you going to do?"

"First I'm going to talk to Wally, and if he hasn't got any answers, I'll call a friend of mine in Las Vegas. It's surprising what funeral directors hear."

Skye could believe it. Both she and Simon dealt with the public during very emotional times in their lives, and often they were told things they'd rather not know. "I'll keep my ears open here. I have a feeling Ruby will eventually let something or other slip."

"No doubt." Simon poured vodka into a chrome shaker. "Why do you think she's here?"

"My guess is she got into some trouble in Las Vegas, and decided to hide out here until things cool off."

"I hope it's not something illegal. Try to find out who Benny is, and why he's in jail." Simon picked up the martini and the glass of Coke and carried them to the two women across the room. "Here you go, ladies." He put his hand on his mother's shoulder. "I've got to get back to the funeral home. There's a viewing tonight. I'll see you tomorrow. You two try and stay out of trouble."

Skye accompanied him to the front door. He kissed her and traced a gentle finger over her cheek. "I'm sorry, I didn't ask earlier how you were feeling."

"My face hurts, but I'll be fine." Skye grimaced. "I just wish I didn't look like a raccoon."

"But you're the cutest little raccoon in Stanley County." He kissed her again and added, "Keep an eye on them. Ruby's up to something, and I don't trust Bunny not to get involved. You know how easily led astray she is."

Chapter 4

Much Ado About Blondes

"I hear one of that woman's trampy friends is in town." Skye's mother, May, didn't look up from the stove as she stirred a water-and-flour mixture into the meat drippings. This was a delicate operation. A lapse in concentration could mean lumps in the gravy, an occurrence not allowed in May's kitchen.

Skye shook out the tablecloth and carefully made sure it hung evenly before answering. Her mother had taken an instant aversion to Bunny, which was both unusual and awkward: unusual, in that May generally liked everyone, and awkward, since Skye was dating Bunny's son. Skye just counted her blessings that Ruby's makeup seemed to work, and so far her mother had not noticed the bruises she had acquired from the morning's umbrella incident. May would really have it in for Bunny if she knew that she had physically harmed Skye, even unintentionally.

"If by 'that woman' you mean Bunny," Skye said, "then yes, there is someone visiting her, but how can you pronounce someone a tramp when you've never even met her?"

May poured a smooth stream of dark brown gravy into the china boat and set it on the counter. She selected a knife from the drawer and started to carve the roast. "Because I saw those awful things Wally had to get rid of." May was a police, fire, and emergency dispatcher. She normally worked weekday afternoons.

"Why were you working on a Sunday?" Skye tried to distract May. Chatting about sex aids with her mother was not something she was eager to do.

"Pat's grandson was being baptized, and she needed the day off."

Oops! The issue of babies was another subject Skye attempted to avoid discussing with her mother. May's fondest wish was for Skye to marry and produce a few grandchildren. As she searched for a safe topic of conversation, Skye centered a plate in front of a chair, aligning the knife and spoon on the paper napkin to the right and the fork to the left.

But May was too quick for her. "You know, Pat's daughter is only twenty-four. That's nearly ten years younger than you." Apparently May assumed Skye's math skills might not be up to the challenge of subtraction.

Skye ignored her mother's dig and asked quickly, "Does Wally have any idea who might have broken into the bowling alley Saturday night?"

"No." May opened the oven door, and the intoxicating scent of freshly baked bread seeped into the room.

Skye was thankful that the low-carb craze had not reached Scumble River.

"He thinks it must be kids." May pulled out a tray of Parker House rolls, and set it on a wire rack. "That woman has been really strict about keeping teenagers out of the bar area of the bowling alley, and one of them is probably mad at her."

"I wish you'd call her Bunny." Skye finished setting the table and started putting the food out.

May sniffed. "Bunny is not a Christian name."

"And Skye is?"

"That's different. Skye is a family name, as you well know, missy."

"Then call her Mrs. Reid."

"No. She hasn't earned that name." May shook her head. "You have to stick around and take care of your husband and children to earn the title of missus."

Skye opened her mouth to suggest May call Bunny Ms. Reid, but snapped it shut without speaking. She already knew her mother's opinion of the word *miz,* and it wasn't positive.

May looked over the table.

Skye stood at attention, waiting to be told what she had missed. Her mother tolerated Skye's presence in her kitchen with thinly disguised unease.

"You forgot the butter. All you've got out is my Shedd's

Spread. You know your dad won't use anything but the real thing." May handed Skye a rectangular dish. "Let's see: Jed, Vince, and Charlie already have their beer, you have your pop, I'll get me some wine, and we're all set. Call the men into dinner."

Skye stepped around the archway that separated the dinette from the living room and said, "Come and get it."

Charlie Patukas, six feet tall and easily three hundred pounds, was first into the room. In his mid-seventies, he was still mostly muscle, but a small bulge was starting to overhang his belt.

Although Skye and her brother, Vince, called him "uncle", he was really their godfather and a special friend of the family. He sat at the head of the table, the sturdy oak chair groaning under his bulk.

Next was Skye's father, Jed, several inches shorter than Charlie and about half his weight. He had a farmer's tan with a white band across his forehead where his John Deere cap had protected it from the sun. The rest of his face was leathery from years of working outdoors. He sat at the other end of the table in the chair with a view out the picture window, so he could keep an eye on the crops.

Finally Skye's brother, Vince, ambled into the dinette and kissed his mother on the cheek before sitting next to Skye. He was far too handsome for his own good. His attractiveness to the opposite sex had already gotten him into *serious* trouble twice; it had gotten him into *minor* difficulties too many times to count. Tall, with emerald-green eyes and long butterscotch hair worn in a ponytail, Vince got his tan from the machine at the hair salon he owned rather than from the great outdoors.

May said the blessing, and then started the platter of roast around the table by handing it to Jed. As the man of the house he got first pick. There was silence as they all filled their plates and started to eat.

After his initial helping had been devoured, Charlie leaned back, took a long swig of beer, and belched. He patted his belly as if it were a pet he was fond of, then said, "I had a really striking-looking lady in one of the cabins last night." He owned the Up A Lazy River Motor Court—the only place to stay in town.

Skye's investigative radar engaged. "Really? Did she have blond hair and drive a pink car?"

"Yeah." Charlie's thick white eyebrows flew up until they nearly met the matching hair on his head. "How did you know?"

"Sounds like Bunny's friend Ruby."

"Ruby? I don't think that's the name she registered under." Charlie frowned. "She paid in cash, so I didn't ask to see any ID."

Skye buttered a roll. Could there be two blondes in town driving pink vehicles? "She was tall and statuesque, right?"

"Yep. That's her." Charlie took the bowl May had handed him, and spooned another pile of mashed potatoes on his plate. "Fine figure of a woman."

"Wally arrested her this afternoon," May announced, a line forming between her eyebrows.

"For what?" Charlie stopped, fork poised midway to his mouth.

Skye took a drink of her Diet Coke and listened to her mother's version of what had happened.

May finished with, "Then she came strutting into the police station, as if she wasn't a wanted fugitive, and demanded that she see the chief and no one else."

"Did you hear what she had to say to Wally?" Skye had been waiting to ask this question since she heard that her mother had been dispatching that day.

"No." May took a sip of wine. "Wally took her into the interrogation room. He usually keeps the door open if he has a female prisoner so I can testify that no hanky-panky took place, but that woman insisted on closing the door and turning on the radio." May stood and started clearing the table. "I couldn't hear a thing, even with my ear pressed against the door."

Skye got up to help. The men stayed seated and waited for dessert to be served. Skye had long ago given up trying to explain the women's movement and equal rights to her family. It might be the twenty-first century in the rest of the country, but in Scumble River they had barely left the nineteenth.

While May cut apple pie and Skye scooped vanilla ice cream, Vince said, "You know, a woman like you described stopped at the salon yesterday afternoon. She wanted me to dye her hair black, but I didn't have time." He took the plate Skye handed him and dug into the pie. Around a mouthful he said, "I told her I didn't think she would look good as a brunette, but she wanted me to color it anyway."

Skye filed away that piece of info with the fact that Ruby seemed to have arrived a day earlier than she had thought, and used a false name to check into the motor court. Evidence was adding up against Miss Ruby.

As Skye set her dad's dessert in front of him, Jed spoke for the first time. "Caboose seems to be pulling the engine with that lady."

Skye considered her father's statement. Ruby *did* seem to be letting events control her life, rather than being in control of her own actions. Jed didn't talk a lot, but when he said something, it was usually worth thinking about. Maybe what he meant was that Ruby was a train wreck waiting to happen.

Chapter 5

Monday-Morning Blonde

When Skye arrived at the bowling alley Monday around eleven-thirty, she kept an eye out for Ruby, but it wasn't until midafternoon that she spotted the blonde descending the steps from Bunny's apartment.

Obviously Ruby was not a morning person; her first words were croaked out in a desperate tone: "Coffee, black." As soon as Skye handed her a cup she took a gulp of the hot liquid, swore when she burned her tongue, than took another sip. Finally she sat down.

Skye joined her. "Did you and Bunny have a good time catching up last night?" she asked.

Ruby nodded, eyes still half-closed.

"How far back do you two go?"

"We met twenty years ago, when Bunny first came to Las Vegas to be a dancer. I was a magician's assistant at the time. Then it just seemed that we always ended up in the same shows and we became best friends." Ruby sipped her coffee. "Bunny had a lot of talent but could never make it to a headliner spot."

"Why?"

"Mostly bad luck." Ruby's gaze became unfocused and she didn't answer right away. "It seemed like whenever she was about to get her big break, something would go wrong. She'd agree to go to Mexico with a boyfriend and their car would break down, so she'd end up missing a rehearsal. Or someone would talk her into going on a skiing trip, and she'd fall and sprain her ankle."

Skye nodded. Ruby's description sounded like the Bunny she had come to know. Easily led, usually to her own detriment. "That's a shame."

"Yeah, it is. Bunny is a good egg and deserves better from life."

Skye allowed a moment of silence, then, edging closer to what she really wanted to know, said, "Was she upset about Benny being arrested?"

Ruby shrugged. "It's not his first dance with the jailhouse band."

"So did they catch him doing the usual?" Skye tried to be casual.

"No. He . . ." Suddenly Ruby stopped. "Never mind. It's not important." She took another sip of coffee and parried, "Are you and Simon engaged?"

Skye shook her head. "No. We're not ready to settle down yet." Refusing to be distracted, she probed, "You know, I'm still not clear as to why you ran away when Wally stopped you."

"Like I said, I panicked, silly me." Ruby fluffed her hair and tried again to sidetrack Skye. "Speaking of the police chief, do you and he have something going on the side? He's really hot."

"No, of course not." Skye felt her cheeks flush. "Why would you ask that?"

Ruby drained her cup. "The vibes, honey, the vibes. You just can't fight the vibes."

Skye opened her mouth to rebut Ruby's claim, but the blonde muttered something about running errands, and hurried away. Skye frowned. What kind of errands could someone new in town have to do?

After a few minutes of unproductive speculation about the older woman's intentions, Skye gave up. She had too much to do to waste any time trying to figure out Ruby.

Skye spent the rest of the afternoon getting the alley's restaurant ready for the night's crowd, and when she finished up around five, Bunny drafted her to help with the talent show.

Even though the program didn't start until seven, the contestants were already crowding the stage. Evidently word had gotten out that there was room for only twenty entertainers, and that it was first come, first perform.

Skye sat at a table to Bunny's left, giving out numbers and taking names. She wondered if the talent show was so popular because Scumble River was full of enough hams to supply Easter dinner for the entire state of Illinois, or due to the prize Bunny had wheedled out of Quentin Kessler, the owner of the dry goods store: a big-screen TV.

So far Skye had registered comedians, singers, dancers, an accordion player, and even a lady who had dyed her poodle pink and taught it to dance on its back legs. The animal's owner had colored her own hair to match, curled it to look like the canine's fur, and wore a rose net tutu similar to the one the dog sported around its hindquarters.

Currently Skye's attention was riveted on a girl standing center stage tossing two burning batons and reciting:

> "The boy stood on the burning deck,
> Whence all but him had fled;
> The flame that lit the battle's wreck
> Shone round him o'er the dead."

Suddenly Ruby erupted through the doors leading into the bar. A hush fell over the crowd as Ruby shouted, "I've been vandalized!"

Skye rushed off the stage. "What happened? Were you attacked? Where?" Ruby looked fine. Her leopard-print miniskirt and black silk blouse were undamaged. There wasn't a hair out of place in her blond pageboy, and her makeup wasn't smeared.

"I'm fine, but when I get ahold of the prick who tore up my car, he won't be." Ruby whirled on her stiletto heels and marched away. "Come look."

Skye, followed closely by Bunny, the talent show contestants trailing them like baby ducks, trooped outside. As they neared the bowling alley parking lot the blare of an alarm assaulted Skye's ears.

She hadn't seen Ruby's car before, but when Wally had told her that Ruby drove a pink Cadillac, she had felt a certain sense of solidarity with the blonde. Skye herself drove a 1957 aqua Bel Air, a big car in an unusual color. She had pictured Ruby's car as a pretty pastel, like the ones the cosmetic ladies drove. She had been wrong—very, very wrong.

The pink of Ruby's car was closer to neon, and the Eldorado had been fitted with a miniature statue of David for a hood ornament. It was anatomically correct—and he wasn't wearing a fig leaf. There were several snickers and pointing fingers in the crowd as people realized what they were seeing.

Ruby, ignoring the group's reaction to her choice of art, threw out her arms in the direction of the decimated vehicle and ordered, "Look what someone's done to my baby."

The doors hung open at odd angles, and objects that had been inside the car now littered the asphalt. The upholstery had been skinned from the seats, chunks of foam had been dug out and dotted the area around the car, the dashboard had been ripped off, and the carpet peeled back from the floor. Even the ceiling fabric hung in shreds like the tassels on a stripper's costume. It was evident the Cadillac had been searched, and the searcher didn't care about the damage inflicted.

Skye examined the destruction. "I'll call the police."

"No!" Ruby grabbed her arm. "I mean, let's not get carried away. Sorry to rile everyone up. I'm sure it was just kids having some fun."

Skye raised an eyebrow. "Kids in Scumble River do not have this kind of fun."

Bunny stepped between the two women, and although she gave her friend a puzzled glance, she said to Skye, "Ruby meant that she didn't want to ruin some kid's life for one mistake, not that the kids in Scumble River are bad."

"We have to call the police." Skye crossed her arms. She knew something was going on, and she wasn't letting Ruby and Bunny float down the river of denial. Wally needed to get to the bottom of it.

"Suit yourself, but I'm not pressing charges," Ruby said. "In fact, I'll tell them I did it all myself." She looked down at Skye, which was easy to do, since she had five inches on her even without the high-heeled shoes. "As long as I don't file an insurance claim, no crime has been committed. There's not a thing the cops can do." Ruby turned her back on Skye and said to the people standing around them, "Anyone know a good garage that can repair this damage?"

Skye ground her teeth in frustration. What was this woman up to? Ignoring the crowd, which was now shouting out places where Ruby could take her car to be fixed, Skye crossed the parking lot, marched into the bowling alley, around the bar, and didn't stop until she was sitting behind the desk in the office. She was going to call Simon. Maybe he'd have an idea.

"What? You're kidding." Simon had picked up on the first ring, and Skye had immediately launched into an account of Ruby's latest escapade. "I'll be right over."

"What's the use? If Ruby doesn't press charges or make an insurance claim, there's nothing the police can do." Skye twirled the phone cord around her finger. "The big question is, Why doesn't she want to involve the police? Did Wally tell you anything when you talked to him yesterday afternoon?"

"No. He avoided answering most of my questions. All he would say was that Ruby had explained her actions to his satisfaction, paid the tickets for reckless driving and obscene display, which is a misdemeanor, and allowed Wally to confiscate the items to be destroyed."

"Did he at least tell you her full real name?" Skye asked. Why was Wally protecting Ruby?

"Jones. The name on her driver's license is Ruby Jones." Simon made a scornful noise.

"I wonder which husband that name's from." Skye tapped her fingers on the desk. "Guess it's time to call your friend in Vegas and see if he can tell you anything."

"I'll do that. Even with a common name like Jones, there can't be that many six-foot-tall, full-figured Rubys who owned sex stores."

"You wouldn't think so, but I've heard some strange things about Las Vegas."

Chapter 6

Out of the Mouths of Blondes

Skye scanned the group of people that had assembled in the bowling alley bar for Team Trivia and wondered if the winner of last night's talent contest had come back. Not that she would recognize him if he were there. The guy had worn a gorilla mask during his comedy routine and signed in as Lenny Bruce.

Since Skye was pretty sure the famous comedian had not risen from his grave in order to perform in Scumble River, she thought it a safe bet that Mr. Anonymous had used a false name. The question was, Why?

Before she could come up with a guess, her attention was diverted to a group of teens attempting to oust people from their seats by tipping their chairs forward. Once someone fell from the chair, the teens claimed the seat. Skye caught the ringleader's eye and pointed to the entrance. The girl pasted an innocent expression on her face and shrugged helplessly. Skye pointed again. The sign hanging on the door was clear. It read: STANDING ROOM ONLY! The teens scowled, relinquished the stolen seats, and marched out of the bar.

Skye let out the breath she'd been holding. She hated to see the kids go—she knew there was little for them to do in town—but the place was too crowded to deal with any group that would cause problems.

Bunny had brought in extra chairs, but still people stood, leaned, knelt, and sat on the floor. Skye was surprised that such a large crowd had turned out on a weeknight just for a game of trivia.

So many wanted to play that Bunny had had to decree that they would use a lottery system to select the contestants. Skye had collected the strips of paper, and now held a recycled pickled-egg jar crammed full of the tickets.

Bunny mounted the stage, dragging a reluctant Ruby after her. She took the mike from Skye and announced, "Our special guest from Las Vegas, Nevada, Miss Ruby, will draw twenty names. There will be four teams of five. Team One will play Team Two, and Team Three will play Team Four; then the winners of the first two rounds will play the third round for the grand prizes.

"Everyone ready?"

The audience roared its approval, and Ruby started picking slips from the jar. Skye only half listened as the names were called out. She recognized most, although one or two weren't familiar. Suddenly she froze as Ruby announced, "Earl Doozier is our lucky thirteenth contestant."

A man wearing sweatpants and a flannel shirt pushed his way through the crowd. He was skinny except for the bowling ball–sized potbelly that hung over the elastic waist of his pants. His mud-brown hair formed a horseshoe around the back of his head.

Skye struggled to keep her expression neutral as he climbed the steps up to the stage, but she just couldn't wrap her mind around the idea of Earl Doozier on a trivia team. She was afraid to imagine his answers.

Earl was the patriarch of the Red Raggers, a clan who always seemed to turn up whenever there was trouble. They didn't necessarily initiate the problem, but they also never missed an opportunity to contribute to the chaos.

The Dooziers were tough to describe to anyone who hadn't grown up with the legend of the Red Raggers. The best Skye could come up with was a tribe of outsiders who didn't want to be insiders. She had established a good relationship with Earl through working with his many children, sisters, brothers, nieces, and nephews in her job as a school psychologist, but for the most part the Dooziers kept to themselves.

So why on earth was Earl at the bowling alley signed up to play Team Trivia? The only reason she could think of was that he had once told her he'd learned everything he knew from the two wise men, Jack Daniel's and Jose

Cuervo; and for tonight's game Bunny had persuaded the owner of the Brown Bag Liquor Store to donate five gift certificates. Maybe he wanted the prize to further his education.

The rest of the participants were chosen, and when the game began, Skye slipped away to check on how things were going in the rest of the bowling alley.

She hurried through her checklist, wanting to be back in time to see Earl play when it was his team's turn. The lanes were doing fine, and the cook appeared to have things under control in the kitchen, but Frannie Ryan, the grill's waitress, was having a rough time.

The teenagers who had been kicked out of the bar had settled at the counter, and they were obviously intent on humiliating Frannie.

Skye narrowed her eyes. Frannie was one of the coeditors of the high school newspaper that Skye supervised, and she had been through a lot with Skye, even once helping to save her life. The mean teens had picked the wrong person, time, and place to attack.

As Skye strode toward them she heard the leader of the pack, a girl named Blair, say to Frannie, "So, do you get all the free food you can eat? Is that why you're as big as an elephant?"

Frannie was solidly built and would never be a size two or even a twelve, a trait that caused her much heartache.

Skye felt a flare of anger. She didn't put up with bullying of any kind, and being on the curvy side herself, she especially didn't allow fat bashing. She paused for a second to get control of her temper, and while she was composing herself, Ruby swooped down on the group.

The older woman put her hands on the back of Blair's stool and leaned over her shoulder. "You know, honey, I've been facing down underfed, ignorant ego busters like you my whole life, and they've never won."

One of the others at the counter jeered, "Maybe if you'd lose some weight, you wouldn't have to keep 'facing people down.'"

Ruby moved over to the boy who was speaking, bent down, and spoke into his ear. "Sweetheart, I've had five husbands, one of them a duke, made and lost millions of dollars, and traveled around the world. Do you really think

your itty-bitty, no-account opinion means anything to me?"
Ruby straightened and flicked him on the arm with her
thumb and index finger. "Kids like you may be big shots
during your teenage years, but in the real world you generally end up digging ditches or working for someone you
looked down your nose at in high school."

The teens exchanged uneasy glances. They weren't used
to people talking back and making them feel bad about
themselves.

Although Skye hated to interrupt Ruby when the older
woman was on a roll, she couldn't in good conscience let
her attack students from her high school, even obnoxious
ones. But she wouldn't let them get away scot-free either.
She preferred to use the behavior-management technique
of consequences, so she said, "Kids, I'm afraid I have to
ask you to leave the bowling alley. We have a no-bullying
policy here, and you've broken the rules."

Blair twitched her shoulders. "Whatever." Then she
turned to the others and said loudly, "Let's get out of here
before we start to look like these three—Fatty, Fatter,
and Fattest."

There was some grumbling, but the six teens grudgingly
got to their feet and shuffled away. As they rounded the
corner Blair's voice floated back toward where Skye, Frannie, and Ruby stood: "We should have known better than
to hang out anywhere Fat Frannie was. People might think
we're her friends. Wouldn't that be mortifying?"

Blair's words had hit their mark. Frannie burst into tears
and fled into the stockroom. Skye and Ruby were quick to
follow. They found the teen sitting on the floor with her
back against the wall.

Skye sat next to her and said conversationally, "You
know, this is what those girls wanted—your crying over
what they said makes them the winners."

Frannie shrugged, drew up her knees, and buried her
face in them.

Skye opened her mouth, then closed it without speaking.
It was tempting to launch into a speech on coping with
bullies, but she knew the real art of counseling was not
only to say the right thing at the right time, but also to
leave unsaid the wrong thing at the tempting moment.

Ruby, on the other hand, felt no such restriction. She

pulled an old chrome chair in front of where Frannie and Skye sat, eased onto the cracked vinyl seat, and crossed her legs. "I'm pretty sure that girl was a skinny, evil witch, but we'd better make sure."

Frannie sniffed, but continued to stare at the floor. "What do you mean, make sure?"

"We need to run her through the test to be positive," Ruby said, maintaining a serious expression but winking at Skye, who shot her a puzzled look.

Frannie straightened and wiped her eyes with the back of her hand. "What's the test?"

"There are five questions, and you have to answer yes to all of them to classify someone as a skinny, evil witch." Ruby held up one finger. "First, would that person split a salad with four friends and call it a meal?"

Frannie nodded. "I've seen Blair do that in the cafeteria with the other 'in' girls."

Ruby put up a second finger. "Would she claim she was full after eating a package of airline peanuts?"

"Definitely." Frannie started to smile. "I've seen Blair eat one M & M."

"Three: Would she count carbs even at a health-food restaurant?"

"Thats one's tougher. We don't have health food in Scumble River." Frannie pursed her mouth, thinking.

"I'm pretty sure we can say yes," Skye contributed. "It's the thought that counts."

"Is her idea of a great conversation one that consists mainly of the words sit-ups, crunches, and treadmilling?" Ruby went on.

"Absolutely." Frannie grinned. "It's all she ever talks about."

"And last, but most important, does she ever say, 'I'm not hungry, I ate yesterday?' "

Frannie was now beaming. "Yes, yes, yes! I've heard her say that."

Ruby nodded solemnly. "Then I pronounce Miss Blair a skinny, evil witch. Do you think she'll want the T-shirt prize?"

Skye left Ruby and Frannie laughing and went back into the bar. She had missed the second round of the trivia game, but by some miracle Earl's team had made it into the finals, and she watched as one of the opposition answered a question correctly.

Next Bunny turned to Earl, and, reading from an index card, asked, "Name the four seasons."

Earl scratched his crotch, then answered confidently, "Salt, pepper, catsup, and . . ." He chewed his thumbnail. "Tabasco sauce."

The audience roared, Skye cringed, and the rest of Team Three scowled.

Bunny went through another group of questions, and when she once again came to Earl, she announced, "The teams are tied at seven points each. If Earl gets this correct, Team Three wins." She waited for silence, then read, "According to the Bible, what happened on Easter Sunday?"

Earl stuck his finger in his ear, dug for a while, then examined what he had mined. Finally he said, "Jesus came back from the dead as a giant rabbit and hid eggs for all the good little kids."

The spectators went wild with laughter, completely ignoring Bunny's attempts to quiet them. Both team captains were shouting that their team had won. Skye stood at the back wondering what to do. She was afraid the crowd would get violent if Bunny didn't regain control soon.

Suddenly, over the commotion, a fire alarm sounded, and seconds later Skye heard the sirens of a fire truck heading their way.

Chapter 7

Blondes Are the Dark Roots of All Evil

The firefighters cleared the building, and while everyone stood around the parking lot trying to figure out what was going on, Bunny declared the trivia contest a tie and promised that both teams would receive equal prizes.

After a half hour, most of the crowd drifted away, disappointed that there were no flames shooting out from the building's windows and no bodies plummeting from the roof. It was past ten on a worknight, and if there wasn't any blood and guts, they figured they might as well go home and catch the late-night news on TV, which could be counted on for at least one shot of a bleeding corpse.

By the time the fire department declared the bowling alley safe to reenter, there were only a handful of people remaining, and most of them had a good reason to be there.

Skye stood between Bunny and Simon, a position she found rather symbolic, since mother and son had been sniping at one another since Simon's arrival minutes after the firefighters had evacuated the place. They were all shivering, since Bunny and Skye hadn't been allowed to go back into the building for their jackets, and Simon had left the funeral home in such a hurry he had forgotten to grab his overcoat.

Frannie, Ruby, and Earl Doozier were an odd threesome sitting on dilapidated lawn chairs that Earl had produced from the trunk of his ancient Buick Regal. Ruby's contribution to the gathering was a silver flask, which she and Earl were passing back and forth while Frannie watched in fascinated silence. Skye kept an eye on the group to make sure

Ruby and Earl didn't decide to include the teenager in their party.

Another trio consisted of Skye's parents and Charlie. Although Charlie's business was operating the motor court, his true avocation was running Scumble River. He held no public office, except that of school board president, but he was the big cheese in town. Between him and Skye's mother, thanks to her job as a police dispatcher, they knew everything that was worth knowing about the community, and some things that were probably better left secret.

Skye's parents had shown up to make sure she was safe after hearing the emergency call on their police scanner, and then withdrew to discuss the situation out of her earshot. Both were convinced that Skye was still a child and needed their help in all matters.

Charlie had heard about the fire the same way that May and Jed had, as had nearly everyone in town, since most people owned a scanner, finding it more amusing to listen to than most television shows. Scumble Riverites had discovered the allure of reality programming long before the TV executives started putting it on the air.

The remaining group hanging around consisted of males of a certain age who turned out to watch whenever there was a fire call. Skye recognized most of them, but a few were unfamiliar. She figured they were probably men who had been at the bowling alley when the alarm sounded.

Something glinted to Skye's right, and she squinted in that direction. A man stood off to the side, in the shadow of the shop next door. Could he be the person who wore the gorilla mask to tell jokes in the talent show the night before? He had the same build and posture, but without a face to go by, she couldn't be sure. Something had struck her about last night's comic, but she couldn't quite remember what it was. What had she noticed that made him stick out?

The fire chief interrupted her rumination by holding out his hand to Simon and saying, "Mr. Reid, good news. There's no sign of a fire anywhere in the building."

Simon shook the chief's hand, and asked, "What caused the alarm to go off?"

"As far as we can tell, it was triggered in the upstairs apartment. It looks as if someone burned something in a wastebasket up there and didn't quite put it out." The chief took off his helmet and scratched his head. "You've got a very sensitive smoke-detection system, and the smoldering paper would have been enough to set it off."

"That's strange." Simon wrinkled his brow. "My mother lives in that apartment, and she was down in the bowling alley." He turned to Bunny. "Did you go back upstairs for anything?"

"No. I haven't been in my apartment since six, when I changed clothes for tonight's contest." Bunny smoothed the pristine white embroidered jeans that clung to her like the peel on a banana. The matching shirt had a mesh vee down the front that reached nearly to her waist.

Skye noticed that the fire chief could barely take his eyes from Bunny's silicone valley, which made her aware of her own less-than-attractive appearance. She wore the same clothes she had put on to come to work at noon—black jeans and an emerald-green turtleneck that matched her eyes. They were both covered with smudges and stains from helping people exit the building in an orderly fashion. How had Bunny remained so spotless?

"Who else has a key to your apartment, Mrs. Reid?" The fire chief withdrew a small notebook from an inside pocket.

"Please, call me Bunny. 'Mrs. Reid' makes me feel so old."

"I'd be honored."

Skye hadn't noticed Charlie join the group until she heard him clear his throat and saw him frown at the chief, who ignored him. Skye made a face. She knew Charlie and Bunny had dated back in November, when the redhead had first arrived in town, but she thought that was over. Had they started up again?

The chief repeated his question. "So, Bunny, who else has a key to your apartment?"

"Let's see." Bunny tapped her cheek with a red-tipped nail. "Sonny Boy."

"That would be Mr. Reid?"

Simon nodded brusquely and frowned at his mother.

"Were you in the apartment tonight?"

"No."

"Anyone else, Bunny?" the chief probed.

Bunny was silent, as was Simon, so Skye suggested, "How about Ruby?"

"What about Ruby?" The blonde had sidled up next to Charlie, and was looking him over appreciatively.

"I thought you might have a key to Bunny's apartment, since you're staying with her," Skye explained. "The fire chief wants to know who has one."

"Yes, Bunny gave me a spare." Ruby turned her attention to the chief, laying a hand on his arm. "I hope that doesn't mean you think I deliberately set the fire. I'd be ever so upset if you thought badly of me."

It was hard to tell, since the chief's face was deeply tanned, but Skye could swear he blushed.

"No," he stammered, "of course not. It looks like an accident. Maybe you burned something in the wastebasket earlier and didn't realize it was still smoldering?"

A strange expression crossed Ruby's face, but she quickly rearranged her features and produced a single tear. "Oh, my, I'm so sorry. I didn't think. How awful of me to abuse Bunny's hospitality like that." She clutched the chief's hand. "I was paying bills and I wanted to destroy the invoices. You know, they keep warning and warning you about identity theft, so I burned them. I was sure the fire was out. I can't believe I was that careless."

The chief put his free arm around Ruby's shoulders. "Don't you worry about it, ma'am. No harm done. My boys needed the practice anyway." He turned to Simon. "I'm sure you agree, Reid, that accidents happen."

Simon glanced from his mother to the blonde cuddling in the chief's arms, and shrugged. "Can't argue with that. Some things are inevitable."

Chapter 8

Nip It in the Blonde

"Trust Bunny to have an alarming finish for something as tame as a trivia game," Simon commented to Skye as she drove them toward her cottage.

After the fire chief had finished talking to them, Simon had gone home to drop off his car. Skye had followed a few minutes later and picked him up.

Six months ago, Skye and Simon had finally taken the big step and spent the night together. Since then, continuing the intimate side of their relationship without the whole town finding out that they were sleeping together had been a challenge.

Despite the casual attitude toward sex that Hollywood portrayed in the movies, small-town Scumble River took a dim view of its unmarried citizens hopping in and out of bed with one another. Not that the town singles didn't have premarital sex; they just had to be a lot more discreet than if they lived in Chicago.

This posed a bigger problem for Skye and Simon than most, because both their jobs put them in the public eye. In addition, each drove extremely distinctive cars, and Skye's mother worked as a police dispatcher—the officer on patrol would definitely tell her if he saw Simon's Lexus parked at Skye's cottage all night.

Now, as Skye maneuvered the Bel Air into her driveway, she wondered if Simon's staying over was a good idea. It had been a long day, and she felt anything but attractive in her dirty clothes with her hair morphed from its usual smooth curtain into a mass of wild curls.

She planned her strategy as she fitted the key into the lock. First, she'd divert his attention. "I was surprised that

Xavier didn't come over to see if Frannie was okay." Xavier was Frannie's father and worked for Simon as embalmer and assistant funeral director. "Did you call him and let him know she was safe?"

"He was in Kankakee. Tuesday nights are his martial-arts classes. I don't think he gets home until midnight or so."

"Oh." As Skye entered her cottage foyer, a big black cat appeared and began rubbing against her ankles. She picked him up and scratched under his chin. "What's wrong, Bingo? Are you a hungry kitty?" The feline purred louder and wiggled out of her embrace.

Simon leaned down to pet him. "What's up, fella? Can't take all this attention?"

Turning to Simon, Skye put phase two of her plan into action—keep Simon occupied while she fixed herself up. "Could you take care of Bingo for me while I take a quick shower? Give him one can of Fancy Feast, fresh water, and sift his litter box."

Skye fled into her bedroom while Simon was still nodding his agreement. Fifteen minutes later, she was clean—smelling of Chanel No. 5 rather than sweat—her hair had been tamed into a French braid, and she was dressed in a jade-green satin chemise and matching kimono.

She was now ready for phase three—seduction. She walked out of her bedroom and purred, "Simon, darling, I'm ready."

There was no response. Where was he? She moved farther into the great room. Simon was sprawled on the couch. He had taken off his suit jacket, tie, shoes, and socks; rolled up the sleeves of his shirt and untucked it; and apparently started to read the paper before exhaustion had won. He was fast asleep.

Skye sighed, draped an afghan over him, and went into the kitchen for a midnight snack. If she couldn't have one treat, she'd have to settle for another kind.

Mmm. What did she feel like? Something soothing. She opened the freezer door. Ah, just the thing, chocolate ice cream with marshmallow-fluff topping—one or two scoops?

She stood with the spoon poised over the carton, listening to her good angel argue with her bad one about portion size, when a husky voice murmured, "Got enough to share?" Simon leaned against the archway separating the great room from the kitchen. He had shed his shirt, and his muscular chest glowed with a bronze sheen.

The underlying sensuality of his words made her tremble.

He moved toward her and wrapped her in his arms, then whispered into her hair, "You weren't really planning to let me sleep on the couch all night, were you?"

She put her arms around his neck and inhaled his scent. "I thought maybe you needed the rest."

Simon tightened his embrace, molding her soft curves to the contours of his lean body. "Do I seem tired to you?" His mouth covered hers hungrily.

Parting her lips, she raised herself to meet his kiss, and she heard him groan deep within his throat.

His hand slid up the silky fabric of her nightgown until it found her breast. His stroking fingers sent pleasant jolts through Skye. Simon's lips left hers and seared a path from her earlobe to her bare shoulder. Her breathing was uneven, and she managed to gasp only one word: "Bedroom?"

He freed one arm and snagged the carton of ice cream from the counter.

Skye thought he would put it back into the freezer so it wouldn't melt, but he said, "Let's take this with us."

She wondered what he had in mind, shivering at the possibilities.

Skye stretched and yawned before turning to look at the clock radio. *Shit!* It was already after eight. Why hadn't Simon woken her? He was always up by six, no matter how late he got to sleep.

She was supposed to be at her mother's by nine to accompany May to the hospital. She had finally convinced her mom to get a mammogram, and she wasn't letting May weasel out of it.

Throwing off the covers, she leaped out of bed, then glanced back, looking for her robe. Simon was still fast asleep, a satisfied smile on his handsome face. She kissed him lightly on the lips and headed for the bathroom.

A half hour later, she was dressed in navy wool slacks and baby-blue twinset. Simon had finally woken up and was showering. While he got ready, she gulped down a cup of tea and a piece of toast.

By the time she went back to the bedroom for her shoes he was zipping his pants.

He kissed her and said, "I need to leave some things over here. I hate putting on dirty clothes the next morning."

Skye froze. Leaving clothes at each other's places was getting perilously close to moving in together, and she was not ready for that. Was she? She murmured something noncommittal, then said, "Sorry to rush you, but I've got to be at Mom's in ten minutes, and if I'm late she'll chicken out."

"No problem, let's go." As they got into the car he said, "I'm going to do some investigating this morning about Ruby. Give me a call when you get back, and I'll let you know what I find out."

"I should be back by noon and at the bowling alley by one. Don't forget tonight is karaoke, and I expect you to sing to me."

"That's about as likely to happen as my finding out that Ruby is working for the CIA."

Chapter 9

I Know Why the Caged Blonde Sings

Skye had discovered one of life's little truths: A karaoke machine brought out every bad singer within a thirty-mile radius, and they were all intent on being first to demonstrate why they shouldn't even consider packing their bags and moving to Nashville or Hollywood.

Skye looked around the bowling alley's bar; once again the room was overcrowded. When they had brought out the equipment, and the horde rushed the stage, she had been afraid they were in for a riot. But Bunny had handed out numbers and assured everyone they would get a turn, which meant that at the rate they were going, some of the people possessing the higher digits might be singing at dawn.

The lady currently in possession of the microphone was droning the longest version of "Danny Boy" ever heard outside of Ireland. Skye narrowed her eyes. Was that pink fur beginning to grow on the woman's arm? No, maybe not, but even so, Skye could detect a distinct resemblance to the Energizer Bunny—she just kept singing and singing and singing.

Normally Skye would have slipped out of the bar and hidden somewhere with a good book until the musical mayhem was over. Unfortunately, tonight she was trapped. The bartender hadn't shown up for work, and she'd been forced to fill in for him. Considering her limited knowledge of mixing cocktails, it was a good thing most of the crowd drank beer or some other form of malt beverage from a can, bottle, or keg.

She scanned the room as she filled two mugs from the

Budweiser tap. Where was Ruby? The blonde hadn't been around since Skye had gotten to the bowling alley that afternoon. When asked, Bunny had claimed ignorance of Ruby's whereabouts, and then become busy elsewhere, avoiding further questions.

The final strains of "Danny Boy" had barely faded when a man weaing a white jumpsuit, dark glasses, and a wig with long sideburns claimed the stage. Somehow Skye wasn't shocked when he started to sing "Love Me Tender," though she was a bit surprised that he was good.

Skye paused in midpour to inspect the Elvis impersonator. He seemed familiar, but with the costume and all it was hard to tell. Was he someone from town?

Her concentration on figuring out Elvis's true identity was broken when Hacker, the missing bartender, materialized at her side, startling her. She dropped the glass she was holding, and it shattered as it hit the floor.

"Damn!" Skye immediately knelt to pick up the jagged pieces, bumping into the power-washing gear the cleaning crew had stored behind the bar. She made a mental note to ask Bunny how long that equipment would have to stay there. It was really in the way.

Hacker lowered himself much more slowly. His hands shook as he attempted to help clean up the shards.

"Are you sick?" Skye asked, keeping her voice low. He looked awful. His eyes were like two poached eggs, and his normally olive skin was yellow. The hula girl he had tattooed on his right biceps appeared old and jaundiced.

"I'm fine." His normal gravelly voice squeaked as though he were just entering puberty.

"Then where were you?" Skye checked her watch. "You're two hours late."

"I got held up. Sorry."

Skye frowned. Hacker had appeared in town shortly after the bowling alley opened. He was not originally from Scumble River, and it was obvious that he had led a hard life. Skye's best guess was that he was in his fifties, but he could be ten years younger or older. His face had a lived-in quality that made his age hard to estimate. He was going bald on top, but wore what was left of his brown hair in a scraggly ponytail.

Bunny had hired him without asking for references, and

Simon had been worried, but up until tonight Hacker had been reliable and an excellent bartender.

Skye wondered if he had been drugging. Soon after he'd begun working at the bar, Bunny had confided to Skye that she had met Hacker at her Narcotics Anonymous meetings.

They finished cleaning up the broken glass and got everyone at the bar served without further conversation. Skye was sitting on a stool, keeping an eye on Hacker and trying to decide what to do, when Simon took the seat beside her.

A woman dressed like Madonna was belting out "Like a Virgin," so he leaned close and asked, "How are things going around here?"

Skye cut her eyes toward Hacker and whispered in Simon's ear, "He was two hours late and looks like crap, but he claims he's fine."

Simon examined the bartender. "Can you cover for him? I want to know what's up."

"Sure. I want to know too."

Simon walked over to the older man, spoke to him briefly, and then headed out of the bar toward the bowling alley office. Hacker reluctantly followed him.

From the stage, Bunny watched Hacker and Simon leave with a worried expression.

Skye had served seven beers, a bottle of hard lemonade, and two Zimas by the time the men returned. Hacker took over without comment, and she joined Simon, who was standing by the door.

Simon put his arm around her. "Let's take a walk."

She nodded and he led her outside, saying as the doors closed behind them, "That's better. The off-key singing was getting to me."

Skye leaned against him. "You should try listening to it for more than two hours."

"Poor baby." His lips brushed her forehead. "Seems like they're having fun, though."

"Yep. So far Bunny's Spring Break Bash has been very good for business." Skye twisted a little to look at Simon. "What's the story with Hacker?"

"He got jumped and was embarrassed to admit that someone got the better of him in a fight."

"Where? Here in town?" Skye was amazed. She had never heard of a mugging anywhere in the area.

"Right here in Scumble River."

Skye knew she had been listening to karaoke too long, because she half expected Simon to start singing a Scumble River version of "Trouble" from *The Music Man*.

To her disappointment, Simon continued without bursting into song. "Hacker says he was supposed to meet Ruby at the Dew Drop Inn this afternoon around four. He was walking into the tavern when he heard a commotion in the alley, so he went over to see what was happening and someone grabbed him from behind, pressed a gun into his back, and said, 'Hand it over.'"

"He was meeting Ruby." Skye shook her head. "Why am I not surprised that she's somehow involved in Scumble River's first mugging?"

"I thought Bunny was a pain when she first arrived, but Ruby could give her lessons." Simon paused, his expression sour. "I just hope she hasn't given her lessons, I mean."

"So what happened?"

"Hacker said he had no idea what the robber wanted him to hand over, and when he said as much the guy hit him behind the ear with the gun and he passed out."

"No wonder he looks so bad. He shouldn't be at work. He probably has a concussion." Skye started to go back inside. "I can finish his shift. He needs to go home. Did he see a doctor or go to the hospital?"

Simon grabbed her hand and stopped her. "He wants to work. He refuses to see a doctor—I offered to pay because I thought he might not have the money. He says he's okay except for a tremendous headache, but he said it's no worse than some hangovers he's had."

"Oh." Skye allowed herself to be drawn back into Simon's arms.

"Hacker did say that when he woke up he had been thoroughly searched, but nothing was missing." Simon stiffened as the door behind them whooshed open, but relaxed once the laughing group walked past them toward the parking lot. "I'm worried that you or Bunny might be attacked next."

"I think it's pretty clear by now that Ruby has something that someone else wants."

"And whoever that someone is, he doesn't care who he hurts to get it."

Chapter 10

Make the Best of a Bad Blonde

"Did Hacker report being attacked to the police?" Skye asked suddenly.

It was three A.M., karaoke had finally ended an hour ago, and they were nearly finished cleaning up. The grill closed at eleven, so Frannie and the cook were long gone.

Simon was washing glasses behind the bar, having persuaded the bartender to go home when they locked the door. He wiped his forehead, leaving a trail of bubbles, and said, "Not yet. He hasn't had the best experience with the authorities in the past, but I assured him Wally was different, and he promised to talk to him tomorrow. I said I'd go with him if he'd feel more comfortable."

"You're a good man, Charlie Brown." Skye smiled at Simon, thinking how few guys would be so kind to someone like Hacker. "Have you told your mother what happened?"

"Yes, she claims she has no idea what Ruby has or who's trying to get it, but I think she knows more than she's admitting."

"I'd bet big bucks you're right." Skye finished emptying the last ashtray and started wiping down the tables. "Is Ruby back yet?"

"Yes. I sent Bunny up to the apartment to check after we closed up, and she said Ruby was there fast asleep."

"How annoying, though it's probably best for us to question her when we're a little more wide-awake ourselves."

Simon put the last glass in the drainer, wiped his hands

216

on a towel, and came out from behind the bar. "True. She won't be an easy one to crack."

"That's for sure." Skye threw the dishcloth into the laundry bag and wiped her hands dry on her jeans. "Done." She sank onto a chair and blew a strand of hair out of her eyes. "Oh, I forgot to ask you, did you get ahold of your friend in Las Vegas? Did he know Ruby or anything about her?"

"I did talk to him. He said something about her sounded familiar, but he couldn't remember." Simon took Skye's hand, tugged her back onto her feet, and led her out of the bar. "He's going to dig around a little and get back to me."

They found Bunny in the office, a pencil poked through the mass of red curls on top of her head, finishing up the bank deposit.

Skye kissed the older woman's cheek. "Good night, Bunny. See you tomorrow afternoon for the Easter-egg hunt."

Bunny didn't look up from the old-fashioned adding machine she was using. "Night."

"Get some sleep, Bunny. You can do that in the morning." Simon awkwardly patted his mother on the shoulder. He still couldn't bring himself to call her Mom, and found it difficult to display affection.

"Night, Sonny Boy." Bunny waved at him, still concentrating on the numbers in front of her. "I'm almost done."

Skye and Simon walked out to the parking lot, and he opened the car door for her. "What time are you getting to the alley tomorrow?"

"The kids arrive at two thirty to dye the eggs, and then Frannie and some other teens I've drafted will take them down into the basement and play a few games while Bunny and I hide the eggs. Charlie's dressing as the Easter Bunny, and is appearing at four to officially start the hunt." Skye slid into the driver's seat. "So I guess I should get here about one to get the egg-dyeing stations set up. We're expecting about a hundred kids."

"Could you come a little early so we can talk to Ruby first?"

"Definitely."

Simon leaned forward and kissed her. "In fact, why don't I pick you up at eleven and we go for an early lunch?"

Skye reached up and caressed his cheek. "Make it eleven thirty. You didn't let me get much rest last night, and I need my beauty sleep."

Skye struggled to wake up. She had hit the snooze button several times and knew that if she didn't get up soon, Simon would be ringing her doorbell while she was in the shower. Maybe she should give him a key. He'd been hinting for the last month or so that he wanted one, and had offered to make her a copy of his, but she wasn't sure that was a step she wanted to take at this point in their relationship.

She had only ever been this intimate with one other man, and look how poorly that had turned out. He had jilted her and left her broke and out of a job.

But now wasn't the time to think about that. She had to get dressed, interrogate Ruby, and help a hundred children dye Easter eggs. Deciding whether to exchange keys with her boyfriend would have to wait.

She rolled over and swung her legs out of bed, her eyes still closed. Her toe encountered something warm and furry, and an infuriated yowl informed her it was Bingo. She had fed the cat when she got home at three thirty, hoping to appease him into letting her sleep past his usual six o'clock hunger alarm.

It must have worked, because instead of rousing her he had been snoozing on the throw rug by the side of her bed. Stepping on his tail had not been the best way to wake him. He narrowed his golden eyes, hissed, and ran out of the room.

Skye swept a sheaf of hair out of her eyes, and dragged herself into the bathroom. She hoped Bingo wouldn't punish her by using someplace other than his litter box for his morning pee. She had tried behavior modification on the feline, but she was afraid he had altered her own conduct more than she had changed his.

After a quick shower, she stood in front of her closet as she blew-dry her hair. What to put on? In her heart she yearned to start wearing spring clothes, but even though it was the last day in March, the temperature was expected to get only into the low forties. Also, there was the question of the Easter-egg dye. Did she really want to risk a new outfit?

Fighting the temptation to give in to vanity, she grabbed a pair of jeans and a navy sweatshirt with a bright orange U OF I printed on the front. Might as well support her alma mater if she couldn't wear something pretty.

Simon arrived as she was lacing up her sneakers. She grabbed her jacket and purse and kissed him, then said, "I'm famished. Let's go." She'd missed supper the night before due to her unexpected bartending duties, and hadn't had time for breakfast.

"We can't have you starving to death." Simon took her hand and led her to his car. "Where would you like to go?"

"Gee, I don't know. We aren't exactly a matched set this morning." Simon was dressed for work in a dark suit, shirt, and tie. Skye felt shabby beside him. "Plus we're in sort of a hurry, so let's just go to the Feed Bag."

"You know you look beautiful whatever you wear." Simon hugged her before tucking her into the passenger seat of the Lexus.

Skye made a face. Simon was always a gentleman, but she knew she was far from beautiful. She had nice hair, when the humidity was low and it behaved itself, and great eyes. On a good day but she could be called pretty, but after less than eight hours of sleep, she was lucky to achieve "doesn't frighten small children and dogs."

As they drove to the restaurant, Simon told her about the wake he had scheduled for that afternoon and evening. The deceased was a popular local man with a big family, which meant there was a lot of work to do preparing for the large crowd that was anticipated.

Other than McDonald's and a sandwich shop, the Feed Bag was the only restaurant in town. The owner, Tomi Jackson, had redecorated in 1984, using lots of mauve and brass, and hadn't touched it since then. Over twenty years of hard wear were catching up with the interior. Rips in the vinyl seats had been repaired with duct tape, and smudges on the walls had been dabbed with a color that didn't quite match the original paint.

Skye and Simon snagged one of the last available booths, and both ordered as soon as the waitress appeared. They ate at the Feed Bag at least once a week, and knew the menu by heart.

While they were waiting for their food, Simon said, "I went with Hacker to the police station this morning."

"What did Wally have to say about his being attacked?"

"It was a little strange. I could tell he was interested, maybe even angry, but he didn't say anything. He just asked Hacker some questions, took a report, and thanked him for coming in."

Skye squeezed a lime wedge into her Diet Coke. "I sure wish we could get Wally to tell us what he knows."

Simon's voice was mild, but there was an underlying tone Skye couldn't quite put her finger on. "Have you tried to talk to him?"

"No." She fought to keep her expression neutral. This was dangerous ground. She and Simon had never discussed the "Wally issue," and she certainly didn't want to do it now. "I don't think he'd tell me anything he hasn't told you."

Before Simon could comment, the waitress served their food, and they dug in. Skye steered the conversation to safer topics, and they ended up discussing a trip they were hoping to take to the lake as soon as the weather got nicer.

When they finished their meal, Simon excused himself to use the restroom. Skye sat back, sipping the rest of her soda and looking around the restaurant. It was a nearly twelve thirty, and the place was packed. Most Scumble Riverites ate lunch strictly between the hours of twelve and one.

Her gaze slipped over the diners until she came to a small table in the corner by the kitchen. It was generally reserved for the restaurant's owner, who did all of her business from that location, but today a man sat there with his back to the wall.

Skye squinted, but she couldn't see his face. He was reading a newspaper that hid all of him but his hands. A huge diamond ring sparkled on his right pinkie.

Wait a minute. She had seen that ring before. Had the gorilla-masked comic been wearing it? She closed her eyes, thinking back to Monday night. Yes, she could visualize it on his hand as he held the microphone. Then Tuesday she had noticed it glittering on the man standing in the shadows after the fire alarm went off. And last night the Elvis impersonator had had on the same ring.

Skye wiggled in her seat. This could be the guy behind all the stuff that had been happening. She kept him in her sight until Simon returned; then she slid out of the booth and grabbed Simon's arm, whispering in his ear, "Don't turn around, but there's a man at the table near the kitchen who I think has been hanging around the bowling alley since Monday. Maybe he's the one after Ruby."

Simon took Skye's elbow, and they started to walk toward the cash register to pay their bill. Suddenly he stopped and turned around, saying loudly, "Just a second. I forgot to leave the tip."

Skye turned too, glancing immediately toward the mystery man. The table was empty. She scanned the rest of the restaurant. He was nowhere to be seen. She touched Simon's arm and said in a low voice, "He's gone."

Simon put a few dollars on the table and moved back to Skye's side. "How did he get past us?"

"I don't know." She shrugged. "We were between him and the exit. You need to check the men's room."

"I just came from there," Simon protested. "People will think I have a bladder problem."

Skye gave him a little push. "Go."

Once Simon left, Skye approached Tomi Jackson. She was a tiny woman, though her platinum-blond beehive added several inches to her height. Ageless, she had been a part of Scumble River for as long as Skye could remember.

During busy times the restaurant owner often doubled as a waitress, and Skye caught her as she approached the kitchen with an order. "Hi, Tomi. Did you see that guy sitting at the back table?"

"Sure, I waited on him."

"Did you notice how he left the restaurant?"

Tomi looked at her a little strangely, but answered, "He asked me to let him go out through the kitchen. He said he wasn't feeling well and his car was parked out back. Why?"

"I thought I knew him from somewhere, but he disappeared before I got over to talk to him."

"Oh, that's too bad. Well, if you see him tell him thanks for me. He left me the biggest tip I've gotten since the place opened." Tomi waved a hundred-dollar bill in the air before returning it to her apron pocket. "He must be a real nice man."

Chapter 11

Of Blondes and Men

"You can't go up there. Ruby's still sleeping." Bunny stood on the bottom step of the stairway with her arms straight out, blocking their way to her apartment.

"It's time she woke up." Simon gently moved his mother aside.

"Then I'm going with you." Bunny followed Simon as he climbed the steps.

Skye trailed them both.

He tapped on the door and waited. Nothing.

"Maybe she left through the outside exit," Bunny offered.

Simon didn't answer, just pounded harder.

Skye bit her tongue to stop herself from commenting. He was obviously not in the mood for chitchat.

Finally, after a third round of knocking, the door was flung open, and Ruby stood before them rubbing her eyes. She wore baby-doll pajamas made out of an eye-catching electric-blue stretch lace. "Where's the fire?"

Simon's face darkened, and he snapped. "I don't know. Did you set another one?"

For a moment Ruby looked sheepish, but she stood her ground. "I said I was sorry about that. Why did you wake me?"

"We need to talk. Now." Simon moved forward.

"I'm not dressed."

"We'll wait."

She started to close the door, but Simon put a foot out. "We'll wait inside."

Ruby grudgingly moved back and allowed them into the apartment, but stopped Bunny. "It's better if I talk to them alone."

"Are you sure?"

Ruby nodded. "You and I'll talk later."

Bunny patted her friend's arm and went back down the stairs.

Ruby closed the door and said to Simon and Skye, "I may be a while." She started toward the bedroom, words floating over her shoulder: "And I could really use some coffee." She turned her head toward Skye. "Bring me a cup when it's ready, hon."

Skye ignored the blonde's request, and tugged Simon over to the sofa to wait for her reappearance.

A half hour passed, and Ruby still had not come out of the bedroom. Simon was pacing up and down the small living room. It looked like a tornado had gone through, strewing clothes, shoes, cosmetics, magazines, and empty plates and glasses on every possible surface.

On one of his passes by the couch where Skye was sitting, he gestured to the mess and said, "Bunny likes things tidy, so this mess must be Ruby's. She's not much of a house-keeper, is she?"

Before Skye could ask where he got the idea his mother liked things tidy, Ruby swept into the room and stated, "There's where you're wrong. I've been married five times, and I always keep the house."

Ruby settled onto the chair facing the sofa. She was now dressed in a bright pink jersey. The pants were tight, though otherwise not too outrageous, but the top consisted of a rectangle in front and crisscrossed straps in the back.

Simon raised an eyebrow at Skye as he joined her on the couch. She shrugged. The woman's clothes were not their problem.

Ruby relaxed back into her seat and yawned. "What's so urgent?"

Simon growled, but got control of his temper when Skye dug her nails into his thigh. "We want to know what's going on. It's obvious someone is after something you have."

"I don't know what you mean." Ruby examined her manicure, making a moue of displeasure when she spotted a chip in the hot-pink polish.

"First the incident with the police; then your car is vandalized; this apartment is almost set on fire; and yesterday Hacker was mugged. We may live in a small town, but we aren't stupid."

Ruby continued to avoid their eyes. "I never thought you were."

"Then tell us what's happening," Skye said, having decided to play good cop. "We just want to help."

"There's nothing to tell." Ruby picked at an imaginary piece of lint on her pant leg. "I've just had a run of bad luck since coming here."

Simon grunted. "Does that 'bad luck' have a name?"

"No. I must have broken a mirror or something."

Skye got up and knelt by the other woman's chair, taking her hand. "Ruby, I know you think you can handle whatever the problem is on your own."

Ruby nodded.

"I know you're a strong, independent person, but everyone needs help at some point in their lives." Skye paused and looked into Ruby's eyes. "People are starting to get hurt because of you, and I'm sure that's the last thing you intended."

A single tear rolled down Ruby's cheek. "I didn't think they'd bother anyone else."

"When it was just your car or a false fire alarm, we could let you deal with whatever is going on by yourself. But yesterday Hacker was attacked. What if today it's Bunny or one of the children coming for the Easter-egg hunt?"

Ruby sniffed. "I'll leave, then everyone will be safe."

Simon offered her his handkerchief and said gently, "No, I'm sorry, but they won't. Whoever is doing this might still think you're here, or that you left behind what he's trying to find."

"Please, please, tell us what you're hiding." Skye squeezed the other woman's hand.

"Okay." Ruby heaved a sigh. "I'm turning them over to the FBI tomorrow anyway."

Skye and Simon exchanged an alarmed glance and asked simultaneously, "Turning what over?"

"Some computer disks that just happened to fall into my possession."

Simon ordered, "Tell us from the beginning."

"It all started when a friend of mine, Benny, who worked on the cleaning crew in one of the new casinos, got busted by the feds for selling land through the mail."

"That's illegal?" Skye questioned.

"It is when there's no land. He put ads in the paper, sent any sucker who answered a slick brochure, and then if they took the bait and wrote him a check, he sent them a fake deed. Most people who bought were yuppies looking for investments, so they never figured out all they owned was a worthless piece of paper. Unfortunately for him, someone found out, got the feds involved, and next thing you know poor Benny is back in the slammer."

"How can you say 'poor Benny'?" Skye asked. "He was cheating innocent people."

Ruby shrugged. "People with the kind of money to invest like that are never innocent. No one gets rich without screwing someone else." Ruby shook her head at Skye's naïveté. "Anyway, this was Benny's third offense, and he was going away for a long time, so he made a deal with the feds. He would turn over a lot bigger fishes if they let him skate on his jail time."

"He stole the computer disks from the casino, right?" Simon guessed.

"Right." Ruby smiled. "The casino owners were up to something shady, and Benny figured it out."

"What were they doing?" Skye asked.

"I don't know, and I don't want to know." Ruby crossed her arms. "I was just holding the disks for Benny. Nothing else."

"I thought it was almost impossible for a casino to do anything illegal anymore." Simon's face was set in hard, tight lines.

"Like I said, I don't know the details." Ruby shrugged. "But you know the old saying—invent a better mousetrap and the mouse just gets smarter."

"Why didn't Benny give the disks to the FBI when he made his deal?" Skye demanded.

"Benny's been around the block a few times, and he doesn't trust the government. He gave them to me to hold until he and the feebs could come to a mutually satisfactory agreement. I got a message from Benny yesterday that it was okay to turn them over now."

"Then it's an FBI agent who's been trying to get the disks?" Simon's brow wrinkled in disbelief.

"No. I told the FBI I would turn over the disks on Good Friday—that I couldn't get ahold of them until that day. Agent Dodd will be here tomorrow morning at eight A.M."

"That's why Wally didn't arrest you," Skye deduced. "You had him call the FBI and they told him to let you go."

Ruby smiled serenely. "It was purely a delight to see that boy's expression when he realized he couldn't put me in jail."

"So what did you burn when you set off the alarm?" Skye asked.

"I didn't burn anything." Ruby's expression was puzzled. "Someone else burned some of my personal correspondence." She bit her lip. "He must have thought it was from Benny, but it was only a couple of notes from my fiancé."

"It must be the casino owner, or more likely one of his goons looking for the disks, but why would they burn your love letters?" Skye questioned.

"Who knows?" Ruby's expression turned serious. "How anyone figured out I even had the disks is beyond me. I would never have come here if I thought for a minute I'd put Bunny in danger. We've been like sisters for nearly twenty years."

"But you must have had some suspicion, since you came a day early and tried to have your hair dyed." Skye suddenly remembered what her godfather and brother had said during Sunday night's dinner.

"I was just being cautious." Ruby tossed her head. "I figured better safe than sorry."

"I wonder if whoever is after you lost your trail, and didn't realize you stayed at the motor court rather than here Saturday night, and that's who vandalized the bowling alley." Skye was starting to put the recent events together.

"Maybe." Ruby squirmed in her seat.

"Who knew you were going to visit Bunny?" Simon asked.

"The only person I told was my fiancé."

"Have you spoken to him lately?" Skye questioned, not liking the way the situation was shaping up.

"Yesterday. I wanted to know how his daughter took the news of our engagement. He told her the day I left Las

Vegas, and I hadn't been able to catch up with him to find out her reaction before then."

"And he hadn't told anyone where you were?" Skye chewed her lip.

"No." Ruby paused. "Well, he gave his daughter this phone number so she could call me, so we can get to know each other, but he didn't tell her where I'm at."

"Maybe she told someone?" Simon suggested. "It isn't that hard to get a location if you have a phone number."

"There'd be no reason for anyone to even question her."

Simon shrugged. "So where are the disks?"

"It's best if you don't know." Ruby got up and straightened the material of her top. "I'll give them to Agent Dodd tomorrow morning, and that will be that." She smiled at Simon. "See, problem's solved."

Chapter 12

Misery Loves Blondes

"Did you know about Ruby and the FBI before today?" Skye asked Bunny as they worked setting up the egg-dyeing stations.

Skye, Simon, and Bunny had discussed whether or not they should shut down the bowling alley and cancel the Easter-egg hunt, but finally made up their minds to go through with it. Bunny had clinched their decision by pointing out that a bad guy among the kids would stick out like a librarian at a book burning.

"Some of it." Bunny had been subdued since hearing what Ruby had told Skye and Simon. "I'm glad Sonny Boy had to leave. He was making me nervous pacing around here and grinding his teeth."

Simon had reluctantly returned to the funeral home. Ruby had agreed to stay in the apartment until she turned over the disks the next morning.

"Did Ruby tell you where she hid the disks?" Skye probed.

Bunny paused and looked over the station she had just set up. Each one would hold five kids and a teen supervisor. Each child would get to dye four eggs.

"No." Bunny moved on to the next table. "And I didn't ask her. Asking too many questions is what gets you into trouble."

The women worked in silence while Skye considered what Bunny had said. Finally she said, "Why didn't you tell us about Ruby's predicament?"

"It wasn't my story to tell." Bunny put her hands on her hips. "What you don't understand is that I've lived a really different life than you have. Las Vegas is like no other place on earth, and the rules are different there. You learn pretty damn fast to mind your own business, and be awful careful about who you try and help, because there's no quicker way of making an enemy than doing someone a favor." She gave Skye a half smile, and then went into the kitchen to get the eggs the cook had been hard-boiling all morning.

Skye contemplated what Bunny had said as she finished setting up the last dyeing station and went over to check on the prize table. Once again, Simon's mother had proven she was far from the airhead she pretended to be.

A deep voice yelling, "Ho, ho, ho," broke into Skye's musings, and Charlie strode into view. He held a purple Easter Bunny costume out in front of him.

Skye hurried up to him and kissed him on the cheek. Laughing, she said, "Uncle Charlie, where did you get such an elaborate costume? It looks like it could walk and talk all by itself."

"I rented it from a place in Chicago."

"Well, it's terrific, but the Easter Bunny does not go 'ho, ho, ho.'"

He frowned. "Well, what does a rabbit say?"

"Nothing. The Easter Bunny just nods and smiles and hands out prizes."

"You mean you ladies talked me into wearing this stupid outfit and it isn't even a speaking part?" Charlie pretended to be upset, but the twinkle in his blue eyes gave him away.

Bunny came out of the kitchen, put down the tray of eggs she was carrying, and walked over to him. "There are other compensations." She took his arm, tugging him toward the storeroom. "Let me show you the present Ruby brought me."

Skye felt her cheeks flush, remembering the objects that had gotten Ruby into trouble when the blonde first arrived in town.

She checked her watch. "The kids will be here in half an hour." Bunny and Charlie walked away without acknowledging her words. Skye called after them, "Don't forget Frannie and her crew will be here any minute, so keep it G-rated."

The teenagers arrived just as Skye started to get the refreshments ready. They pitched in, and as they all worked

Skye went over their duties one more time. "Each of you is in charge of five kids. Miss Bunny and I will be available if you need help with anything. After the eggs are dyed, take your group into the basement. We've got three games for you to play with them. Try and give us at least thirty or forty minutes to hide the eggs before you bring them back upstairs. Everyone with me so far?"

They all nodded.

"Great. Once they come back upstairs, hand them each a little basket and let them start hunting. There'll be the regular eggs they dyed, and also plastic eggs with slips of paper inside indicating prizes ranging from a chocolate bunny to the grand prize—a bicycle. Try to make sure all of the children find at least one plastic egg. Understand?"

More nods.

"Okay. Let me show you the games we set up in the basement." Skye led the teens to the stairs.

They encountered Bunny as she came out of the store-room. The redhead's hair was mussed and her makeup smeared. She waved at the kids and said to Skye, "I'll be right back. I want to freshen up and see if Ruby needs anything. Charlie is changing into his costume."

"Good." Skye looked at her watch. "We'll unlock the door in five minutes, so don't be long."

After the tour of the basement, Skye led the teens back upstairs and to the entrance. There were already twenty or thirty kids and their parents waiting outside. As soon as Skye unlocked the door they dashed inside, and Frannie and her team snapped into action, registering kids, taking coats, and separating them into groups.

Skye made her way through the crowd, reminding parents to pick up their kids no later than five.

The last parent had finally left when Bunny rushed over to Skye, took her arm, and pulled her aside, frantically whispering, "Ruby's gone! The apartment's been ransacked, and there's blood all over."

Skye felt her chest tighten. "I'll call Simon and Wally. You go ahead with the hunt."

Bunny looked torn.

"There's nothing else we can do right now. We have a hundred kids here, and we can't tell them to leave. Most of their parents dropped them off and they're here alone."

Bunny nodded and pasted a smile on her face, turned to the kids, and said, "Let's go have some fun."

Skye made the calls. Simon was stuck at the funeral home, but Wally said he'd go directly up to the apartment. He also said that one of his officers would be at the bowling alley soon to keep an eye on things while the children were there.

She thanked him and went back to the party.

Everyone seemed to be having a good time. Skye dealt with the small emergencies that popped up, like broken eggs and fights over the red dye, but otherwise things were running smoothly.

By three thirty, all the kids were in the basement playing games, and Skye and Bunny were hurriedly hiding eggs.

They finished just as the first wave of hunters crested the stairs. Skye checked her watch. Where was Uncle Charlie?

She said loudly, "Maybe the Easter Bunny is feeling shy today. Let's all call his name to make him feel welcome. Ready? One. Two. Three."

"Easter Bunny!" the kids shouted together.

Nothing.

Skye smiled at the kids, but there was a line of worry between her eyes. "One more time."

"Easter Bunny!" the kids shouted again.

Nothing; then after a long moment the storeroom door burst open and the Easter Bunny hopped out. The kids went wild and the hunt began.

A half hour later, all the kids had prizes and the parents started arriving to pick them up. By five thirty the kids and parents were gone and the cleanup had begun. Wally had come down from the apartment after everyone left and said that he had called out all of his officers to look for Ruby, and he had the county sheriff's department processing the crime scene. If they didn't find her soon, Wally would call the FBI.

After Wally left, Skye paused in gathering discarded candy wrappers from the floor and asked Bunny, who was wiping tables, "Have you seen Charlie since he made his appearance as the Easter Bunny?"

The redhead stopped in midswipe. "No. Maybe he can't get out of the costume. It looked complicated."

Skye stood. "I'll go check. It's been at least an hour

since I've seen him. Surely he'd have come for help if he
needed it."

Bunny followed her. The storeroom was dark, and when
Skye switched on the lights she gasped. Charlie was duct-
taped to a chair with a gag in his mouth.

Chapter 13

Blondes of a Feather Flock Together

Skye cradled the receiver between her ear and shoulder as she straightened the rental shoe racks. It was six P.M. Friday night and the lanes were full. "Mom, as I already told you in our previous hundred phone calls, Charlie's fine."

"Are you sure?" May demanded.

"Yes. The guy held a gun to him and duct-taped him to the chair but didn't hurt him." Skye repeated what she had been telling her mother every time May called. "Hey, I've got to go. I haven't talked to Bunny yet, and I need to check and see if things are ready for tonight's Marilyn Monroe look-alike contest. 'Bye." Before May could answer, Skye hung up and headed downstairs.

"Oh, my gosh." As Skye entered the basement, she stopped dead in her tracks and gazed at the sea of Marilyns. There were Marilyns of all shapes and sizes crowding the room. A half a dozen dressing tables had been set up in the middle of the space, so the impersonators could add the finishing touches to their costumes before making a grand entrance when it was their turn to go onstage. Several battles over the use of the mirrors were currently in progress.

Bunny fought her way through the throng and clutched Skye's arm. "Ruby's still missing, and that FBI agent was here this morning demanding the disks."

Skye steered Bunny to the side of the room. "Did he search the place?"

"Well." Bunny's gaze slipped from Skye's. "Not exactly."

Skye felt the urge to shake Bunny until whatever she was hiding popped out. "What do you mean, not exactly?"

"I . . . uh . . . you see, I sort of knew where they were, so I gave them to him."

"What!" Skye's roar caused an ocean of blond heads to turn in her direction. She bared her teeth in what she hoped resembled a smile, and motioned to them to go back to getting ready. "You told me you didn't know where Ruby had hidden the disks."

"No. I told you Ruby didn't tell me where she hid them, not that I didn't know where they were hidden."

Skye took a deep breath to stop herself from strangling the woman. "Where were they?"

Bunny grinned. "In the ceiling of the ladies' room. I figured she stashed them there the day she got here when she was hiding from Wally."

"But Simon looked there, remember?"

"He was looking for a large woman, not a small white envelope that blended in with the tiles." Bunny smiled smugly. "I, on the other hand, knew what I was looking for."

Skye shook her head. There was no use in being upset with Bunny; she just marched to a drummer most people couldn't even hear, let alone keep step with. "Now that the FBI has the disks, I wonder if they'll still help look for Ruby."

"Damn!" Bunny's expression was stricken. "I'm so stupid. I shouldn't have given them to the feebs. They aren't going to care what happens to someone like Ruby now that they got what they wanted."

"That's not what I meant." Skye put her arm around Bunny and squeezed. "Of course you should have given the FBI the disks. It was the right thing to do."

Bunny didn't look convinced, but she let the subject drop and asked, "Any news from Wally?"

"No. He said Officer Quirk saw the guy who tied Charlie up and stole the Easter Bunny outfit leave dressed in the costume, but he thought it was Charlie. Ruby wasn't with him at the time."

Bunny's nails dug into Skye's flesh. "Charlie's really okay, isn't he?"

"He's fine." Skye thought she would scream if one more

person asked her that. "It's too bad he didn't get a good look at the guy, but Charlie said he wore a cap, sunglasses, and a bandanna over the lower part of his face."

Bunny nodded and Skye turned to leave as one of the Marilyn look-alikes tapped the older woman on the shoulder. "You said I could go first, but that lady with the baby insists she's first. It's essential that I be first. I'm doing Marilyn before she was discovered."

Baby? Skye glanced in the direction the Marilyn had pointed and saw a woman who had dressed her infant in a satin gown and put a tiny blond wig on its head. Skye sure hoped the child was a girl.

Before Bunny moved away to settle the dispute, she said, "What I don't understand is how Charlie's attacker got into the bowling alley without being seen by someone."

"The only thing I can think of is that he came in with the kids and parents, and we just assumed he was someone's dad. I figure he slipped into the storeroom to hide, was surprised to find Charlie there, and after he tied him up he saw the costume and decided that would be a good way to search the place without anyone being suspicious of a stranger poking around." Skye narrowed her eyes. "In fact, I think he's been here every night this week, dressed in various outfits and looking for those disks, or trying to get to Ruby."

The prestar Marilyn had been joined by a Marilyn dressed in a white halter dress, its skirt somehow wired into a permanently flipped-up position. They were both tugging on Bunny, trying to get the best spot in the show.

Bunny shook them off. "You're right. He was probably the guy in the gorilla mask, and the Elvis impersonator. The creep even won two prizes. When he's caught, I want those back. He's disqualified."

Skye grinned. Trust Bunny to see a different slant to things.

A Marilyn in a slinky evening gown pushed the other impersonators aside and grabbed Bunny. In the trademark breathy Marilyn Monroe voice, she said, "Some son of a bitch stole my lip gloss. Call the police."

Skye shook her head and edged over to the stairs, escaping the mad Marilyns before Bunny got her involved in the case of the missing makeup.

The bar was already full. They sure were making a lot more money than usual on drinks and food this week. If the FBI didn't shut them down for harboring Ruby, and the Las Vegas goon didn't burn them out, Bunny's attempt to increase business would be a success.

Skye was checking to see that everything was ready when she heard her name being called. Simon and Uncle Charlie, seated at a table near the front, were beckoning to her.

Skye joined them and said to her godfather, "You don't look any the worse for wear."

"I'm fine," Charlie huffed. "I should have beat the crap out of that punk."

Skye patted his hand. "I'm sure you would have if he hadn't had a gun."

"Damn straight I would."

Before anyone else could say something, Bunny stepped onstage. She had changed into a crocheted dress with fringe trim hanging from the short hem.

Skye tipped her head. Was the dress lined in a flesh-toned fabric, or was that Bunny's skin showing through? Skye glanced uneasily at Simon, who was scowling at his mother's latest fashion statement.

Bunny tapped the mike to make sure it was on, then announced, "Good evening, everyone. Sit back, have a drink, and enjoy the world of Marilyn Monroe."

The lights dimmed, the music from "Diamonds Are a Girl's Best Friend" started, and the first Marilyn appeared to thunderous applause.

Some of the impersonators were good, a couple great, and a few awful, but everyone was having a fine time. Skye had relaxed and was chatting with Charlie and Simon when the sixth Marilyn made her appearance.

Skye stopped in midsentence and turned her full attention to the stage. This one was amazing. The dress, the hair, the makeup were perfect. Even the voice seemed dead-on.

Skye squinted. Everything but the hands was right. They were much too large for a woman . . . and the diamond ring on the right pinkie was obviously not a woman's piece of jewelry.

Oh, my gosh! She knew that ring. It was the same as the one the man at the restaurant had been wearing, the same as that on the comic in the first night's talent show, the same as the one on the Elvis impersonator. It had to be the goon from Las Vegas. What did he do, travel with a trunk full of costumes?

Skye whispered to Charlie, "Did you notice if the guy who tied you up was wearing a ring?"

"Yeah, a god-awful diamond pinkie ring on his right hand. Why?"

Skye nodded toward the Marilyn onstage. "Like that one?"

"Yeah!" Charlie leaped from his seat, thundered up the steps, and tackled the impersonator, yelling, "Pull a gun on me, will you? This'll teach you to treat an old man with more respect."

Chapter 14

Survival of the Blondest

Before anyone could react to Charlie's attack on the impersonator, Bunny came flying from the wings, jumped on the guy's back, grabbed his ears, and started pounding his head on the wooden floor, screaming, "What have you done with Ruby? If you've hurt her, you're a dead man."

The gender-challenged Marilyn's blond wig flew off, soaring into the audience, where two women attempted to catch it as if it were a bridal bouquet and they were the last single females in town. Neither lady made a clean catch, and a tug-of-war ensued, escalating into a wrestling match that both the women's escorts felt obligated to join.

Most of the spectators froze, enthralled with the show, but then someone yelled, "Fight!" and several men rushed the stage, joining in the melee. They might not know what was going on, but they weren't about to miss a good brawl.

Hacker, the bartender, sighed, scooped up his baseball bat, and waded into the frenzy.

At the same time, Skye shot out of her chair, but Simon grabbed her arm as she sprinted past him. "Hold it. You'll only get hurt if you go up there."

"We've got to stop it!" Skye tried to free herself from Simon's grip.

"How?"

That was a good question. There were now at least a dozen men and a couple of additional Marilyns throwing punches and smashing one another over the head with anything available. Skye winced as one guy lifted the karaoke machine and brought it down on another guy's back. Simon was right: At this point, it wasn't as if she could break things up with mere words.

What could she use to cool the combatants off? *Cool off!* That was it. She hastily explained what she needed to Simon, who took off at a run, ducking between clusters of fighters. He quickly found the hose that the cleaning crew used to wash down the cement floor behind the bar and connected it to the faucet back there.

After he had it ready, he tossed the other end to Skye, who turned the dial on the nozzle to "power-wash" and aimed it at the fracas on the stage. She nodded to Simon, who turned the water on full force, and almost instantly a powerful torrent slammed into the fighters.

Ten minutes later drenched people were trooping out the bar door, and Simon, Bunny, and Charlie were tying up the male Marilyn Monroe. Bunny had contributed her panty hose, Simon his necktie, and Charlie his belt to secure the impersonator.

After making sure everyone who was supposed to leave actually did, and that the fighting was not going to start up again, Skye put down the hose and turned her attention to the guy tied to the chair. She poked him in the shoulder with her finger. "The FBI picked up the disks this morning. You're too late, buddy."

"Disks? I ain't after no disks. And my name's not Buddy; it's Lance."

Bunny pushed Skye aside, sloshing water as she moved. "Where's Ruby?"

"Gimme the ring and the letters and I'll tell you where the old broad is." Lance sneered, attempting to look tough but failing. A man wearing a wet evening gown and a nylon stocking on his head loses a lot of his ability to appear dangerous.

Skye looked at Bunny and demanded, "What's he talking about?"

Bunny pushed a sheaf of wet hair from her face, spraying everyone in her immediate vicinity like a lawn sprinkler. "I have no idea. Honest."

"Forget it; he's just stalling," Charlie said to the women, and then hit the kidnapper on the side of the head with his open palm. "Where's Ruby?"

Lance howled. "Police brutality!"

Simon smiled darkly. "Charlie's not a cop. And if you don't tell us where Ruby is, he'll beat it out of you."

Skye thought Simon was bluffing about Charlie's inclination toward violence, but the kidnapper wasn't sure. He eyed the big man, whose fists were clenched and lips were drawn back in a snarl.

"Enough of this." Before Skye, Simon, or Charlie could react, Bunny grabbed Lance by his family jewels and twisted. "Tell me what you did with Ruby, or the next time you sing in the church choir, you'll be a soprano."

The man let out a shriek, then gasped as Bunny tightened her grasp. "Vacant factory . . . edge of town . . . office . . . but she might already be gone." Bunny gasped, but did not release her grip on Lance's privates. "What do you mean?"

"The guy who hired me was sending someone to pick up the old broad. I was supposed to stay behind and get the letters and ring."

"She'd better still be there or you're going to spend the rest of your life as a eunuch." Bunny gave one more twist before letting go; then she wiped her hands on her dress and ordered, "Charlie, you and Sonny Boy stay here with Lance. Skye, get the car."

Skye hesitated, meeting Simon's eyes and asking, "Isn't it time to call the police?"

Before he could answer, a female voice from the doorway said, "Did you all throw a party and forget to invite me?"

"How did you get here?" Lance squeaked, apparently still feeling the effect of Bunny's interrogation methods. Ruby shot him a dirty look and snapped, "You better just shut up or I'll scalp you. You made me miss the Marilyn Monroe look-alike contest."

Lance sneered. "I'm such a better Marilyn than you anyway. You're too fat to do Marilyn the right way."

Ruby huffed. "I do the queen-size version, and I could have mopped the floor with you."

Before he could retort, Bunny ran over and hugged her friend. "Ruby! You're not dead."

"The rumors of my death have been highly exaggerated." Ruby pried herself away from Bunny's soggy embrace. "Why are you soaking wet?"

Everyone began to explain at the same time. Finally Skye managed to get the others to quiet down, and filled Ruby in on the evening's activities. She concluded with, "What ring and letters is he talking about? I thought he was after the disks."

"So did I, at first." Ruby pulled out a chair and sat down. "But it turns out the casino owners didn't send him. My fiancé's son-in-law did."

"Who?" Bunny asked.

"Why?" Skye got right to the point.

Charlie and Simon were silent, perplexed looks on both their faces.

Ruby stared pointedly at the bar. "Someone make me a martini and I'll explain as much as I know."

"Make mine a double and I'll fill in the rest." A tall, handsome man in his sixties stood framed in the doorway.

Ruby leaped out of her chair and threw herself into his arms. "Darling, how did you get here?"

"When this dunderhead kidnapped you, he called my son-in-law to report that he had you. My daughter overheard her husband arranging to send someone to kill you, and she told me everything. I boarded the next plane to Chicago."

Everyone tried to talk at once, and Skye thought she would need to resort to the hose for a second time that day. Instead, she put two fingers in her mouth and let out a piercing whistle. In the ensuing silence she said, "Why don't we just let Mr. . . . ?"

"Masterson," Ruby supplied. "Everyone, this is my fiancé, Archie Masterson."

Skye nodded and completed her sentence, ". . . Mr. Masterson and Ruby tell us everything from the beginning." Skye turned to the blonde and directed, "Ruby, you start from when Lance kidnapped you."

"The kids at the Easter-egg hunt were so loud, and I had a horrible headache, so I decided to sit outside until it was all over." Ruby clung to her fiancé. "When the Easter Bunny came up to me, I thought it was Charlie, but then he pulled a gun and demanded I give him the ring and the letters. I refused and he tore the apartment apart. Luckily I had put the ring and most of the letters in my safe-deposit box before leaving Las Vegas. I managed to slam a lamp across his face, but he didn't drop the gun, and when he couldn't find what he wanted he forced me to go with him."

"That explains the blood," Bunny murmured. "We were worried it was yours."

"Nope. That sucker's nose bled like a stuck pig."

"You almost broke it. If I'm too disfigured to do my act, I'm going to sue you." Lance whined until Bunny made a squeezing motion with her hand.

"Why did he want your ring, and what letters are you talking about?" Skye asked, getting more and more confused. "What act?"

"I'm able to solve the first part of the mystery." Archie smiled, displaying straight white teeth under a clipped gray mustache. "When Ruby consented to be my bride, I gave her the Masterson diamond as an engagement ring. The letters are no doubt from me to Ruby declaring my love and intention to marry her."

Skye was entranced with Archie's slight accent; it wasn't quite British, but what was it? She shook her head. She wasn't going to let his charm distract her from getting the whole story. "And?"

Archie sighed. "And when I told my daughter about my engagement to Ruby, and she told her husband, my twit of a son-in-law was afraid Ruby's rather vivid past would leak out and ruin his chances to become governor of Nevada." Archie's blue eyes twinkled and he winked at Ruby. "What he really should be afraid of is that *my* past might get out."

Ruby swatted him playfully and giggled. "Oh, Archie."

Skye ignored the interruption, intent on getting this whole thing settled once and for all. "So he hired this goon to get back the ring and the letters," she guessed.

"Exactly. They're the only physical evidence that we plan to marry. Once he had them, his next step was to have someone get rid of Ruby. He fooled my daughter into giving him the phone number here, ferreted out Ruby's location, and sicced this cretin on her."

Skye turned to Ruby. "How did you get away from the factory? Didn't he have you tied up?"

"I could have gotten free from the ropes anytime—remember I was married to both a contortionist and a magician—but I had to wait until he left me alone." Ruby shook her head. "Luckily, I was already free and walking down the road when the next thug showed up or I'd be dead right now. I hid behind a tree and watched. The new guy was a professional, and had his gun drawn as he went into the building. He was ready to shoot me."

Archie hugged her as everyone else made sounds of distress.

Finally, Skye said, "There's only one thing I still don't understand."

"What?" Ruby and Archie asked together.

"How Lance just happened to have all the costumes handy to disguise himself all week."

Everyone's eyes turned to the guy tied to the chair. He shrugged. "They're part of my act. I'm not really a crook, but I owed Mr. Masterson's son-in-law a favor, and Mr. Carretti called it in. In my real life, I do a show at the Majestic Casino impersonating dead movie stars."

Charlie grunted, unimpressed. "What are we going to do with this guy?"

"Turn him over to Wally," Skye said firmly.

Lance cringed. "Mr. Carretti's going to kill me."

"Don't worry." Bunny patted his shoulder. "Maybe Wally can put you into the witless protection program."

Skye snorted, not sure if the redhead knew what she had just said. Either way, Skye was glad that school would be starting up again on Monday and that this was her last day working at the bowling alley. Dealing with hormonal teenagers had to be easier than this past week with crazy Bunny and her even crazier friend.

Read on for an excerpt from
Denise Swanson's next
Scumble River mystery

Murder of a Smart Cookie

Coming from Signet in July 2005

Cookie Caldwell died the third Sunday in August, and the Scumble River First Annual Route 66 Yard Sale almost died with her. She had lived in town only a few years, and no one seemed to really know her. This isolation would suggest that no one would have a reason to murder her, but obviously that supposition would be incorrect.

Cookie's death raised a lot of questions. Two of the most puzzling ones were: What had she been doing at the Denison/Leofanti booth in the middle of the night, and how had a piece of jewelry managed to kill her?

For the next week, until the crime was solved, these questions were asked over and over again on the TV news, while a picture of Cookie stuffed into Grandma Denison's old Art Deco liquor cabinet, one hand thrust out as if she had tried to claw her way to freedom, flickered on the screen.

The Heartland TV channel had been on location taping a program about the Route 66 Yard Sale, and thus managed to get exclusive footage of the postdiscovery activities. While the other news stations managed to get a shot of Cookie's body, Heartland's film clip included a group of locals who were ignoring the dead woman and arguing amongst themselves. It was not an attractive depiction of the citizens of Scumble River, Illinois. It was an especially unflattering portrayal of its mayor, Dante Leofanti.

Leofanti's niece, Skye Denison, didn't look much better. Playing tug-of-war with her uncle over Cookie's purse was not the image she wanted to project as the town's school psychologist.

Even though her profession had nothing to do with her

involvement in the mess being broadcasted via HTV into homes across the Midwest, the reporters tended to play up her occupation in their stories. That, and the fact that she had solved several of Scumble River's previous murder cases.

If the journalists had dug a little deeper, they would have discovered that it wasn't her full-time job, but how Skye spent her summer vacation, that had gotten her into the purse-wrestling predicament. However the media tended to focus on the here and now, even though the real story started nearly eight weeks ago, after Skye had already lost two summer jobs and was forced into accepting a third.

The first loss of employment was due to geese with loose bowels and poor toilet habits, and the second was because of her inability to keep her mouth shut. It was too bad that the only job she had been able to keep came with a dead body attached to it.

BLIND SIGHTED

A PSYCHIC EYE MYSTERY

VICTORIA LAURIE

For Laurie Comnes,
whose dedication, support, and
friendship mean the world to me

Chapter 1

As I joined the cattle call to baggage claim, and pushed against the throng of people trudging their way through Tampa International Airport, all I could think was, if Abel was even half the pain in the butt my sister was, he definitely had it coming.

Now, that isn't to say that I don't think Cain should have at least counted to ten, like I was trying to do, but maybe Abel was a meddler, just like my sister. And perhaps, even though Cain had *repeatedly* told him to back off, Abel decided to stick his nose into his brother's business one too many times—thus deserving a good wallop on the noggin after all.

"Abby!" I heard across the lobby.

"Speak of the devil," I muttered as I cocked an eyebrow in my sister's direction.

"Abby!" she repeated, waving at me like a prom queen. "Over here!" I waved back with far less enthusiasm and mumbled, "Seven, eight, nine, ten," under my breath.

Nope. No good. I still wanted to kill her. It didn't really matter that I was angrier with myself for being suckered when I should have known better; at the moment, I was too focused on giving my sister what-for. Squaring my shoulders, I grabbed my blue suitcase and duffle bag off the turnstile and began marching with purpose in her direction. Before I could get to her, however, I smacked right into a pair of bodacious ta-tas the size of cantaloupes.

"Excuse me!" I said as my duffle bag bounced off the cleavage and off my shoulder to land on the floor.

"Watch where you're going!" an angry voice snapped back at me.

Quickly I grabbed my duffel and righted myself, red with embarrassment and wanting to make amends. But as I looked up at the owner of the cantaloupes, I nearly thought better of it.

The ta-tas belonged to exactly the kind of woman who makes my upper lip snarl in distaste. Her hair was blond, a shade of platinum one tint shy of albino, shoulder length, with long bangs that bounced when she blinked her heavily mascaraed eyelashes. She looked to be in her mid to late thirties, with enough collagen, Botox, and silicone pumped into her to make her the next Bionic Woman. Her face was square and angular, except for her lips, which puffed out unnaturally, probably due to a recent injection.

She towered over me by about four inches, but that could have been the red stilettos talking, and she was dressed in a skintight black minidress that showed off legs better kept hidden. The dress was also cut low enough in the front to give the cantaloupes plenty of sunlight—to ripen, I guess.

Snuggled between her cleavage was a huge crystal of the diamond variety, which, because of its gargantuan size, I could only assume was fake, but the Gucci bag on her arm and the mink coat around her shoulders were definitely real. *Good thinking,* I mused, *bringing a full-length mink down to Florida. I mean, who knows when the next Ice Age is going to hit?*

"I'm sorry," I said tightly as the woman stood over me, her hands on hips and those huge fishy lips puffed out in a frown.

"You need to look where you're going!" she barked.

"Okay," I said, reining in my temper. There was only so much of this I was going to take. "Again, I'm sorry about that."

"Mother?" a voice called from behind Fish Lips. "Are you all right?"

"I'm fine, Gerald," she said, turning slightly so that I could see the man who had just walked up behind her.

My eyes widened as he came into view. I would never have guessed in a million years that these two were related. Gerald looked the same age as, if not older than, his mother. He was short, stocky and tubby around the middle. He had dark brown hair, a bulbous nose, and some sort of bright red rash that was making its way along his arms, which were lightly smeared with white cream.

"Are you sure?" he asked, putting a concerned hand on her arm.

"Get away from me with that poison ivy!" she spat at him, and instantly he retrieved his arm.

Ah, now I knew the source of the rash. "Listen," I said to the two of them, "I'm sorry I bumped into you."

"Fine, now move along and get out of my way," she said testily.

Gee, no invite to spend the holidays together? Sheesh.

Just as I stepped out of the way to let her pass, however, I heard a *buzz, buzz, buzz* in the back of my mind. *Oh, crap!* I thought.

"Uh," I stammered as she moved to step in front of me. "Wait a second," I said quickly and thrust out my arm to bar her passage.

With a snarl she regarded me the way you might eye a mosquito right before smashing it into oblivion. "What is it now?"

"Did you just come in from out West, like from California or something?"

"Excuse me?" she asked, looking at me oddly.

"Yes," Gerald said helpfully, "we're from Burbank. Why?"

"Well, this is going to sound really weird to you, but there's something you need to know. You must get back on the plane immediately, and go back to Burbank. There's some sort of danger lurking here for you. I get the feeling that if you stay here in Tampa, there could be grave consequences—someone you know is about to betray you, and you really shouldn't be here."

Fish Lips chuckled humorlessly and said, "You have got to be kidding."

"No," I insisted, "I'm really not. I'm telling you that if you stay here you could be in real danger. Someone you know is waiting to stab you in the back and betray you if you're not careful, and—"

"Oh, don't tell me you're one of *those*," she said, folding her arms and smirking as if she were suddenly amused.

" 'Those'?" I repeated, still trying to sort out the message blipping through my head.

"Psychics," she said, but the word sounded disturbingly more like *psychos* the way she said it.

"Uh, yes," I said hesitantly, "yes, I am. My name is Abby Cooper, and I am a professional psychic, so as I was saying—"

"Forget it, honey," she snapped, cutting me off with a flip of her hand. "If you think this little performance of yours is going to make you a millionaire, you'd better think again."

"I don't understand," I said, furrowing my brow.

"Oh, cut the con. You know who I am," she said.

"I'm afraid I haven't the slightest clue," I replied, but now that I looked at her, I thought she did look a little familiar.

"Sure you don't," she said with a sneer. "Well, let me assure you that the Ballentine Fund will not be awarded to a scam artist like you. Celeste Ballentine wasn't born yesterday, sweetie, so take your little song and dance and go try some other sucker." And with that she clicked her high heels together and walked away, leaving me to blink in surprise at her derriere.

"Abby?" My sister's voice sounded into my ear, causing me to jump.

"Oh! Hey, Cat," I said, forgetting my earlier irritation with her and bending to give her a quick hug.

"Who was that?" she asked, pointing to Celeste and Gerald.

"Have you ever heard of Celeste Ballentine?"

"Was she that cynic we saw on *20/20* a couple of months ago who's offering the two-and-a-half-million-dollar reward for absolute proof of psychic phenomena? The one blabbing on about how every psychic out there is a con artist and there's no way she'll ever have to award the prize money?"

"That'd be the one," I said, marveling at my sister's remarkable memory for names and details. "My intuition went haywire when I bumped into her, so I tried to pass along the advice."

"What did you tell her?"

"I told her to get out of Dodge and go back the way she came."

"Really? How'd she take it?"

"All things considered?" I said, watching as Celeste walked through the double doors to the outside and into the back of a cab. "Pretty well."

"I see," Cat said, a small grin forming at the corners of her mouth. "That's all you brought?" she asked me, pointing at my small suitcase and duffle bag.

"Yeah."

"Well, grab them and let's go. Our driver is waiting for us outside." And Cat turned to lead the way through the crowded airport.

I picked up my bags and began following her, belatedly remembering that I was furious, but her pace and the crowded airport weren't the best conditions under which to open up a can of whoop-ass. I'd have to wait until we got to the car.

Watching the two of us wind our way through the airport, you'd be hard-pressed to guess we're siblings. My sister, Catherine, is tiny, something like five-foot-nothing, with a frame that's thin, bordering on skinny. She wears her hair short and messy, like Sharon Stone's, and it complements the fragile features that frame her enormous light blue eyes. Her clothing often hides the fact that she's so petite, and her sense of style can be described in one word: *expensive*. She prefers couture to practical, and because she often takes advantage of the talents of a very good stylist, it's not until you're standing next to her that you notice you're looking down. Her size and femininity, however, are at complete odds with the tiger she can become in the boardroom. You can bet the farm that Cat has never been underestimated—at least not twice, that is.

Her success dates back to several years before, when Cat came up with a brilliant marketing idea that sold huge and made her a ton of money—which she now spends like water. She currently lives on a sprawling estate in a suburb of Boston, where she still holds court at the now megasize corporation she started.

As for me . . . well, I've got six inches on Cat, with roughly the same build but broader shoulders and longer legs. My hair is very long, reaching just past my waist, and I wear it straight and simple most of the time. I'm brunette by nature—but helped along by Clairol—and I prefer the jeans-and-a-T-shirt kind of attire my sister wouldn't be caught dead in.

Professionally we're even more different, divergent paths started years ago when Cat was pursuing an MBA at Harvard, and I'd settled for a BA in finance from a local university, and ultimately a modest career in banking. I'd left that field about three and a half years ago to launch a stint as a professional psychic. Even as a child I'd had a natural propensity for picking up things about strangers that I couldn't possibly know beforehand, and when I reached adulthood the ability just became too obvious to ignore.

While what I do for a living may be unusual, I genuinely like the work, and in my own way I feel more than satisfied with my career. I have a small office in the town where I live, Royal Oak, Michigan, and a three-month waiting list for a clientele I've built solely by word of mouth. I work five days a week, and see about six clients a day. I'm not wealthy per se, but I am very happy to be making a living in a relatively easy, low-stress way.

As we reached the exit and walked through the double doors out into the warm, slightly humid atmosphere, I drew in a deep breath, filling my lungs with as much fresh, tropical air as they could hold. I then closed my eyes, tilting my face to the sky, and felt the weight of a long winter melting away with the burst of sunshine greeting my pale northern skin. "Ahhhhh," I said exhaling, "that's the ticket."

My eyes were still closed when I felt someone gently lift the handle of my suitcase out of my hand, and, startled by the movement, I opened my eyes to a tall Hispanic man dressed in black suit coat and slacks, his head sporting a chauffeur's hat.

"This is Juan," Cat said, noting the surprise on my face. "He'll be our driver to the Seacoast Inn."

Juan tipped his hat at me and walked my luggage to the open trunk of a long, black stretch limousine. "Do you do *anything* economy?" I asked my sister, looking at the decadence of our transportation.

"Oh, please, Abby," my sister said, rolling her eyes. "If you can afford to go first class then by all means, *go* first class," she finished, as Juan opened the car door for her and waited for both of us to get in.

Once the limo pulled away from the curb I was reminded about the whallop I owed my sister, so I began subtly with, "This is really wonderful of you to arrange a nice, restful, relaxing three-day getaway, Cat. I'm really looking forward to just doing nothing but lying on the beach and lazing the next few days away."

My sister squirmed uncomfortably in her seat and began to pick imaginary lint off of her slacks.

"I mean, it's just been work, work, work for the past couple of months, and this is going to be such a nice breather for me. Three days where I don't have to do anything even remotely psychic, just sand, surf, and sleep . . ."

"Okay, okay, so you know," Cat said, looking at me with a face that suggested she wasn't the least bit sorry.

"You mean about the huge psychic seminar going on in the very same hotel we are about to check into? No, don't know a *thing* about it," I said sarcastically.

"How'd you find out?"

"I met a lovely little old lady on the plane who was clutching 'famed psychic' Deirdre Pendleton's latest book like it was the family Bible and gushing about all the festivities Deirdre was hosting at the Seacoast Inn this weekend."

"So I wanted to surprise you," Cat replied, avoiding eye contact. "Where's the harm in that?"

"Do you think I'm stupid?!" I said, raising my voice an octave. "The only reason you arranged this little getaway, Cat, was so you could continue to hammer the publicity campaign at me."

"Well, can you blame me? I mean, Abby, you're so talented, and no one even knows about you!" she insisted, using the same tired argument she'd used on me so many times before. "I just thought if you came down here and took Deirdre's seminar and saw what having a national audience can do for your career, you might be inspired to branch out and use some of Deirdre's techniques to get your own name on the map."

"That's just it, Cat," I spat, losing all patience with her. "I don't *want* to be on the map. I am happy with my career just the way it is, thank you very much, and I don't need to do work while I'm on vacation!"

"Who said anything about making you work?" Cat

pressed. "I merely invited you to listen. You don't have to perform, Abby. No one even has to know you're a psychic. All I'm asking is that you sit through at least one seminar, and if you're not impressed, then fine; I'll join you on the beach and we'll never speak of it again."

I sat quietly for a moment, silently smoldering. It irked me that she'd found a compromise I could definitely live with. I didn't want to let her off the hook that easily. But after a minute or two common sense prevailed; after all, she'd paid for the entire weekend, and all I had to do was sit through one stinking seminar. "Fine," I said grudgingly.

"Really?"

"Whatever," I answered, rolling my eyes. "When's the first seminar? I want to get this over with as quickly as possible."

"That's the spirit," my sister said sarcastically. "Deirdre's first seminar is tonight, and dinner is included."

"Yippee," I said flatly.

"Abby," Cat said sternly, "are you going to be this much of a pain in the butt all weekend?"

"Depends on how much of this stuff you drag me to," I answered, still irritated.

Cat sighed loudly and reached for the door to the small refrigerator in the back of the limo. She pulled out a plastic pitcher of iced tea and poured us each a glass, handing me one before filling the other. After she'd put the pitcher away she turned back to me and asked, "So how's the house hunting going?"

"Funny you should ask," I said, taking a sip of tea and struggling to let go of my residual anger. "My Realtor called me right before my flight and said that there's a house listed in the neighborhood I like, and the price tag fits my budget." For the past several years I'd been squished into a thirteen by ten studio apartment, and after diligently saving my pennies I finally had enough to venture into the big grown up world of home ownership.

"Meaning there's something wrong with it," Cat said.

"No," I said getting defensive again, "not necessarily. It's listed as a handyman's special, but my real estate agent insists it's got lots of potential. I'm going to take a look at it next week when I get back home."

"A handyman's special?" Cat asked, looking at me doubtfully.

"What?" I asked, taking offense. "I'm handy!"

"Right," Cat said, hiding a grin. "Well, my offer still stands to help you out financially. I don't know why you're settling for dilapidated housing when I'm more than happy to make you comfortable."

"Thanks, but I really want to do this on my own."

"Have it your way. Say, how's Theresa? Did you have fun at the wedding?" she asked me, referring to my best friend and business partner.

"She and Brett are enjoying their honeymoon, and yes, the wedding was wonderful. They'll be back late next week. Oh! And get this! Some television producer heard about her and wants her to come out to California for a meeting!" Theresa was an exceptionally gifted medium—the kind of psychic whose expertise is connecting the living with the dead.

"You know," Cat started, "if Theresa could teach you to do that whole 'I see dead people' thing, you'd have Hollywood producers calling you too."

"Thanks for pointing that out, but it's either an ability you have or you don't, and I'm in the 'don't' category. So if it's all the same to you, I think I'll just stick to my particular forte of predicting the future."

"I'm just saying—"

"Oh, look!" I said pointing out the window, desperate to change the subject. "There's our hotel!"

Chapter 2

Our limo rounded the large circular driveway of the Seacoast Inn and came to rest next to a gigantic water fountain spraying water ten feet in the air. As Juan held our door open and Cat and I exited, a little of the mist coming off the fountain caught on the wind and peppered my upper arm with cool refreshment.

As our driver got our luggage out of the trunk I looked around at the scenery and began melting into the surroundings as I felt my shoulders relax and the tension ooze out of my taut neck muscles.

Our hotel was a large, beautiful affair with giant palm trees framing the six-floor building of white brick and tinted windows. Balconies jutted out in neat little rows along the top five floors, and several guests could be seen taking in the view from on high.

The driveway was flanked by several gardens of tropical trees, and flowers like hibiscus, jasmine, gardenia, oleander, and bougainvillea all mixing together in a gorgeous cacophony of hot pinks, yellows, purples, and oranges, while a symphony of sweet perfumery scents dazzled my nose.

Off to the side I could see the coastal waters of the Gulf of Mexico, and sighed contentedly at the soothing sound of surf meeting sand and the smell of salt lightly scenting the air.

When I'd had my fill of the outdoors, Juan led us inside, carefully maneuvering the revolving door of the front lobby as he carried our luggage, which was an odd mixture of Louis Vuitton meets Rubbermaid. Once inside, Cat walked slightly ahead of me as my eyes ogled the lobby, which dazzled with its mixture of lush tropical flowers, huge skylights, overstuffed furniture, and simple white marble floors. While my sister checked us in I was free to wander around and get familiar with the layout.

I found the hotel to be a simple rectangular structure with a large dais lobby bubbling out like a Buddha belly at the building's base, with two one-story wings jutting off to each side. I walked over to the right wing first to see what was down that hallway, and took in the signage that the hotel's restaurant was at the end of the corridor. Heading over to the left wing I saw more signage indicating that the convention halls were on this wing. To one side I noted a large poster with Deirdre Pendleton's black-and-white photo welcoming patrons to her three-day seminar, which would begin promptly at six this evening.

I ran an eye down the itinerary for the event and held back a groan. Each topic heading was preceded by a big gold star and the list began with dinner and an introduction by Deirdre for that evening, followed by such fun times as "Meet your spirit guide!" or "What your angels want from you!" and, of course, "How to lead a more fulfilled life!"

I couldn't help but notice that after each individual seminar there were twenty-minute intervals where "Deirdre's Fairyland Magic" books, tapes, cards, clothing, crystals, and jewelry could all be purchased; Visa, Mastercard, and American Express accepted.

Oh, boy.

After shrugging my shoulders, I moseyed back over to the lobby and resisted the urge to whine to my sister about having a perfectly good vacation ruined by sitting indoors at some boring psychic convention. My disappointment was compounded by the spectacular view of the ocean I found off to the right of the check-in counter as a crystal-white beach and azure-blue ocean beckoned my bikini-clad bottom for a little sit-down time.

Lured by the beauty of the beckoning surf, I walked over to the beach entrance and was staring out the window when a door to my right opened and the sound of splashing and children at play caught my attention. Curious, I walked over to the other door and peeked through the windowpane. A large pool complete with waterfall and huge deck peppered with lounge chairs called alluringly to me. I gawked at all the people sunbathing and relaxing or playing in the pool, and my shoulders slumped. God, I wanted to join them.

"Ready?" Cat asked, suddenly appearing beside me and attempting to hand me a room key.

"Huh? Oh, yeah . . . ready," I said smearing a huge plastic grin on my face the way I did when I was little and my parents announced a vacation to historical Gettysburg, Virginia. *Yippee-friggin'-yee.*

I followed after Cat as we headed to the elevator and waited beside two other women who looked like they'd just gotten off a Grateful Dead tour. Both women were dressed in wildly colored tie-dyed cotton dresses, with bangles on every possible appendage. They wore no makeup, their hair was long and stringy, and each had a rather dreamy smile on her face that made me wonder if they'd just chowed down on an entire batch of "happy brownies".

While we were waiting for the elevator Cat and I checked out the Peace Sisters, who were alike enough to be twins, and they, in turn checked us out, and suddenly an almost palpable air of hostility seemed to permeate the space between us, for reasons I really couldn't name. When the elevator doors opened, the girls pressed "2" and Cat pressed "P" after inserting her card key into a little slot on the control panel. The twins studied the movement, and the dreamy smiles turned snide as they gave each other a knowing look. The exchange made me bristle slightly, and I moved protectively closer to my sister.

We didn't have to put up with them for long, as a few moments later the double doors opened and the girls quickly stepped out. Cat elbowed me in the arm and said, "Gee, and I was going to invite them to dinner."

I chuckled and added, "And I was going to ask them for some fashion advice."

Cat flashed me the peace sign and we both rolled our eyes. By that time we'd reached the top floor, and the doors opened to a brightly lit hallway with pink floral wallpaper and rose-colored carpeting. Cat looked at the signage and nodded her head toward the right. We walked down to the end of the corridor, then came to a stop in front of a double door with a plaque that read, PRESIDENTIAL SUITE, and Cat swiped her card key through the control panel to the right.

The door clicked and she pushed it open, and I caught my breath as we traversed the threshold.

The suite was enormous, at least fifteen hundred square feet covered in thick white Berber carpeting and dreamy velvet furniture of a soft moss green. I walked into the sitting area and ran my hand across the top of one overstuffed couch and smiled at the ticklish texture while eyeing the rest of the room. Across from the seating area was a large bar, complete with top-shelf liquors and mixes, a blender, and a refrigerator that I assumed was filled with some type of delicacy.

All along the far wall were sliding glass doors that opened up to a gorgeous terrace. One of the sliding doors was already open, and a warm breeze fluttered the linen curtains and carried the scent and sound of the ocean only a few hundred yards away.

I drifted outside and onto the terrace and stood gripping the railing and squinting into the sunshine of the day as I watched the waves roll in and seagulls hover on currents of air. I took a seat in one of the lounge chairs and allowed a most satisfied smirk to plaster itself onto my face. *This is the life,* I thought.

A little while later I heard a blender at work, and within a few minutes Cat had joined me out on the terrace, where she took a seat next to me and handed me a glass of frozen margarita.

"I hope you don't mind if we bunk together; this was the only suite on this floor still available," Cat said.

"Oh, I'll make do," I said dramatically, adding a sigh for effect as I took a huge swig of margarita and marveled at my sister's bartending skills. I noticed she had changed out of her silk suit and into a pair of linen pants and a knit top. "Did our luggage arrive from downstairs?"

"Yes, I put yours on your bed. You can change whenever you're ready."

"Cool! You want to hit the beach?" I said excitedly, jumping up from the chair ready to rush down to the beckoning sand.

"Uh, no," Cat said, holding out her wrist and pointing to her watch. "We won't have time. Deirdre's dinner seminar begins in an hour."

I glanced at my own watch and moaned. This was gonna stink. I took my chair again and pouted for a good ten minutes before I asked, "So what's for dinner?"

"Sea scallops or chicken, I think," Cat said, tilting her face to the sun.

"I hate sea scallops," I grumbled moodily. "And the chicken will probably be overcooked."

"That's what I love about you, Abby, your positive attitude," Cat said dryly as she leaned back in her lounge chair and closed her eyes.

I scowled at her and stuck out my tongue, punching the plastic straw into my drink testily. I waited for Cat to continue the conversation, but she seemed content to quietly soak up the sun for a while, so I drank the rest of my margarita; then went inside to unpack and change.

I entered the bedroom, which was large and splendid, with light rose-colored comforters topping two queen-size beds layered with soft cotton sheets. After unpacking my clothes I walked my toiletries into the bathroom and couldn't help saying, "Wow," out loud.

The bathroom was extravagant, with a large Jacuzzi tub, enclosed shower, and, next to the toilet, a bidet. Good for getting sand out of those hard-to-reach places, I guess.

Once I was finished unpacking I went back into the bathroom and looked longingly at the tub. It had been a long time since I'd been in a Jacuzzi. I glanced at my watch again and decided I had time for only a quick shower, and even that was pushing it.

I rushed through the shower and combed my hair, thinking I'd just leave it down and au naturel for the evening. I changed into a pair of black cotton slacks, a sleeveless coral-colored blouse, and black sandals just before Cat came looking for me.

"Abby? You ready to go? We don't want to be late," she said, poking her head into the bathroom.

"I'm just putting on some mascara," I said as I tucked the tube back into my makeup case and turned to follow her out of the room.

We exited the suite and walked the hallway to the elevator, where Cat pressed the down button. While we were waiting I asked, "So how long is this little soiree supposed to last tonight?"

"Three hours," Cat answered.

"*Three* hours? What the hell is she going to talk about for three whole hours?"

"Well, there's an hour-and-a-half lecture, then an hour and a half of audience readings."

"Audience readings?" I asked, perking up.

"Yeah, according to the information sheet, Deirdre is going to cruise the audience and give out messages to people."

"Hmmm," I said thoughtfully. Even though I wasn't interested in the topical portion of the evening, it still might be cool to watch another professional at work. I mean, maybe she had a technique I could use for my own clients.

Just then two more people joined us in the hallway. I turned to my right as they came into my peripheral vision, and caught my breath. Standing right next to Cat was the same buxom blonde and her son whom I'd met at the airport. Quickly I ducked my head, hoping Celeste wouldn't recognize me and lavish me with another taste of her frosty attitude.

To my relief the elevator doors finally opened, and I followed Cat into the boxcar with head bent and eyes on the floor. Celeste was too consumed with inspecting her manicure even to acknowledge us, and I was grateful that we would probably make this descent in silence.

One floor down the elevator stopped, and the doors opened onto a small group of hotel guests. As the first in the group stepped forward, I did a double take when I realized Deirdre Pendleton was about to stand right next to me. Although I'd never seen her in person, it wasn't hard to recognize her as the woman from the picture on the signage downstairs.

Deirdre was taller than I expected, close to five-ten by my estimate. She had light, wavy brown hair with small traces of gray streaming through the blend. Her face was deeply tanned, and lined more than it should have been for a woman her age. Her eyes were dark green, and her features fine and feminine. She wore a long, flowing gown of canary yellow belted by a gold cord about her waist that billowed when she moved. The cut and style of the gown reminded me of something out of the Middle Ages.

She was flanked by a tall, balding man in a tweed blazer

and with beady little eyes, and two women who bore a striking resemblance to the Peace Twins my sister and I had encountered earlier in the day while waiting for the elevator. They also wore tie-dyed dresses, with bangles and sandals, and kept their eyes adoringly on Deirdre.

As I stepped to the side to make room for Deirdre and her entourage, I watched as she took two steps forward, then snapped her head in the direction of Celeste and abruptly stopped.

"Deirdre," Fish Lips said, inclining her head with a malicious grin.

"Celeste," Deirdre said in a way that made you think the name left a nasty aftertaste. "My spirit guide told me you'd be here."

Liar, liar, pants on fire . . .

I cocked my head slightly as the playground chant sang through my head. One of the odd talents I have is something like an inboard lie detector. Whenever I'm within hearing distance of a lie, the chant pops into my head. I consider the skill a terrific perk when it comes to negotiating the price of a new car, or taking a check from a client. It was interesting to hear that even though she covered it well, Deirdre was shocked to find Fish Lips in the same hotel.

"*Really?*" Celeste replied, "*Did* he now?"

"Yes, and Great Wind Talker also said that I was not to acknowledge your existence," Deirdre said as she backed right out of the elevator, folded her arms, and waited for the doors to close.

As the doors shut, Celeste turned to her son and let go a sharp, hard laugh, as if someone had just told her a very funny joke. Gerald flinched at the sound but forced a smile to his lips as he nodded his head in agreement. The entire exchange between Deirdre and Celeste was so odd that Cat and I looked at each other as if to say, "Huh?" but in the next instant the elevator began moving again and we were headed back down.

When we reached the ground floor, Celeste pushed her way off first, and Cat and I held back as she and her son departed at a clipped pace. "What was that about?" Cat asked when they were out of hearing range.

"I have no idea, but that woman," I said pointing at Celeste's back, "shouldn't be here."

"Why? What do you mean?"

"I'm not sure, just that every time I'm near her these alarm bells go off, like she needs to get on a plane and head home—pronto."

"Didn't you already try telling her that?"

"Yeah, but that doesn't mean that I can just turn off the message."

"Well, maybe we can talk to Deirdre after her seminar. I mean, I'm sure she's had plenty of experiences like this before. Maybe there's a way she can tell you to turn it off if the person won't listen?"

I bristled slightly at my sister's suggestion. "Cat, just because she's famous doesn't mean she's better at the whole intuitive thing than I am."

"I'm not saying she is, Abby. Jeesh! Don't get so defensive."

Just then Cat and I reached the entrance to the hall where Deirdre would be speaking. A small line had already formed, and just in front of us I spotted the same little old lady I'd met on the plane who'd filled me in on the weekend's festivities. Her back was to us, so as Cat and I stepped into line, I tapped her lightly on the shoulder.

"Oh! Hello, there, Abby, isn't it?" she asked, turning around.

"Yes, good memory, Millicent," I answered her warmly. Although Millicent had talked mostly about Deirdre and her excitement about the weekend, I still genuinely liked the woman, finding her to be sweet and endearing. "Cat, this is Millicent Satchel; we met on the plane this afternoon."

"How do you do, Millicent," Cat said, extending her hand. "I'm Abby's sister, Catherine Cooper-Masters, or Cat for short."

"Hello, Cat," Millicent said, switching the now dog-eared copy of Deirdre's book from one hand to the other so that she could shake hands. "Are you a fan of Deirdre's too?"

"Let's just say I have a very open mind about all of this," Cat answered. "And that is a lovely suit you're wearing," she added, referring to Millicent's light blue attire with a pink blouse and a matching corsage pinned to one lapel. The ensemble matched her perfectly coiffed, short, curly hair that was also a subtle shade of blue.

"Why, thank you," Millicent said, beaming at my sister from behind huge bifocals. "I wanted to look my best for Deirdre—I'm even wearing blusher tonight," she confessed in a whisper.

I smiled at the pair of them, because in forty years I imagined that Cat would probably look very similar to Millicent. The two were even close in height, with my sister having a slight edge in her three-inch heels.

"Do you think Deirdre will have time to sign my book after the seminar?" Millicent asked us.

"Oh, I'm sure she'd make time for you, Millicent," Cat answered with a smile. If I knew my sister, I was sure she'd make it a point to get Deirdre's attention for an autograph signing.

Just then the line shifted, and a man with a clipboard approached the three of us. "Are you all together?" he asked.

"Oh, no," Millicent said. "I came alone; here's my registration," she added, pushing a neatly folded piece of paper at the usher. The man took Millicent's ticket and checked it against his clipboard, then motioned for her to follow him into the large dining hall.

A minute later he was back for us, and Cat handed him our reservations. We then followed him into the large hall.

When we were inside the grand room I was a little startled at the quantity of tables set out for the event. There must have been close to thirty tables, with six place settings apiece. I didn't know what the plate price was, but by the sight of the linen tablecloths and fancy swan-folded napkins, I assumed it must be a pretty penny.

The usher led Cat and me to the front of the hall, arriving at table number one, which was front and center to a raised platform where Deirdre would be speaking. I wondered how Cat had managed to get us the best seats in the house, but then smiled at my own naïveté. Cat used money like a gunslinger used a six-shooter, and she was quick on the draw when she wanted her way.

We took our seats and were soon joined by two more

guests. A couple took their places across from us, and Cat and I smiled gamely at them. They looked to be in their late forties and were at that point in their marriage where they had begun to look alike. Both of them had rounded features, with apple-red cheeks and plump figures. Their clothing and jewelry indicated they had some cash, and I began seeing how the seating arrangement had been worked out for the evening.

To confirm my suspicions I turned to my sister and whispered in her ear, "How much did it cost to get a seat up front?"

My sister looked crossly at me and said, "Oh, Abby, for God's sake. I'm not letting you pay me back, so just relax—"

"No," I insisted, "I'm just curious. I want to know what this table cost as opposed to one in the back."

"Oh, well, in that case it was five hundred dollars a person, as opposed to two-fifty for something in the middle, and I think about a hundred in the back."

My jaw dropped and hung there. Finally I sputtered, "You are *kidding* me!"

"No, it's the truth," she said. "*Now* do you see why I want you to take notes? This is a very lucrative business if it's done right."

I scowled distastefully. This entire setup was really starting to bug me, and I felt the beginnings of something sinister seeping into my bones.

A short time later we were joined by the man in the tweed jacket I'd seen flanking Deirdre, and one of the Peace Twins from our first elevator ride. When the two joined us they nodded briefly at all of us, then occupied their time looking over the rest of the crowd joining the event.

Before long our waiter appeared and took our orders. I opted for the chicken, while Cat gamely went with the scallops. Our drinks and salads arrived, and Cat and I talked about mutual acquaintances and other members of our family. Even though we talk every day, Cat and I never seem to run out of things to say to each other.

Finally, just after our food arrived, Deirdre walked into the long hall and through the crowded room to thunderous applause. I clapped politely and watched her take the stage, forming her hands into a steeple and bowing demurely at her adoring fans.

"Thank you," she said humbly as the applause began to wane. "Thank you all so much, my brothers and sisters, for joining me on this spiritual journey here in beautiful Clearwater, Florida."

As I cut into my chicken—which was, in fact, over-cooked—I noticed out of my peripheral vision about a dozen women flanking the sides of the room, all wearing tie-dyed dresses and jingling with bangles. The way they all gazed adoringly at Deirdre made me a bit squeamish, and I looked around at the audience to see if anyone else took notice. Everyone seemed transfixed by Deirdre, who was launching into her speech.

"So what I will talk to you about tonight is my own spiritual journey and all the wonderful gifts that have resulted from my experience as an internationally renowned psychic.

"My journey began some twenty years ago, when I was in college pursuing a Ph.D. in psychotherapy. One day while I was walking to class, a man wearing a black mask and hold-ing a gun stepped in front of me and demanded my purse.

"Now you can imagine my terror as I looked at this thief, willing to do anything he said as long as he didn't shoot me, when all of a sudden I heard a loud, distinctive male voice call my name. It was so loud and clear that I thought someone had come up from behind me to rescue me, but when I turned to look, no one was there. The voice spoke again, and this time he said, 'Deirdre, listen to me and you will not be harmed.'

"Meanwhile, the mugger was growing impatient with me, because as I was listening to the angelic voice, I forgot to hand over my purse, so the thief again waved his gun at me, threatening to shoot me, and reflexively, I started to hand over my purse. But just as I was giving it to the mugger, the voice shouted in a thunderous tone, 'No! Deir-dre, do not hand over your purse!'"

The audience gasped as Deirdre imitated the detached voice. "So," she continued, "I said, 'Well, what am I sup-posed to do then?' And the voice said, 'I am Great Wind Talker, and I am your spirit guide, and you must do as I say!'"

I stopped eating my food and pushed my plate aside, my appetite gone. All around me people were hanging on Deirdre's every word, waiting for her to tell them more about this "Great Wind Talker," while in my head all I'd heard since Deirdre began her story was, *Liar, liar, pants on fire* . . . And I knew, well before Deirdre talked about hitting the mugger with her purse and knocking him out, and the appearance of an angel-like figure who claimed to be her spirit guide and set her on the path to deliver heavenly messages to all the world, that Deirdre Pendleton was a complete and total sham.

The more she talked the more disheartened I became. Her story was rife with the overly fantastic and illusionary, angels, fairies, and Indian spirit guides appearing before her and giving her messages to deliver in her books and writings. There seemed to be no end to her abilities, as she took credit for predicting the last presidential election, the war in Iraq, and the fall of the Twin Towers. I couldn't help but notice that she offered no proof to back up her claims, as the constant drum of, *Liar, liar, pants on fire,* beat dully in my head.

I glanced over at my sister, knowing there was no way she could be buying this, but to my astonishment Cat sat slack-jawed during Deirdre's speech, and her eyes seemed to widen as every tale grew bigger and more fantastic.

Finally, just about the time I was looking for something sharp and pointed to impale myself on to put an end to my misery, Deirdre switched topics and said that her newest mission was to take some of her "flock" to the Hawaiian Islands to visit a vortex that allowed the emergence of spiritual beings to pass freely from one plane of existence to another. She said that there were only a limited number who would be able to attend the retreat, but the first one hundred to pay the ten-thousand-dollar fare would be guaranteed a reservation.

Around the hall the rainbow-clad women, who were obviously Deirdre's assistants, moved into action, handing out flyers and brochures about the Hawaiian trip to everyone in the room. When a brochure was handed to me, I promptly handed it back and gave a pointed scowl to Cat as she held her hand out to accept the flyer. "What?" she asked as my scowl deepened when she took the pamphlet.

"There is no way you're going, Cat," I said with a hiss.

"Why?" she whispered back, and I noticed the man in the tweed jacket to my right quickly turn his beady eyes in my direction.

"I'll explain later," I said, and pulled the pamphlet from her hand, folded it in half, and put it underneath my plate of half-eaten chicken.

After we'd all had time to peruse the Hawaiian trip, Deirdre claimed to be ready to read the audience. She held out her arms dramatically, and the twin sitting next to Tweed Jacket jumped up and joined her sister onstage, where they each held one of Deirdre's arms and assisted her down the steps.

It was so over-the-top that I wanted to vomit right there: Deirdre swaying slightly as she mimicked a trancelike state, and her two attendants steadying her like servants as they descended the stairs. For a moment she stood at the bottom and eyed the audience, her eyes going unfocused as she seemed to concentrate, and then, with deadly precision, she turned her attention directly on Cat. Motioning to her two attendants, she fluttered over to our table, her gown billowing softly as she walked, and flickered to a stop when she came directly in front of my sister and smiled wisely down at her.

Cat was caught a little off guard as a spotlight turned on, illuminating her to the audience as Deirdre asked her to stand. My sister complied, and one of the twins shoved a microphone into the space between Cat and Deirdre.

I watched with disgust as Deirdre exaggerated her movements, enhancing the belief that she was spiritually charged as she closed her eyes, putting her hand on my sister's shoulder and asking, "What is your name, dear?"

"Catherine."

"Ah, yes," Deirdre said, her voice all breathy and dramatic, "Great Wind Talker told me there was a C connection to your name. Now, Catherine, I see an older female figure standing over here," she said as she waved at an area just over my sister's left shoulder, "and she says she loves you very much and she's glad that you came to visit her when you were a child. She says she was petite, just like you, and that she loved to bake cookies. Does this sound familiar to you?"

"Oh, brother," I said to myself, and rolled my eyes.

"Uh . . ." My sister said thinking hard. "It could be my grandmother?"

"Yes!" Deirdre practically shouted. "Yes, it is your grandmother, and she's nodding her head acknowledging that. And to her side is an older gentleman who says that he loves you very much as well and he's so proud of you, and he says he's glad that you made a recent decision . . . did you recently make an important decision?"

I rolled my eyes again at all the generalities spewing out of Deirdre's mouth, but the audience begged to differ with my opinion, as all around me people sat slack-jawed and gawking as if they were witnessing the Second Coming.

"Uh, it could be a new product line I'm launching for my business?" Cat supplied, unsure what Deirdre was looking for.

"Yes! He's nodding his head, Catherine, and saying that's it. And he's also talking about a nickname you had as a child. Did you have a nickname when you were little? Maybe something he called you?"

"Uh . . ." Cat thought.

"Yes, he's insisting there was a nickname that he called you when you were little," Deirdre pressed, nodding her head at my sister while her two attendants mimicked her agreeably.

I could see Cat growing uncomfortable at the pressure to recall an imaginary nickname that never existed. "Well . . ." She hesitated, and then, in an instant, Deirdre's demeanor shifted, and she abruptly dismissed her.

"Well, I'm sure you'll remember it later," Deirdre said tightly, and pointed my sister back to her chair.

As Cat took her seat again, her face flushed with embarrassment for not having remembered an imaginary nickname, Deirdre moved on to the portly man sitting across from us. For some reason I felt the need to turn my intuition to the "on" mode, and as he stood I pointed my radar at him and began assessing his energy.

"Now, what is your name?" Deirdre asked as she placed her hand on the man's shoulder.

"Stanley," he answered obediently.

"Ah, yes, and people call you Stan, don't they?" Deirdre said knowingly.

Stanley nodded, eager to cooperate, and Deirdre continued: "Well, Stan, Great Wind Talker is telling me that you are a very successful man."

"Uh-huh," Stan acknowledged.

"And he is also telling me that you are about to close a rather large business deal," Deirdre said.

"Really?" Stan asked, his hopes rising.

"Yes, and this will bring you even greater success. More than you've ever had before," Deirdre said.

Stan was near bursting with excitement as he hung on her every word. "Really?"

"Yes, it's the truth. It has something to do with a contract. Do you work with contracts, Stan?"

"Uh, well, I own my own company," Stan offered.

"Yes, that's it. That's what your guides are saying. And your guides want you to celebrate, Stan; they want you to take your lovely wife on a vacation—someplace warm and tropical. They're telling me that both of you should go someplace wonderful to kick back and celebrate the success that's coming your way. . . ."

"Maybe we should go to Hawaii with you?" Stan offered.

Deirdre smiled benevolently at him and said, "Yes, I feel that is a good fit for you and your wife. Just remember there are only a hundred seats available, so why don't you see my associate, Mr. Hamilton, here, and he can sign you up?" Deirdre suggested, indicating Tweed Jacket to my right.

Stan nodded his head, so happy to have such fantastic news, and as he took his seat I began to seethe with rage. What I picked up from Stan was far different from what Deirdre had indicated, and the harm she was inflicting on these trusting people was making me fume.

Deirdre then turned her attention to the table next to ours, and I recognized a familiar face. Even before she got there, I knew Deirdre was going to pick Millicent Satchel as the next contestant on *The Price Is Right,* and sure enough, like a wolf to a sheep, Deirdre made a beeline to the sweet old lady.

"Would you stand up for me, dear?" Deirdre said, her voice dripping with honey.

Millicent popped up quickly, so excited she was shaking and still clutching her book. "Would you tell us your name?" Deirdre asked.

"I'm Millicent Satchel, Miss Pendleton, and I'm such a huge fan of yours!" she gushed in a voice cracked with age and quaking with excitement.

"That's sweet of you to say, Millicent. Now the first thing I'm seeing is a large crowd of people standing behind you and waving at me. These people claim to be your friends and family who have already crossed over into heaven," Deirdre said.

"Oh?" Millicent asked, already a small line of doubt crinkling her forehead.

"Yes," Deirdre said confidently, "and they're saying they love you and they are holding your place beside them. And one of them is talking about knitting; does that make sense to you?" Deirdre asked.

"Knitting?" Millicent questioned, her brow furrowing even further.

"Well, maybe it's needlepoint, or crochet—someone you knew used to love to needlepoint or knit, didn't they?"

Millicent thought long and hard and finally said, "Why, yes! I have a cousin who likes to knit hats for her grandchildren."

Deirdre nodded her head knowingly and said, "Yes, they're saying that's correct, it's your cousin they are talking about. Has your cousin's health been bothering her lately?" Deirdre asked.

"No, not that I know of," Millicent said, trying hard to make all the square pegs fit the round holes.

"Well, tell your cousin that her family wants her to watch her health and get plenty of exercise," Deirdre said.

"But she's in a wheelchair," Millicent said.

Deirdre opened her eyes and smiled at Millicent, already finished with her and beginning to turn away. "Well, see? Then she does have some health problems."

As Deirdre began to turn away, Millicent urgently tugged on the gown and asked desperately, "Oh, Miss Pendleton, please, can you just tell me about my Harold?"

Deirdre's smile returned full wattage as she came back to Millicent and dramatically placed her hand on the older woman's shoulder. "You want to know about Harold?"

Millicent nodded vigorously up and down. "Yes, please! I just have to know if I made the right decision in moving on to Jack."

Deirdre nodded wisely and closed her eyes. Concentrating as she took deep exaggerated breaths, she finally said, "All right, I see him. I see Harold, and he is telling me that he doesn't hold anything against you, and he knows that you had to move on and find love with someone else. He's glad that you're taking care of yourself and that this other man seems to be just what you've been looking for. He says that you should marry this man and that the two of you will care for each other until your dying days. . . ."

Millicent gaped at Deirdre, her face a furrow of utter confusion as Deirdre talked on and on about Jack and Harold, and just about the time that Deirdre was describing the upcoming nuptials I'd had more than enough. Fueled by my own anger I stood up so fast that my chair fell over backward, clattering to the floor and startling the room. I was enraged at the load of crap spewing out of Deirdre Pendleton's mouth, and I couldn't take it one more nanosecond. *"Oh, for crying out loud!"* I shouted.

The entire audience gasped at my outburst, my sister the loudest among them, but I didn't care. Deirdre's eyes snapped open as my voice reverberated off the walls. Quickly I used the stunned silence to my advantage as I walked around the table to point an accusing finger at Deirdre and her entourage. "She wants to know about her frigging *dog,* you miserable fake!" I shouted. "Harold was her *dog,* and Jack is her new *dog*! Millicent's husband is still *alive,* right, Millicent?"

Millicent nodded dumbly as I continued to rattle off my own impressions of her energy, which I had been gathering since she stood up for Deirdre. "Millicent, you did make the right decision. Harold was a little white fluffy dog, right?"

"Yes! He was a bichon frise!"

"And he had some sort of liver problem, didn't he?"

"The vet diagnosed him with liver cancer," Millicent confirmed, her eyes growing misty, "and I just didn't want him to suffer anymore . . ." she added, dabbing at her eyes.

"Well, the feeling I have is that Harold is in a better place, and you did the right thing by putting him to sleep. Jack, however, is getting too fat, and you need to stop spoiling him with so many treats. Also, your husband needs to come home from the golf course and fix that leak under the sink."

"Oh, my goodness!" Millicent gasped. "My husband *does* play too much golf, and we *do* have a leak under our sink!"

I sneered at Deirdre, who was watching me in horror; then I quickly turned to point at the man from our table whom Deirdre had ordered to take a twenty-thousand-dollar vacation. "And you, Stan, is it?" I asked.

Stan nodded hesitantly, watching me with wide eyes.

"Your company is in major financial trouble, and you have a little problem with the IRS, don't you?"

Stan's face turned slightly pink, but he obliged me by nodding vigorously.

"Well, here's my advice; your lawyer is a female with blond hair, right?"

Stan sucked in a breath of surprise and said, "Yes, yes, she is!"

"Well, I hate to tell you this, but the woman is crap as lawyers go, and it's time to kick her to the curb, 'cause she's charging you an arm and a leg and she doesn't know what the hell she's doing. There's another lawyer, a man in his thirties—like thirty-five-ish—who can really help you negotiate a better deal with the IRS, and save your company from going under. There's a connection to a family member here too. Has anyone in your family—a female, like maybe a sister—suggested using their attorney?"

"Yes!" Stan said, jumping to his feet. "My sister used a lawyer friend of hers to help her with her business, and he's just like you describe. She's been after me for months to give him a call, but I kept hoping that my current attorney could work it out."

I nodded at Stan and quickly moved on to the next topic for him. "That's great; give him a call. Now, you also have an employee who's been stealing from you. I'm guessing that the books are totally screwed up, and you don't know where your money is, am I right?"

"Yes!" Stan said.

"Okay, this employee has a connection to a motorcycle, and I think it's red. He either has a model of it on his desk or he owns a red motorcycle. . . ."

"Oh, my God!" Stan sputtered as his wife gasped and

clutched her chest. "Our comptroller has this model of a red motorcycle on the shelf in his office. He's always going around telling everyone how he's saving up to buy a real one!"

"I see. Well, there's something up between your accounts and this man, and you need to investigate the matter—pronto. Your business will survive, and that's important for you to know, but *no way* should you and your wife be spending money frivolously on vacations to Hawaii. Am I clear?"

Stan nodded his head vigorously and leaned over to shake my hand as the room erupted in applause. Just then another hand gripped my upper arm like a vise, and I turned to see Tweed Jacket clutching me tightly as he turned to the crowd and declared, "Thank you so much for that demonstration, miss! One of Deirdre's protégés, everyone! Isn't she wonderful?"

The room again erupted in applause, and before I knew it, I was being escorted through the dining hall in the direction of the entrance. "Hey!" I hissed as we neared the door. "Let go of me!"

"Your money will be refunded to you, as your invitation to the rest of the lecture has been revoked," the man hissed in my ear, and before I could say "boo," we were outside. the hall doors and I was pitched roughly forward with a shove as the man brusquely disappeared back into the hall, slamming the double doors behind him and leaving me to look blankly about.

For a minute I thought about pounding on the doors and making a ruckus, but after counting to ten—twice—I decided to walk away with my head held high. I turned on my heel and harrumphed my way down the narrow corridor, thumbing my nose at most of the vendors waiting hungrily for intermission and the chance to sell their crystals, charms, and snake oil to any gullible attendee.

When I got to the end of the corridor, I stopped and waited for Cat to come barreling out of the hall after me. I pictured her giving Deirdre and her people a little whatfor at my less than courteous removal and stomping out of the hall to join me in support, but as I stood at the end of the hall, tapping my foot impatiently, she failed to appear.

I thought about just heading up to our room, but the

card key was in my purse, which was still back in the dining hall, so I had no choice but to wait for my sister. The longer I waited, the angrier I became, so, to distract myself, I looked around for something to do. It was then that I noticed a display just off to my right that seemed to be slightly removed from the rest of the vendors. Curiously, I read the sign tagging the display that read: TEST YOUR PSYCHIC IQ!

Behind a table sat a woman with carrot-red hair and freckled skin who ogled me with interest behind enormous horn-rimmed glasses as I surveyed her exhibit, which was mostly comprised of three computer monitors hooked up to a central P.C. and accompanying chairs. What can I say? Curiosity got the best of me, so I moseyed over. Nodding to Carrot Top as I sat down in front of one of the terminals, I put my hand on the mouse, and clicked the button that read "Start."

The screen flashed from black to blue, and across the monitor five cards aligned themselves up in a neat little row at the top of the screen. The caption at the bottom read, *Find the picture behind the card!* After pausing with the cursor for a moment I clicked on the fourth card over from the left. I was instantly rewarded with a picture of a chocolate fudge sundae loaded with sprinkles and a big fat cherry accompanied by the words, *A perfect hit! Great job! Please try again!*

"Okay," I said aloud, as I smiled and waited for the cards to line up once more. I played this little game for a few minutes and made it through two trials of twenty-five, missing twice the first trial and only once the second. Midway through the second trial the redhead came up behind me and watched curiously as I clicked my way to the end.

When I was finished with the second trial I looked back at her and was taken aback by the woman's expression. Her mouth was hanging open, and her eyes had grown even bigger behind the glasses.

"You're amazing!" she whispered breathlessly.

I flushed slightly, a little embarrassed by the way she was looking at me, and smiled sheepishly in return. "This? Aww, this is nothing. Just luck, really."

"No," she said shaking her head vigorously. "It's nearly impossible for it to be luck. That's why I've designed this test this way. According to your results," she said, taking

the mouse from me and clicking at the bottom where the
button for "results" was, "it's nearly mathematically impossible for you to have done so well based solely on chance."

I looked to where she had clicked and saw that the odds
against my performing so well were right around four bazil-
lion to one. "Well, it's not that hard once you get the hang
of it," I offered.

"Try this one," Carrot Top said, and made a few clicks
with the mouse to another test. This one displayed a small
blue square, and the instructions indicated that I was supposed to click on the place where a little red dot would
appear. I focused for a moment, swirling the mouse in a
circular motion before choosing a spot and clicking in the
bottom left corner. Instantly a little red bull's-eye appeared
just a fraction to the right of my blue dot. I cleared the
screen and tried again, this time clicking in the upper right-
hand corner, and was rewarded with an almost perfect hit.
I played this game through twenty-odd more trials, and
allowed Carrot Top to click on the results again. I was
surprised to see that I'd performed even better on this test,
the odds against chance being in the six-bazillion-to-one
range.

"What's your name?" Carrot Top asked in a voice growing bolder with excitement.

"Abby Cooper," I said, extending my hand by way of
introduction.

"Zoë Schmitt," she said, grasping my hand and holding
on tightly. "Listen, you're the best I've ever had take these
tests. I would love to study you. Do you think we could
set up a time this weekend for a little more testing?"

My response was less than enthusiastic. As a rule, I try
to avoid being a human guinea pig. "Well, I really came
here to avoid work, if you can believe it. . . ."

"What kind of work do you do?" she persisted, sitting
down next to me, her interest piqued.

Her intensity was starting to give me the creeps, and
nervously I looked to the hall door again, silently cursing
Cat for taking so long. "Uh . . . I'm a psychic."

"*Really?* That's wonderful! Listen, I know it's a huge
imposition, but I've spent the past ten years researching
and cataloging psychic phenomena, and, to put it bluntly,
I've been waiting for someone just like you to come along.

If you could just spare me an hour or two, it would really help my research—"

Just then the double doors of the hall opened and out stormed Fish Lips, her giant boobs dribbling like basketballs as she stormed by us, her clothing torn, dirty, and disarrayed, and her platinum locks tossed and frenzied, while her son hurried to catch up to her as he pleaded, "Mother, please! I had no idea she would attack you like that! Really! I'm sorry!"

Zoë and I stood transfixed by the scene as the two brushed past us, followed by a massive wave of seminar attendees streaming out the door, chattering excitedly as they exited the dining hall. Somehow, in all the confusion, I still managed to spy Cat, and while Zoë's attention was turned to the crowd I sneaked off and made my way over to her.

"What the heck's going on, and *where* have you been?" I demanded as I took my sister by the arm and tugged her to one side, out of the flood of people.

"Oh! Abby, there you are!" Cat said brightly, her eyes merry with excitement. "I was hoping you'd be close by."

"Why didn't you come out after me?" I said, the hurt ringing slightly in my voice.

"I was about to, but as I got up to follow you I noticed that my diamond tennis bracelet had fallen off my wrist again, and while I was looking around the table for it, Celeste Ballentine—you know, that woman we saw in the elevator on the way down—took advantage of the situation you created and jumped right up onstage! And, that's when the show *really* began!"

"Ohhh, tell me," I said excitedly, finding a sofa in the lobby for Cat and me to sit down on.

"Well!" Cat began. "It's a shame you left so quickly, because things really got good the moment you disappeared."

"It wasn't exactly like I had a choice in the matter," I reminded her.

"Yes, yes." She waved at me, wanting to get to the juicy part. "After you left, the audience was just stunned. They were all looking around wondering what had just happened, and Deirdre was simply standing there looking at her manager and the audience, trying to decide what to do. Meanwhile, I couldn't find my bracelet, so I was just about to duck under the table to see if it had fallen there—remind me to report it to hotel security by the way; I couldn't find it anywhere—when Celeste Ballentine walks out onstage like she owns it, and a spotlight turns on her as she introduces herself and starts telling the audience all about Deirdre and her checkered past!"

"No way!" I exclaimed, and for just a moment I felt sorry for Deirdre Pendleton. "Go on," I encouraged.

"Well, Celeste started talking about what a fraud Deirdre is. She had a long list of affidavits from people who had gone to Deirdre for a reading and swore that nothing Deirdre had predicted had come true—and one woman even claimed to be *suing* her! I guess Deirdre told this woman that she absolutely *had* to quit her job of twenty years, mortgage her house to the hilt, and start her own dot-com, where she'd be very successful within a matter of months. So the woman follows Deirdre's advice, and right around the time the woman gets her name on the NASDAQ, the entire bottom fell out of the dot-com industry and she ends up in foreclosure and bankruptcy!"

"Get out!" I said, a chill spreading to my neck. As a psychic, I am extremely conscious of boundaries that are *never* appropriate to cross. Telling someone to mortgage their house, quit a steady job, and throw caution to the wind to become an entrepreneur was just so careless and stupid that, if it were true, Deirdre deserved to get the pants sued off her.

"Yes, and there were several other stories just like it, Abby," Cat said shaking her head back and forth.

"So what did Deirdre do?" I asked.

"Well, for the most part she just stood there mutely with her eyes lowered and her cheeks flushed, and then when Celeste talked about the lawsuit, she started to cry a little. And then I guess she got so angry that she jumped up onstage and threw herself on top of Celeste!"

"You're *kidding*!" I said, slapping my knee, chagrined that I'd missed it. Although I'd never admit it to anyone, at heart I'm a true-blue WWF fan.

"No, really! The two of them were rolling around onstage, punching and pulling hair and hitting each other! It was wild!"

"You're talking about the catfight?" a feathery voice off to our right asked.

Cat and I turned at the sound of the voice and saw Millicent Satchel standing close by, looking at us with interest.

I beamed a smile at Millicent and moved over on the couch, patting the cushion next to me and offering her a spot. After Millicent shuffled over and sat down, she turned to us and asked, "You were talking about Deirdre and Celeste?"

"Yeah, I can't believe I missed it!" I said.

"Well, it's a shame that two grown women have to settle their differences that way, but if you ask me it's just too bad that Deirdre didn't get her ass kicked after all the harm she's caused!"

Cat and I both gasped at Millicent's outburst. It seemed She wasn't quite as sweet as we had assumed.

"Excuse my French," Millicent said sheepishly, noting our expressions, which made both Cat and I burst into a fit of giggles.

"Millicent, you are too funny!" I said companionably, giggling some more.

"Well, it burns my toast that I've been so gullible all these years, buying her books and telling all my friends what a wonderful person she is, when all this time she's been pulling the wool over my eyes. I feel like such a fool."

Cat and I quickly stopped smirking, concerned by the sudden change in Millicent. "Don't be so hard on yourself," Cat offered. "We were all taken in. I mean, the woman does a great job of marketing herself. And I think we all really want to believe in things that give us comfort, like angels and spirit guides. In fact, if it weren't for Abby, here, I doubt I'd be as spiritual as I am, and that would mean that something very important would be missing from my life."

I beamed at my sister. Sometimes Cat said absolutely the right thing. "Yes," Millicent agreed, "I suppose you're right. That's a good perspective, Catherine."

"Thank you," Cat said, and squeezed Millicent lightly on the shoulder. "You know what, ladies?" she asked us, jumping up from the couch. "All this excitement has made me hungry. That dinner they served was pathetic. Why don't we all go up to my suite and order room service?"

"Music to my ears," I said, jumping up too and helping Millicent to her feet.

"Oh, but before we go I need to report my missing pocketbook to the hotel's lost and found," Millicent said.

"You lost your pocketbook?" I asked, something tickling the hairs on the back of my neck.

"Yes," Millicent said, bobbing her head. "I had a small antique pocketbook in the shape of a seashell that I use on special occasions like tonight. There wasn't really anything in it, but when I stood up to leave I noticed it wasn't where I thought I'd left it on the table next to me. It was my mother's from a very long time ago, and I'd be crushed if I never got it back," Millicent said sadly.

"That's weird," I said. "Cat lost her bracelet tonight too."

"Oh? It must be something in the air then," Millicent said gravely. "Come on, Catherine; we can report our missing things together."

After Cat and Millicent had reported their lost items, we made our way over to the elevators, and Cat depressed the "up" button. While we were waiting, someone came up behind us, and we all turned to look. My eyes became slits when I realized it was Tweed Jacket, Deirdre's manager, looking rather disheveled himself, as if he'd been caught in the middle of a windstorm.

As we stared pointedly at him, he avoided eye contact for a moment, then sneaked a quick glance in our direction. He must have recognized me, because in the next moment he turned with a scowl and stomped off.

The way he stormed away made the three of us laugh in spite of ourselves, which caused Tweed Jacket to quicken his step as he paused only slightly before ducking into the hotel bar.

A few minutes later we were in Cat's suite with the room service menu out and the blender whirring another round of my sister's famous margaritas. As I wrote down everyone's food orders, preparing to call room service, it dawned on me that the weekend wasn't going to be a total wash after all—now that there were no more seminars to attend, I could look forward to two days of sun, surf, and relaxation. When my left side felt thick and heavy, my sign for "no," I barely noticed, mostly because I wouldn't know how wrong that assumption would be for several more hours yet.

Chapter 3

By two in the morning I was exhausted. Cat had thrown in the towel around one A.M., but Millicent showed no signs of slowing down, and out of sheer politeness I stayed up with her, listening to her unfold her seventy-three years from start to finish. The three rounds of margaritas had gone right to my head, but seemed only to make Millicent more lucid. Through her colorful stories, Cat and I had learned all about Millicent and found her to be an extraordinary woman with an interesting past and an intelligence that belied her rather old-fashioned appearance.

When my head began bobbing forward and my drooping eyelids made it apparent that it might be polite for Millicent to stop talking, she patted my arm gently and got to her feet. "Listen to me, going on and on about myself when it's well past your bedtime, young lady," she said kindly.

Acknowledging her point I rubbed my tired eyes and stood up with her, stretching as I said, "No, really, I've enjoyed getting to know you." A yawn escaped from my tired frame.

"You're a kind woman Abigail Cooper and, if I might add, an extraordinary psychic."

"Thanks," I said, smiling broadly. It suddenly meant a lot to have Millicent's approval. "Can I walk you back to your room?"

"Oh, no, dear, I couldn't impose. Besides, I'm in the mood to go for a walk along the beach before I turn in."

My face turned down in a small frown. I didn't like the idea of Millicent walking along the beach by herself. It was dark outside, and who knew what nefarious type could be wandering around out there just waiting for someone vulnerable to come along?

I stood up straight and popped my eyes wide open, shaking the sleep out of them as I announced, "You know, a walk on the beach sounds like just the ticket! Mind if I join you?"

Millicent chuckled softly and replied, "Abby, you're exhausted, and I've spent a lot of years taking good care of myself. I'll be fine. You go on to bed now . . . I insist."

My shoulders slumped; I really *was* tired, but felt dutybound to take care of Millicent, so I pushed back and said, "No, no, I'm fine, really. I'll take a short walk with you—"

"Oh, you'll do no such thing," Millicent said firmly. "Now go on. Go to bed. You look exhausted, and I've kept you up far too late. I'll be fine; don't you worry."

I looked at her skeptically, my responsible side pushing me to do the right thing and make sure she got back to her room safely. But my entire body was yawning for sleep. In the end, Millicent gave me a look that said she meant business, and the fear of offending her by insisting I come along won out, so I settled for walking her to the door with the promise that she wouldn't walk off hotel property, and she promised to be careful.

As the door closed behind me I limped my way to the bedroom and dove headfirst into the pillows, kicking off my sandals and not bothering to change into pajamas as I sighed deeply and curled into a fetal position.

I closed my eyes and was just drifting off to sleep when my intuition buzzed loudly in my head. Annoyed, I ignored it and squeezed my eyelids tightly closed. *Buzzzzzzzz!* it called again. *Buzzzz! Buzzzzzz! Buzzzz!* my intuition demanded.

What?! I shouted inside my head, thoroughly annoyed.

Go find Millicent!

You've got to be kidding me, I said in my head.

Go find Millicent! my intuition shouted.

"Crap," I said aloud, and rolled to a sitting position, the urgent feeling to run down to the lobby and find Millicent pushing my exhausted frame off the bed.

In the dark I fumbled for my sandals, shoving them on, then stumbled toward the door, remembering to grab the card key. Quietly I made my way out the door and down the corridor to the elevator.

The hotel was oddly quiet at this time of night, a stillness settling over the building that seemed strange given the level of activity that I'd observed over the course of the day. Groggy with exhaustion, I pushed the elevator's "down" button and waited with my head resting against the wall. I was going to give my guides what-for if this turned out to be a false alarm. When the doors finally opened and I got in, I felt the tug again to find Millicent quickly. The urge was filled with intense alarm, and it sent a small jolt of adrenaline through me, waking me like a double shot of espresso.

By the time the elevator reached the lobby my foot was tapping anxiously on the floor, and even before the doors had opened wide enough I'd pushed my way out, glancing quickly around for any sign of Millicent. I rushed through the entrance hall looking this way and that, taking in that the room was empty and no clerk was sitting at the front desk. I darted around the side of the lobby, heading down the left corridor, in the direction of the beach.

Just as I got to the French double doors leading to the beach I felt an intuitive tug to go to my right but ignored it, my anxiousness to find Millicent pushing me to move quickly. I shoved open the doors and found myself on a small patio that led to a set of stairs winding down to the beach. I paused on the patio, swiveling my head left and right, scanning the beach for any sign of Millicent. Luckily, a full moon hung brightly over the gulf, illuminating the sand in silvery shadow, but as I squinted into the distance, searching for Millicent's small, bent frame, I couldn't see anyone making their way along the water's edge.

The longer I stood there the more anxious I became. What if I'd come too late? What if she had fallen into the water and the tide had taken her? Quickly I rushed down the stairs, but with each step I had the feeling I was going in the wrong direction. Again I paused at the bottom and searched the beach with my eyes, trying to see any movement in the darkness.

Anxiously, I took two hurried steps forward, when all of the sudden a bloodcurdling scream pierced the darkness like a knife. I jumped three feet at the sound and screamed a little myself, scared silly by the noise.

The outburst had come from behind me, up the stairs and to the right of the way I'd come. Without pause, I scrambled back up the stairs and tore back through the double doors. Instinctively I knew who had screamed, and I was in a complete panic to rush to Millicent's aid.

As I burst through the entrance, however, I nearly crashed headlong into her, and stopped just in time to catch her as she fell into my arms, white with fright and covered in blood. With shaking limbs I lowered her carefully down to the ground, searching for the wound that was bleeding so profusely.

"Millicent!" I said to her huge eyes and pale face, "tell me where you're hurt!"

"Oh, God!" Millicent moaned, and crossed her arms over her chest protectively. She was visibly shaking, and this only intensified my fear.

"Millicent," I said again, trying to lower my voice into a tone of forced calm, as I began to feel along her arms and body, looking for the source of the blood. "Look at me, honey! Tell me where you're hurt!" I pleaded.

Just then I was joined by a wild-eyed night clerk, who looked like he'd just been jolted awake trying to comprehend that he wasn't still dreaming. As he reached us he quickly bent down and asked in a shaky voice, "What happened?"

"I don't know yet, but we need to call for an ambulance—"

"She's . . . she's . . . she's . . ." Millicent interrupted as she pointed behind her with one bony, shaking finger.

"What, honey?" I asked, wanting to keep her talking and thinking it was a good sign that she was still conscious.

". . . *dead!*" she gasped, and the night clerk and I both stared first at her, then at each other, and finally in the direction Millicent was still pointing.

"What?" I asked, a chill growing at the base of my neck and working its way down my spine. "What did you say?"

"Out there," Millicent said, swallowing hard and trying desperately to collect herself. "She's dead out there. . . ."

I looked again in the direction Millicent was pointing and suddenly noticed the dark splotches of red on the tiled floor leading from the pool and marking Millicent's footsteps to my arms.

I turned to the night clerk and barked, "Call nine-one-one!"

The clerk—a kid really, probably not a day over nineteen—didn't move, but stood stock-still as he stared transfixed by the red footsteps leading from the pool.

"Yo!" I shouted into his ear, jolting him to look at me. *"Go call nine-one-one!"*

This time the command spurred him to action as he jumped up and ran back to the check-in counter.

Gingerly I got Millicent to her feet, then carefully moved her over to the couch and sat her down. I swallowed hard as I looked at her pale face and blood-soaked clothes; then, carefully, I asked, "Millicent, how did you get so covered in blood?"

Millicent was looking toward the door she'd just come out of, her eyes out of focus as the memory of what had happened out by the pool played behind her eyes. Finally she swallowed hard, and in a voice clogged with emotion she said, "After I left your room I figured it probably wasn't a good idea to wander out to the beach by myself, so I settled for a walk by the pool. You can see the beach from there, and I didn't think I could get into trouble if I went that way instead."

While she unfolded her story, I patted her on the back reassuringly, nodding my head and encouraging her to go on. She continued after a moment: "So I was walking around the deck and looking out at the gulf when it happened. . . ."

"What?" I asked, when her voice trailed off, my own voice low with anticipation.

"I tripped over her," Millicent said simply, still looking toward the pool.

"You tripped over who?" I asked, following her gaze.

"Celeste Ballentine. She's been stabbed."

My jaw dropped, and I sucked in a breath of surprise. For some reason the message I'd given Celeste at the airport about getting back on the plane she'd come in on came rushing back to my memory, and, following that, I remembered how I'd mentioned something about a betrayal and that she would be stabbed in the back if she wasn't careful. It occurred to me then that Celeste, though injured, might still be alive. Feeling stupid for sitting with Millicent when Celeste might need some form of CPR, I jumped up and moved quickly to the pool door.

"Abby? Where are you going?" Millicent called urgently after me.

"If she's hurt then maybe there's something I can do for her," I said as I shoved the pool deck entrance open. As the door swung shut behind me I could hear a muffled call from Millicent that sounded like, "No, it's too late!" but I had to make sure for myself.

On the other side of the entrance I paused for a moment as I slowly scanned the pool deck, following with my eyes the trail of bloody footprints made by Millicent's hasty retreat, when I finally spotted her. Even in the dark it was possible to tell Celeste Ballentine was already dead, and no amount of CPR was going to help her.

Carefully I picked my way through the lounge chairs and over to within three feet of her, and as I squatted down my face scrunched up in distaste as a small amount of bile bubbled up to my throat in reaction to the horror of the scene.

Celeste lay on her stomach in an enormous pool of blood that nearly encircled her. Her face was obscured by a tousle of platinum-blond hair that was half-caked with drying blood, and the knife used to kill her remained sickeningly lodged out of the middle of her back. I wanted to check for a pulse, but thought better of it because I couldn't bring myself to touch her. Judging by the tremendous amount of blood, and the fact that some of it had already dried in the night air, she couldn't possibly still be alive. I settled instead for watching her bloody back to see if there was even the slightest rise and fall, but nothing moved, and that was somehow more disturbing than the scene itself.

I wanted to leave but hesitated for a moment, leaning in just a little closer as morbid curiosity got the best of me. I saw that the back of Celeste's shirt was ripped in several places, and it appeared she had more than a dozen stab wounds peppering her upper back and lower neck.

About then, it dawned on me that I could be contaminating a crime scene, so quickly I retraced my steps, making my way back to the lobby, when the night clerk rounded the corner and announced, "Police and an ambulance are on the way."

I nodded to the clerk as I again took my seat beside Millicent, picking up her hand and squeezing it with a pained smile. "Thank you, uh . . . Bradley," I said, scanning his rumpled shirt for a name tag. "Do you think you could possibly get us a towel and some water so that I can help Millicent, here, clean up a bit?"

Millicent smiled gratefully at me, the color just beginning to return to her cheeks, as Bradley darted off to find the requested towel and water.

"Did you see her?" Millicent asked.

I nodded and squeezed her hand again. "Yes. I didn't touch her, but you were right: There's nothing we can do for her now."

Millicent sighed heavily. "Poor woman. She was a real bitch, of course, but no one should go like that. . . ."

Millicent's direct observation made me smirk in spite of the dire situation, and I nudged her lightly with my shoulder. "You're a pretty cool cucumber, aren't you, Millicent?"

Millicent smiled slyly and replied, "Well, it's the truth."

I sighed myself and said, "Yeah, I suppose you're right. . . ."

A few moments later Bradley returned with a moist towel and a glass of water, and at the same time we heard the distant sound of sirens approaching. Quickly I used the wet towel on Millicent's hands and face, wiping off as much blood as I could while my stomach squirmed at the sight of so much red.

"Thank you, Abby," she said when I was finished.

I didn't get a chance to say, "You're welcome," because in the next moment the revolving door at the hotel's entrance burst to life as several sheriff's deputies and two paramedics came rushing into the lobby. For some reason everyone approached me instead of the night clerk, who seemed only too happy to relinquish the details to me. A tall deputy in army-green sheriff's uniform stopped in front of us and bent down, eyeing Millicent but looking to me for answers. "What seems to be going on here?" he asked in a voice rubbed raw by cigarettes.

"This is Millicent Satchel," I began calmly, the idea that

I just needed to state the facts forcing me to keep my cool. "She was having trouble sleeping tonight and decided to take a stroll around the pool. When she was at the far end she tripped in the dark over someone who has apparently been murdered—"

"What's that?" the deputy asked sharply, already looking toward the door to the pool. "You say someone's been murdered?"

"Yes. Celeste Ballentine has been stabbed to death out by the pool, and Millicent tripped over her body as she was taking her walk—"

The deputy stood up abruptly, interrupting my statement as he moved quickly to the door of the pool. The other two deputies fell in behind, flanking him, and each took up a position on either side. Looking back at us, the first deputy asked Millicent, "Ma'am, do you know if the assailant is still out there?"

Millicent immediately tensed, her shoulders shaking slightly, and I knew what she was thinking even as the same thought sent similar shivers down my own spine. What if the killer was still out by the pool? Could both of us have passed right by him and never even known it?

"I . . . uh . . . I don't know, Deputy," Millicent said in a trembling stutter. "I only saw Celeste, and everything else is just a blur."

The deputy looked to his two companions and motioned them silently to follow him in. The three of them drew their guns simultaneously and eased their way through the door, leaving us to wait anxiously for their return.

Quicker than I would have expected they were back in the lobby, and the first deputy raised the walkie-talkie attached to his lapel and said, "Dispatch, this is Unit 651. We're here at the Seacoast Inn, and we're going to need Detective Stokes and CSI out here ASAP. . . ."

The next several hours were a complete blur of movement, questions, and activity. Detective Stokes was a woman, Wanda Stokes, who was short, with sandy-blond hair and a tough-as-nails attitude. She had a thick boroughish accent that made me guess she probably hailed from parts much farther northeast than Florida. She was also quite good at getting information, which Millicent and I were only too happy to give.

We told her about staying up late and talking until two A.M., then Millicent's desire to take a walk and my feeling uneasy about her safety pushing me to come down and find her. We told our story together, then separately, then together again, and Stokes finally seemed satisfied that we had nothing to do with the actual murder.

In between sessions with Detective Stokes, the paramedics attended to Millicent, advising the elderly woman that, given her age and the extent of her shock, a trip to the hospital might be in order. Millicent staunchly refused, and eventually got snippy when they kept insisting she consider it.

"I'm perfectly fine, just a little shaken. In my seventy-three years I've seen car accidents just as terrible. I didn't need to go to the hospital then, and I'm not going now, so you two can just run along and go treat someone who's really in need of your services, thank you very much!"

By this time other hotel guests, who had awoken to the noise of police and ambulance sirens, were beginning to crowd into the lobby. One by one each guest was questioned by the county sheriffs. While the procession of possible suspects, witnesses, and bystanders crowded into the lobby, I sat with Millicent on the couch and watched the crime scene technicians file in and disappear behind the pool door. As we watched law enforcement work the scene, we were able to pick up little tidbits of information as snatches of conversations floated over to us.

Things like, ". . . vic suffered multiple stab wounds and has been dead at least four hours, putting approximate time of death between midnight and one-thirty A.M. . . ." and ". . . crime scene in line with someone who knew their killer, evidence of a struggle present . . ." and finally, ". . . several witnesses claim the vic had a real knock-down, drag-out fight with one of the other hotel guests, someone named Deirdre Pendleton, earlier in the evening . . ." floated over to our hungry ears.

Eventually, the bustle died down, and by seven A.M. the crime scene technicians were packing up and Celeste's body, cloaked underneath a maroon-colored blanket, was wheeled through the lobby and out a side handicap door.

Millicent and I got up as the coroner's van drove out of the parking lot, and together we walked tiredly over to the elevators. I was so drained and exhausted I could have slept for a month, but as luck would have it, at that moment Cat walked out of the elevator and right into us, nixing my opportunity for a little R & R.

"Abby! I've been looking for you everywhere. Did you hear there was a murder here last night?"

Twenty minutes later I was still no closer to going to bed, as Cat insisted we tell her everything, detail by detail . . . again. As Millicent was recounting the ordeal for the sixth time she was suddenly struck dumb when the handcuffed figure of Deirdre Pendleton, escorted by two deputies, passed by us on the way to the revolving front door.

Collectively we each uttered a gasp as Deirdre's bent frame shuffled past; her head bowed and her long wavy hair hiding her shamed face as she walked woodenly beside the officers escorting her to an awaiting police cruiser. As one we each turned and mouthed, *Oh, my God!*

"Deirdre murdered Celeste?" Cat gasped.

My left side instantly felt thick and heavy—my intuition wasn't buying it.

"I *knew* it!" Millicent added, "The way she attacked Celeste yesterday, of course she was mad enough to finish the job!"

Again my left side felt thick and heavy. "I don't know . . ." I said thoughtfully as we all watched a deputy duck Deirdre's head into the waiting county car.

"Oh, come on, Abby!" Cat insisted. "Of course she did it. Celeste practically ruined her career last night. The woman will never get another book deal, and Celeste had threatened to go public about what a sham Deirdre was."

"Yeah," I said, still uneasy, "I know she's the obvious choice here, but I'm just not buying it. My intuition says it wasn't her."

Millicent darted a look at me, interest lighting up her features. "You mean your psychic sense can tell she didn't do it?"

I thought about that for a moment and nodded my head. "Yeah, that's right. My intuition says that it wasn't Deirdre.

In fact," I added as I shifted into psychic mode for a moment, "my intuition is screaming that there was more than one killer. I keep seeing the number two, so my guess is that one lured her down to the deck, and the other stabbed her to death."

"Deirdre and her manager!" Cat said, excited to put the pieces together.

"Yes!" Millicent hurried, catching on to Cat's excitement. "It makes perfect sense!"

One skeptical eyebrow shot upward as I gave both women an unconvinced look. "Ladies, ladies . . ." I began, trying to insert a little reason into the lynch mob forming in front of me. "Listen, I think it's fairly safe to say that at this point we don't know who did it, and I believe it's best if we let the police handle—"

"Oh, Abby, grow up," my sister interrupted, swatting away my good reasoning with a small condescending flick of her hand.

"Excuse me?" I asked, offended.

"You know very well the police aren't interested in anything that's going to involve work, and since Deirdre is the most obvious suspect, it's clear they'll focus on her to make the murder stick. And if *she* didn't do it . . . well, I think we should absolutely devote the rest of our stay here to helping them discover who did."

I ogled my sister for a full ten seconds. She couldn't be serious. "Are you *crazy*?" I finally spat, looking to Millicent for support, only to find her excitedly nodding her blue-haired head in support of Cat.

"Oh, come on, Abby! We can do this! We can solve this crime! We have everything we need between the three of us—especially given our considerable resources," my sister persisted.

"And what exactly are our 'considerable resources'?" I asked caustically, folding my arms stubbornly across my chest.

"Well, there's your sixth sense," Cat said, ticking off her index finger and directing it toward me, "and Millicent's trusting appearance—I'll bet you know everything about every one of your neighbors, don't you, Millicent?"

"Absolutely." Millicent nodded. "People will tell a little old lady just about anything," she added smugly.

"And then, of course, there's my money—which has opened many a door, let me tell you," Cat said triumphantly.

"Cat," I said sternly, wanting her to see reason, "this is crazy! There is no way I'm going to be party to this. I'm tired," I insisted, ticking off on my own hand, "I haven't slept in, like, *days,* the sun is coming *up,* I'm still *pale,* and I want my *vacation*!"

"Fine," Cat said, giving me her "I'm sooooo disappointed in you" look and turning to wrap an arm around Millicent. "If you won't help us then Millicent and I will just have to work this case without you. Come on, Millicent; let's go see what we can dig up." And with that the pair actually turned and began to walk away from me.

I slapped the top of my forehead and snarled in frustration. My sister lived to play dirty. *"Fine!"* I said when they'd taken several steps away.

"Pardon me?" Cat called over her shoulder. "Did you say something?"

I took a very deep breath and hissed it out through clenched teeth. "I said, 'Fine,' as in I will help you, but only after I take a nice long nap, and only if you promise that the moment this gets hairy we will turn over what we know to the police," I added, my voice all business.

Millicent and Cat nodded their heads vigorously, their eyes large with innocence, which I wasn't buying for a second.

"That's very fair," Cat said happily. "Now why don't you go on to bed and we'll come for you in a few hours, okay?"

I nodded dully and was about to turn away when I remembered that Millicent hadn't slept all night either. Tiredly I turned back to the two of them and asked, "Millicent, aren't you exhausted too? Shouldn't you get a couple hours' sleep before we start snooping around?"

"Oh, no," Millicent replied, a huge smile spreading across her face. "I'm fine. I rarely sleep more than a few hours a night anyway. Been an insomniac all my life, and it's never been as exciting as it was last night. I could go all day without any trouble at all. Well . . ." she added, looking down, "perhaps I should just change into some new clothes first. All the blood might scare people."

Cat nodded and took Millicent by the arm, walking her

in the direction of the gift shop. "Come on, Millicent; I know the perfect little ensemble for snooping. I saw it in the hotel store here yesterday. . . ." And the two disappeared around the corner.

Watching them go, I sighed heavily and shuffled over to the elevator, waiting impatiently for the double doors to open. When they finally did I nearly ran smack dab into one of the Peace Twins who smirked at me as I mumbled my apologies. As she and her sister brushed by me my intuition began to buzz. Sleep-deprived and lethargic, I turned in the elevator slowly and cocked my head, listening for the message. The feeling that I had was that there was something not quite right about the two girls, and they deserved a second look. I was about to trudge out of the elevator after them when a family of four barreled in, blocking my exit, and just then the double doors closed. As the elevator moved up, my whole body ached with fatigue, and I figured that before I did any sleuthing I might as well get a little rest. I had a strong suspicion the twins weren't going anywhere with so many police personnel around. They'd still be there in a couple of hours, and I could follow up later. Looking back, I can't help but think that if I'd only followed them when I'd had the chance we could have saved ourselves a whole lot of extra time and effort.

Chapter 4

Around one o'clock that afternoon I'd pretty much gotten all the sleep I was going to get for the day and sluggishly rolled out of bed. My eyes felt itchy, my brain was foggy, and my limbs dragged along behind me as I propelled myself in the general direction of the shower. Sleep and I are great friends; in fact, I visit with the old guy regularly right around eleven every night, and leave him only when I've had my fill about eight hours later, so having to go through a twenty-four-hour period when I hadn't gotten a chance to linger with my dear friend for longer than a catnap was making me feel very neglected.

Under the spray of the shower I managed to revive a little and clear some of the cobwebs from my sluggish thoughts. The idea of joining up with Cat and Millicent for some supersleuthing was never far from my mind, and I'd had some weird dream about the three of us walking around trying to find someone's lost cat and coming across Deirdre, who said that she'd seen the cat bouncing a basketball and to look over by the pool. The dream ended with an image of Celeste lying dead and facedown in a pool of milk while a calico cat licked at the liquid and intermittently stopped to twirl a basketball with one paw.

I wasn't even going to try to figure out what the hell my subconscious was trying to tell me.

Just as I was rinsing the shampoo out of my hair I heard my sister call from the bedroom, "Abby?"

I sighed heavily, then yelled back, "I'm in the shower! Be out in a minute!"

Annoyed that I had to rush now, I quickly ran some conditioner through my hair, rinsed, and grabbed a towel

and my robe. I padded out to the sitting room, where Cat
and Millicent sat bubbling with excitement.

"So what's up?" I asked as I mopped at my hair with
the towel.

Millicent nearly squeaked with excitement as she said,
"Oh, we got such good dish!"

"Do tell," I said smiling at her enthusiasm and sitting
down on one of the large chairs with brush in hand to comb
out my wet hair.

"Well! Word has it that Deirdre wasn't doing so well in
the finance department as of late. Her last two books
bombed, and we've learned that she just bought a huge
house in Malibu that she's having a really hard time making
the payments on. So in desperation she signs on her manager, a man named Mark Hamilton—I believe you're already acquainted," she added, tongue in check.

"Are you talking about the guy in the tweed jacket who
was sitting at our table and who manhandled me out of the
hall last night?"

"Yes, that's the one." Millicent nodded. "Anyway, Deirdre talked him into bankrolling this seminar in order to lure
people to her spiritual retreat in Hawaii. We hear Mark's
background is selling timeshares there, and he agreed to
put up the cash for this little shindig and split the profits
with Deirdre on the Hawaii deal. The markup was ridiculous, from what I understand."

I nodded, remembering the ten-thousand-dollar price tag
attached to the Hawaii adventure Deirdre had been
peddling.

"So when Celeste got up onstage and ruined the whole
thing, you can imagine how angry Mark must have been,"
Cat said, jumping into the conversation.

"Uh-huh," I agreed, working on a small tangle in my
hair.

" 'Uh-huh'?" Cat demanded. "That's all you have to
say?"

I stopped working on the tangle and stared at my sister,
wondering why she'd suddenly become offended. "Well,
what would you like me to say?" I asked.

"How about, 'By Jove, Watson, I think you've solved
the crime!' "

I resisted the urge to roll my eyes and settled for staring

pointedly at my sister. She had to be kidding. "Cat," I began, forcing patience into my voice, "first of all, while I will admit that it sounds like a pretty good lead, we're a long way from solving the crime. I mean, a lot of people get angry when they get screwed financially, but that doesn't mean they're willing to resort to murder."

"Abby, you said yourself that another person was involved in the murder of Celeste. I remember looking at Mark after he'd pulled Deirdre and Celeste apart. He was furious!"

I sighed again and sat down, my intuition humming slightly in the background of my thoughts. "Okay, okay, it's motive, but I don't think that with just that small piece of evidence we're going to convince the police that Mark did it."

"So what would you suggest we do?" Millicent asked, her large owl-like eyes blinking at me.

I stood up again and looked at the two of them, resignation settling in my shoulders. "Well, let's do this: Let's go to the scene of the crime and see if my intuition can pick up anything to help tie Mark to the murder."

Cat and Millicent beamed at me as my sister jumped up and said, "Perfect! I knew we could count on you! Go get dressed; we'll wait right here."

On lead feet I walked back to the bedroom and got dressed, still aching with sleep deprivation and wishing I hadn't suddenly agreed to use up more energy to play Sherlock Holmes.

Fifteen minutes later we were back in the lobby and I was standing just outside the pool entrance, which had been roped off by yellow crime-scene tape and a gigantic sign that read, POOL CLOSED UNTIL FURTHER NOTICE.

Along the way, we had passed a long line of people hurrying to check out of the hotel, and I really couldn't blame them, given the circumstances. Who wanted to stay in a hotel where someone had been stabbed in the back a half dozen times?

I looked at the yellow tape and wondered what to do. It would be best if I could go out to the actual scene of the crime, but there was no way I wanted to risk getting caught snooping around—I was pretty sure it wasn't worth the trouble.

"Can you get a feel from out here?" Cat asked, looking at me anxiously.

"I don't know. I hope so," I said, leaning against the wall just to the side of the door. "Cat, do me a favor and take some notes, okay? I'm going to try to tune in and just tell you my impressions. No matter how kooky they sound, just write them down."

I'd brought along a pad of paper and a pen and handed these to Cat.

"No problem," she said, taking them from me and waiting for my cue.

I smiled gamely at Cat and Millicent, then closed my eyes and tried to clear away all other thoughts, centering my energy and concentrating. When I felt focused I shot my intuition like an arrow from a bow through the wall and over to where I thought Celeste had been murdered. Several images came to mind right away, and I began to rattle them off to Cat. "The first thing I'm getting is the number two, as in two people were definitely involved. There's a feeling of betrayal, like I definitely think Celeste had a close connection to her killers. The next impression is something about a tree. . . . This is weird. . . ." In my head swirled the image of an apple tree, and as I watched an apple dropped to the ground. "Something about apples or an apple tree, and now they're showing me poker chips . . . something about apples dropping and poker chips . . . hmmmm." I was having a hard time coming up with the meaning for these metaphors, but decided not to dwell on it. "The next impression I'm getting is something about basketball, or someone who plays basketball. Also there's this image of a cat. . . ."

"Me?" Cat asked.

"Uh . . . no . . . not you. It's more like someone's pet. . . . No, that's wrong. . . . I don't know, they keep showing me this calico cat, and there's a connection to *Little House on the Prairie*. . . ."

"*Little House on the Prairie?*" Cat asked.

"Yeah, this calico cat is coming out of that school from *Little House on the Prairie* . . . remember? The one that Laura Ingalls and her sister Mary went to?"

"Abby, this is so bizarre," Cat said.

I snapped my eyes open, frustrated that the clues were

so all over the place and completely nonsensical. "Yeah, I know. This is so weird. My antenna doesn't work well when I'm tired, and I think maybe my guides are trying to help me by keeping it simple and just showing me pictures. I know there are some good clues here, but I'm not sure how they fit."

"Well, maybe one of the killers has a cat and he likes to play basketball," Millicent suggested helpfully.

I shrugged my shoulders. "Yeah, maybe . . ."

"Only one way to find out," Cat said, and began walking toward the checkout counter.

"What's she doing?" Millicent asked.

"I have no idea," I said, "but if I know Cat, it's going to be good."

Millicent and I watched as my sister strolled around to the side of the desk and tapped one of the harried clerks on the shoulder. She then pulled the clerk aside and whispered in his ear. This was followed by emphatic head shaking on the part of the clerk, at which point Cat subtly reached into her purse and extracted several folded bills, delicately tucking them into the clerk's palm. After a slight moment of hesitation the clerk moved quickly over to his computer terminal, typed furiously on a few keys, scribbled something quickly down on a piece of paper, and handed it discreetly to Cat.

Moments later she was back by our side, triumphantly waving a small piece of paper.

"What gives?" I asked.

"Mark Hamilton's room number ."

"How is this going to help us?" I asked.

"Well," Cat began patiently, "what if there's something to what Millicent said and your guides are talking about, someone who has a pet cat and who likes to play basketball? Mark Hamilton is certainly tall enough. . . ."

"Uh-huh," I said skeptically, not liking the direction this was taking.

"So I think we should just go ask him, and if all the clues about cats, basketball, apples, and poker chips fit, then we've found ourselves the killer. And the beauty of it is that he doesn't even have to know *we* know he did it! We can just thank him for his time and go directly to the police!"

"Cat, that is the craziest thing you have ever—"

"What are we waiting for?" Millicent said over me as she sauntered over to Cat and took her by the arm, and the two began trotting in the direction of the elevators.

"Coming, Abby?" Cat said over her shoulder.

"Oh, for Christ's sake!" I said, giving her the full eye roll before stomping after them just the same.

Five minutes later Cat was knocking confidently on Mark Hamilton's door, and after a short wait it opened abruptly to a bleary-eyed and much-disheveled man who looked like he'd just been run over by a Mack truck. The three of us recoiled as the smell of vomit filled the hallway from the open door.

"Yeah?" he asked, swaying a little in the doorway.

"Good afternoon, Mr. Hamilton," Cat said gamely. "We're so sorry to disturb you; however, we were wondering if we could ask you a few questions?"

Mark bobbled slightly in the doorway as he tried repeatedly to focus his bleary, bloodshot eyes. "Wha?" he managed after a series of rapid blinks.

"Some *questions*?" Cat tried again. "We have a few questions for you?"

"You the police?" he mumbled. " 'Cause I've already talked to you guys once today . . ."

Cat laughed politely and waved her hand as if she were shooing a fly. "Of course not! No, you see, we're actually members of Deirdre Pendleton's fan club, and we're trying to get the monthly newsletter out to our members. We just wanted to do a small blurb about Deirdre's manager . . . you know . . . for the newsletter."

Mark blinked furiously a few more times, trying to focus on us. As he looked at me I could tell his memory was working to place my face, so I discreetly moved a little farther out of view to the side of the door. "Where you from again?" he asked Cat, scratching his head and sighing with the effort it took to concentrate.

"From the Deirdre Pendleton Fan Club, which, as her manager, I'm sure you know all about. We have a lot of members, and the fan base is always growing. So anyway, as I was saying, we'd like to do a story on you, if you could spare us just a few minutes of your time."

Suddenly what Cat was saying must have sunk in, because Mark seemed to take an interest. "Newsletter? How many members did you say you had?"

"Oh, close to a couple thousand, I think," Cat said, pumping her head up and down in an honest Abe, Scouts honor, cross my heart and hope to die kinda way.

"You going to mention anything about this murder business?"

"Of course not," Cat said dramatically. "We *know* Deirdre didn't do it, and I'm sure she'll be exonerated before the day is through—"

"Good," Mark said, cutting her off. "How about mentioning her retreat to Hawaii?"

Cat smiled demurely and caught my eye with a hidden wink. Now we had him. "That's actually our cover story. We're devoting the whole front page to it, in fact. We're hoping that most of our members sign up for it."

"Really?" Mark asked, a trace of clarity returning to his squinty eyes. "Well, then, count me in. What did you want to know?"

Cat smiled broadly, so happy that it had been this easy. "Well," she began, looking at the notes she'd taken from our little psychic session downstairs, "I'd like to know a little about your personal life, like . . . oh, I don't know . . . do you have any pets?"

"No. No pets. I'm allergic to most animals."

"Not even as a kid?" I tried. "Like, did you ever have a favorite cat or something?"

"Nope. Had asthma instead."

"I see . . ." Cat said, crossing off the calico-cat connection. "How about sports—what kinds of sports do you like?"

"Well," Mark said, thinking, "I'm not really into sports, but I do like to play a round of golf every once in a while."

"Ever play basketball?" I tried again.

"No," Mark answered, looking at me quizzically. "Remember me? The kid who had asthma?" he asked with a sarcastic sneer.

"Right," I said, pointing a finger gun at him and looking at Cat with a slight shrug of my shoulders.

"I see . . ." Cat said again, scratching off another clue. "How about gambling? You like to play poker at all?"

"Uh . . ." Mark thought. "No. I like money way too

much to risk losing it in some dumb game. Say, you gals aren't very good interviewers, you know?"

"Oh, don't mind them," Millicent jumped in. "The questions were my idea. Most of our club are elderly, and they love little tidbits like this."

"Really?" Mark asked, suddenly believing our legitimacy because it was now coming from a sweet little old lady. "Well, okay, what else do you have?"

Millicent peeked over Cat's shoulder at the list of clues and tried one last time. "How about apples, Mr. Hamilton? Do you like apples?"

"You mean like apple pie?"

"Yes," Millicent said gamely.

"Hate it," Mark said flatly. "I'm a blueberry man."

By this time I'd had enough of beating around the bush and impatiently asked, "So where were you last night between midnight and two fifteen A.M.?"

Cat and Millicent both took in sharp breaths, but I was going to get some straight answers if it killed me. Mark blinked a few times, rather shocked himself at the dramatic shift in questioning. "I-I-I . . ." he stammered.

"Yes?" I said, tapping my foot impatiently and staring him down.

"I was at the bar!" he said at last.

"All night?" I pushed.

"Yeah! I left the bar right around two and came straight up here to my room. The police already asked me this anyway, and they checked it out with the bartender."

I listened intently for my inboard lie detector to sound off, but it remained silent, so with a shrug I accepted that he was probably telling the truth.

Looking him over, I didn't think he had it in him anyway, and this only spurred my foul mood for having wasted so much time. "All right," I said sullenly, "then what's your theory on who killed Celeste Ballentine?" It was worth a shot.

"Say, who are you anyway?" Mark asked, finally getting uppity at my interrogation.

"I'm investigating Celeste's murder, and I'd like my question answered," I said in my best tough-as-nails voice, playing the bad cop for all I was worth.

Just then Millicent stepped in and explained, "You see,

we're trying to clear Deirdre's name, Mr. Hamilton. We really want to go to Hawaii with her, and if she's in jail, well, then there goes my vacation. Won't you please help us?"

Good old Millicent got the job done. "Well, I don't know for sure," Mark said, softening to her, "but you might want to check out two of the Rainbow Sisters, Willow and Waverly."

"The Rainbow Sisters?" Cat asked.

"Yeah, there are these twins who recently joined Deirdre's little entourage—Deirdre likes taking a couple of psychic wannabes to each seminar; she calls them her 'Rainbow Sisters'—and these two joined the group a few weeks ago. At first Deirdre thought they were great; I mean, they stick to her like glue and practically worship the ground she walks on. But recently even Deirdre began to get creeped out."

"Why?" I asked.

"Well, for one thing, they insist on standing right next to her when she does her audience readings. Normally all of the Sisters rotate positions from seminar to seminar, but these two kept butting out all of the other women. The other Sisters are a little intimidated by them. The twins also follow Deirdre constantly. It's like they're obsessed with her or something. Anyway, I remember how pissed off they got when Celeste showed up at the seminar, and when I heard the news this morning . . . I just figured they might have had something to do with it. They think of Deirdre as a . . . I don't know, like a goddess or something, and there's just something not right about the two of them, you know?"

The three of us stood there nodding our heads as Mark rambled on about Willow and Waverly. Something felt dead-on about what he was saying, and, at the same time, something didn't.

"Okay," I said, wanting to wrap this up. The smell coming off Mark was making me nauseous. "We'll check this out. Thanks for your help, Mr. Hamilton."

"By the way," Mark offered as we left him in the doorway, "the deadline for the Hawaiian retreat is in three weeks, you know . . . so your readers know to book their

reservations right away," he called after us as we headed
down the hallway.

"Okay," Cat sang, and gave him a "tootles" hand wave.
Once we had safely rounded the corner we all stopped
to catch up. "So what'd you think?" Millicent asked me.

"Well, I hate to say this, but I believe him. Just to be
on the safe side, though, I think we should double-check
with the bartender this afternoon. But the guy can barely
stand up, and he's had more than eight hours to shake off
his little binge from last night. I really doubt he'd be able
to overpower Celeste and stab her umpteen times, as drunk
as he must have been."

Cat and Millicent nodded regretfully. "I really wanted it
to be him," Cat said. "It would have made things really
easy."

"Well, there's still the Rainbow Sisters," I offered.

"Willow and Waverly?" Cat asked. "Yes, I think that's
a good logical next step. Come on, girls, let's go purchase
us a room number," she added, already hurrying to the
elevator.

Fifteen minutes and a hundred dollars later we were
standing in front of room 266, with Millicent taking the
knocking honors while Cat and I stood off to one side.
Millicent knuckled the door several times, but no one answered. Finally we all turned and headed back down the
hallway, weary about coming to yet another roadblock. As
we got around the corner I heard a door open behind us,
and something told me to quietly halt the other two women
and step back against the wall.

Cat and Millicent both looked at me curiously, but I only
supplied a finger to my lips in a "shhh" motion, and nodded
my head in the direction of the twins' room. Sure enough,
we could hear someone around the corner saying quietly,
"Are you sure they're gone?"

"Yeah, about time too. I thought they were gonna
knock forever."

"Got your luggage?"

"Yep, let's go." And with that we all heard footsteps
growing louder and heading in our direction.

Just as the twins were about to round the corner I
stepped away from the wall, Millicent and Cat following my

cue as we blocked the sisters' path. "Going somewhere?" I asked boldly as the twins rounded the corner and came up short in front of us.

"Excuse me," the twin on the right said politely. "We need to get by."

"Oh? Do you now?" Cat said, taking a threatening step forward.

"Yes," the other twin said firmly. "We're checking out, and we need to get by."

"Why didn't you answer our knock?" Millicent demanded.

"What knock?" Left twin asked innocently.

I scowled menacingly at her. Did she think we were stupid?

"Oh!" right twin said in fake recollection. "I thought I heard someone knocking, but it sounded like it was coming from next door." *Liar, liar, pants on fire . . .*

"No," I said. "We were knocking on your door and you had no intention of answering. But now that we have your full and undivided attention, we need to ask you a few questions."

"We don't have time," left twin insisted. "We need to catch a plane and we're in a hurry." *Liar, liar, pants on fire . . .*

"Nope," I said.

"Excuse me?" right twin asked.

"No, you don't have a plane to catch, and no, we are not going to let you by until you answer a few questions."

"Who do you think you are?" left twin demanded, beginning to grow angry.

"*We* are the people blocking your path, honey, and until you answer our questions *you're* not going anywhere."

"Listen here—" left twin began.

"Where were you last night around two A.M.?" I spat out, cutting her off.

"What?" Right twin.

"You heard me," I said. "I want to know where you were last night between one thirty and two A.M.?"

Both twins scowled at me and replied in unison, "In bed, sleeping."

Liar, liar, pants on fire . . .

"Baloney," I said smugly, crossing my arms and looking

at them with intense dislike. My intuition was buzzing rapidly, and I knew I needed to press these two. "Did you kill Celeste Ballentine?" I asked boldly.

"No!" right twin said quickly.

I waited but my lie detector remained silent. "How about you?" I asked left twin.

Left twin rolled her eyes and said, "Of course not, you idiot! We had nothing to do with that!"

Again my lie detector stayed silent, and it puzzled me, because I knew these girls were up to something.

"Now I think we have answered all we're going to, so if you don't mind!" right twin said, and shoved violently against Cat, knocking her out of the way.

"Hey!" Cat shouted, and shoved back, but it was too late. Right twin had made it through the blockade, and just as quickly her sister took advantage of the distraction and pushed through the opening too, joining her twin on the other side of us. Quickly the two trotted down the corridor in the direction of the elevators, leaving Cat, Millicent, and me burning holes in the back of their heads.

"That was rude!" Cat said, rubbing her arm where she'd been shoved.

"Should we go after them?" Millicent asked.

"No," I said as we watched them stop in front of the elevator and stab at the button. "They didn't do it."

"You're sure?" Cat asked me.

"Yeah," I said moodily. "My lie detector didn't go off when they said they had nothing to do with it."

Millicent sighed tiredly and asked, "So what do we do now?"

"I don't know," I said, rubbing my temples at the start of a nasty headache. "Maybe go down to the bar and check with the bartender to corroborate Mark's story? He probably gets in around three. Cat, what time do you have?"

"Uh, it's about . . ." Cat began lifting her right wrist to look at her watch. *"Ohmigod!"* she said suddenly, lifting her wrist high and widening her eyes in shock.

"What?!" Millicent and I said together.

"My watch! My Rolex watch! *It's gone!*"

As one, we looked at each other in startled amazement; then, just as quickly, we each turned our heads in the direction of the twins just as they were getting into the elevator.

"Hey!" I shouted, and began sprinting in their direction. "Stop!" I commanded, nearing the doors, which were beginning to close. "Thief!" I hollered at the top of my lungs. *"Thief! Thief!"*

Five yards from the elevator I watched with mounting fury as the doors closed and one of the twins waved snidely at me as she disappeared behind the steel doors. Propelled by anger I swung a hard left and bolted to the door leading to the stairs, swinging it open furiously and charging down the steps. Behind me I could hear Cat yelling at me to hurry as she clattered down the stairs herself, hampered by her expensive Manolo Blahnik high heels.

At the bottom of the stairs I yanked at the door and ran out into the lobby, swinging my head in the direction of the elevator, which had already opened, and with a flood of adrenaline I spotted the twins already rushing toward the revolving front door.

Infuriated, I sprinted in their direction and watched as they both picked up their luggage and began running to the exit, which was all that stood in their way to freedom. We reached the enclosure at the same time, and, thinking quickly, I let them jump into the glass revolving door just ahead of me. As the gate turned and both girls moved one step closer to freedom, I jumped in between the frame of the door and the next opening, wedging my back against the outer frame while propping my feet against the window, effectively jamming the door from moving forward. As the girls pushed forward I merely locked my knees, straining hard with all my might, and refused to allow the door to progress.

Just then Cat reached my side and wedged herself into the frame of the door with me, lending her support as both twins strained against our resistance to move the door forward, without avail.

As Cat and I strained to keep the door locked a hotel clerk approached us and asked crossly, *"What* is going on here?"

"Call the police," I said, my voice tightening under the pressure of keeping the door from moving. "Those two women are thieves." I added, "They just stole my sister's Rolex, and I'll bet dollars to doughnuts their luggage is full of stolen merchandise."

The clerk stood gaping at us without moving as a crowd began to gather and the twins pounded on the glass and screamed to be let out.

"Go!" my sister shouted at the stunned clerk, impatient for him to hurry.

Just then Millicent came across the lobby and took the clerk by the arm, saying, "Come, dear, I'll explain everything on our way to the telephone . . ."

An hour later we had finished giving our statements to the sheriff, and Cat had retrieved her diamond tennis bracelet and her Rolex watch, while Millicent was happily toting her mother's pocketbook again as we watched Willow and Waverly being led away in handcuffs. The police found all sorts of valuable objects taken from the hotel, and a stack of credit cards belonging to some hotel patrons and other victims stuffed away in the twins' luggage. We now understood why Willow and Waverly insisted on sticking so close to Deirdre during her readings; while the audience member was distracted and focused on Deirdre, one of the twins could pick them clean.

Soon after they were taken away, Cat, Millicent, and I gathered in the dining room for much-needed sustenance, and to discuss our next steps.

"So," Cat said, stirring her potato soup to cool it off, "any ideas on where we go from here?"

I sighed heavily and replied, "I'm not sure. I mean, where do we even begin? The bartender confirmed Mark's story about being nearly too drunk to see last night, let alone wield a knife, and Willow and Waverly may be bold enough to rob someone blind, but I doubt highly that they'd be motivated to murder, so I'm not sure where that leaves us."

Silence fell on the three of us as we sat alone in thought, each trying to decide what next step to take, when a gasp sounded among the very few patrons who were left in the hotel and eating in the dining room with us. We all snapped our heads up to look for the cause; then we too released our own gasps of surprise.

Standing at the hostess stand at the entrance to the dining room and gazing intently about was none other than Deirdre Pendleton.

For a moment no one in the room seemed to move; the hotel patrons sat nervously still and waited to see if perhaps the suspected murderess would lunge for another knife and claim her next victim, while Deirdre moved only her eyes, which combed each face within the dining room. In the next instant she locked eyes with me, her lids narrowing menacingly as her body came to life, moving with marked determination, and clenched fists in my direction.

Alarmed by her manner, I clutched my chest while frantically scanning the table for an available weapon to defend myself. In three strides she reached our table, and with one long accusing finger pointed it directly at me and said, *"You!"*

Cat had scooted her chair a little closer to me as Deirdre approached, and when she started pointing fingers, Cat jumped up and put her small frame directly in front of Deirdre's line of fire.

"Listen here," Cat said in her most boardroomlike tone, "you can get your bony finger out of my sister's face and just go back the way you came or I will call the police and have you arrested . . . *again*!"

Deirdre, who had been holding my eyes and was clearly undaunted by Cat's protective movements, suddenly snapped them at my sister when she heard mention of the police. Lowering her arm slowly, she said, "No, that won't be necessary. I just wanted to talk to her for a moment, if that's all right with you?"

Cat eyed Deirdre for a long tense moment and refused to back down, so I gently put my hand on her arm and said, "Cat, it's okay. I'll talk to her."

"Fine," Cat said dismissively. "But you'll play nice, Miss Pendleton, agréed?"

"Yeah, yeah." Deirdre waved tiredly and took the fourth seat at the table, eyeing our breadbasket hungrily while she was at it.

Cat sat down as well and pulled the basket of bread to the middle of the table a little closer to us as she continued to flash Deirdre a warning look.

"So what do you want?" I asked, cutting to the chase.

Deirdre looked at me and leaned in close so that we couldn't be overheard. "You have ruined my career," she said bluntly, her voice hard as iron, "and for that, you owe me."

"I don't owe you diddly, Deirdre. I'm not the fraud here; you are," I retorted.

"Listen here, missy: I have talent, you know—"

"For misleading people," I snapped.

"People want to believe what they want to believe. . . ."

"Oh, cut the crap, Pendleton. Everybody's onto you. You're a phony. All I did was set things right, and I can't understand why you think I did more harm to your career than Celeste did. After all, she had all the proof; I just provided some expertise."

"Yes, and you did it at *my* show, Miss Cooper, where people paid to see me, not you. You should have kept your damn mouth shut, because now I can't afford to pay my own rent!"

"So are you gonna kill me now too?" I snapped, losing all patience and raising my voice.

The room fell silent, and all eyes turned to us as Deirdre eyed me with large, shocked eyes. Finally, after a long, tense moment, Deirdre said, "I didn't kill her," in a voice that had lost all hint of aggression. And then her eyes welled up and tears slid down her cheeks.

Crap. Now I'd done it. "I know," I said after a moment.

"You do?" she asked, looking up, her eyes pleading as she wiped at her cheeks.

"Yeah," I said, squirming uncomfortably.

"But how do you know?" Deirdre asked.

I tapped my temple in answer, and she said, "Oh. Of course. Well, then, it's only right that you'll help me."

"Help you?" Millicent asked, finally jumping into the conversation.

"I need her to help clear my name," Deirdre answered, fully recovering herself and reaching across the table to snatch at a roll before my sister could pull it away.

I was taken by surprise at Deirdre's request, and it was a moment before I could respond. "Why do you think I can help clear your name?" I finally asked.

"Because," she said, stuffing a small bit of roll into her mouth, "I didn't kill Celeste, and I need to find out who did before the police collect enough circumstantial evidence to pin the murder on me. You've got real talent," she said, wagging a finger at me. "With your abilities and my connections you could go far, you know, and besides, you owe me," she said again.

One of my eyebrows arched tightly upward. "Oh, really?" I drawled. "Gee, Deirdre, *tempting* as that offer sounds, I think I'll pass, because, like I said before, I don't owe you diddly." What can I say? This woman got under my skin, and clearing her name suddenly became something I didn't feel like doing.

"Abby . . ." Cat hissed through the side of her mouth, "She said she has *connections*."

The arched eyebrow came down hard and joined its twin in a look of death that told my sister to clam it. "Hire a private detective," I suggested, turning back to Deirdre. "I'm sure they're better suited to the task of clearing your name. . . ."

"Didn't you hear me when I said I can't even afford to pay my own rent? How am I supposed to pay for a private detective now that my career is ruined?" Deirdre asked, putting down the butter knife she'd stolen from Millicent's plate and looking at me honestly for the first time. "I'm in trouble, Miss Cooper, and if you don't help me I'm going to go to jail for something I swear I didn't do, and a killer will go free."

Damn . . . why'd she have to appeal to my sense of justice? I sighed heavily and checked in with my intuition to see if I should help her clear her name.

Right side light and airy, my sign for "yes."

"Fine," I said, rolling my eyes and letting my shoulders droop. "But it's going to cost you, Deirdre."

"What is it about not having any money you don't understand?" Deirdre snapped.

I looked over at Millicent and considered an idea for a long moment. Then I smiled when I had the answer, and said, "Oh, I don't want your money, Deirdre. I'll just bet that all this publicity is probably going to work to your advantage, and once your name is cleared your fans are going to come out of the woodwork to support you. My guess is that the Hawaii retreat is still a go, so after you get through peddling ninety-eight of those one hundred tickets to Hawaii, you're going to reserve the last two slots, free of charge, for my dear associate Millicent Satchel and her husband . . . uh . . . ."

"Ernie," Millicent said quickly, excitement building in her eyes.

"Yeah, Ernie. And they'd better be first-class tickets to boot. And while she's there you'll make sure her accommodations are the best and that she has plenty of food vouchers and coupons for her touring pleasure," I added.

Deirdre's own eyebrows lowered dangerously. I was asking for the moon, and it must have irked her that I wasn't falling all over myself to help her out of her little predicament. "Fine," she said flatly. "But *only* if you find the murderer and I am completely exonerated."

I nodded at Millicent, allowing her to make the decision.

"Deal!" she sang sweetly. "This is so exciting! I've always wanted to go to Hawaii!"

"Okay, now that that's settled," I said, getting down to business, "we can move on to identifying suspects. We've already done some of the preliminary work."

Deirdre looked a question mark at me and asked, "Preliminary work?"

"Yeah," I said smugly, "I've already tuned in on the murder."

"So you were already working on the case even before I came here?"

"Yup," I said, allowing a small, "nah-nah-nah-nah-nah" smile to form on my lips.

"Great," Deirdre said rolling her eyes, "just great. So tell me, what have you come up with?"

"Well," Cat said, jumping in, "Abby has been able to home in on several clues about the murderer, and from the very beginning she didn't think you did it."

"Thanks," Deirdre said flatly to me, no real gratitude reaching her eyes. She then turned back to Cat and asked, "What clues?"

Cat pulled out the piece of paper with my flashes of insight on them and ticked them off like a grocery list. "Two killers—most likely they knew and betrayed Celeste. A reference to an apple tree, some poker chips, a calico cat, *Little House on the Prairie,* and basketball."

Deirdre's face hung heavy with disappointment as she listened to the laundry list of odd clues and snapped, "You have *got* to be *kidding* me."

I couldn't help it; my dander kicked in, and I snapped testily back, "They're *metaphors,* you know, like the type that come through a psychic message? Oh, that's right . . . you wouldn't know what that felt like, would you, Deirdre?"

Deirdre half stood at the insult, her upper lip curling menacingly, and Cat jumped in quickly. "Ladies! Ladies . . . no reason to get upset here; we're all on the same team, after all, right?" she asked, looking around at Millicent and me for support.

Deirdre collected herself with effort and sat slowly back down, glaring intently at me as I glared just as intently back, neither of us blinking or looking away from the other, but waiting it out to see where Cat would take us next.

"So let's try to work together on this, shall we?" Cat said in a soothing tone. "Deirdre, let's start with the first clue; do you know anyone who has an apple orchard or who likes apples, or even someone with that for a last name?"

"No," Deirdre said flatly, folding her hands together and tucking them snootily underneath her chin as she gave me a look of disdain.

I glared at her in warning, but Cat—ever the optimist—persisted. "I see. So how about poker? Do you know anyone who might want to kill Celeste who gambled or played poker?"

"No."

Buzzzzz, buzzzzz, my intuitive phone rang. Shifting in my chair I homed in on the thought wanting to come into my head, and after a quick flash of insight I asked her, "Are you sure?"

" 'Am I sure' what?" she repeated.

I scowled as I tried to make sense of the clue in my head, which insisted that Deirdre knew about a connection like Cat had just asked about. "That you don't know someone connected to Celeste who gambles?"

"I already told you I didn't," she answered. *Liar, liar . . . pants on fire.*

I sighed heavily in frustration. Why wasn't she cooperating? She wanted to clear her name, didn't she? "Deirdre," I began, trying to rein in my attitude for the sake of moving this train forward, "you're holding something back on us, and I'm telling you that it's important that you come clean. If you want our help clearing your name—"

"I told you I don't know!" Deirdre snapped, cutting me off and making several patrons look in our direction. *Liar, liar . . . pants on fire . . .*

I counted to ten and waved a hand at Cat to continue. This was going to get us nowhere, but what could I do?

"How about someone who owns a calico cat? Anyone you know who might want Celeste dead who owns a calico cat?"

Deirdre shook her head and said, "This is ridiculous! How the hell are we going to find the killer if all we have to go on are these idiotic metaphors?"

"We're doing our best," Cat tried, still holding on to the hope that Deirdre would help us narrow the field.

"Well, this is crazy," Deirdre said. "I thought you had talent."

That did it. "Listen to me, you no-account scam artist," I said angrily. "I have more talent in my little finger than you have in your entire head! Despite appearances, these *are* valid clues, and you can either work with us to figure them out, or against us and go to jail. About now, I'm looking forward to sitting front and center as they lock you up and throw away the key, so what's it gonna be?"

There was a long, stunned silence as Cat and Millicent bounced glances between me and Deirdre, waiting to see if things were about to explode or calm down. Finally Deirdre lowered her head into her hands and said tiredly, "You're right. . . . Of course you're right. I'm being stubborn and I'm not helping." She lifted her face then and looked at each of us in turn. "It's just been a very long day, and I'm sorry. Please continue. What's the next clue?"

"Little House on the Prairie."

Deirdre rolled her eyes slightly and fought to bite back a remark I was sure wasn't pleasant. "Could you give me a little more to go on?"

"Well," Cat said, referring to her notes, "Abby had a vision of a calico cat coming out of the schoolhouse from *Little House on the Prairie.*"

"Hmmm," Deirdre said, "you said schoolhouse?" And after Cat nodded she continued, "I wonder . . ."

"What?" I asked.

"Well, it's a little bit of a stretch, but one of my vendors at this seminar came from a school out west that teaches psychic intuition. Her name is Zoë Schmitt, and she teaches at the Institute for Metaphysical Studies in Kansas. I've been to the school, and it's in one of those old, nineteenth-century schoolhouses that looks very much like the one from *Little House on the Prairie*."

"I've met Zoë," I said. "She was conducting some tests on psychic ability during your seminar last night."

"Yes, she wrote to me a few months ago and asked permission to join the other vendors. I agreed because I've been to the school, and they do amazing things there. The interesting thing about all this, however, is that I know for a fact that Zoë has been submitting her research to Celeste's foundation for years, hoping to win the two-and-a-half-million-dollar prize. It's common knowledge that she's been turned down every time."

"Hmmm," I said, becoming interested. "Do you know if she owns a cat, or maybe has a gambling problem?"

"She looks like she would be the type to own a cat, now, doesn't she?" Deirdre said with a smirk. "The truth is that I really don't know much about her personal life. You'd have to ask her to find out."

"What are we waiting for?" Cat said, standing up and tossing several bills into the middle of the table. "We have a room number to purchase. Let's go, ladies."

Deirdre looked longingly at our leftovers and said, "You three go on ahead. I'm going to grab a quick lunch and take a hot shower. The sheriff's station is filthy, and the interrogation room they had me in smelled like urine."

"Charming," I said, getting out of my chair. "We'll catch up with you later then." And with that, the three of us went in search of a certain redhead who just might be a sadistic killer.

Chapter 5

Zoë Schmitt was not in her room, but Cat was able to glean
that, as far as the front desk knew, she was still checked
into the hotel. After much discussion, we decided to call
Zoë and leave her a message from me, stating that I was
down on the patio and wanted to offer my services as a
human guinea pig to help her with her research. We then
trotted down to the patio by the beach to wait and hope
that Zoë got the message and came down to investigate.

Just as I was starting to really enjoy the warm waning
sun of the late afternoon and the cool breeze coming off
the coastal waters, a shadow appeared over my head, and
I squinted up to see a patch of red hair sticking out from
underneath a gigantic straw hat. "Hi, Abby," Zoë said
sheepishly.

Stifling a groan, I sat up in the chair and forced a smile
as I greeted her. "Hello! I'm so glad you found me. Zoë,
I'd like you to meet my sister, Catherine Cooper-Masters,
and our dear friend Millicent Satchel," I said, making the
introductions and indicating a spare seat underneath the
shaded area of our umbrella-topped table.

"Nice to meet you," Zoë said politely, switching her laptop from right hand to left in order to shake everyone's
hand before taking her seat. "I'm so glad you called me. I
didn't have a chance to get your information last night before everyone came storming out. It's been quite a show
here this weekend, huh?"

"Yes, it certainly has," Millicent answered, beaming her
trusting smile at Zoë.

"So! Abby, you want to participate in my research," she
announced, swiveling the laptop around and opening it in

one fluid movement. "I've got everything loaded onto my computer, so if you'll just—"

"Uh . . ." I interrupted. "About that, Zoë. You see, before we begin I'd just like to know a few things first—you know, so that I have a level of comfort with these 'tests,' as you call them."

"Okay," Zoë said, slightly caught off guard but recovering quickly. "What would you like to know?"

"Well, first I'd like to know some background on you . . . like where you're based, what you're trying to accomplish, et cetera, et cetera."

"Well, let's see . . ." Zoë said, thinking. "I come from Kansas, and I'm a member of the faculty at the Institute for Metaphysical Studies, which is a school completely dedicated to helping naturally gifted intuitives develop their abilities while gathering evidence of psychic phenomena."

"Uh-huh," I said, nodding my head as if fascinated. "So tell me about this research. Why are you so intent on proving the existence of our sixth sense?"

"Well, for one thing, our school doesn't get much in the way of funding, and if we were able to prove the existence of psychic phenomena then we would be eligible to win a two-and-a-half-million-dollar prize that's currently up for grabs."

My brow crinkled, alarm bells clanging in my head. "Two-and-a-half-million-dollar prize?" I asked carefully.

"Yes." Zoë nodded eagerly. "In fact," she continued, leaning forward conspiratorially, "you know the woman who was murdered here this weekend?"

"Yes," I said almost casually.

"Well, she ran a foundation that had a trust fund set up for any person or institution that could scientifically prove the existence of psychic phenomena."

"I see," I said. "But now that she's dead, doesn't that pretty much nix your chances?"

"No, not at all. In fact, it actually improves them."

"How?" I asked, looking at Cat and Millicent, who were glued to the conversation and the direction it was going.

"Well, now that Celeste is dead, the trust will go to her heir, Gerald Ballentine. And I know for a fact that he's not nearly as critical of my research as his mother was. I figure I'll give him a little time to come to grips with what's happened, and then submit my work. With any luck the check will be mine by next summer."

"Uh-huh," I said, nodding. This woman was practically tripping over herself to throw the shadow of suspicion her way. "So can I see this research?" I asked, really curious to see some of her results.

"Sure!" she said happily, and reached into her briefcase to extract several sheets of paper. "These are the people I've tested over the years, and yours is right on top," she said, pointing to the top sheet.

I looked over some of the pages, and was quite impressed with most of the results. Then, because I felt a tug from my intuition, I began to look more closely at my own test results. I was shocked to discover that my psychic IQ results had actually improved and expanded from the night before. "Zoë?" I asked, my brow furrowing slightly.

"Yes?"

"On this page here," I said, swiveling the paper toward her, "this is showing that I missed only *one* card out of *four* trials, when in fact I missed *three* cards between *two* trials."

Zoë immediately flushed red and snatched the page out of my hand. "Ah, yes . . . sorry about that. Must have been a keying error," she said quickly. *Liar, liar . . . pants on fire . . .*

"Really?" I asked, my heart dropping, because in spite of myself I was starting to like her. "Well, it happens."

"So shall we begin?" Zoë asked, tucking the papers away and smiling innocently.

"Uh, okay . . ." I said, wondering how I was going to get out of this now that I'd opened Pandora's box.

Just then the patio door burst open and out came Deirdre, who stormed over to our table and slapped her hand dramatically against her heart while pointing an accusing finger at Zoë as she bellowed, "*You!* You're the murderer!"

"*What?*" The four of us gasped in unison.

"I've just been talking to some of your colleagues, and they told me all about how you could hardly wait until Celeste was in her grave before you started talking about getting your dirty hands on her money! I've asked my guide, Great Wind Talker, to confirm it, and he insists that *you* murdered Celeste so that you could finally claim the prize!"

"That's ridiculous!" Zoë said, standing up defensively. "I had nothing to do with it! *I* didn't kill Celeste—*you* did!"

"I did no such thing!" Deirdre shouted back. "I didn't do anything of the kind! But how *convenient* for you, Zoë, I mean, now that Celeste is out of the way and all. Your research was turned down year after year. That must have just *galled* you, didn't it?"

"You don't know what you're talking about!"

"Oh, don't I? I know for a fact that you've been submitting your test scores for years, and you'd think that after all this time you would have figured out that it wouldn't have mattered how good your research results were; Celeste was never going to pay you! She was never going to pay *anyone!* The whole thing was a scam just to get publicity—"

"I've checked the records!" Zoë screamed. "The trust's balance was public record! There was two and a half million dollars in the account!"

"Of course there was, honey," Deirdre said, her voice dripping with condescension. "But as long as she could benefit from the interest—which she did—she was never going to pay that money out! Stupid girl, you've wasted all this time, and now that you've killed her you're still never going to get the money."

"You're wrong!" Zoë screamed, her face growing a brilliant shade of red as she folded up her computer and stuffed it back into its carrying case. "You're wrong, wrong, *wrong*!" And with that she stomped off, leaving us to make sense of the scene we'd just witnessed.

When the patio door slammed shut behind Zoë, I looked at Deirdre, who had taken a seat in one of the available lounge chairs and was looking at us expectantly. With mounting irritation I asked, "What the hell did you think you were doing?"

"Excuse me?" Deirdre said, looking down her nose in my direction.

"We were in the middle of getting some good information from her. She was willing to cooperate with us—that is, until *you* showed up with guns blazing like some scene out of *Gunsmoke*. What the hell were you thinking?"

"My guide, Great Wind Talker, told me she had something to do with Celeste's murder—"

"For Christ's sake, Deirdre! Drop the act already! You and I both know you're about as psychic as a doorknob! You can't hear your guide! He's never appeared to you, and he sure as hell isn't some old Indian chief with a name like 'Great Wind Talker'! His real name, if you must know, is Fred, and in a former life he lived in Missouri . . . on a farm . . . growing wheat!"

Deirdre looked at me for a long moment, her features unreadable, until finally she said, "Did you just make that up?"

I sighed heavily and replied, "No, it came to me last night when you were onstage."

Deirdre's lower lip trembled a little, and her eyes grew a bit misty as she said softly, "My mother used to tell this story about when I was a little girl and I had an imaginary friend named Fred who lived on a farm and grew hay for the horses."

"Well, there you go then," I said gruffly, not really knowing what else to say.

"So what do we do now?" Millicent asked when the silence stretched out among us.

All eyes turned to me for an answer, but all I could do was shrug my shoulders. "Well, I'm not sure. I think we blew our chances getting anything useful out of Zoë . . ."

"What other leads do we have?" Deirdre asked.

"There's always Celeste's son," Cat said reasonably. "Maybe we could all go and give our condolences and ask him if he knows of anyone who may have wanted to hurt his mother."

"You know, Cat, that's a really good idea," I said, brightening.

"So what are we waiting for?" Deirdre asked, standing up.

"Oh, no," I said as I got up too. "There's no way you're coming along."

"What? Why not?" Deirdre asked huffily.

"Because, dear, you don't know how to keep your big yap shut," Millicent answered, and flashed Deirdre her sweetest smile as she shuffled past.

Cat and I both nodded and trundled after Millicent, leaving Deirdre standing there with her hands on her hips, her eyes making holes in the backs of our heads.

*   *   *

Ten minutes and another room-number purchase later we were in front of Gerald's door, with Millicent doing the honors of knocking and being the point person. The door opened quickly after just a few taps, and there stood Gerald, looking like he'd been kicked in the stomach, his eyes bloodshot and weepy, the sound of a television blaring ESPN in the background of his room. "Yes?" he asked softly, looking at each of us, trying to place our faces.

"Hello, dear," Millicent began. "We're so sorry to trouble you like this after you've experienced such a terrible loss. . . ."

"Thank you," Gerald said, politely nodding his head and wiping at his eyes. "I'm sorry; who are you, exactly?"

"Where are my manners?" Millicent said lightly. "I'm Millicent Satchel, and up until your dear mother, Celeste, got up onstage the other night I was a devoted fan of Deirdre Pendleton's. Do you know I almost bought a ticket to her Hawaiian retreat? And I'd even booked a reading with her for later in the month. Can you imagine what she would have taken me for?"

Gerald looked uncomfortably at Millicent, unsure where the conversation was leading and probably wondering what, if anything, it had to do with him. "Uh-huh," he said tentatively.

"So you see, dear, we just wanted to come up here and express to you our deepest sympathies. If not for your dear mother doing her diligence, so many more people could have been taken for a ride. And we're also so deeply saddened that her commitment led to such tragedy."

"Thank you," Gerald said, wiping his fatigued face. "I'm just so relieved the police have fingered Deirdre Pendleton as their prime suspect," he added, his voice growing suddenly darker.

"Yes, I know," Millicent agreed, slightly startled by the venom in his voice. "But may I ask you why you're so sure Deirdre is responsible?"

"Well, for one thing, she had motive. She hated my mother," Gerald answered.

"Yes, your mother did ruin her career."

Gerald barked out a laugh that was short and hard. "No, not because of that; although that would have been reason enough. See, Deirdre hated my mother because her father, my granduncle, loved Mother more than Deirdre."

"Come again?" I asked, completely confused.

"It's not really public knowledge," Gerald explained, "but Deirdre and my mother were first cousins."

"You're joking," Cat sputtered.

"No, it's true," Gerald insisted. "Years ago my granduncle Jerome, Deirdre's father, had a huge falling-out with her. It was right after Aunt Deirdre claimed to have all of these so-called psychic abilities, and my granduncle—a true-blue atheist—refused to have anything more to do with her.

"Then, a few years later, when she published her first book and basically lambasted him, he got even by setting up a prize to be held in trust for anyone who could prove beyond a shadow of a doubt that psychic phenomena really existed. The one rule he put on the reward was that it couldn't go to a family member.

"To add further insult to the daughter who turned on him, right after he and Aunt Deirdre had their falling-out, Uncle Jerome and my mother became very close, so it wasn't a surprise when he named mother executrix of the trust, and for an extra bonus, even made her his sole legal heir.

"Uncle Jerome was a very wealthy man—worth millions, in fact—and by making my mother the sole heir to his estate it guaranteed that, other than watching over the trust fund for a possible winner, my mother would never have to work a day in her life.

"So the other night, when Aunt Deirdre saw Mother up onstage, revealing her for a fraud, I can only imagine that it must have galled her to no end to see her own family exposing to the world what a liar she really is."

"Wow," was all I could muster as we soaked in Gerald's story. "We had no idea."

"No one did. Both women wanted to keep the truth about the family tree quiet for professional reasons. Mother was highly connected in our community, and she really didn't want anyone to know someone like Deirdre came from our family. We come from a long line of devout atheists, after all, and I'm sure Aunt Deirdre wanted to keep it on the down-low for the very same reasons. But after my mother found out that Deirdre was affecting people's lives . . . well, she just couldn't take it anymore and decided to show up here to expose the fraud. And now she's dead, and although the police have named Deirdre their prime suspect, she's still out there, roaming around free and probably gloating."

"I can assure you she's not gloating," I said quickly. *Especially not after I got through with her.* "We apologize for having disturbed you, Gerald, and we're even sorrier for your loss."

"Thank you," he said, and moved back into the room, ready to shut the door.

Just as he was about to close the door something occurred to me, and I quickly stepped close again. "Just one more thing, Gerald. I'm sorry to bring this up at such an awful time, but I want you to be aware that Zoë Schmitt's research results are skewed, and I suspect that she may have made up or exaggerated many of the results. I want to add that I would love nothing more than to have psychic phenomena proven true once and for all, but I'd rather have it done on honest research and wait a few dozen years than have it flounder on a fraud."

Gerald looked at me quizzically for a long moment, then said, "Thank you, miss. I appreciate your bringing this to my attention, and I'll take care of it immediately."

I gave him my sincerest smile as I turned away and walked with purpose back toward the elevators.

"Where are we going now?" Cat asked.

"To throttle a certain 'internationally renowned psychic,'" I replied, using finger quotes as I ticked off the last three words.

"Uh-oh," Cat said as she hurried after me. "That's never good."

"This is the best vacation ever," Millicent said happily. "Wait until I tell Ernie!"

We found Deirdre still sitting on the patio, gazing moodily out at the gulf. I didn't bother to mince words as I approached her and caught her eye. "Hello, Deirdre," I sang. "Or should I call you 'cousin'?"

"Excuse me?" Deirdre asked, unsure about my tone and manner, which were quickly approaching hostile.

"Why didn't you tell us you and Celeste were cousins?" I demanded.

"Who told you that?" Deirdre asked sharply as she looked around to see if anyone else had overheard.

"It doesn't matter who told me. Now answer the question!"

"It was Gerald," Millicent added helpfully. "He told us, and he told us about the money your father left to Celeste, too."

Deirdre's reaction startled all three of us; she actually laughed. "Did he now? Well, that's rich, no pun intended," she said, and giggled some more.

"What's so funny?" I demanded.

"Don't you see? Don't you get it?" Deirdre said through a fit of giggles. "It's just *so* hilarious!"

"What's hilarious?" Cat asked, sitting down and looking at Millicent and me to see if we got the joke or were as much in the dark as she was.

Deirdre was now clutching her sides and wiping her eyes at the effort the laugh was causing her. For the life of me I had no idea what she was talking about. Finally she calmed down long enough to motion to Millicent and me to sit, and then she began to fill us in. "Yes, it's true that Celeste and I were first cousins, a secret I would have preferred to take to my grave. It's just so embarrassing, you know? Your first cousin is your mortal enemy and represents all that's antithetical to your cause. I mean, I come from a long line of atheists, if you can believe it. Not exactly the best pedigree for a psychic out there promoting herself."

"Is that why you didn't tell us you two were cousins?" Millicent asked.

"Yes, my reputation got thrown into the crapper enough this weekend. I didn't need the world to know that Celeste was my cousin and have the toilet flush on what's left of my career."

"So now that we know, why don't you fill us in on the rest of it?" Cat asked.

"Fine," Deirdre said with a sigh. "You might as well know that it's also true that, due to my father's rather myopic view of the world, he left Celeste the bulk of his estate and guardianship of the trust he set up to entice the scientific community to *disprove* the theory of psychic phenomena, even while he touted publicly that the money was an incentive to prove it existed. You see, he reasoned that if the scientific community set out to find proof and failed, then eventually people would come to the conclusion that no such proof existed, and reason that psychic phenomena was all bunk."

"Sounds like a clever man," I said dryly.

"Oh, yes, that he was," Deirdre said with a bit of nostalgia. "But that's not what is truly funny here, ladies," she continued. "The irony of ironies is that Celeste blew through all the money and was nearly as broke as I am the day she was murdered."

"She blew it?" Cat asked. "How?"

Deirdre sighed sadly and said, "She gambled it away and lost just about every penny. The really tragic thing for her was that she was reduced to living off the interest from the trust, because even though my father put the limitation on the prize that it couldn't be awarded to any blood relative, he allowed for Celeste to benefit from the interest the trust earned. So you see, this woman had become accustomed to living on millions, and after she wasted every penny she was reduced to making ends meet on only one hundred and fifty thousand dollars a year, which sounds easy enough unless you've got spending habits that calculate up to ten times that."

Although we were all listening to Deirdre intently, her point was still elusive, so I asked, "What does this have to do with anything?"

"Don't you see?" she said, her eyes willing me to understand. "That's why she was here in the first place. That's why she had decided to come after me. Celeste figured she could dig up some dirt and build on my success to write a book about debunking psychics. My agent flat-out told me she was looking for a book deal, and I think someone must have bought into it, because about six weeks ago I heard she was out there fishing around some of my clients. So my theory is that someone knew she and I would get into it, and this same someone knew this would be the perfect opportunity to frame me for the murder."

"So when we asked you earlier if you knew anyone who gambled, and you said no, *this* didn't ring any bells?"

Deirdre sighed heavily and lowered her chin. "Well, yes, but I didn't think it was especially relevant."

"Are you stupid, or just simpleminded, Pendleton?" I said, my hands clenching into fists as my frustration mounted.

"Don't get snippy, Cooper. The reason I didn't tell you was because I had a similar problem about fifteen years ago. But unlike Celeste, I got help for my addiction. So when you asked me about a gambler, I didn't know if you meant me or Celeste. And I didn't want you to think I had something to do with the murder, so I just thought it would be better to focus on some of your other . . . uh . . . so-called 'clues,' " she finished, using finger quotes to finish her sentence.

"What the hell is that supposed to mean?" I asked, growing really angry now at having wasted so much time.

"Well, so far, Miss Cooper, your abilities on this case are failing to excite me."

"Ohmigod, I'm gonna *kill* you!" I said, jumping up and moving menacingly toward her.

Cat jumped up too and got right in front of me, blocking my way. "Abby! Abby, calm down! This isn't the way to handle this!"

"She's purposely trying to stonewall our investigation!" I stormed.

"No, she's not, Abby," Cat said sensibly, with a pointed look over her shoulder at Deirdre. "She's just jealous of your abilities, and even though she desperately needs your help she secretly doesn't want you to succeed, because that would mean she really is a failure. So you see? She's clearly not thinking it through, because *if* she were, Deirdre would understand how much you've sacrificed on her behalf; how all you wanted to do was come down here and enjoy a little time in the sun, and instead you've been working your tail off trying to keep her out of jail—"

"You know what, Cat?" I said, my anger mounting with every breath. "You're absolutely right, and I think it's high time I got back to my original plan. Deirdre?" I said sweetly over Cat's shoulder.

"Yes?" Deirdre answered, Cat's words clearly ringing in her ears as she looked at me nervously.

"I quit. Millicent, Cat," I said, looking determinedly at

both of them, "if you need me I'll be up in my room ordering room service and planning my day tomorrow at the
beach."

As I turned to walk away I heard Deirdre call out desperately, "Abby! Please don't quit on me! If you leave now
how will I clear my name?"

"Ask your guide, 'Great Bag of Hot Air'! I'm *sure* he
can help!"

Later that night, just as I'd finished eating my lobster
salad, Millicent and Cat came back to the room and sat
down carefully next to me. "How you feeling?" Cat
asked nervously.

"Me?" I asked, looking at her like she'd asked a silly
question. "Why, I'm *fine.* I'm finally going to get a day to
rest and enjoy the beach, which is the *sole* reason I came
here in the first place."

"Don't be mean," Cat said reproachfully.

"I'm not being mean, Cat, I'm just sick of this whole
thing. We've been on this wild-goose chase for what feels
like an eternity, and it's gotten us nowhere—and for
what?"

"A trip to Hawaii?" Millicent asked meekly.

I looked quickly at Millicent, and my mouth fell open a
little. I'd completely forgotten about the deal we'd made
with Deirdre. "Damn," I said, "I forgot about that, Millicent. I'm sorry."

"It's all right, dear. I'm sure it's not as wonderful as
everyone says it is."

Guilt, guilt, guilt. "Millicent," I tried, "I'm out of leads
here. I don't know what Celeste's gambling problem has to
do with her murderer, and I don't know who to question
next—"

Just then there was a knock on the door, and the three
of us looked a question mark at one another as Cat went
to answer it. When the door opened we could see Zoë
Schmitt standing in the hallway, and Millicent and I stood
up quickly.

"Hello," Zoë said sheepishly.

"Zoë!" Cat said excitedly. "We thought Deirdre scared
you off."

"Oh, her? No way. I normally wouldn't give her the time

of day. Do you know that I tested her before the seminar, and her results were actually worse than chance? Really, the woman's a total scam."

"So we've heard," Cat said, letting her in.

"How did you find us?" Millicent asked.

"Well, I went to the front desk and inquired about whether or not you had checked out yet, and the clerk said no, and then he asked if I wanted to buy your room number for fifty dollars."

"Fifty?" Cat gasped. "He charges me a hundred!"

"What?" Zoë asked, looking at Cat.

"Nothing," I said quickly. "Listen, Zoë, I'm glad you're here. We have a couple of additional questions we'd like to ask you, if you have a minute." What can I say? I'd made a promise to Millicent, and I was having a hard time looking at her sweet face and feeling okay about letting her down.

"Sure, and after that can you sit down with me and take a few more tests?"

"Uh, sure," I said, "that'll be fine. So," I said, searching for a place to begin. Just then my intuition buzzed, and the image of the calico cat came into my mind's eye very crisp and clear, so I decided to lead with that. "Let me ask you something personal. Do you by any chance own a calico cat?"

Zoë chuckled like I'd just asked her a joke and said, "That's a weird question. Why would you ask?"

I chuckled myself and replied, "Sometimes my intuition just homes in on something obscure, and every time I'm around you I see an image of a calico cat coming out of an old school building."

"Wow!" Zoë said, her eyes widening in surprise. "Abby, that's pretty good!"

"So you do own a calico cat?" I asked, getting excited.

"Uh, no, but I know what your intuition is referencing. The Institute for Metaphysical Studies is run by my boss, Kitty Lowenstein. She's actually the one who encouraged me to try for the Ballentine reward money. She thought it would do wonders for the school, and she's been so supportive through this whole process. Most people think I'm crazy to give all the money away to the school, but it's really important to me that our mission continue. I have so many students who benefit from our courses, and it would be a shame if we had to shut our doors. The prize money would guarantee we could continue our mission for a long, long time."

All of the sudden my intuition went haywire, and I knew Kitty was a piece of this puzzle. Trying to hide my anxiousness, I asked, "Oh? Wow, that's great. Listen, is your boss, Kitty, back in Kansas?"

"No, actually. She's here for the retreat too. She thought she could do some recruiting of potential students identified by my research. She has the room next to mine, in fact."

I stole a glance at Cat, who was looking at me with eyes that were dancing with excitement. "I would love to meet your boss!" Cat said, and came forward to stand next to me. "Listen, Abby, I know you said earlier you were pretty exhausted from all the goings-on at the hotel today, and I know how your antenna doesn't work as well when you're tired as when you're rested. Why don't you and Zoë get together tomorrow morning, after you've had a chance to get a thorough night's sleep?"

Zoë's shoulders slumped in disappointment, and she looked at me with resignation. "Would you rather get together in the morning?" she asked politely, even though I could tell she'd be crushed if I put her off again.

"Yes, Zoë, I think I would," I answered, lifting my arms above my head for a gigantic stretch and throwing in a big, fat yawn for effect.

"Oh, all right. I guess it is getting kind of late," Zoë said, lifting her watch up and noting the time. "And I haven't had a chance to eat dinner yet."

"Then it's settled," Cat said quickly, taking Zoë by the shoulders and escorting her to the door. "Abby will come down to your room promptly at nine A.M.—what room number did you say you were?"

"Number four fifty-seven," Zoë answered obediently, "second to last door on the left."

"Perfect," Cat said, and squeezed her arm even as she began to shut the door. "We'll see you then."

We waited fifteen anxious minutes after practically closing the door in Zoë's face, and then filed quickly out the door. A few minutes later, and after a very short debate on which side of room number 457 to knock on, we took a chance and tapped briskly on number 459. The door was opened a little bit later by a rotund woman with short black hair streaked with several odd patches of white all about her head. The pattern was so unusual and fit so perfectly with the calico-cat analogy that for a moment I was caught off guard. "Uh, hello . . ." I stuttered, smiling uncomfortably.

"Can I help you?" she asked.

It was then that I noticed she was wearing a bathrobe, and I quickly apologized, "I'm so sorry; I didn't realize I'd caught you at a bad time."

"It's fine," she assured me. "I was just getting ready to jump in the tub."

"Uh-huh . . ." I said, unsure how to proceed.

"Hello," Millicent said, moving in and nudging me out of the way. "I'm Millicent Satchel, and I believe I'm psychic, but I don't know how to develop my intuition. We heard that you run a school for the gifted, and we'd like to find out some more information. Oh, and by the way, we're all rich, so money is no object."

I nearly blew it by laughing inappropriately, but caught myself just in time. Kitty hesitated in the doorway for a moment, weighing Millicent's statement, but then slowly let the door open and motioned for us to come in.

The inside of Kitty's hotel room was comfortable and atypical. There were two queen beds, one unmade and very rumpled, and a television blared on top of a dresser. Television addict that I am, I couldn't help but check out the program, and noted with disappointment that the broadcast was covering an NBA game. In the background the sound of a bathtub filling with water could be heard. It appeared that Kitty was telling the truth about preparing to take a bath.

Millicent took the lead again, asking Kitty about the school and the programs they offered, as my eyes wandered the room and my intuition buzzed for me to look closely because something felt out of place. Distracted, I homed in on the message and kept seeing the apple tree and its fruit dropping to the ground. I didn't understand the metaphor, so in frustration I shook my head again and tried to focus on Kitty and her answers to Millicent's questions.

It was then that I noticed Kitty scratch at her arm, and

when she did so she lifted the sleeve of her robe to reveal a rash creeping up her arm, masked slightly by a light white cream.

"Ohmigod!" I said, and pointed at her, the shock of each and every clue suddenly falling into place making me forget to be discreet.

"What?" Kitty asked, turning to her left and right to see if I was pointing to something behind her.

"You!" I said, still pointing. "You've got poison ivy!"

Cat and Millicent stood frozen in place, mute to my outburst, confusion clouding their expressions.

"So?" Kitty asked, already backing up a little and pulling down the sleeves of her robe.

"You've got the same rash as Gerald!" I said, getting excited. "It was the two of you, wasn't it? You two killed Celeste!"

Millicent and Cat gasped, as they turned wide eyes on Kitty, waiting for her to say something. She, however, did not make a sound, but in the bathroom all four of us heard the sound of the bathtub faucet squeaking as it was turned off, and only a second later the bathroom door creaked open to reveal Gerald Ballentine, clad only in jeans, holding a .45 and sporting a menacing grin.

"How'd you figure it out?" he asked as he stepped into the room.

"The apple never falls far from the tree," I said, looking nervously at the gun.

"What's that supposed to mean?" he asked.

"Your mother was a gambler, and so are you." I pointed at the blaring TV, which was tuned to ESPN. "You bet on basketball, don't you, Gerald? That's why you were upset earlier today. You bet on a game and lost. You weren't upset about your mother at all, because you killed her."

"Not bad," Gerald said, walking into the center of our group, aiming the gun in my general direction.

Nervously, I eyed the gun and decided to keep talking and stall for time. "And because your granduncle set up the trust so that the money couldn't go directly to a member of the family, you and Kitty, here, were working on getting the money from the trust by granting it to Zoë, because you knew she'd give it to the Institute of Metaphysical Studies."

"Yes, that was our plan—Miss Cooper, is it? At least, it was until you showed up with your good intentions and informed me about Zoë's flawed research. All afternoon I've been worrying how I could still get around to granting her the money after you'd exposed her, and now I don't have to worry about it anymore."

"Why not?" Millicent asked meekly.

"Because I'm going to kill you," Gerald said evilly. "And with you out of the way, I can grant the money to Zoë, and Kitty and I can retire to Mexico, right Kitty?"

"That's right, baby," Kitty purred, and the way the two of them looked at each other made the lobster salad I'd eaten earlier do a flip-flop in my tummy.

"Now, all of you, move over to the bed," he said, waving the gun at us.

"You'll never get away with it," I said as I felt my way along the bed, trying to make room for Cat and Millicent but never taking my eyes off the gun. "I mean, you might have gotten away with Celeste's murder, but three more added to the list, Gerald, is a little much to—"

"Shut up!" Gerald yelled my way while taking aim at me with the gun. He didn't have to tell me twice; I went instantly quiet. "That's better," he said; then he looked at Kitty and said, "Take the lamp cords and tie them up. We can put socks in their mouths until it's safe to move them."

Kitty jumped to do Gerald's bidding, and walked over to the nightstand, where she unplugged the lamp, then tugged the cord free and proceeded to head to the other lamp around the bed. Millicent, thinking fast, shoved her foot out, tripping Kitty, who went down like a big sack of calico potatoes.

This was all the distraction Cat and I needed as we each instantly sprang forward, Cat leaping on Kitty, and me ducking low under the sight of the gun and tackling Gerald as he played with the safety, hitting him waist high.

Kitty and Cat rolled around, locked in a firm embrace on the floor. Their high-pitched wailing, hissing, scratching, and biting seemed for all the world like one great catfight.

At one point Cat managed to get the neck of Kitty's robe pulled up high over her head, obscuring Kitty's vision long enough to roll her over onto her stomach and yank back both arms, pinning her in place and sitting on her back even as Kitty continued to buck and kick, frantic to get loose.

I, on the other hand, wasn't having nearly as much luck, because Gerald proved to be a rather worthy opponent. When I tackled him I'd managed to knock the gun from his hand, and it landed across the room. But instead of pinning him to the floor, I barely managed to hold on to him as he crawled across the carpet in the direction of the gun. At first I gripped his considerable waist tightly and braced my legs against the bed, trying for dear life to keep him from gaining ground, but he was a sweaty, slippery beast, and my grip just wouldn't hold.

Next I tried holding on to his pants, but they were fitted to hug his pudgy belly, and once they cleared that, his pants came easily down to his calves. At that point all I could do was grip his legs somewhere around his knees, while staring at his tightie-whities and praying for a miracle.

At that moment I actually got one when just two feet from the gun, after dragging me nearly all the way across the room, Gerald was knocked unconcious with the same lamp Kitty had pulled the cord from. Standing triumphantly over the broken lamp and Gerald's bleeding head stood Millicent, who also managed to kick the gun clear to the bathroom and out of reach.

Quickly letting go of Gerald's limp legs, I stood up, kissed Millicent firmly on the cheek, and dove for the phone.

Half an hour later Kitty Lowenstein and Gerald Ballentine were being escorted away in handcuffs. We learned later that the two had met at another psychic convention, when some other poor target had caught Celeste's attention. They had been secretly rendezvousing and planning Celeste's murder for months, waiting for Deirdre and Celeste to cross paths so that they could frame her for the murder. We also learned that Gerald owed several bookies with very checkered reputations hundreds of thousands of dollars, and his life probably wasn't worth a plugged nickel if he ever got out of prison. Now that Zoë's boss was being taken away to jail, she was named interim director of the Institute of Metaphysical Studies, and luckily her new duties required her to get back to Kansas immediately, relieving me of my human-guinea-pig obligations.

Right after Kitty and Gerald were carted away, Cat and I attended to our various scratches, bites, rug burns, and bruises. Millicent, however, who had avoided even the smallest scratch, was busy telling anyone who would listen about the big battle and how she, a little old lady of seventy-three, had saved the day.

The Seacoast Inn was so relieved to have the murder of Celeste Ballentine solved that they comped Cat for the entire weekend, and offered us each an extra three days on the house, all expenses paid. Cat, unfortunately, couldn't take them up on their offer of extending her visit, but had to fly home for some important board meeting.

Millicent left early Sunday morning, so excited to tell her husband, Ernie, about her great adventure that she nearly forgot to leave us her address so that we could keep in touch.

Deirdre promised Millicent she would keep her end of the bargain, and sure enough, mere hours after Gerald and Kitty were led away she could be seen pacing the lobby with a cell phone pinned to her ear, making reservations and talking to her agent about her next book, tentatively titled, *Deirdre Pendleton and the Seacoast Killer: How One Psychic Detective Solved a Gruesome Murder*.

As for me . . . well, let's just say I took the hotel up on their offer and made a few calls to my clients, pulled in a few favors from some other psychic friends of mine to cover me, and wasted no time hitting the beach.

Ah, sun . . . Don'tcha just love a good, *restful* vacation?

Read on for an excerpt from
Victoria Laurie's next Psychic Eye mystery

Better Read Than Dead

Coming from Signet in June 2005

The three cardinal sins to be avoided by *legitimate* professional psychics are:

1. Never make up or alter a psychic message
2. Never betray the trust of a client by revealing details of a reading to others
3. Above all, never, *ever* use your intuitive gift to cause harm to another person.

As I stood in the thickening pool of blood leaking from the man I had effectively killed, I didn't care that I had flagrantly committed not one, but all three of these cardinal sins. Instead, as my karmic debt for such crimes mounted to new and overwhelming heights, my only thought was the sick satisfaction of finally getting my eye for an eye.

I wasn't always like this, you know. A mere three weeks earlier I could have been the poster child for ethical intuitives. I believed in my work as a professional psychic, giving helpful advice, lending my talent wherever it was needed, and using my "gift" for good. All that changed one rainy autumn afternoon the day before Halloween—don'tcha just love irony?

"Kendal, you *cannot* do this to me!" I complained into my cell phone as I navigated the rainy-day traffic of downtown Royal Oak, Michigan.

"Abby, I swear, I have called everybody else. You are the only person left who can pull this off—and besides, you owe me," Kendal answered unsympathetically.

"Kendal, of all the times to call in *that* favor, you had to pick tomorrow night?"

"Not my wedding, Abby; I didn't pick the date. The bride and groom did."

My breathing was coming in irregular short bursts of frustration. I didn't want to say yes; in fact, I had a very strong feeling I should say no, but Kendal, another professional psychic, was in a jam, and he had helped me out a few months previously, when I'd had to take a few weeks off from my own business to recuperate from a tango I'd danced with a psychopath. He was right: I did owe him, big-time, and owing people was not something I was particularly comfortable with.

Debt in general bothered the hell out of me, which is why I never borrowed money if I could possibly avoid it. Just ask my wealthy sister, who had to engage in a ten-minute "discussion" with me every time she wanted to pay for lunch.

The problem with Kendal's request was that my boyfriend was due back from his training with the FBI at Quantico, and tomorrow night was supposed to be *our* night, if you get my drift.

My boyfriend, Dutch, used to be a detective for the Royal Oak PD, until he'd been recruited by the FBI. We hadn't dated very long; in fact, we had yet to consummate our relationship—hence why the following evening was such a big deal.

"Kendal, I'm *begging* you, isn't there *anyone* else? Another psychic-in-training? Some guy off the street who could fake it?"

"Abby, there is no one else, I swear. And this gig is really important to me. I could use the cash—and besides, you owe me," he repeated inexorably.

I pulled the cell phone away from my ear and stuck my tongue out at it. If he said that one more time I was going to crawl through the thing and tie his nose in a knot. I sighed audibly and gave it one more valiant try. "Can't you just do it alone?"

"An entire wedding party? Are you nuts? Even with the two of us we'll still be lucky to make it through thirty people. I promised the bride two psychics, she's already paid for two psychics, and she is going to *get* two psychics, because *you owe me*!"

My eyebrows lowered to dangerous levels; damn it, he'd

said it again. "But I don't even know how to read tarot cards!" I shouted.

Kendal had informed me at the start of our conversation that the bride had insisted on using tarot card readers. Kendal had booked the event with a friend of his who also used tarot. Unfortunately Kendal's friend had been wheeled into the OR for an emergency appendectomy an hour earlier, thus his frantic phone call to me.

"I can teach you; just meet me at my house an hour before the reception and we'll go over it when we get to the reception hall. It's pretty easy; you'll probably pick it up right away. Besides, if you get stuck you can just put down a card and say whatever comes to mind. You're pretty much free-form as it is, aren't you?"

I had pulled into my assigned parking space in the parking garage across the street from my office by now, and, smelling defeat, I let me head bang forward onto the steering wheel. I wasn't going to get out of this.

About the Authors

Professional psychic **Victoria Laurie** drew from her career as a gifted clairvoyant and police psychic to create the character of Abigail Cooper. She lives in Arlington, Massachusetts, with her two spoiled dachshunds, Lilly and Toby. For information about upcoming novels and appointments for readings, visit her Web site, www.VictoriaLaurie.com.

Like her heroines, the Blackbird sisters, **Nancy Martin** comes from a distinguished Pennsylvania family whose ancestors include Betsy Ross and a signer of the Declaration of Independence. She has written numerous novels, directed a few Shakespeare plays, and raised two delightful daughters. Visit her Web site at www.nancymartinmysteries.com.

Denise Swanson has worked as a school psychologist for more than twenty years. She lives in Illinois with her husband, Dave, and their cool black cat, Boomerang. For more information, visit her Web site at www.deniseswanson.com.

Elaine Viets's new *Dead-End Job* series from Signet was named one of the hot new series by *Publishers Weekly*. Elaine has been nominated for seven awards this year, including three Agatha Awards and an Anthony for her mystery fiction. In each *Dead-End Job* book, her character, Helen Hawthorne, works a different minimum-wage job. *Just Murdered*, due out in May, is at a bridal shop. She has served on the national boards of the Mystery Writers of America and Sisters in Crime.

Signet

Denise Swanson
The Scumble River Mysteries

When Skye Denison left Scumble River years ago,
she swore she'd never return. But after a fight with
her boyfriend and credit card rejection, she's back to
home-sweet-homicide.

MURDER OF A SMALL-TOWN HONEY
0-451-20055-1

MURDER OF A SWEET OLD LADY
0-451-20272-4

MURDER OF A SLEEPING BEAUTY
0-451-20548-0

MURDER OF A SNAKE IN THE GRASS
0-451-20834-X

MURDER OF A BARBIE AND KEN
0-451-21072-7

MURDER OF A PINK ELEPHANT
0-451-21210-X

Available wherever books are sold or at
www.penguin.com